The Castle of [...] *Brighton*;

unaccounta [...] marigolds, whatever was sown in them; and where snails were constantly discovered holding on to the street doors, and other public places they were not expected to ornament, with the tenacity of cupping-glasses. In the winter time the air couldn't be got out of the Castle, and in the

There were two other *very* small boarders, *these two rooms* in it, where Little Dombey (first called so of Mrs Pipchin) arrived. These were one Master Bitherstone from India, and a certain Miss Pankey. As to Master Bitherstone, he objected so [...] much to the Pipchinian system, that before Little Dombey had been established in the house five minutes, he privately asked that young gentleman if he could give him any idea of the way back to Bengal. As to Miss Pankey, she was disabled from offering any remark, by being in solitary confinement in ~~the Dungeon~~, for the offence of having snorted three times in the presence of visitors. At [...] o'clock there was dinner, and then this person (a mild little blue-eyed morsel of a child, who was shampoo'd every morning, and seemed in [...]

Endpapers: pages from Little Dombey privately printed by Dickens for his reading tours and annotated by him.
Reproduced by courtesy of the Charles Dickens Museum, London

THE LAST DICKENS

Also by Matthew Pearl

The Dante Club
The Poe Shadow

THE LAST DICKENS

Matthew Pearl

Harvill *Secker*
LONDON

Published by Harvill Secker 2009

2 4 6 8 10 9 7 5 3 1

First published in Great Britain in 2009 by
HARVILL SECKER
Random House, 20 Vauxhall Bridge Road,
London SW1V 2SA

www.rbooks.co.uk

Addresses for companies within The Random House Group Limited can be found at:
www.randomhouse.co.uk/offices.htm

The Random House Group Limited Reg. No. 954009

A CIP catalogue record for this book
is available from the British Library

ISBN 9781846550843 (hardback)
9781846550850 (trade paperback)

The Random House Group Limited supports The Forest Stewardship
Council (FSC), the leading international forest certification organisation. All our titles
that are printed on Greenpeace approved FSC certified paper carry the FSC logo.
Our paper procurement policy can be found at www.rbooks.co.uk/environment

Typeset in Dante MT by Palimpsest Book Production Limited,
Grangemouth, Stirlingshire
Printed and bound in Great Britain by
Clays Ltd, St Ives plc

FIRST INSTALMENT

I

BENGAL, INDIA, JUNE 1870

EITHER OF THE YOUNG MOUNTED policemen fancied these subdivisions of the Bagirhaut province. Neither of them fancied jungles where all manner of things could happen unprovoked, unseen, as they had a few years before when a poor lieutenant was stripped, clubbed and drowned in the river for trying to collect licensing taxes.

The officers clamped the heels of their boots tighter into their horses' flanks. Not to say they were scared – only careful.

'You must be careful always,' said Turner to Mason as they ducked the low branches and vines. 'Be assured, the natives in India do not value life. Not even as the poorest Englishman does.'

The younger of the two policemen, Mason, nodded thoughtfully at the words of his impressive partner, who was nearly twenty-five years old, who had two brothers also come from England to be in the Indian Civil Service, and who had fought the Indian rebellion a few years before. He was an expert if ever one was.

'Perhaps we should have come with more men, sir.'

'Well, that's pretty! More men, Mason? We shan't need any more than our two heads between us to take in a few ragged *dacoits*. Remember, a high-mettled horse stands not for hedge nor ditch.'

When Mason had arrived in Bengal from Liverpool for his new post, he accepted Turner's offer to 'chum', pooling incomes and living expenses and passing their free time in billiards or croquet. Mason, at eighteen, was thankful for counsel from such an experienced man in the ranks of the Bengal police. Turner could list places a policeman ought never to ride alone because of the Coles, the Santhals, the Assamee, the Kookies and the hill tribes in the frontiers. Some of the criminal gangs among the tribes were *dacoits*, thieves; others, warned

Turner, carried axes and wanted English heads. 'The natives of India value life only as far as they can kill when doing so', was another Turner proverb.

Fortunately, they were not hunting out that sort of bloodthirsty gang in these wasting temperatures this morning. Instead they were investigating a plain, brazen robbery. The day before, a long train of twenty or thirty bullock carts had been hit with a shower of stones and rocks. In the chaos, *dacoits* holding torches tipped over the carts and fled with valuable chests from the convoy. When intelligence of the theft reached the police station, Turner had gone to their supervisor's desk to volunteer himself and Mason, and their commander had sent them to question a known receiver of stolen goods.

Now, as the terrain thinned, they neared the small thatched house on the creek. A dwindling column of smoke hovered above the mud chimney. Mason gripped the sword at his belt. Every two men in the Bengal police were assigned one sword and one light carbine rifle, and Turner had naturally claimed the rifle.

'Mason,' he said with a slight smile in his voice after noticing the anxious look on his partner's face. 'You are green, aren't you? It is highly likely they have unloaded the goods and fled already. Perhaps for the mountains, where our *elaka* – that is like "jurisdiction", Mason – where our *elaka* does not extend. No matter, really, when captured, they lie and say they are innocent peasants until the corrupt darkie magistrates release them. What do you say to going tiger shooting upon some elephants?'

'Turner!' Mason whispered, just then, interrupting his partner.

They were coming upon the thatched-roof house where a bright red horse was tied to a post (the natives in these provinces often painted their horses unnatural colours). A slight rustle at the house drew their eyes to a pair of men fitting the description of two of the thieves. One of them held a torch. They were arguing.

Turner signalled Mason to stay quiet. 'The one on the right, it's Narain,' he whispered and pointed. Narain was a known opium thief against whom several attempts at conviction had failed.

The opium poppy was cultivated in Bengal and refined there under English control, after which the colonial government sold the drug at auction to opium traders from England, America and other nations. From there, the traders would transport the opium for sale to China, where it was illegal but still in great demand. The trade was enormously profitable for the British government.

Dismounting, Turner and Mason split up and approached the thieves from two sides. As Mason crept through the bushes from around the back, he could not help but think about their good fortune: not only that two of the thieves were still at the suspected confederate's house but also that their argument was serving as distraction.

As Mason made his way around the thick shrubbery he jumped out at Turner's signal and displayed his sword at the surprised Narain, who put up two trembling hands and lay flat on the ground. The other thief had pushed Turner down and dashed into the dense trees. Turner staggered to his feet, aimed his rifle, and shot. He fired a wild second shot into the jungle.

They tied the prisoner and traced the fugitive's path but soon lost the trail. While searching up and down the curve of the rough creek, Turner lunged at something on the ground. Upon reaching the spot, Mason saw with great pride in his chum that Turner had bludgeoned a cobra with his carbine. But the cobra was not dead and it rose up again as Mason approached and tried to strike. Such was the peril of the Bengalee jungle.

Abandoning the hunt for the other thief, they returned to the spot where they'd left Narain tied to a tree and freed him, leading him as they took the horses they'd borrowed back to the police outpost. There, they boarded the train with their prisoner in tow to bring Narain to the district of their station house.

'Get some sleep,' Turner said to Mason with a brotherly care. 'You look worn out. I can guard the *dacoit*.'

'Thank you, Turner,' said Mason gratefully.

The eventful morning had been exhausting. Mason found an empty row of seats and covered his face with his hat. Before long he fell into a deep sleep beneath the rattling window, where a slow breeze made the compartment nearly tolerable. He woke to a horrible echoing scream – the kind that lived sometimes in his nightmares of Bengal's jungles.

When he shook himself into sensibility he saw Turner standing alone staring out the window.

'Where's the prisoner?' Mason cried.

'I don't know!' Turner shouted, a wild glint in his eyes. 'I looked the other way for a moment, and Narain must have thrown himself out the window!'

They pulled the alarm for the train to stop. Mason and Turner, with the help of an Indian railway policeman, searched along the rocks and found Narain's crushed and bloody body. His head had been smashed open at impact. His hands were still tied together with wire.

Solemnly, Mason and Turner abandoned the body and reboarded the train. The young English officers were silent the remaining train ride to the station house, except for some unmusical humming by Turner. They had almost reached the terminal when Turner posed a question.

'Answer me this, Mason. Why did you enrol in the mounted police?'

Mason tried to think of a good answer but was too troubled. 'To raise a little dust, I suppose. We all want to make some noise in the world.'

'Stuff!' said Turner. 'Never lose sight of the true blessings of public service. Each one of us is here to turn out a better civilisation in the end, and for that reason alone.'

'Turner, about what happened today . . .' The younger man's face was white.

'What's wrong?' Turner demanded. 'Luck was with us. That cobra might have done us both in.'

'Narain . . . the suspected *dacoit*. Well, shouldn't we, I mean, collect up the names and statements of the passengers for our diaries so that if there is any kind of inquiry . . .'

'Suspected? Guilty, you meant. Never mind, Mason. We'll send one of the native men.'

'But, won't we, if Dickens, I mean . . .'

'What mumbling! You oughtn't chew your words.'

'Sir,' the younger officer enunciated forcefully, 'considering for a moment Dickens—'

'Mason, that's enough! Can't you see I'm tired?' Turner hissed.

'Sir,' Mason said, nodding.

Turner's neck had become stiff and veiny at the sound of that particular name: *Dickens*. As though the word had been rotting deep inside him and now crawled back up his throat.

II

BOSTON, THE SAME DAY, 1870

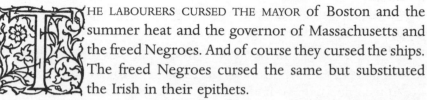

THE LABOURERS CURSED THE MAYOR of Boston and the summer heat and the governor of Massachusetts and the freed Negroes. And of course they cursed the ships. The freed Negroes cursed the same but substituted the Irish in their epithets.

In other months, some dockworkers sang. But in the summer they'd curse.

'Damn moss to hell!' said one labourer. He did not specify whether it was his own poor wages he was damning or the money lining the pockets of the cushion-faced rich folks whose goods they hauled.

A second labourer added: 'Damn *all* moss! Straight to the devil!' At that, three cheers and another were called out in unison.

They didn't yet notice, walking across the pier, a large stranger dangling an ivory toothpick from his lips. His dark eyes darted ahead into the lanes of stevedores and express wagons. 'Say!' he called out to the clique of Irish labourers, though he failed to attract their attention. Then he raised his gilded walking stick.

That did it.

At the top of the stick was an exotic and ugly golden idol, the head of a beast, a horn rising from the top, terrible mouth agape, sparks of fire shooting from its outstretched tongue. It was mesmerising to behold. Not just because of its shining ugliness, but also because it was such a contrast to the stranger's own mouth, mostly hidden under an enormous ear-to-ear moustache. The man's lips barely managed to prise open his mouth when he spoke.

'I need,' said the stranger, addressing the dockworkers, 'to find a lad. Have you seen him? He wears a heavy suit and carries a bundle of papers.'

In fact, the dockworkers had seen a passerby fitting the description just a few minutes before. The young man had stopped at an over-turned barrel outside the Salt House. Just to look at the fellow's thick suit added to the heat. Steadying himself with a self-conscious air, he had removed a bundle of papers tied up with black string from underneath the barrel and staggered through the pack of labourers. Naturally, they had cursed him.

'Well,' said the stranger when recognition came into their eyes. 'Which way did he walk?'

The four dockworkers exchanged evasive glances. Not so much at his question, but at his decidedly English accent – and at his brown-parchment complexion. Under his hat, a chocolate-coloured cotton turban stuck out. He wore a tunic-style garment that hung over the knees of his silk trousers, and a woollen cord was wrapped around the waist.

'You some kind of Hindoo?' a wiry labourer finally asked.

The swarthy stranger paused and took a momentous breath. He turned with only his eyes to the labourer who had proposed the question. With a sudden ferociousness, he thrust his stick against the labourer's neck and slammed his body down to the ground. His companions rushed in, but a single look from the attacker kept the would-be rescuers at bay.

That grotesque head had crooked, razor-sharp fangs. These were now biting into the soft flesh of the prostrate worker's jugular. A thin drop of blood trembled down his Adam's apple.

'Look at me. Look at me in the eye now,' the stranger said. 'You'll tell me where you saw that lad go, or right here I rip your Dublin tongue out through your throat, God save us all.'

Fearing the fangs would dig deeper into his neck, the felled stevedore answered with a just perceptible motion. He raised his arm and pointed a shaky finger in the direction the young man had taken, his eyes closing in dread.

'Good boy, my young Paddy,' said the stranger.

No wonder the Irish labourer had closed his eyes. The stranger's teeth and lips, seen from that low vantage point, looked to be stained an unnaturally bright red. As though painted by blood. As if this man had just chewed up a rabid animal for breakfast.

Armed with the new information, the dark-eyed stranger soon regained the trail on the street leading away from Long Wharf and into Boston proper. There, straight ahead, weaving around the market carts of produce by Faneuil Hall, he spotted the one he was after. It was as though a strong wind were pushing the young man. His locomotion was wild, his disoriented eyes urgent; if anyone had paid attention, it would seem that he was possessed of a mission – vital to Boston, vital to the world. He tossed back looks of concern as he hugged the water-stained packet tightly with both arms.

The pursuer pushed aside fish dealers and beggars through the aisles of Quincy Market.

'Beer by the glass!' cried a hawker before being jostled to the ground.

At the end of the market, as predator and prey crossed through the exit, the large hand had latched on to the other's sleeve.

'You'll be sorry you ran from me!' he growled, pulling him by the arm.

'No!' The earnest eyes of the young man lit up with defiance. 'Osgood needs it!'

The lad's free arm rose as if to strike his assailant – at which gesture the enormous man did not even flinch. But instead of striking, the lad used the free hand to take hold of his own captured sleeve and pull down on the fabric, ripping his suit open at the shoulder. Freed from the stranger's clutches, he was sent pirouetting from the force across the street and almost to the safety of the other side.

An inhuman shriek combined with an awful cracking sound.

The stranger with the golden idol, panting at the bottom of his throat, pulled his rounded hat to shield his eyes from the clouds of dust as he stepped to the kerb. For a moment he could not find the young man, but then he saw what had happened. When a large assortment of people had gathered, *too many people*, the watcher shuffled away as though he'd never had any interest.

The swarthy stranger hadn't been the only one out hunting in the lusty traffic of the docks that morning. There were, at the moment, two or three others among the hives of workmen, wharf rats and holiday revellers. These were familiar faces on the docks, many mornings out before the stevedores. They were familiar most of all to each other, though odd as it sounded they didn't know one another's names.

Not their christened names, that is. There was Molasses, so titled humorously for his always harried pace. Esquire was a coloured gentleman, a former cabman, who taught fencing and dancing in the Negro neighbourhoods. Kitten was one of the females of this elite and grimy clique and could have charmed the drink right out of the hands of Whiskey Bill, another of their rivals.

It was Molasses, today, in a black neckcloth and moleskin jacket, who was a hair's breadth from sweet victory. Victory! During the War of the Rebellion, Molasses had been a professional bounty man, paid to take the place of rich lads in the draft who did not want to serve. Using various aliases to get his money and then vanishing as eagerly from each regiment, the powdery days of war helped Molasses pocket five thousand dollars in two and a half years. Since then he had taken to dyeing his hair and beard colours never known to grow on any man naturally. The beard was also overlong. He had sworn that he would not shave until a Democrat was president and those cheating Republicans out of business.

There. Right in front of Molasses's eyes was hidden what he wanted. He had been ordered by wire from Philadelphia to retrieve the treasure for a hefty reward. Stationing himself in one of the fish houses on the waterfront with his long spyglass, he had seen the young man in the suit hide it earlier that morning. Now it would be his.

A wharfinger was taking up an abandoned barrel.

'Beg pardon,' Molasses said, approaching and picking his tweed cap off his head as if in polite greeting. 'I'll take that, sir.'

'Who are you?' asked the wharfinger in a firm German accent. 'Go away from my barrels, wharf rat.'

Molasses kicked over the barrel with his unlaced boot. To his dismay, nothing but stray fish bones poured out. He couldn't believe it. He crouched down, rummaging through the mess. When he looked up, there was Esquire standing over him, gallantly chuckling.

''Squire, you copper bottom rascal! Where are they?'

'They're not here! Calm down, 'lasses, I didn't procure the papers neither. You didn't get them, I didn't get them, and I saw Kitten – I think she's working for C. today – at an old tug with a face like she'd been slapped on the back while eating a stick of butter. Why, they've likely vanished safely altogether by now to their rightful owner, I s'pose. Rotten luck.'

The German wharfinger became red in the face. 'If you do not leave my wharf, I shall send for the police.'

Molasses kicked violently at the barrel until it was in pieces.

Then he cried out a warning to the wharfinger in German. This time, the wharfinger backed away.

'Whiskey Bill? Was it him?' asked Molasses, turning back to Esquire.

'Nay, 'lasses,' Esquire answered grandly, raising himself on to the top of a bench, his feet dangling as he looked out at the water. 'Bill didn't get sent on this mission.' A light breeze now played against the bay and the heavy sun illuminated the sailboats. In the distance, they could hear a bad snarl of traffic, the shouts of drivers and whipping of horses, by Quincy Market.

Molasses, cleaning his reeking hands on his coat and trousers, suddenly paused. 'There was a whaler of a fellow following the young man – browned skin, lantern jaw, with a turbanned head. You think one of the bigwigs put him on the bounty, too, 'squire?'

'Oh, I seen him earlier,' replied Esquire eerily. 'His eyes big and black, like they were all hollow, and his mouth just like a skeleton's? No, he wasn't one of our kind, Molasses, that's sure. Not a man bent on dollars and dimes.'

Just about that time in the middle of Dock Square, the omnibus called the 'Alice Gray' rolled to a lumbering stop. Its driver and passengers dismounted to learn the source of the noise – that long blood-chilling crack they had all heard from below the vehicle a moment before.

'Good God!' 'Why, he must've just been dragged!' 'Crushed flat!' 'Git the ladies away from here, will you?'

Below the back wheel, a pale young man in a torn wool suit. The first wheel had passed over his neck and the next over his leg, nearly severing it below the knee.

One of the gentlemen coming out of the bus was the first at the body. The young man's head jerked slightly. His pupils contracted and his mouth opened. 'He's alive!' someone shouted. 'Is there a doctor?'

'I am a lawyer,' said the gentleman as if to improve on the question by answering a different one. 'Sylvanus Bendall, attorney-at-law!' The dying man reached to grab this lawyer's collar with surprising insistence, as his mouth formed a word, then another. Bendall listened carefully, and then the lad's strength seemed to fail and he stopped.

After a few moments of sober examination befitting an actual doctor, the kneeling man who called himself Bendall removed his hat to signal the young man's death. A tall gentleman pointed to the bundle of papers in the dead man's hand. 'What's he got? His will?' He chuckled at his own morbid joke.

'Pooh!' Bendall the lawyer said very seriously. Untying the string, he removed one sheet and put his eyeglass up to his face to examine it. 'I have seen many wills before, and this is no will, sir! Wills do not tend to have engravings . . . See here,' he muttered, his lips opening silently as he read for a few moments. His expression slowly shifted. 'I believe – yes! I believe this is . . . *By heavens!*'

'Well, man?' asked the tall bystander.

'Who could have told,' said Bendall, 'whether he had ever known ambition or disappointment?'

The lawyer wasn't soliloquising over the dead: he was reading the pages taken out of the man's hand. Sylvanus Bendall looked up from the page, his face flushed bright.

III

AMES R. OSGOOD HAD GREETED his visitor with, 'Mr. Leypoldt, a great pleasure,' which was the truth. Leypoldt was the editor of one of the principal journals for the book trade. The short-statured German immigrant was supremely well liked by those in publishing for his cordial manner and the fact that he reported with a fair, even hand.

'I hope to share with our readers the latest intelligence of your and Mr. Fields's firm, Mr. Osgood,' said Leypoldt.

'The firm is receiving A-1 notices lately on all sides,' Osgood remarked with an air of humble gratitude rather than pride.

The visitor cross-examined him. 'Your publications upcoming? Very well, very good. Number of books published this year so far? I see, very good. Number of employees currently? Very well. I see you have many bookkeepers of the female sex.'

'Things have changed so quickly,' Osgood said.

'Indeed you're right, so many things in our field are changing, Mr. Osgood! I have even been weighing a change of title for our journal. So that it will reflect more a concentration on the trade.'

The visitor's journal was presently titled *Trade Circular and Publishers' Bulletin: A Special Medium of Inter-Communication for Publishers, Manufacturers, Importers, and Dealers in Books, Stationery, Music, Prints and Miscellaneous Goods Sold at the Book, Stationery, Music and Print Stores.*

'We wish something, in a word, that will stand out as memorable for a national readership. Here is what I am considering.' Leypoldt wrote: *The Publishers' Weekly Trade Circular.*

Osgood said diplomatically, 'Our firm should continue our subscription whatever the title you decide on.'

'Many thanks, Mr. Osgood.' A pause signified that Leypoldt turned now to the true subject of his interrogation. 'Many in the trade who read our columns do wonder, Mr. Osgood, how you shall vie with so many of the larger publishers in New York. And with so many cheap republications of English editions threatening the ones published by your firm.'

'We shall choose the best-quality authors, print the best-quality books, and not yield to standards less than those that have brought us here, Mr. Leypoldt,' Osgood said earnestly. 'I am confident we'll succeed if we uphold those principles.'

The visiting reporter hesitated. 'Mr. Osgood, I would like our journal not only to report on publications of books but, in a word, the very story of publishing – its bloodstream, its soul, if you will. To encourage cooperation in the trade and to illustrate why those in our fraternity choose to elevate this calling. Why are we not black-smiths, or politicians, for instance? If you should have such a story, I should like very much to tell it in this column.'

'It was when I read *Walden* that I knew I wanted to be a publisher,' said Osgood, not a philosophical man but one who always wanted to be helpful. 'Not that I wished to experiment as a hermit in the woods, mind! But I realised that behind the unusual insights of this strange spirit, Thoreau, there was yet another person, far from Thoreau's woods, who was going to great lengths to ensure that every person in America had a chance to read his writing if they so desired. Someone who did so not because it would instantly prove popular, but because it could be important. I wrote a letter to Mr. Fields, asking for the chance to learn from him as his shop boy.'

'And now, as a man, what is it that you hope to find?'

Osgood was considering this question quite seriously when he was interrupted with the entrance of his bookkeeper. The young woman, whose pretty face was tightly framed with raven hair, bowed her head to both men as if to acknowledge her interruption was bold. She walked over to the desk with a light but confident stride and whispered a few words.

Osgood listened attentively before turning apologetically to his guest. 'Mr. Leypoldt, would you be kind enough to excuse me? I'm afraid something has arisen and I will need to continue this interview another time.' After the reporter had departed from the room, Osgood, twirling his pen between his forefinger and thumb, said to himself, 'A policeman is here?'

His bookkeeper Rebecca Sand spoke quietly as if they might be overheard. 'Yes, Mr. Osgood. The officer wishes a private word with a partner, and Mr. Fields is still out. He wouldn't say what it is about.'

Osgood nodded. 'Show him in, then, Miss Sand.'

'Mr. Osgood, I wasn't clear,' Rebecca said. 'The officer said that he'd wait outside.'

Osgood, gripping the back of his neck with one hand, thought that strange. He also saw a doubt in Rebecca's usually stoic face, but he could not stop to think about it now. James Osgood always was ready to move ahead to the next problem.

The policeman was standing outside the street entrance by the peanut vendor, who took the opportunity to complain about a band of street musicians who had been driving away his customers with solicitations for money. Osgood presented himself.

'Are you that one?' said the policeman.

'Pardon, Officer?' replied Osgood.

'That Osgood up there?' the officer asked, squinting at the shingle rising over the entrance to the three-storey building at 124 Tremont Street: FIELDS, OSGOOD & CO.

'Yes, sir,' Osgood said. 'James Ripley Osgood.'

'Never mind all that,' the policeman shook his head sternly. 'Ripley and what-you-will. I suppose I expected a partner of your firm to be a somewhat, now then . . . a gentleman somewhat . . .' He was trying to find the most sensitive and yet deliberate word. 'Somewhat older, perhaps!'

James Osgood, a trimly fitted man not yet thirty-five and not yet looking thirty, even with a well-shaped shadow moustache, was accustomed to this. He smiled generously and handed the officer a book. 'Please accept this token, Officer Carlton. One of the finest from our presses last year.'

The firm's senior partner, J. T. Fields, had taught Osgood that no matter what the circumstances, presenting a book as a gift – a rather inexpensive gesture for a publisher – improved the mood of the gloomiest recipient. Regardless of the volume, the book was weighed, its title leaf examined with pleasant surprise, and the object finally fancied as precisely right for the recipient's interests. Accordingly, Carlton weighed the book that Osgood handed him and studied the title. *A Journey in Brazil,* by Professor and Mrs. Agassiz.

'I have spoken to my wife more than once on how I would enjoy Brazil!' the officer exclaimed. Then, with an astonished gaze, looked up and said, 'Sir, how is it you know my name?'

'You called upon our firm some years ago for a minor problem.'

'Yes, yes. But do you say we met?'

'We did, Officer Carlton.'

'Well,' the policeman said definitively, 'you must have changed how you wear your moustache.'

In fact, Osgood had not changed a hair since he was twenty, but he agreed wholeheartedly with the speculation before asking what had brought the officer to their firm.

'It is not my desire to startle anyone, Mr. Osgood,' the policeman said, reclaiming a grim demeanour. 'I asked you to come down because I did not wish to frighten that girl – I mean the very young lady only steps from your office door.'

'I think you will find that Miss Rebecca Sand does not frighten easily,' Osgood said.

'That so? Bless her! I esteem that sort of fortitude of character, even in a woman. I only hope you prove just as strong hearted.'

The young publisher climbed into the back of a carriage while the policeman ordered his driver to the dead house.

It was impossible not to feel possessed of heightened caution when entering the halls of the city coroner's chambers of Boston. Upon their arrival, the officer led Osgood through an anteroom with little air and a dusty half window. Ascending a narrow staircase to a dark room on the floor above, the police officer turned up a lamp and looked down impatiently at his shoes, as though it were Osgood's turn now to guide them.

'We don't have the entire day, I'm afraid, Mr. Osgood.'

Then he noticed. Officer Carlton was not looking at his shoes, but at the floor.

Osgood stumbled backwards as though about to fall, for the floor below them was made entirely of glass. Below it was a tiny room, twenty feet square, containing four stone slabs. On one, a woman whose skin was shrivelled and blackened by cholera. Another displayed an old man whose face was burned on one side, and a third, a bloated victim of drowning. Beside each stone was a hook with the clothing the dead had been in when found.

On to each body, a gentle stream of water flowed from a series of pipes.

'It's new. This is where dead bodies not yet identified are kept for viewing, at least for forty-eight hours before being placed in a pauper's grave if no one claims them,' Carlton explained. 'The water keeps the bodies fresh.'

The fourth slab. The body was covered below the neck by a white sheet. A familiar heavy suit on the hook at its side was ripped at the left sleeve. Osgood took off his hat and clutched it against his heart when he saw the dulled eyes staring back up at him.

'You know the young man then?' Officer Carlton asked at the publisher's reaction.

He was so distorted by death Osgood had to force himself to recognise him. Checking the catch in his throat and looking up at the policeman with misty eyes, Osgood lowered himself on one knee and touched the cold glass below. 'He is one of my employees. His name is Daniel; he's a junior clerk at our publishing firm. Seventeen years old.'

Osgood did not know how to maintain his usual poise. It was Osgood who had hired Daniel as a shop boy three years earlier. He had been determined to give him a chance in spite of his un-propitious circumstances. Daniel quickly proved himself honest and dedicated – and for longer than two weeks, the usual expiration. He had risen to the post of clerk, and even Mr. Fields had soon called him Daniel (instead of *that one*, short for 'that poor country boy you wanted to hire').

'What happened?' Osgood asked the police officer when he was able to speak again.

'Run down by an omnibus in Dock Square.'

'Did he have anything with him?' Osgood asked, trying to piece it together, make sense of anything that he could. As he kneeled, Osgood was so close to the glass that the reflection of his own face was imposed over his clerk's lifeless form.

'No, he had nothing on his person. We connected him to you because one of our patrolmen had remembered seeing him coming and going from your building. Do you know where he was today?'

'Yes, of course. He was to be receiving important papers at the harbour and delivering them to our vaults.' Osgood hesitated but remembered he was speaking to a police officer, not a rival publisher.

'They were the advance sheets of the next instalments of *The Mystery of Edwin Drood* sent from London.'

The Dickens novel had been published in serialised instalments at the beginning of each month. As with his other novels, the serial publication would gradually add readers who would then praise the story to friends and relatives who had not read it. The serial format made readers feel present at the very moments the story unfolded, as if they were among its characters. After the publication of the final monthly instalment, the novel would be published in its entirety in book form.

'Hold!' said the officer. 'I have been reading about young Mr. Drood's fortunes – misfortunes, I should say – with great interest in the magazines! I suppose this isn't the best time to ask. But pray tell me, Mr. Osgood, do you know how it will all end for Eddie Drood, now that Mr. Dickens has died?'

This very question had in fact been consuming Osgood's mind more than the officer could know – *how it will all end, with Dickens dead* – yet suddenly he had no response. Not now, not at the sight of good Daniel, motionless and broken on a cold board. The figure undulated strangely from the stream of water, as if he might still awaken.

'Daniel never failed his duties to me,' Osgood said. 'To be lost to such a senseless accident!'

'Mr. Osgood, this was not merely an accident,' Carlton said as he delivered a long sigh.

'What do you mean?'

Carlton led Osgood down the stairs and into the room of the unknown dead. There was an entirely different feeling inside the little room with the glass ceiling than there had been in the viewing space above; it was like the difference between watching an exotic and dangerous animal through bars and entering the cage. The floor was white and black marble and cooled by the running water. Close up, the young clerk's stomach was grossly distended under its sheet.

Carlton explained. 'Your clerk appears to have forfeited the responsibilities you assigned him and indulged in some variety of intoxicants. Before his death, he was deep out of his senses and wandering blindly through the streets, according to witnesses we interviewed. I'm afraid the young man's last act *has* been to fail you.'

Osgood knew he should restrain his anger, but he couldn't. 'Officer, I'd suggest you mind your words. You are slandering the dead!'

'Ha!' clacked the old coroner, Mr. Charles Barnicoat, coming from around the corner and hunching his sweaty face and whiskers over the body. 'Officer Carlton speaks only the truth, wouldn't know how to speak anything else.'

'I *know* Daniel,' Osgood insisted.

'Spine bent like a question mark, see?' said the coroner with confirming nod. 'Common sign of the habitual opium eater.'

'He was run down by an omnibus!' cried Osgood.

Barnicoat yanked hard at the dead clerk's arm. The skin there had turned a horrible blue tint. 'You need more?' he asked.

The sight revealed around Barnicoat's fingers instantly silenced Osgood. There were several small holes pierced into the arm.

'What is it?' the publisher asked.

Barnicoat licked his lips. 'These are marks from a new sort of needle called a hypodermic treatment – it was used by our doctors in the war. It serves like a lancet but the dose can be precisely controlled. It is now employed by doctors to inject certain potent medicines through the skin and into the cellular tissue. But the kits are used without a doctor's consent by the opium eaters who are habituated to it, as your young clerk must have been by the looks of it. Some even inject these needles directly into their veins, a thing that would never be permitted by doctors! "Portable ecstasies", these young men call the drug.'

'God save the commonwealth,' Officer Carlton intoned morosely.

'They wish to be the heroes of their dreams, you see, rather than live their real lives,' Barnicoat lectured with his chin stuck out pompously. 'They prefer to feel in their brains they are floating through fire in China or India instead of trudging Boston in the monotonous treadmill of life. It *is* a shame but somewhat less of a shame to remember a young tramp with these habits rarely will attain the age of forty, something you or I can do quite without fail.'

Osgood interrupted. 'Daniel Sand was no tramp. And no opium fiend!'

'Then explain the marks on his arm,' Barnicoat said. 'No, the omnibus and its passengers, waylaid from their pressing travel, were more the victims than this lad. Now, you needn't feel any personal responsibility fall on yourself, Osgood,' Barnicoat said with a rude informality.

'What happened to his chest?' Osgood asked, forcing himself to look more closely at the mangled remains of his clerk. There were two parallel cuts in Daniel's skin. 'It is almost like a bite mark. And his suit. Over here, it looks as though someone tore it at the seam.'

The coroner shrugged. 'From the mechanisms beneath the bus, perhaps. Or perhaps the boy had injured himself while in the spell of his narcotic. Sad to reflect on, the shadows of this danger fall not uncommonly on young men of low station and more and more even women – if you can call them that still, for they are much degraded. I'm afraid this boy was one of the *fallen*.'

'I cannot say it is a surprise,' Carlton said to Barnicoat, 'after seeing the office today.'

Osgood had begun to feel the heat of anger rising to his ears and lips against Daniel for what seemed an undeniable secret life. Now he could direct his emotion elsewhere. 'Since I have entered, you have insulted the decent name of my clerk, and now my business. Exactly what do you mean to say about our office?'

Carlton raised an eyebrow, as though it were too plain. 'Why, an office in which the men are mixed together with unmarried women – it is bound to corrupt young boys! Could awaken certain uncontrolled physical urges in the females, too, I dare fancy, that should make any gentleman colour.' Though he himself did not.

Osgood steadied himself to rebuke the policeman, when he realised something . . . In his astonishment at seeing Daniel lifeless on the slab, it had unaccountably fled his mind.

'My God. Rebecca!' Osgood said softly.

'Yes, Rebecca! That was the name of the little miss, Mr. Barnicoat, and a pretty one with blooming cheeks, sitting by Mr. Osgood's office door,' Carlton said with a lugubrious frown. 'The place almost seemed all women, in truth. Before long the dear strong-willed creatures will have the ballot – mark my having said that, Mr. Barnicoat! – and there will be no one left in all Boston for housekeeping.'

'Rebecca,' Osgood whispered, gently clutching the stiffening hand of his clerk. 'Rebecca is Daniel's sister.'

IV

OUGH IT HAD BEEN THERE for thirteen years, give or take a month, 'the New Land' was still new in the eyes of Bostonians. The area had been a wasted basin for many years before being filled in as hundreds of new acres, where streets and sidewalks were put down and gradually extended west. The region was widely pronounced as having even more potential than the South End for a luxurious and prestigious collection of houses. But though the old blue bloods liked to speculate in the markets, they did not like to gamble with the value of their neighbourhoods and children's inheritances.

Sylvanus Bendall was a different breed. He welcomed risk. He opened the door and invited risk in, taking its coat and brushing its boots and serving it tea in his living room. He was one of the first men to have purchased one of the tracts of land in Back Bay as far west as possible when the commonwealth announced it would sell them. He liked the idea that the street he lived on – Newbury Street – was so aptly named that it had not even existed a few years back. At times, at least twice a day, he boasted to himself that he was not unlike Sir William Braxton, the sturdy Englishman who had lived on this peninsula by himself for five years before 1630 when Governor Winthrop came and founded Boston. In the days of Braxton, Boston would have looked far more rugged and hearty, capped by its three potent hills that were now barely distinguishable, faintly remembered in the name of Tremont Street. To the lone pilgrim Braxton, they would have been like the Alps.

Bendall enjoyed rushing into the unknown. Just as he had at the scene of the omnibus accident a few days earlier, sacrificing his good summer trousers to the pavement to be nearer to the dying lad. It was Bendall who'd examined the papers the dead man clutched, while others stood by dumbfounded by what to do, and found them to be the latest episode of Mr. Dickens's current (and, alas, final) novel.

The company present at the scene of the accident had been split between those most fascinated by a dead man and those most fascinated by the mysterious pages.

Among the latter, each pleaded his and her case to Bendall – who held the papers like the auctioneer holds his hammer – as to who was most deserving of a sheet or two from the packet. A poetic brick-maker noted that he had attended all of Dickens's public readings at the Tremont Temple in Boston two and a half years earlier, waiting in line when it was so cold the mercury was clean out of sight. Another man, rosy and cheerful, had kept his own ticket stubs in his family Bible and vowed that if he did not truly love the genius of the great novelist more than anyone else did, then he would wish Dickens never born. A buxom lady listed a series of household pets – two cats, a yellow dog, a bird – that she had named for Dickens characters (Pip and Nell, Rose, Oliver); a mechanic perched near the corpse announced he had read Dickens's *David Copperfield* four times, but this was eclipsed by *six! eight!* and *nine!* from others. One old man began to cry and it seemed to be for the accident victim's sad fate, until he whispered, 'Poor dear old Dickens, noble Dickens.'

As the bystanders quibbled with each other over the pages, Bendall silently made a bold decision: he himself would be the treasure's custodian. Folding the pages up, he quietly made his exit, pausing only to leave his name with the driver of the 'Alice Gray', should he happen to be arrested for mowing down the lad.

'Sylvanus Bendall,' he said to the nervous omnibus driver, 'two words to remember, and you shall not have reason to fear Boston justice!'

Sylvanus Bendall. His name itself sounded far more like the name of an adventurer than an attorney-at-law for the indigent and un-fortunate classes of Boston. It was the name of one who had penetrated deep into the New Land. His friends from Beacon Hill may have put up their handkerchiefs at the smell of the nearby marshes and the dust of construction, but Bendall inflated his nostrils each morning like a war horse.

Not to say that the Back Bay was an Eden; there were problems and he faced those with a manly demeanour. In fact, there was one waiting for him on this day when he returned to his house.

The plate-glass window at the side of his porch was shattered into pieces. Bendall walked quietly to the street door and took the latch in his hand. Inside, he faced a mess: desks and secretaries overturned; up a flight of stairs, holding tightly to the oak balustrade, coming upon dishes and china shattered; up another flight, shelves emptied of books. He heard a shuffle and a sudden noise from another room. The thieves at large! He grabbed a walking stick and an umbrella and raised them together like a Japanese samurai. 'I shall knock your head clear off!' he shouted as fair warning.

A small, white-haired woman cried out, 'Mr. Bendall!' His housekeeper, who had arrived to prepare supper shortly before him, now stood dead still with a look of terror.

'Don't be afraid, my dear Mary, you will be safe now with me,' Bendall said.

It did not seem that any objects of value were missing. His much-prized pages were undoubtedly safe, for he had been keeping them on his own person, in his waistcoat.

'Should I send a boy for the police?' asked Mary.

'No, no,' he said dismissively.

'But they must be on alert!' the housekeeper protested.

'Pooh, Mary!' said Bendall. 'You read too many sensation novels. Police are of an old mind-set and know nothing of the Back Bay. I shall root out the source of this evil myself.' There, once more, a bold and undoubtable decision by Sylvanus Bendall.

V

ANIEL SAND'S DEATH WAS YET another crisis at the bustling 124 Tremont Street office building of Fields, Osgood & Co. It was the nature of the publishing trade to shift from crisis to optimism back to crisis, and the master of those rhythms was James Osgood. It had been back in March, three months before Daniel Sand fell lifelessly in the street, when the senior partner, J. T. Fields, stopped Osgood on the stairs. Fields's long, stiff, greying beard and a rumbling undercurrent in his voice lent him an inflated gravity at all times.

'Mr. Osgood, a word please.'

A word never failed to add a burden to Osgood's shoulders. He knew Fields's troubled expressions like he knew the halls of the publishing firm and could guess the sort of business emergency at a glance. Osgood had been in this man's employment for fifteen years since he had written him that first letter praising *Walden* with the vivid enthusiasm of a neophyte. It had been five years since Osgood introduced bright colour binding to replace the drab maroon covers they had formerly favoured. And it had been almost two years since his own name was added to the stationery – transforming *Ticknor, Fields & Co.* as though by magic fulfilment of his once dreamlike ambitions into *Fields, Osgood & Co.*

But there was no shortage of problems. Their neighbours, the shrewdly evangelical Hurd & Houghton, with their young lieutenant George Mifflin, had transformed from their reliable printer into a competing publisher. And their chief rival in New York more than ever was Harper & Brothers.

'It is Harper this time!' Fields cried out to Osgood when they were alone. He leaned his elbows over a pulpitlike standing desk in the corner of the room, where there always sat open his massive appointment book. 'It's Harper, Osgood. He's plotting.'

'Plotting what?'

'Plotting. I don't know what *yet*,' Fields admitted, the last word coming with a stinging warning as though the chief partner of Harper & Brothers, Major Harper, was looking down from the chandelier. 'He is filled with rancour and spite against our house.' Fields stabbed a pen in ink and wrote in an appointment. 'Fletcher Harper is coming from New York soon to recruit more Boston authors – to poach more from us, let us be blunt – and has requested an interview here. You ought to be the one to meet with him. Blasted hand! I will have to call one of the girls in to write.' Fields opened and shut his hand, which suffered from painful cramps. 'I daresay I haven't written a letter in my own hand in a year, except those to Mr. Dickens, of course. My other correspondents must think I have grown womanly with age.'

Osgood was still surprised at Fields's instruction about Harper. With a casual downcast glare, as though checking the shine of his left boot, the younger man commented, 'I would expect that Major Harper will prefer the interview be with you, my dear Mr. Fields.'

Fields became silent. His recent tendency to fall entirely quiet had struck Osgood as worrisome. The senior publisher stepped out from behind the high desk and began a slow breathing exercise. Finally, he responded in a softer tone. 'Everyone likes you, Osgood. It is an advantage I hope you keep long after I am quietly laid away in some uneditorial corner far from this business. Why, it is something to say of a publisher, that everyone likes him! We are like lawyers, except instead of being blamed for the loss of a mortgage, we are blamed for lost dreams.'

When Osgood looked up he was startled to find Fields with his fists posed in a fighting position.

'You've boxed, eh?' Fields asked.

Osgood shook his head confusedly and replied, 'At Bowdoin, I fenced.'

'I had my first boxing lessons from an old pugilist when I lived in Suffolk Place as a lad running errands under Bill Ticknor. I paid the fellow in books Ticknor threw out! Could have been a prizefighter if I'd kept at it. Start with a jab.'

Fields demonstrated his moves. Osgood reluctantly imitated.

'This,' Fields said as he pantomimed an exchange of severe blows and quick escapes, 'is how you stand up to a Harper brother! There is only one thing worse than the coming war with the Harpers, Osgood: and that is being afraid of it.'

Osgood had been correct in his prediction: when the appointed day came later in March for Fletcher Harper's interview and Osgood greeted him in his best suit and with the offer of a brandy, the New York visitor peered around impatiently through his wire-framed eyeglasses.

'Mr. Fields sends his sincerest regrets, Major,' Osgood said. 'I am afraid he has been drawn away suddenly by the press of business.'

'Oh! Trying to stop one of your authors from drowning himself in the Frog Pond?'

Osgood gave his most gentlemanly laugh, though Harper did not. How could a man scowl at his own joke?

Harper was called the Major not to signify any service during the war but because of his battlefield style of command at his offices in New York. He scratched the line of his jaw under his wide mutton-chop running down his face. 'Do you *have* authority here, James R. Osgood?'

'Major,' Osgood said with equanimity, 'I am a partner of the firm now.'

'Well! Junior partner, yes,' he grumbled. 'I must have read about it in Leypoldt's columns. And you are an honest man?'

'I am.'

'Good, Mr. Osgood! You did not hesitate in your answer; that means it is true.' Harper accepted the glass of brandy. He began to raise it to his lips, then paused and held it in a toast. 'To we happy few, the publishers of the world! Individuals who kindly assist authors to obtain an immortality in which we do not ourselves participate.'

Osgood raised his glass without comment.

'Men in our line know me well for being direct,' Harper said, sacrificing his drink to a long gulp and putting the glass down, 'and I am too old to change. So this is what I have come to say. Ticknor and Fields – I mean by that, of course, Fields and Osgood – this house cannot survive its present circumstances.'

Osgood waited for Harper to continue.

'Your magazine, the *Atlantic Monthly*, for all its merit, hardly turns a penny, does it? Now, take New York City.'

'What about it, Major?'

'Come! I like Boston, I do. Well, except for your priest-ridden Paddy camps, which are worse than ours in New York. But that can't be helped these days, we open our shores and soon we are corrupted. Still, I wander into the world of politics. We speak of the literary world. Writers by species are creatures more and more of the New York breed. We have the cheaper printing presses, the cheaper binders and the cheaper ideas at our fingertips. An author's fame will no longer last twenty-odd years in the fashion of your Mr. Longfellow – no, an author's name will survive one book, two perhaps, and then be replaced by something newer, bolder, bigger. You must produce *quantity* going ahead, Mr. Osgood.'

Osgood knew how the Harper family treated *their* authors at their Franklin Square building in New York, where an iron bust of Benjamin Franklin, through a shrewd squint, looked down judgementally on all comers to their kingdom as though to suggest he was the last author worth any fuss. There was the anecdote known throughout the trade about Fitz-James O'Brien's marching outside the massive Harper building holding a sign, 'I AM ONE OF HARPERS' AUTHORS. I AM STARVING', until the Harpers would agree to pay him what he was owed. There were, besides, tales of great satisfaction in the Harpers' offices when they collected back the pitiable $145.83 that they had paid in advance to Mr. Melville for his queer sea tale, *Moby-Dick, or The Whale*.

To the Harper brothers publishing was power. It was a power that had reached a crescendo in the 1840s when the eldest of the quartet, James Harper, became mayor of New York City as part of the anti-Catholic Native Party. James instituted what was known as Harper's Police, before dying in a bloody accident, when his carriage cracked and his horses dragged him bodily through Central Park. Fletcher, formerly their financial manager, had since ascended to the top of the publishing firm and earned the sobriquet of Major.

Osgood felt an urge to scream bubbling up, a rare and uncomfortable feeling. Osgood was the oldest of five siblings and, growing up, it had always been left to him to be the sturdy, sensible one who would preserve order at any cost to his own personal feelings. Others could be permitted to give way to their emotions but not him. That was how he was known in youth in Maine, that was how he had made his stamp at their firm and on the trade at large. These same traits, his workmanship and steadiness, had attained his admission to college at only twelve years old – though his family waited until he was fourteen at the request of the Bowdoin administrators.

'We like our local authors very much,' Osgood assured his guest as calmly as he could. 'You might say we believe our house works for our authors, rather than the other way around.'

'If you talk metaphysics, I can't follow you, Mr. Osgood.'

'I shall be happy to try to speak more plainly.'

'You can tell me then, why Mr. Fields wished you to meet with me instead of him. Because,' he said without giving Osgood the chance to answer, 'Fields knows he is in the after-dinner hour of life. You are the eager young man, you are the enfant terrible with a sharp eye and smart ideas, and can break with sleepy tradition.'

Harper went on with only a slight pause for breath: 'Books are to be mere lumber in the future. Articles of trade, you see, Mr. Osgood! The bookstores already are filled with empty space, cigar boxes, Indian prints, toys. *Toys!* Before long there will be more toys than books in this country, and it will matter not who is the author of the new book any more than who is the manufacturer of a new paper doll. The publisher's name will be far more important than any author's and our job will be to mix the ink of a book together like the pharmacist's chemicals.

'Well, I come to you with a proposal: that Fields, Osgood and Company shutter its doors here in Boston, give up this dying hub and move to New York – combining with us, under the Harper name, of course. Oh, we'd give you full swing for your own peculiar literary tastes. And you will forgo a slow demise of this great old house to be part of our publishing family. You will be to us as your own sons are to you – haven't you children, Mr. Osgood? Oh! You are a bachelor, I do recall. Childless Fields having been your prototype.'

Osgood blinked away the last aside. 'Your idea is simply not in our authors' interests, Major. We shall always see our books as wiser and better than objects, and I think I speak for Mr. Fields in saying we would rather continue in that light even if it means we do not last. I'm afraid you cannot ever de-Bostonise this house.'

Osgood decided to swiftly end the meeting using one of Fields's techniques. He passed his foot down on a pedal hidden under the desk and Daniel Sand came to alert Osgood of an 'emergency' that would forestall any further conversation. But Harper stood and signed his understanding.

'You needn't bother with the performance,' Harper called out before the clerk had the chance to speak.

Daniel, acting out his urgent entrance, looked to Osgood with sad eyes. Osgood nodded permission to go.

Harper continued, a dark cloud passing over his face. 'I know every trick, every plan, every purpose in this trade, Mr. Osgood, and I know it ten times better than my dear brother the mayor did, God bless the proud man. Come! The old methods will not save you from the truth I have delivered to you today.'

They eyed each other, taking stock.

Harper suddenly laughed, but a laugh that said the joke was his and his alone. 'Well, it is true what they say, I suppose. Courtesy is courtesy but business is business.'

'Who says that, Major?'

'Me. And you shouldn't believe Mr. Fields and yourself are so different from us, Mr. Osgood, shielded from the world around you by sunshiny talk and your high ambitions. We've watched you. Remember, the angel may write, but 'tis the devil that must print. You should have gone into the ministry if you wanted to remain a believer.'

'Major, I wish you good afternoon.' Osgood waited silently until Harper had no choice but to gather his belongings.

'Oh! By the by, the new mystery that Dickens is writing, I hear, shall be enthralling,' Harper said offhandedly to Osgood as he brushed the rainwater from his hat. 'Chapman in London, they say, is paying a fortune to publish it. *The Murder of Edward Drory*?'

'*The Mystery of Edwin Drood*, I believe he has decided to call it.'

'Yes, yes, that is it! I am on the very tiptoe of expectation to see where Dickens, the Great Enchanter, will take us this time.'

Dickens! – that strange word, that name of names, the man – meant the world to the firm of Fields, Osgood & Co. The Major knew it, which is why his mention of the new novel was also a threat.

Fields had a few years earlier made two big propositions to the world's most popular novelist, Charles Dickens: first, that Dickens come to America on a grand reading tour, and second, that their firm be the author's exclusive publisher in America. From his estate in the English countryside, Dickens agreed to both terms, which prompted the loud grousing of all the other American publishers – especially the Harper brothers.

There was no international copyright agreement between the United States and Britain. This meant that any American publisher could publish any British book without permission of the author. There did exist what was known as trade courtesy, however: when an American publisher made an agreement to be the publisher of a foreign book, other American publishers would respect it. The Harper brothers were notorious, though, for printing cheap, unauthorised editions (making their own changes to the text, sometimes carelessly and sometimes to suit an English topic better to an American audience). They'd leave the Harper torch off the title page and sell the spurious edition in railway cars or on the street or by subscription.

Thus, Major Harper's alluding to *The Mystery of Edwin Drood* was a reminder that Harper could undermine the enormous investment by Fields, Osgood & Co. in *Drood* by flooding their own cheap editions into the marketplace. The demand would be high for Dickens's new book, and what would the typical hardworking American reader choose? Spend two dollars for the book from Fields, Osgood & Co. – or seventy-five cents from one of Harper's hawkers or pedlars?

The Boston publisher would be powerless to stop it.

Charles Dickens's five-month-long reading tour of the United States arranged by Fields and Osgood in the winter of 1867–68 had proven an enormous success. It felt historic even as it was happening. Thousands heard him perform. Osgood worked industriously during the tour, charged with the duties of a treasurer and with meeting Dickens's sometimes-fickle demands, in addition to smoothing over conflicts and troubles. At the end of the tour, there were a hundred thousand dollars in profits in the pockets of the 'Chief' – as he was called by Dickens's manager, Dolby.

Fields, Osgood & Co. made money on the readings – 5 per cent of gross receipts – but their real reward for the faith they had shown in Charles Dickens was yet to come. That would come with the publication of *The Mystery of Edwin Drood*.

The whole world awaited it, as had been true of each Dickens novel since *The Pickwick Papers* and *Oliver Twist* placed the former court reporter's name before the public thirty-five years before. Dickens alone, among all the writers of popular fiction of the day, could employ wit and discernment, excitement and sympathy, in equal parts in each one of his books. The characters were no mere paper dolls, nor were they thinly veiled extensions of Charles Dickens's own persona. No, the characters were utterly themselves. In a Dickens story, readers were not asked to aspire to a higher class or to hate other classes than their own but to find the humanity and the humane in all. That is what had made him the world's most famous author.

This time the wait for a new book had been nearly five years, longer than any other interval between books in the past. 'The public is ripe for it!' Fields had said. *Drood* would tell the story of a young gentleman – Edwin Drood – an honest though ambling character who vanishes after provoking the jealousy of a devious uncle named John Jasper, a respectable citizen with a double life as a drug fiend. Dickens promised in his letters to Fields that the book would be 'very curious and new' for his readers.

Ralph Waldo Emerson had been sitting in Fields's office when Fields and Osgood had read Dickens's letter about the novel.

'I am afraid Dickens has too much talent for his genius,' Emerson announced in his way of an old oracle bored by his own pronouncements.

'How do you mean, my dear Waldo?' asked Fields. A publisher in the trade as long as Fields would never be roused by one writer kicking another.

'His face daunts me!' Emerson exclaimed at the Dickens photograph on the wall showing a strong but weather-beaten profile, the far-off look in the strict military eye. 'You and Mr. Osgood would persuade me that he is a genial creature. You would persuade me that he is a sympathetic man superior to his talents, but I believe he is *harnessed* to them. He is too consummate an artist to have a thread of nature left.'

Emerson did not realise how much his publishers needed Dickens and could no longer depend only on the likes of Longfellow, Lowell, Holmes – nor even their Concord Sage, Mr. Emerson – to keep them afloat. Years earlier, the mutual admiration society of Boston brought floods of readers to the publishing house for their novels and poems.

Effortlessly, Longfellow's sensation, *The Song of Hiawatha*, had flowed from the presses and out the doors of bookshops in Osgood's first months of working at the firm! Now the best Osgood seemed able to do was to persuade Dr. Holmes to write a pale sequel of *The Autocrat of the Breakfast Table*; smile at Mrs. Stowe over a well-intended morality novel half as courageous as *Uncle Tom*; or encourage Longfellow's slow labour on his long, sombre poem about Jesus Christ, *The Divine Tragedy*, though republishing Longfellow's controversial *Divine Comedy* translation, yet again, would be more lucrative.

Osgood felt the Furies chasing him: each day, having to meet irritated authors' demands for free copies or for solace when books passed into the dreaded land of the out of print. *Drowning themselves in the Frog Pond in disappointment*. Montague Midges, from two offices down the hall, would report the higher author payments needed to fill the pages of their magazine, the *Atlantic Monthly*. Osgood would look over his shoulder at sluggish, heavy literary productions always reported as '*almost* half finished!' like Bryant's translation of Homer and Taylor's *Faust*, neither of which could realistically sell enough, even once completed, to make up for their costs. Osgood was overseeing a ship rocking at sea, with the storms worsening.

Dickens's new book could change that.

Harper had a point, Osgood had thought the day of their meeting, though he would never admit it. Maybe a publisher had become little different from the toy maker, and maybe an author's name couldn't survive twenty years. 'Except for Charles Dickens,' Osgood said to himself. 'He transcends the rest. He makes literature into books, and books literature. Harper's toys be damned.'

Then, early that summer, the news arrived.

'James!' Fields had rushed into Osgood's office breathlessly. 'We received it over the cable wires! God grant it as some mistake!'

Osgood panicked before he knew what to panic about. It was so rare that Fields would address his young partner informally, or that he'd exhibit such a show of emotion in proximity to the female book-keepers – who all looked up from their copying and probably blotted a dozen words in one instant – or that he would be running at all. Then Osgood noticed one of their employees crying into her bare hands before she could find a handkerchief. And Rebecca was looking over at Osgood as though she had a thousand words waiting on her lips. He had the sickening feeling of everyone else knowing something terrible had transpired.

The sympathetic look of her green eyes made Osgood want to take Rebecca's counsel – to have the news, whatever it was and however bad – delivered by her.

But Fields had already flown through his office door, gesticulating wildly as he pushed it shut. 'Charles Dickens . . . dead!' he finally managed to blurt out.

The Boston newspapers had received the obituaries from that morning's London papers and had sent a wire on to their office. Fields read from it aloud, emphasising the details as though the subject might still be saved by quick thinking: 'The pupil of the right eye was much dilated, that of the left contracted, the breathing stertorous, the limbs flaccid until half an hour before death, when some convulsion occurred . . .'

Further details included that Dickens had spent his final day working on *The Mystery of Edwin Drood* when, pen in hand, he had begun to feel sick. He had just finished the final words of the sixth instalment of the story – the halfway mark through the book, which was to be composed of twelve serialised parts. Soon after, he fell down and never recovered.

'Dickens dead!' Fields exclaimed, shaking bodily. 'How is it . . . ! I cannot believe it! A world without Dickens!'

Men and women wept or sat bewildered and silent in the offices as word spread. 'Charles Dickens is dead,' was repeated by all who heard it, to whomever they saw next. Nearly everyone in the publishing house had met Mr. Dickens when he had come for his tour two years before. Though it was difficult to feel Charles Dickens to be your friend, it was instantaneous to feel oneself his. How much life was in him – not just his own but each of his characters whose lives he had performed in front of so many thrilled audiences during his visit! No one who had ever met Dickens could imagine him gone. A man who had – Osgood remembered someone saying – a man who had exclamation points for eyes. How could such a man die?

'Charles . . . Dickens . . . Forty miles . . .' Fields was mumbling still in a crestfallen fog after they had sat in silence almost an hour. 'I must remain on watch at the wires in case it was a mistake.' Dickens had only been a few years older than Fields – whose own sick headaches and hand aches had grown worse. Fields turned back to Osgood on his way out, 'Forty miles, you said so!'

'I did indeed,' Osgood replied with a patient kindness.

It had been March 1868, near the end of Dickens's visit to Boston, at dinner at the Fieldses' on Charles Street. The talk had somehow turned, in the way such things happened at the Fields dinner table, to calculating how far all of Charles Dickens's manuscripts would extend in a single line if the pages were laid end to end.

'Forty miles,' Osgood had said after careful mental calculation of the number of novels and stories and a quick census of their average length.

'No, Osgood,' Fields had called out. 'A *hundred thousand* miles!'

'Thank you, my dear Fields,' Charles Dickens had said, as though conferring knighthood on him, then turned to Osgood with a stern countenance, his large blue-grey eyes seeming to burrow deep into the young publisher's soul, and his eyebrows darting far up. 'Mr. Fields, I am inclined to be down on your young associate here until he rather changes his calculation of how many words I have surrendered in my day. More than forty miles, surely!'

There were Fields and Osgood in a nutshell: the younger man sought the correct answer, the older gave the answer one wanted to hear.

'Does it not give you a weird sensation, Mr. Dickens?' said beautiful Annie Fields, laughing at her husband and his partner. 'How could words with so much value cover so light a portion of the earth?'

The writer put up his large hands in an expressive gesture that pulled all attention to him. He had an ever-changing face that could not really be seen properly unless he was caught sleeping. 'Mrs. Fields, you *do* understand my odd lot. Once I publish, my words are mangled, pounded, and robbed on both sides of the ocean. I have many readers and booksellers in league with me: and yet I stand alone. I suppose I am fated to be a Quixote without a Sancho. That is how my fellow authors fall as this life fight of ours progresses. There is nothing to do but close up the ranks, march on, and fight it out.'

Osgood felt a confusion and diminishment come over him at the memory now as he followed Fields into the corridor and his office. The senior officer sat and slumped over on his manuscript-filled window seat, pressing his forehead against the cool glass of the window until it fogged over from his breath.

Osgood felt if he could make a strategy for business instead of sinking into depression, Fields would be grateful. He would earn the faith placed in him with this partnership. He could hear Major Harper's voice in his ear from three months earlier speaking of *junior partner, yes,* and then of *Drood. I am on the very tiptoe of expectation.*

'Mr. Fields,' Osgood said, 'I am concerned now more than ever about the Harpers.'

'Yes, yes,' Fields replied languidly. He was lost to grief. 'What? I cannot understand it, Osgood. How could you think of Harper?'

'When the Major hears the new novel was only half finished – and Dickens dead – well, Mr. Fields, Harper will claim no trade courtesy even applies for anything *unfinished.* He will try to rush out and publish *Drood* right under our noses without hindrance or disguise.'

Fields snapped to attention. 'Harpy Brothers, Lord! A deadly stab. Osgood, our house cannot survive it!' He moaned in a voice of surrender and rolled himself across the room in his desk chair. 'No man can see the end of this. The business world now is depressed and wavering. Major Harper was right about what he told you of New York, you know. It will be over for us.'

'Do not say that, my friend,' said Osgood.

Fields's energy had seemed to expire as he sat with his limbs hanging flaccidly from the chair. 'New England has been a brilliant school of literature. But it has the feature of a single generation, not destined to be succeeded by another. Edinburgh gave away its publishing over to London, and so we will be bought and swallowed by New York. Dash it all! We might as well just hawk books of quotations and law textbooks, like poor Little and Brown, God rest their souls. Why undergo the pain of literature?' Fields's mind suddenly wandered. 'Say, you have a taste for salt at the moment, as I do, Osgood? I would run a mile for it. I want you to go to the stand on the corner and get a quart of peanuts. Yes, something salty.'

Osgood sighed, feeling suddenly like a junior clerk again – and feeling the solid forms around him were ready to disappear. Then he tossed his hat on the chair and turned back to his senior partner. 'We must not sit by,' Osgood said. 'Perhaps nothing can be done, but we must try. We will publish it and publish it well. Before Major Harper does. Half a Dickens novel is half more than any other novel on the shelves!'

'Bah! What good is a mystery novel without the ending? We become invested in the story of young Edwin Drood and then . . . nothing!' Fields cried out. But he started to pace up and down the room, with a reassuring clarity kindling in his eye. He blew out a long sigh as if expelling the old despair. Suddenly he was Osgood's Fields again, the invincible businessman. 'You are in part right, Osgood. Half right, I should say. Yet we mustn't be content with half of the thing at all, Osgood!'

'What choice do we have? This is all he left.'

'The man just died – all is in disarray and grief in England, I am sure. We need to discover everything we can about how Dickens intended to finish the book. If we can reveal *exclusively* in our edition alone how it was meant to conclude, we shall defeat all the stealthy literary pirates.'

'How shall we do it, Mr. Fields?' asked Osgood, increasingly excited.

'Courage. I shall go to London and use my knowledge of its literary circles to investigate what was in Dickens's mind. Perhaps he even wrote more before his death that he did not have the chance to hand over to his publisher – it may be sitting in some locked drawer while his family is crying out their eyes and putting on mourning clothes. I must go about coolly until I find at least a hint of what he intended. Yes, yes. Take it quietly, tell no one outside these walls our plan.'

'Our plan,' Osgood echoed.

'Yes. I will find the end to Dickens's mystery!'

On that day in June, Osgood went from quietly mourning the death of Charles Dickens to plunging neck and heels into spinning out their practical plans. He asked Rebecca to cable John Forster, Dickens's executor, with an important message: *Urgent. Send on all there is of Drood to Boston at once.* They had the first three instalments and needed to receive the fourth, fifth, and that sixth instalment that the newspapers had reported he'd been finishing when he died. Osgood ordered the printer to begin setting the existing copy of *The Mystery of Edwin Drood* immediately from the advance sheets they already had. In this way they'd be ready to add in whatever could be gleaned of the end and go to press immediately.

Osgood busied himself over the next week helping draw up details for Fields's trip to London. The senior partner would leave as soon as he'd settled some pressing affairs of the firm.

Not long after Dickens's death, Officer Carlton had delivered the shocking news about Daniel. Osgood had sent him to the docks to retrieve those three latest instalments sent from England in response to Osgood's cable. It was yet another test to prevent emotion from becoming paralysing.

Daniel Sand's senseless accident caused Osgood to feel a sadness of heart more intimate and strange than that brought on by Dickens's death. The loss of Dickens was shared by millions around the world as though a personal blow to every home and hearth. Stores were closed the day of the news, flags flown low. But poor Daniel? Who would mourn? Osgood, certainly, and naturally Daniel's sister, Rebecca, Osgood's bookkeeper. Otherwise, it was an invisible death. How much more real this seemed, in a way, than Dickens's apotheosis.

When Daniel died, Osgood expected Rebecca to stop coming to work for a period. But she did not. She was as stoic as ever in her black crêpe and muslin, and she did not miss one workday.

The police had left it to Osgood to inform Rebecca about Daniel. As he told her, she began to tidy her surroundings, as if too busy, with no time to listen. Her teeth clenched as a struggle brewed behind her steady face. Wide eyes closed, her thin mouth cracked, and soon the battle was lost as she fell back into her chair, head in hands.

'Are there relatives I may send for?' Osgood had asked. 'Your parents?'

She shook her head and accepted a handkerchief. 'No one. Did Daniel suffer greatly?'

Osgood paused. He had not told her about the police suspicions of opium use, about the telltale puncture marks on Daniel's arm. He decided at that moment not to tell her. His sympathy for Rebecca was too strong, the details of Daniel's death too painful to utter. It would be a blessing for them both to hide it from her.

'I do not think he did,' Osgood said gently.

She looked up with red-rimmed eyes. 'Would you tell me one thing more, please, Mr. Osgood? Where was he coming from?' she asked and gave him her full attention.

'From the harbour, we believe, as it happened in Dock Square. He was to pick up some papers at the docks before . . . before the accident.'

Her lips pursed and her eyes filled before he could say more. Though he would not have judged any kind of reaction on her part, he admired how Rebecca had neither attempted to put her grief on display nor to hide it. Without thinking, he had taken her hand and held it in his. It was a touch of competence and comfort. It had been the first time he had touched his bookkeeper – any physical contact between men and women being against firm rules. He held her hand just until she had seemed calmer, then let go.

After a week passed and she had continued to come to work without any time off, Osgood invited her into his office, the door left open for decorum's sake. 'You know it would be seen as acceptable if you'd take time to grieve for Daniel.'

'I will stop wearing mourning dress to the offices if I am a distraction, Mr. Osgood,' she said. 'But I will not leave, if you please.'

'Upon my soul, Rebecca – do not always wear such a brave face,' said Osgood.

'I do not want to disappoint you or Mr. Fields by staying away, Mr. Osgood.'

Osgood knew Rebecca's work meant much more to her than to many girls. Some who applied for positions with eager pronouncements counted the days on their desk registers until they could find a man to marry, though since the war women far outnumbered men in the city and the search for suitors could be protracted. He also knew Rebecca was concerned that she show no weakness to Fields, even under the circumstances. The idea of young working women in the office was one thing for the liberal-minded senior partner. Divorced women was another.

'I shall respect your wishes,' Osgood had said, upon which she returned to the tasks waiting at her desk.

The end of Rebecca's marriage had first brought her from the country to the city, with her younger brother accompanying her as both her ward and guardian. Osgood had needed two and a half days to persuade Fields how impressive and prepared she had been in their first meeting, though Osgood would never mention that private campaigning to Rebecca after she was hired. He did not see her divorce as a liability nor did he wish to suggest anyone would. 'You say we need employees here willing to fight,' Osgood had told Fields at the time, 'and Miss Sand has had to endure the meanest treatment imaginable for a young woman.'

Osgood thought about Daniel's mission that day at the harbour. He was to meet the ship from London, where a messenger would hand him – and only him – the advance sheets for the fourth, fifth and sixth instalments of *The Mystery of Edwin Drood*. Fields, Osgood & Co. was publishing the only authorised American edition of the serial novel in one of its periodicals, *Every Saturday*. Readers would find the new parts of *Drood* there first, set from the 'advance sheets furnished us by the author'. This fact they proudly announced in each issue, as well as the fact that their publication was the only one for which Charles Dickens received any compensation. Other American magazines – including *Harper's* – could obviously make no such claims; nor would theirs appear until several weeks later.

For this reason, because of this competition, Daniel Sand's missions to the harbour had been kept quiet. Sending a young clerk would be far less conspicuous than sending a well-known partner like Osgood. Pirates from other publishing houses would loiter at the piers to try to intercept popular manuscripts coming from England before they were claimed by the authorised publisher. This breed of fiend called themselves Bookaneers and had vulgar names: Kitten, Molasses, Esquire, Baby. They sold their services to publishers in New York and Philadelphia or local Boston firms, and Osgood himself had been approached by some of them over the years, though he'd adamantly refused to engage in such techniques.

Daniel had known how important it was to secure the next instalments and deposit them into the Fields, Osgood & Co. vault. That is why Osgood had asked Officer Carlton whether any papers had been found on Daniel – and was astounded to learn none had.

Could Daniel have been deliberately forced into the street by one of those Bookaneers attempting to take the papers? Osgood dismissed the idea from his mind as soon as he had thought it. Publishing had known some shady practices in the art of procuring a manuscript – bribery, theft, spying – but not physical assault nor, even by the shadiest Bookaneer, *murder*! The instalments lost to Daniel's accident could be replaced from London – that was not what kept Osgood awake. But he did not want to admit that the police and coroner were right about his clerk and the opium. *This boy was one of the fallen*, they'd said. Had he forsaken Osgood, the firm, his own sister?

A few days later, Rebecca paused before Osgood's office door before leaving for the day. She was still wearing black – even the little jewellery she wore had been dyed black, as was custom – but she no longer wore the crêpe over her dress. 'Mr. Osgood,' she said, her dark hair straying from under a bonnet. As she fixed it, a ragged scar from years before was visible on the back of her right ear. 'I need to thank you,' she said, and nodded knowingly.

Osgood, caught off guard, nodded and smiled back. Only after she walked away did he realise he did not know what it was she thanked him for. Was she referring to some business matter that had occurred during the day, for having given Daniel a position there years before, for holding her hand when she had cried, even though it broke the rules? Of course, it was too late now to ask her. He could not stop her the next morning and say, suavely, after giving instructions for letters and memorandum for the day, Oh, and what was it you wished to thank me for yesterday, my dear? Osgood was kicking himself for his slow brain, when a less welcome face appeared in the same place in the doorway.

'Ah, Mr. Osgood, still here? No rich dinner parties tonight with the literary sort? No "swarry", as they're called?' This was Montague Midges, the circulation clerk for their magazines, the *Atlantic Monthly* and *Every Saturday*. He was an unctuous and grimly talkative little man but efficient. He was there to deliver the latest accounting numbers for the *Atlantic*. 'I see sturdy Miss Sand is still in mourning,' he added with a sidelong glance out the door.

'Midges?'

'Your girl-keeper.' This was Midges's name for the firm's female bookkeepers. 'Oh, I won't cry when Miss Two Shoes finally folds the mourning garb back in her drawer. The black makes their ankles look big, don't you think?'

'Mr. Midges, I'd prefer . . .'

Midges broke into whistling, as he often did in the midst of another person's sentence. 'Guess she'll be breaking down without her brother in Boston, poor wretch. Ten to one she wishes now she hadn't given that husband of hers the mitten. Good night, sir!'

At that, Osgood had sprung up from his chair, but he knew if he defended Rebecca in hearing of the other female bookkeepers in the office, whispers would fly. It would only make things worse for her at a bad time. Sitting back, Osgood wondered if Midges had recognised the reality of Rebecca's situation better than he had. The palms of his hands began to sweat. Did the terrible loss of Daniel for Rebecca also mean the loss of Rebecca for Osgood?

Rebecca didn't want to move to a new room, but the landlady insisted. With Daniel gone, she was to take her belongings to a smaller one at the top of the narrow stairs of the second-class boardinghouse for which she'd pay an additional one dollar per month.

Rebecca didn't argue – she wouldn't dare. Many boardinghouses did not take single women not living with relatives, especially divorced women, or charged them much higher rates than men. Those houses with too many needle girls from the factories feared being mistaken for brothels, and the landladies always preferred newlywed couples and male clerks when they had a choice. Rebecca's landlady, Mrs. Lepsin, made it clear that she originally had taken Rebecca in for two reasons: because she was not a shiftless Irish girl and because she was sharing the room with her brother. Now, though still not Irish, the other reason was dead, and it was clear Lepsin would prefer Rebecca gone.

Rebecca packed her clothes and her belongings by the light of a solitary candle. There were no closets in the room, so some of her clothes were already folded and the rest hanging by rusted nails on the wall. As she did, she ate a small cake of chocolate she kept with some red and white peppermint sticks inside a glove box for what she called emergencies. Like when she was hungry before bed after a meal downstairs of cold vegetables and watery rice pudding at the crowded table. Or when having to suddenly dismantle one's whole room in a matter of hours, or be put on the street!

The five-dollar monthly rent for the smaller room was more than Rebecca could possibly pay without Daniel's help, even with whatever reductions she'd find to make in her expenses. Savings accounted for, she would be able to pay two more months. If the firm's partners achieved their plan to defeat the pirates and profit as they deserved from *The Mystery of Edwin Drood*, it was widely expected that they would raise the bookkeepers' salaries by seventy-five cents. If the pirates triumphed, the financial worries in the back offices of their building would worsen; salaries might even be reduced by twenty-five cents. The raise in salary had been a given before Dickens's death, but now it – and Rebecca's prospects to remain in the city – hung in the balance.

When Rebecca had lived out in the country, with her carpenter husband, his income had been sufficient to keep up with the needs of a comfortable home with room to spare for young Daniel. He'd come to live with her and Ambrose on the death of their mother.

Then the war came and Ambrose left with the army. In the brutal battle of Stones River, Ambrose had been captured by the Confederates and kept as a prisoner in Danville. By the time he returned two years later, he was a skeleton of himself, debilitated and withdrawn. His temper had grown worse; he beat her regularly on the head and arms and hit Daniel whenever he intervened. The triangle of beatings and retaliation became a pattern that seemed to be the only way to keep up Ambrose's spirits. Rebecca had done her best to steer Ambrose away from his violence, but when it proved impossible to protect herself and her brother she gathered her courage to leave. She'd taken Daniel away to Boston, where she had heard there were new positions opening in offices for young women in what the newspapers proclaimed the postwar economy.

That had been more than three years ago now. When she was able to afford the fees, and after a long process in the courts, she had secured a divorce from her husband. Ambrose, once notified by a country lawyer, did not object, remarking through a letter to the Boston judge that Rebecca's too slender body had refused him any sons, anyway, and that her meddling brother was a worthless pest.

Under the standards of Massachusetts law, it was two years before the divorce would be final and she could remarry. Until then she was legally barred from entering any romantic relationship with a man. During that waiting period – of which there was another year remaining – any violation, or even any appearance of violation, would nullify her divorce immediately and she would not be allowed to marry again.

Being a wife was not foremost on her mind as she readied for the move upstairs. The other bookkeepers could talk all they wanted about weddings and where they would meet the coming mythical husband and how the latest ladies' magazine advised that shaving one's entire head would lead to more lustrous hair once it grew back. All that wasn't her. Rebecca, despite everything, felt fortunate about her present situation. She had experienced marriage, and it had brought her only distress. Her post at the firm was different. True, she and the other girls at the office were 'bookkeepers', not clerks, and were paid a quarter of that paid to most of the male workers at Fields, Osgood & Co. – just as at all the other companies. But she relished her work and it supported her in a city full of young women waiting to snap up both her job and room. For that, and for the trust Osgood put in her to take care of herself, she had spontaneously thanked him before leaving the office.

It may have been a strange thing to feel relief at trading a house and a husband for a shrinking boarding room and office work all day, but that's how she felt. She thought of the words of Mrs. Gamp, Dickens's garrulous character: 'It is little she needs, and that little she don't get.' The little Rebecca needed, she got.

Books, especially. When she lived as a young girl with her family on the farm, the books were her companions, sustenance feeding her mind. They had received a boxed-up library from an elderly man a few houses away who had died without family. She would stay up late with her candle adventuring with Robinson Crusoe and Dr. Frankenstein, Jane Eyre and Oliver Twist. Living in the city, she found Bostonians particular and critical about their reading material, for she had never thought about books being judged rather than devoured. She felt that working in a publishing firm, she might learn to have a more discerning eye for books' moral and literary merits. And if she were to be called a book*keeper* for the rest of her days, should she object?

It was when she had to pack Daniel's side of the room that she began to feel exhausted. Her momentum broke. Before their move to Boston, Daniel used to talk about going to sea. When Rebecca had escaped Ambrose and sought a divorce, Daniel never spoke of those seafaring dreams again, never used them as an excuse to abandon her after she ran from her husband. He quietly had taken to building model ships in small glass bottles. Sometimes she liked to watch him as he worked nimbly and think how one day in the future she would insist on Daniel's taking a two years' voyage before the mast on a merchant passage. He'd finally break out of their bottled lives. These objects she now carefully wrapped in paper, watching that not one tear would spot the glass.

A part of her tried to pretend that Daniel had not died, that he was only on that ship on some far-off commercial adventure to the Orient or Africa. As she closed her eyes and opened them again on his amazing creations, she saw herself on the ships inside those bottles, surviving his dreams. An uncommon thought for a young woman whose whole life was now about survival and isolation, the opposite dream of every other girl she knew, of every ribbon in their hair and feather in their hats.

When the Sand siblings had first arrived in Boston, Daniel had become companions with a distant cousin of theirs, an indolent and hypocritical older boy. Together Daniel and his cousin drank and it became a matter of chronic intoxication. At one point, he fell off a horse they had stolen from a stable and nearly broke his neck. She alone nursed him through it, and when fourteen-year-old Daniel vowed he was through with his vice, she believed him wholeheartedly and brought him to Fields, Osgood & Co. seeking a position as shop boy.

It was the first thing she had thought of when Osgood told her about Daniel's accident. Had he returned to his old state of habitual drunkenness? Had he been coming from one of the crumbling taverns that studded the wharfside? Then she thought about it and realised . . . Impossible. It was impossible! She would have known. She'd lived with this. She knew the signs – she would have known.

She had seen him working the very day before his death with a steady hand on the painstaking arrangements of the battlements with the tiny pliers inside the spout of the bottle. That was the pursuit of the very sober.

The next afternoon, J. T. Fields appeared in Osgood's office to commiserate. He had been reading the remaining chapters of *The Mystery of Edwin Drood* that had arrived after being resent from London. Fields took Osgood's arm and led the way downstairs.

Sitting in the firm's employee dining room, Osgood studied the newly arrived packet of pages and listened to his partner's ideas. Fields ate cold tongue and a salad, wiping food from his chin whenever he paused to speak. 'A mysterious and marvellous story. So the young man, Edwin Drood, disappears and his uncle John Jasper is suspected not only of having done some foul thing but also of desiring Drood's young fiancée. So an investigation begins, led by some mysterious newcomer called Dick Datchery. But we cannot know from these pages how Edwin Drood was meant to come back and enact his revenge.'

'Come back?' Osgood asked.

Fields held up a hand as he swallowed another bite of tongue. 'Yes, why, you don't think Charles Dickens would leave the innocent young man missing? I think that Datchery fellow will find him and rescue him from whatever fate Jasper had planned.'

'It seems quite plain to me that Edwin Drood is dead, Mr. Fields. The mystery will turn instead on how John Jasper will be successfully exposed as the villain by Dick Datchery, Grewgious, Tartar and the others in the book seeking justice for the deed against young Drood.'

'Really?' Fields exclaimed, not the least bit persuaded. 'Well, I shall read it all again.'

The next days, Osgood went through his routine around the offices but was distracted by thoughts of poor Daniel. One memory especially kept coming back to him, from the time when Daniel learned he was to be promoted from shop boy to clerk. Osgood had taken Daniel to his own tailor for his first proper suit – and Daniel had insisted on purchasing one exactly like Osgood's.

'That may be more money than you should spend,' Osgood had said. 'I did not wear this quality wool as a new clerk.'

'Surely I'll be able to afford more sometime, if I remain at the firm and devote myself to work?' Daniel asked.

'I should think,' said Osgood, stifling a smile at his big plans.

'Then I shall already have it, instead of needing to buy a better one later.'

'How do you feel in it, young sir?' asked the tailor.

'I feel an inch taller, sir!'

Osgood laughed at the lean young man, who was already taller than him. 'Perhaps after it fits properly, you will feel like a giant.'

He offered to loan Daniel money for the purchase but Daniel was proud to buy the suit with money he had painstakingly saved and even prouder of the suit itself. When the summer arrived, Daniel still had only this same heavy wool suit and no money for another of serge or flannel. But he never complained and only removed his coat when carrying the heaviest boxes of books to the cellar to pack. He kept on hand a supply of cheap cotton handkerchiefs to scrub his forehead. The strain of overuse eventually loosened the seams at the shoulders, and Rebecca would repair them at their boardinghouse a couple of times a week as best she could.

VI

NLY DAYS AFTER HIS HOME had been ransacked, Sylvanus Bendall had arrived to work one morning and found his office in similar condition. Just as at home, nothing had been removed. The lawyer no longer could attribute the original assault on his property to being a Back Bay pioneer since his office was in a more conventional district. No, the crimes were personal. Perhaps the petty revenge of a client Bendall had failed? There were enough names in that category.

Bendall had questioned a number of his more reliable underworld connections for clues. Then one day he came to his office to find two men waiting in the anteroom. One was a young riffraff, the likes of which often frequented his offices, and the other was a gentleman. The gentleman was dressed in fine clothes and had a fresh, brave face that was instantly admirable and thus suspect in its openness.

Sylvanus Bendall did not ask who had been waiting longer; he simply introduced himself to the young gentleman as attorney-at-law and invited him into his inner office.

'I wish we had set an appointment for our interview another day, Mr. Osgood, so that you would not have had to share the waiting room with such class of people.'

'I make no complaints about the company. It is important I obtain certain facts as soon as I can.'

'I see. Important to a court of law, I suppose.'

'Not exactly,' Osgood said. 'Important for myself. I have come to ask about Daniel Sand, a man in my employ who died a few weeks ago.'

'I do not believe I had the opportunity to be acquainted with him,' said Bendall. 'Though I am counsel for many a poor and ignorant young man.'

'He may have begun life poor, Mr. Bendall, but he worked industriously and was not ignorant in any field he was given the chance to learn. He was killed in an omnibus accident, and I believe you were present.'

'Oh?'

'The policeman told me the name of the omnibus, and the driver remembered that you announced your name and profession.'

'Did I?' Bendall asked, bewildered.

'Several times. They recalled that you stood close to Daniel's body.'

'I see,' Bendall nodded with a new stiffness to his expression. 'I suppose I did, now that you remind me. That was a tragic scene, Mr. Osgood. I hope you have been able to fill the young man's vacancy well enough and, if not, that I might suggest a candidate or two needing work. You shall hardly guess they had ever been to prison.'

'Did you see the accident, Mr. Bendall?'

'I merely heard the *whap!*, I mean,' Bendall said, 'the sound as we struck the unfortunate young man.'

'The driver said he believed Daniel was holding something when the accident occurred, but that it was gone by the time the police arrived. Mr. Sand, I should explain, was to be delivering some papers belonging to our firm.'

Bendall involuntarily caressed his waistcoat where he still kept his treasured advance sheets of the Dickens story, then chewed at his thumb's nail. He had grown uncommonly fond of these pages; as fond, come to think of it, as of his own thumbnail. The last story of Dickens! Of course, the publisher sitting across from him would no doubt already have sent for a duplicate of the advance sheets from England. So what harm was there in keeping his souvenir?

'No,' Bendall answered Osgood's query blandly. Then, after waiting a moment to see the reaction in Osgood's face, added, 'He wasn't holding a piece of paper, Mr. Osgood. Not even, to speak between gentlemen, the smallest dirt-coated scrap of thin quality stationery.'

'The driver must have been mistaken,' Osgood said with disappointment. 'I only wish there were more clues. The police believe that my clerk was suffering in a narcotic state, and I do not want to – I cannot believe it.'

'Pooh! I cannot say, really. He *was* speaking mumbo jumbo, certainly –'

'What?' Osgood interrupted with a revived attentiveness. 'Do you mean Daniel Sand was alive when you reached him?'

'For a few seconds only,' Bendall replied.

'The police didn't say anything about it.'

'Well, they didn't – I mean, the police! They are often so negligent. I myself have suffered break-ins twice of late, you know!'

'Please. What did Daniel say?'

'Nonsense! Gibberish, that's what. He looked at me and said, God – that's right, imagine my breathing very shallowly if you will, when I say that, and a hoarse whisper as suits a man fading from the mortal state of life – "It is God's," said he. It was much like a sentimental novel.'

'That was all he said? "It is God's" what?'

'He did not finish the statement, I fear. It is God's will. It is God's desire, perhaps. Intention? No, too long winded. To tell the truth, if he had said more, I think I would have chosen not to hear, for to eavesdrop on a man making his peace with his maker is to do a disservice to both those parties. At any rate, I took his hand after he spoke and held it there tightly as he expired.' Bendall had not in fact taken Sand's hand after Daniel spoke his final words, but this embellishment had appeared in his retelling and the lawyer by now believed in it more sincerely than if it had occurred.

Sylvanus Bendall could have been seen toiling around the streets of Boston for several more hours that day after meeting James Osgood, hurrying distractedly between his office, the courthouse, the bleak expanse of the Charlestown prison, then running heroically through the rain to board the horsecars on his return home. As he read the evening newspaper in his seat, he began to feel the pungent breath of a tobacco-chewing man sitting behind him and, upon leaning back in the seat, feel the man's fingers pressing against his neck. 'It is not polite,' said Bendall into the air, for he was determined not to turn around, 'to infringe on another person, no matter how cramped the space.'

The fingers withdrew slowly from the back of his seat. Satisfied, Bendall read on, though through a filmy lens of distraction. Ever since his meeting with Osgood, a thought was growing inside

Bendall's mind. Those final words of the clerk's – *it is God's*. Now that his mind returned to that moment, he could not avoid feeling a helpless sense of misunderstanding. Had the poor lad actually been trying to say something in particular, to convey some kind of warning to Bendall?

Black liquid showered down on the floor by his feet.

'It is not polite to spit tobacco inside the cars, either!' the lawyer exclaimed. He heard his voice shake with a lack of control and hated that it did.

But he would not give any satisfaction to the rude imp by turning around in his seat, even when the disgusting black ooze continued to spray his neck and the man's wet umbrella dripped on him. Were the slimy head of Medusa presented to the lawyer's view, he would still not divert his gaze. Instead, Bendall got out at the next stop – three stops early. The summer rain had given way to wind and a thick, hot mist that filled a man's mouth with bitterness.

This was an empty stretch of land. Bendall's plot was far west, almost approaching the corner of Exeter Street, beyond which there was not a soul.

Unseen by Bendall, the man who had been sitting behind him also had exited the cars, only a moment before the door closed again. The heavy, wet footfalls followed just behind him until there was no way to ignore them.

Bendall, realising he was shivering, stopped. 'What is your purpose, sir?' he said sternly, this time finally turning around to face the wretch.

The stranger's umbrella was open and along with a thick fur hat, it shadowed his face. He glared, allowing his eyes to rove across Bendall's suit and down to his rubber boots. The stranger laughed with a deep, discordant bass movement of his throat. The man's sheer bulk was imposing, and his skin was dusky without being quite Negro – perhaps a Bengalee of some sort? From under the shadow of the umbrella, it could be seen that he dangled an ivory toothpick on the top of his lower lip.

Sylvanus Bendall froze. He came to an immediate and urgent conclusion: not only was he in danger, but this swarthy moustachioed man with the dark eyes and the baritone laugh – *this very man* – was his worst enemy. It is God's vengeance, that is what the lad had meant to imply!

Bendall said, his instinct outracing his logic, 'It is you, isn't it? It was you who tore my home to pieces and then my office?'

The stranger shrugged his shoulders and continued to laugh.

Bendall demanded, 'What do you want with me? Why do you trifle with a gentleman? Come, now. Speak, man!'

'What . . . do . . . I . . . want? Dickens!' The man repeated: 'Dickens!' He pronounced his words like an Englishman – or perhaps a 'dude', that particular species of American that imitated English manners – though the rumbling gruffness sounded more exotic. 'You didn't give those pages back to Mr. Osgood, did you?'

Bendall answered righteously, furrowing his brow, 'Pooh! Did Osgood hire you to find those papers?'

'Did you *tell* him of the papers, sir?' asked the man.

'It is none of his concern, nor yours. This is a free country. I kept it to myself.'

'Good fellow. Yet they are not anywhere in your office or at your home, which means . . .' The stranger grabbed him by the arm as the attorney felt the blood drain from his head in terror. Methodically, the man patted Bendall's waistcoat until he located the paper bundle. 'You try to order me? Give them here before I make you swallow them!' He yanked out the pages and pushed Bendall hard, sending the lawyer right into a puddle.

Bendall drew a first breath of relief to have suffered only scrapes, but only a moment later, grew incensed. He'd been assaulted and muddied in the middle of the street and by the man who had also ransacked his home and office. *I shall root out the source of this evil myself*, he had told his housemaid, and here he had done so! Now was the time to grab the moment by the throat. Bendall, recovering his courage, rose to his feet and chased after the thief.

'Wait!' Bendall cried.

The stranger kept walking.

Bendall caught up, waving his fist. 'If you don't come back and give an account of yourself, I shall go directly to the police, and complain to Mr. Osgood at once. Tell me your name!'

The stranger slowed down. 'Herman,' he responded in a compliant voice. 'They call me Herman.' As he said it, in one unhesitating motion, he turned around and slashed Bendall across the throat with the fangs of his cane head. Bendall gasped for air before he fell. In the dreary landscape of the New Land, there was no one around to see Bendall take his last, struggling breath.

Herman bent down and lodged a knife into the neck several times. He kept the toothpick and umbrella in place even while the knife sawed through the lawyer's bone.

VII

BENGAL, INDIA, JUNE 18, 1870

—————◆—————

THESE LAST TWO WEEKS FOR Officers Turner and Mason of the Bengal Mounted Police could have been measured out in drills, parades and treasure escorts. Since the bullock cart convoy had been robbed, they still had not traced the second fugitive that had escaped their raid in the jungle. Worse, they had yet to recover the chests that were each filled with one picul, or 133⅓ pounds, of valuable opium that had been stolen that day.

Their supervisor in the mounted patrol, Francis Dickens, was agitated. He called the two officers to his desk. 'Gentlemen, headway?'

'We received intelligence from one of the native patrolmen on some of the thief's comrades,' said Mason excitedly. 'In the hills. He could be hiding there, waiting for us to abandon our investigation.'

'I rarely trust information from the native men, Mr. Dickens,' Turner interjected, countering his junior's optimism.

'There is corruption to be found in native officials, Turner, I understand that well enough,' said Frank Dickens, a light-complexioned and slender twenty-six-year-old man wearing a flaxen moustache. He spoke with an air of one too rapidly hardened by his own authority. 'That *dacoit* is the only fellow we know of who can lead us to the stolen opium – which I daresay they have not been bold enough to try to sell on the illegal market. We've had guards at the border to the French colony watching for just that.'

'Yes, sir,' answered back Turner.

'You understand our interest, gentlemen,' Frank Dickens added sternly. 'The peace of the district depends greatly on our police department's appearing effective. We mustn't tempt thieves into thinking they are free to operate in Bengal, in our jurisdictions. The railway police and the village police are on the alert. I have an appointment today with the magistrate of the village where the escaped thief lived. I daresay he will enquire into our progress, and I rely on your service.'

The officers saluted and were dismissed. Before they exited, Frank asked to speak privately with Turner.

'Officer Turner. This *dacoit* – should you find him – be certain he arrives here.'

'Sir?' Turner bristled.

Frank crossed his arms over his chest. 'With Narain dead, that thief may be the only way we can trace those opium chests. I want you to ensure his physical safety. *You* take the seat by the window.'

'By all means, Superintendent Dickens.'

As the two mounted policemen rode on their mission, Turner could not stop curling his hands into fists. He knew, *everyone* knew, Francis Dickens was only superintendent because of his name. Why, Turner could hold a command every bit as well as Dickens! The bloke's father, dead this month, was a poor Cockney from the back country who happened to know how to pick up a pen. And how respectable was the family, in any case, with a wife in banishment from her own home, and a pretty actress having taken her place, according to the gossip Turner had read in the London columns? The great genius himself was dead and buried. It galled Turner to be ordered about by the son of such a man. And for what reason? All because Charles Dickens could sketch out maudlin stories that made women cry and men laugh. Was that all there was to becoming a rich and popular author?

He'd said to Mason more than once, 'I'd rather be a son of Charles Dickens than the heir of the Duke of Westminster when it's time for promotions.'

Frank Dickens, meanwhile, rode to the magistrate's bungalow. Finding the bungalow empty, he crossed the compound to enter the *cutcherry*, a building of mud walls and a thatched roof. The magistrate was only a year older and his study at Calcutta University had resulted in English that bore hardly a trace of his native accent. Frank and other English officials had become rather fond of him.

Passing across the compound, Frank noted with satisfaction the newest lamps and footpaths. The more signs of civilisation spread around the native villages, the less trouble. Natives rose and salaamed to him as he walked, placing their hands to their faces and bowing low. Some were lying down across the grass in the shade. One, sitting with his elbows balanced on his knees, shuffled away at the sight of the visitor – perhaps it was because Frank was European, perhaps it was the uniform.

As the Englishman entered the court, the Indian attorneys and guards also salaamed. The magistrate was sitting at a table on a platform before a dimly lit room crowded in every corner with impatient natives. Dressed in ornamental costume with gold and silver patterns, the magistrate walked around the table and took the police supervisor's hand warmly.

'Don't let me interrupt your proceedings, baboo,' Frank insisted.

'You don't disturb me at all, Mr. Dickens,' replied the magistrate jovially. 'I am not very busy today. Will you take a glass of wine?'

Frank ran his gaze over the anxious men and women filling the *cutcherry*. 'Please, go on with your proceedings.'

Despite Frank's demurral, the magistrate ordered glasses and wine to be brought from his bungalow. He brought out a case of fine cigars while his servants yelled, *'Og laou!'* and built a fire. The crowd in the *cutcherry* began to murmur among themselves and then grew louder until one of the court officials demanded silence. After the two gentlemen drank wine and *brandy pawnee* before their restless audience, Frank again anxiously insisted, 'Please, baboo, proceed.'

The cases were tedious, and included the matter of a stolen cow, then an attempted extortion of a European traveller by a Bengalee. At two o'clock, the *cutcherry* emptied and the magistrate invited the police superintendent to his home for tiffin in the English style. First, however, he insisted on bringing the visitor on a full tour of the village. They began at the schoolhouse, called the Anglo-Vernacular Academy, where the master was leading a circle of potbellied pupils, covered only with threadbare sheets of muslin, in chants of the English alphabet. One of the students was unsuccessfully trying to stammer out the letter R. Frank grew pale watching this and indicated to his guide that he was ready to go.

After leaving the schoolhouse, the two officials walked across a new bridge and then visited several drains that had been installed along the streets under the magistrate's guidance. Wherever they walked, the magistrate boasted of the absence of beggars.

Back in the magistrate's bungalow at last, tiffin was ready. Wine was poured by the servants as quickly as the officials could drink.

'So your department is still hunting our escaped thief,' the magistrate commented.

'We believe he may be in the mountains – I have two of my men searching for him even now.'

'You know, Mr. Dickens, that my own villagers wish for the thief's arrest every bit as much as the white police. As you saw in the *cutcherry*, when a cow is stolen, it is my countrymen who suffer.'

'This is no cow,' Frank said, raising one eyebrow. 'This is opium, baboo. The inspector generals shall be around about it if it is not resolved.'

'Yes, yes, the opium – important!' He raised his glass in tribute. 'Let us drink to those who are paid to grow it to sell to China but also to those natives weak enough to ingest it before it is sold abroad. Young Bengal is still but a child growing too large for its first proper garments. Until my people understand to accept a life like the English, they benefit from a dulled sense of reality, a sluggish frame of mind, if I may say. No one desires another revolt, Superintendent.'

After further conversation, Frank removed his watch chain.

'Ah, one moment more, Superintendent,' said the magistrate at his visitor's restlessness. 'You see?'

The magistrate was looking up at a row of books over the policeman's head. It was an expensive collection of Charles Dickens's novels.

'Illustrated editions. I am as much an admirer of your father's books as any of your own countrymen, I can assure you. I was deeply saddened to imagine his chair empty upon hearing the tidings. When will you travel back to England to pay respects?'

'You know as well as I the amount of work at the police department. I shall take a holiday month in England when things are quieter. Perhaps next year.'

The magistrate, for the first time, regarded his guest as a foreigner. 'I suppose some of the English fashion is rather too cool for us Bengalees to make out,' he murmured.

Frank put the glass down, glancing up with a defensive pout emboldened by the wine. 'Do you know what my father said when

I told him I wished to go abroad, baboo? I had asked him to supply only a horse, a rifle and fifteen pounds. My father laughed and then assured me that I would be robbed of the fifteen pounds, be thrown from my horse, and shoot my own head off with the rifle.' Frank paused, then added, 'Bengal, in time, has become my home, and I have earned respect for my work among the Europeans and natives alike, respect never offered in England.'

'You have siblings, sir?'

'Five brothers and two sisters, yes.'

'I have seven sons and daughters myself, Mr. Dickens, and I fear fathers sometimes wish too much for their children,' the magistrate replied solicitously. 'Especially, I would fancy, for you.'

'What do you mean?'

'Go to that looking glass over my dresser, Mr. Dickens! The resemblance about the eyes and mouth to your father is remarkable. Every time he saw you, he surely saw himself.'

'My f-f-father,' Frank stopped. He began again, this time mastering his emotion, 'My father never saw himself in me. Though the groundlings fancy him to have been the most tolerant of men, they did not ever have occasion to come under his lash. Having the world at your feet for thirty years gives you the idea that your nature is perfect. He told us that his name was our best capital and to remember that.'

The discussion was interrupted by a sudden commotion outside the bungalow. The men hurried outside and found an Indian man struggling against the hold of several of the native policemen.

'What is happening here?' demanded Frank.

'Superintendent Dickens! This is the missing opium *dacoit!*' cried out one of the dark-skinned policemen. After some questioning, it was revealed that it was indeed the thief who had eluded Turner and Mason in the jungle. He had been hiding in a mud cellar several villages away in the jungle. When a compatriot had seen Frank walking through the streets, he'd run through the woods to warn the thief the police were near. The compatriot had been followed and the thief had been apprehended as he attempted to sneak away.

Frank ordered the native policemen to secure the prisoner and place him in a cart to be brought to the station house.

'You see, Superintendent, that even now, in our intellectual infancy, my countrymen would not mock justice,' the magistrate said with a face-devouring grin. 'I look forward to hearing his case before my *cutcherry.*'

Frank, after he watered his thirsty horse, climbed into his saddle and lowered his gaze at the baboo.

'Our tour through the footpaths, the bridges, the school . . . You wanted me to be seen by everyone in the village to be certain someone would alert the thief so that he would be captured. And in order to delay my exit until your plan was executed, you introduced the topic of my father.'

His host retained his wide smile. 'We have our mutually desired result.'

'That teaches me, baboo, that the people in your jurisdiction fear the British, but they do not fear you. What does that mean for your promise to keep order? Remember that though you may be a native of this soil, you are a representative of Her Majesty the Queen.'

'I never forget it, Superintendent,' the magistrate replied, salaaming.

'Officers, mount up with your prisoner!' Frank now spoke loudly enough for the surrounding speculators of the village to hear. 'Baboo, you may be assured of my deepest gratitude – I suggest you inform any family and friends of this scoundrel that assisting a villain, even if one's own blood, shall not be looked upon kindly by the British authority. This will be their warning.'

VIII

BOSTON, THE NEXT
MORNING, 1870

———◆———

'IMAGINE IT,' FIELDS SAID, SHAKING his beard into a wild mess. 'Taking up the newspaper this morning with my coffee, I read that this pettifogger lawyer with whom you consulted – Sylvanus Bendall – is dead on the street. His throat is cut ear to ear, his head hanging by a thread! The police are dizzy about it. The public who had our corrupt detective department abolished are calling for them reconvened. The mayor is blaming the railroad tracks for bringing strangers into the city!'

It was early in the morning and Fields was pacing the plush rug of his office, throwing his hands up as he spoke. It was as if he were pointing to the various illustrated portraits and photographs on the walls of the firm's past and present. These were the artists who had brought literature to the masses, who had changed minds about politics and prejudices, who had rebuilt bridges between England and America all through the pages of their novels and poems.

Osgood was sitting quietly in one chair beside another recently vacated by Officer Carlton.

'Bendall was not telling me the whole truth about Daniel Sand's death, Mr. Fields,' replied Osgood, after waiting to see if Fields would say more.

Fields stared at Osgood as though he had never seen him before in his life. 'So you think that is why Bendall was killed?' he asked sarcastically. 'I very much doubt the reason had to do with Daniel Sand, a seventeen-year-old lad, an ordinary clerk.'

Osgood did not want to overstep the limits of his position. In the requirement of their trade to be decisive, the younger man knew about himself that he could sometimes be too quick to accept an idea heartily before fully understanding it, and other times might disagree too readily. But he could not shake his opinion.

'Bendall was there when Daniel died. The advance sheets of the instalments Daniel was to pick up, which we were to use to publish in serial, disappeared, although the driver believed he had seen him holding a bundle.'

'We already know young Sand was in a flight of opium, Osgood. He could have dropped the bundle into a gutter without even knowing it. As for Bendall, a man's throat can be sliced open for nothing more than a watch chain and one gold button! Even in this,' Fields paused theatrically, 'the seventieth year of the nineteenth century!'

'What about the fact that Dickens writes of opium users in the very first pages of *Drood*, and that is how the police say Daniel died. Is it a coincidence?'

'How could it not be? Daniel was an opium eater, and so are many more every day. That is why Dickens turned to write of it in the first place, surely, because of the many who have lost themselves in the clouds of such drugs, here and in England! Dickens has always been conscious of social ills from his earliest novels. Do you think the omnibus driver wanted to stop Daniel from his charge? Hang Daniel Sand – he is not your concern any more. Nobody expects anything more from you.'

'I know. And yet something is –'

'Osgood, pray consider . . .'

Osgood would not yield. '*Something* is not right about all this, Mr. Fields. The police explanation from the first seemed wanting. I trusted Daniel Sand as I would my own son!'

Fields frowned. 'In our calling, our authors are our children, Osgood, and it is our duty and our only duty to protect them. Do you not think I could have imagined having my own children, if Annie were more disposed to it? But what time would I have, and what would be sacrificed?'

Osgood changed his tactic. 'If I can devote a little of my time to make enquiries. For his sister Rebecca's sake, if for nothing else.'

'Think about it, Osgood! What if you had been with Sylvanus Bendall when this happened? You could have been left for the dogs and vultures, your head could be in the police station today, too, with that lobster-eyed coroner poking his fingers through your brain. Indulge me: what is the name of this place?'

Osgood assumed a contrite posture. He knew what Fields meant by the question, and even the eyes of the lofty portrait gallery seemed to wait for an answer. From the left, the face of Mr. Longfellow, their first truly national poet, patient and good in his remote gaze. From the right, the eyes of Emerson's strict ministerial countenance, with a hint of a smile in the pupils, knowing and demanding better from the world just like his famed essays. Straight ahead, the glare of manly Tennyson, holding in it private, dreamy confessions of epic verse. Above the standing desk, the eyes looking down from the sad Hawthorne's fantastically intellectual head.

Osgood answered Fields's question dutifully, 'Fields, Osgood and Company.'

Fields lit a cigar and convulsively puffed out circles of smoke. 'Now look around, my dear Osgood. Stop for a minute and look. We could lose all of this. Everything you see, everything Bill Ticknor and I built up, and that you, my dear old friend, you will be called on to command if our house can but survive this period.'

'You are right,' said Osgood.

'An unfortunate mystery, the human spirit. Why Daniel Sand chose the path he did, we cannot know; why he would leave his poor sister alone. But you must leave him behind. Remember that there are two things in this life that are never worth crying about: what can be cured and what cannot be cured.'

Then Fields paused, before saying, 'I know precisely how you shall engage again in what's before you. You will sail for London to address the Dickens problem.'

Osgood was taken by surprise. 'But who will take charge of things here if we are both away?'

Fields removed a packet from his desk and handed it to his junior partner while shaking his head. 'Not we. I am to stay right where you see me. As for any appointments you have here, I shall entertain them for you.'

'You have been preparing for your trip, Mr. Fields! Gathering letters of introduction, sending word of your arrival . . .'

'You can use them in my stead, and besides, your honest face is your letter of introduction! To be perfectly candid, Annie has not wanted me to go ever since she heard of it. She wants me the rest of the summer to stay weekends in Manchester-by-the-sea – says it will be wholesome for me. Besides, you know what a dead-gone sailor

I am. My last trip to England I won the favour of being the sickest on board – even worse than the cows. Come, no arguing. Remember what our dear Hawthorne used to say: "America is a country to boast of, and to get out of!"'

Perhaps The *Mystery of Edwin Drood* had exerted a wild influence over him, making him see spectres of ill doings where there were none. There was no mystery about poor Daniel Sand, no connection between that terrible accident – which all men and women risked stepping out into the busy Boston streets – and the vicious murder of Sylvanus Bendall! There was only sadness and loss in real life, not given boundaries and significance by serial instalments.

A casual visitor to Boston could be forgiven for thinking that everyone in the so-called Hub of the Universe spent that afternoon hurriedly preparing for James Osgood's journey across the ocean. There was an avalanche of arrangements to be made by him and on his behalf both for the home front and for his travels. To see Osgood himself hurrying from destination to destination all a-fluster would have shocked those who knew the ever-composed publisher.

In the exclusive neighbourhood of Beacon Hill, inside his three-storey brick house at 71 Pinckney Street purchased with his earnings from the Dickens tour, Osgood gave detailed instructions to his help for the maintenance of his quiet abode and its second master, Mr. Puss, his rather self-satisfied and snobby orange and white longhair cat. Mr. Puss, who was usually content to lie among Osgood's books in the carpeted library, was almost startled out of his normal trance by the rush of the servants polishing boots and preparing suits for the publisher's luggage.

Osgood went to the Fieldses' around the corner on Charles Street to procure Annie Fields's list of hotels and friends in London. Fields himself arrived home from the office as Annie finished copying out this list for the junior partner at her table.

'Here you are, dear Ripley,' said Annie to Osgood, handing him a slip of her stationery.

'Oh, good, Osgood, are you coming back to the office when this beautiful lady is through with you?' Fields asked. He crossed the light-filled parlour and leaned in to kiss his smiling young wife on the cheek.

'Indeed, my dear Fields,' Osgood said. 'I will walk back with you. I honestly don't know how I will finish all that I must do if I am to sail tomorrow.'

'I find whichever of my tasks must be finished *are* finished, Mr. Osgood,' said Annie. 'Won't you have some assistance in England?'

'I suppose I will not,' Osgood said.

'How about Mr. Midges? He wields a reliable pencil,' Fields suggested. 'On second thought, the magazines might crumble to the ground without his arithmetic behind them.'

Osgood, cringing inwardly, agreed the magazines' very survival really required Midges's staying in Boston.

'A bookkeeper, then,' Annie proposed. 'Why, you mustn't send Mr. Osgood on such a chore without proper resources, Jamie,' she scolded her husband.

'A bookkeeper!' Fields said, puffing out his chest as though to protect any innocent parties from the idea. 'How shall it look to all the world for our respectable Osgood here to be crossing the sea with a perfectly unmarried or, for that matter, married young woman?'

'It shall look perfectly modern,' Annie replied airily.

'What about Miss Sand?' Osgood heard himself saying.

'Miss Sand?' Fields repeated slowly, stopping to see if there was anything unspoken in Osgood's expression. He found nothing, so he continued. 'She is rather an enigma. Is she not unmarried as well?'

'It's a fine idea,' said Annie, the words bestowing a queenly benediction on the junior partner.

'Why, how is it any different?' asked Fields, though merely for sport, as an argument with Annie was already lost when she had made up her mind.

'If I understand correctly, my dear,' said Annie, 'the terms of Miss Sand's divorce set out that she can have no romantic relationship. She is neither married nor unmarried. Why, to take her has as chaste an appearance to the world as to take Mr. Midges.'

'She makes a mite more handsome travel companion than Midges, certainly,' concluded Fields with an ambivalent agreement. 'Very well, I shall have my girl see about securing Miss Sand's passage in the third steerage straight away.'

Osgood smiled and thanked Annie for the suggestion. He was more pleased with the surprise decision than he would have expected. For one thing, he wouldn't be all alone in the undertaking. He would

have someone along who was both pleasant company and supremely competent. And if Osgood needed an escape from Daniel's death, certainly Rebecca of all people needed it more.

'How does it sound?' Osgood asked Rebecca after explaining the idea when he had returned to the office and found her hauling a bundle of contracts to Mr. Clark in the financial department.

'I'm honoured you would entrust me with this responsibility. I'll see to the rest of the preparations tonight,' she said.

It was hours later, and already several hours since Osgood had gone home for the night, before Rebecca found herself smiling at the amazing chance to travel, to contribute, and to preserve her future in Boston by helping Osgood's quest. She knew she could make a difference, even if it were just a small one. The publishing offices were almost completely empty, but Rebecca still remained in the office, energetically gathering stacks of papers and documents for their trip. She hurried down into the cellar, where rows of metal bins were arranged with periodicals and records, the different lanes of bins having been named for authors, like Holmes Hole. She was so excited, she began a little dance through Longfellow Avenue.

'Hope you haven't any swarrys you're missing being here tonight, Miss Sand.'

'Oh!' Rebecca jumped. 'Why, Mr. Midges. I'm sorry. I didn't know anyone was down here so late.'

Midges, sweating profusely, was sitting on the floor attacking a ledger. His head uncovered, his thinning hair stuck straight up as though he had seen a ghost. 'Late! Not for me, why, this firm would crumble into ruins if I weren't here half my life. I wish I *weren't* here in some nasty cellar, love. But these subscriber lists must be just *so*, and they've been a mess since we've been short a clerk.'

At the thoughtless reference to Daniel's death, Rebecca looked away. 'Good evening, Mr. Midges.'

'Wait! Don't!' Midges stammered awkwardly, then piped out his arbitrary whistle to put her at ease. 'I'm deeply sorry about what happened to your poor brother, upon my word. It's thunderously sad. I had a baby brother die right in my lap when I was four. Just stopped breathing, and I never stop thinking of that moment.'

'I'm sorry about your brother, Mr. Midges – and I appreciate your saying so. Now I must finish my work for Mr. Osgood.'

'Yes, yes, you are very industrious,' Midges mumbled with meek embarrassment, as though rejected for the last dance at the soiree in favour of Osgood. 'If I may say one more thing. I am especially sorry, being a man who respects a moral character, to hear of the terrible way Danny died. I had always thought highly of him.'

A fearful look crept over Rebecca's face, making it clear she didn't understand.

Midges went on, a spasm of pleasure in his words, 'Why, I heard Mr. Osgood speaking about the opium with Mr. Fields as they sat together in the dining room. Well, it's downright sad, I say! He seemed such a forthright boy. Now, if I had a sister, love, and she were pretty and sensible as you, for instance . . .'

Rebecca lifted the bottom of her skirts and hurried up the stairs, away from Midges, as quickly as possible.

'Good evening, Miss Sand!' Midges called out after her with a heartbroken, confused stare. 'Plucky, manlike creature!' he marvelled to himself.

Rebecca went upstairs, her hands clenched in fists on her desk. She felt a great weight resting on her chest, and a tear fell down her red cheek. These were not tears of sadness; these were tears of anger, frustration, rage. These tears were difficult, they didn't want to come out and didn't want to stay in. Hardly conscious of what she was doing, she found the handkerchief Osgood had given her when telling her the news, and looked at the pretty design of the *JRO* monogram. In his personal letters, he'd sign an informal 'James' but would add (R. Osgood). The rest of the world would see him genial and prepared for anything, but she had appreciated the fact that she saw him in his moments of consternation – he would always sit with one or sometimes both hands on the back of his neck, as if to support the weight of the thoughts in his head. In the evenings when back home, she would sometimes think of him as James instead of Mr. Osgood. That he would say such things about her brother was devastating – and within earshot of everyone! She'd been a fool to believe him their advocate.

She waited for a horsecar that would take her close to Oxford Street, which would be a fast passage, but in the swirl of her emotions Rebecca could not stand the crowd of other homebound workers. The walk home seemed to be both instantaneous and cruelly tedious.

Back in her room at the second-class boardinghouse, the stillness and quiet after the hurry of her journey home felt suffocating. Were these blank walls all that was left of her life? No family, no Daniel, no husband, and now not even the trust she had always imagined she had earned specially from Mr. Osgood, a man she had admired more than anyone in Boston for giving her an honest and respectful vocation. The anger had burned up her tears and she was left with panic. Without knowing why, the orderliness of her tiny quarters newly befuddled her, and she pulled out her chest from under her bed and began to reorganise her belongings.

It crossed her mind not to go to the piers in the morning and, furthermore, not to ever return to the firm or Boston. If she chose, she would never see Mr. Osgood again. But this room, old Mrs. Lepsin and her family of sorrowful boarders, this could not be what remained of Rebecca Sand; this could not be what remained of her Boston; this minuscule life must have existed in some other universe. She needed the voyage held out to her. And she knew the one thing she needed right now, more than anything, was an explanation from Osgood's own lips.

IX

BOARD THE OCEAN LINER TO England, Osgood handed out books liberally in the grand saloon, instantly counting a dozen gentlemen and half that number of ladies whose names and tastes he knew by way of this introduction. This transatlantic ship, the *Samaria*, was an ideal place for Osgood's natural sociability. Away from normal occupations in the world, the passengers – at least in fine weather – were inclined to be polite, courteous and open. Nothing could brighten up a publisher and an oldest sibling like James R. Osgood more than helping a shipful of people be happy. He was not the type of man to crack jokes, but he was usually the first to laugh at them. When he did tell jokes, he would remind himself not to later – for too often there would be someone to take what he meant in jest very soberly.

The men of commerce in the first steerage, with an eye towards a bargain despite their long purses, lined up to receive Osgood's gifts. The young publisher's most sociable travelling companion was an English tea merchant, Mr. Marcus Wakefield. Like Osgood, he was young given his significant achievements as a businessman – though the lines in Wakefield's face suggested one hardened beyond his years.

'What is this I see?' Wakefield asked after introducing himself. He was handsome and well groomed with an easy, self-confident, almost jaunty air when he spoke. He stepped closer to Osgood's case of books. 'I've been in this ship's library many times, and I declare you have the better selection, sir.'

'Mr. Wakefield, pray take one to begin the journey.'

'Upon my word!'

'I am a publisher, you see. Partner of Fields, Osgood and Company.'

'It is a trade of which I am entirely uneducated, although I could tell you every spice that makes up the strongest tea in twelve countries and whether the new season's tea is pekoe, congou, or imperial. Forgive the liberty of my question, but how can you give away the merchandise you own instead of selling it? I'd like to shake hands with the man who can succeed like that!'

'We do not own books. Only an author can own a book. It is the honourable position of the publisher to find people to buy stock in it. I like to say, Mr. Wakefield, that one good book will whet a reader's appetite enough that he shall take up ten more in the next year.'

'It is more than kind.'

'Besides, at customs in Liverpool they must look through every book carried off the ship for reprints of English books, so those could be confiscated. I say, Mr. Wakefield, that if I do not dispense with these as planned, I will be held up there for hours while they are examined.'

'I shall be a willing thief, then, if you insist, but I will pay you back ten times on our passage in friendship – and in pekoe.'

It was not until the second morning, when the reality of being trapped at sea away from home and friends floated down upon each passenger, that Osgood questioned Rebecca Sand. Though she always tended to keep her own counsel, she had been unusually distant towards her employer since boarding. At first, Osgood had thought she only wished to ensure a professional demeanour in this new setting, surrounded by strangers, some of whom would disapprove of young women travelling for business.

'Miss Sand,' Osgood said as he met her on deck. 'I hope you have escaped feeling seasick.'

'I have been so fortunate, Mr. Osgood,' she answered curtly.

Osgood knew he would need to be more direct. 'I cannot help but observe a change in your demeanour since we have left Boston. Set me right if I am mistaken.'

'You are not, sir,' she replied steadily.

'Is this change towards me in particular?'

'It is,' she agreed.

Osgood, perceiving a steeper hill to climb in their terse catechism than he'd thought, found two deck chairs across from each other and asked if she would say more. Rebecca folded her gloves over her lap and then calmly explained what she'd heard from Midges in the office cellar.

'Midges, that ogre!' Osgood cried, his hand curling into a fist against the arm of his deck chair. He stood up and kicked an imaginary miniature Midges overboard with his boot. 'How unthinking and cruel. I should have taken better care that he did not overhear my private conversations with Mr. Fields. I am very sorry about all of this.'

Osgood told her how the police officer, Carlton, and the coroner had concluded Daniel had become an opium eater. This time he did not spare any of the details. 'I did not believe it,' he said. 'Then they showed me marks on his arm, Miss Sand, that they say were from a "hypodermic" kit to inject opium into his veins.'

Rebecca thought about all of this, staring out on to the water, then shook her head. 'We shared our rooms. If Daniel was an opium eater, I would have recognised even the smallest sign, God knows that. When my husband returned from Danville after the war, he required phials of morphine or Indian hemp on hand at all times. He carried around a look of blankness, an emptiness that would not let him work or sleep or eat. He wanted nobody around him and no visitors except those he found in his solitude in our books and in dreams. He had survived the battlefields but his soul was shattered by the evils of what his doctor called soldiers' disease. Daniel had been bent on his own form of intemperance when we moved to Boston, and when I first heard of the accident I had to wonder whether he had renewed his habits of gin. No, I would have noticed the marks. I would have seen it in his face. There would have been no doubt, Mr. Osgood, I would have, and immediate action would have been taken.'

Osgood said sympathetically, 'I couldn't fathom it either.'

'You couldn't fathom the police being right, or you couldn't fathom why Daniel would fail your trust?' Rebecca asked.

Osgood turned and met her glare. An intense bloom had risen on her soft cheeks and her eyes narrowed. Osgood, chastened, nodded in surrender. 'You are right to be angry about my not telling you all this. You are angry? I wish you to speak freely of this.'

'I cannot believe you'd hide the details of the police report from me – whether or not they are correct. If I am to take care of myself like a man does and be dependent on no man, then I expect not to be treated like a helpless vessel. You deprived me of the chance to defend his name! I am grateful for my position, and my livelihood depends upon it, so I ought never demand much in my circumstances, I know. But I believe I deserve your respect.'

'You have that. I assure you,' said Osgood.

Rebecca resided in the drabbest class of cabins on the ship. No electric bells to call the stewards, no ornate chandeliers, painted panels and domed ceilings like in the higher steerage filled with superior society. Rebecca used the time she spent in her small stateroom to read. Unlike most of the other girls she knew in Boston, she did not read for sensation but to understand her own life in a more direct way and to learn more about the publishing trade. Aboard the liner, she had brought a rather technical book on the history of sea travel.

She had also brought one of Daniel's bottled ship models. To think that it was her sailing across the ocean and not her brother who'd yearned for such a voyage. If there were an immortal part of Daniel, surely it was her companion here.

At night, she would sometimes stand outside by the rail and quietly watch the sea and stars and the horizon where they met.

'There is such romance to a sea voyage!' a young female traveller exclaimed one morning when she observed Rebecca in this attitude. Christie, a green-eyed girl covered head to toe in freckles, shared the compartment with Rebecca. 'Don't you think, miss?'

'Romance,' repeated Rebecca, shaking her head. 'I don't know.'

The freckled girl insisted on the point. 'You're a goose, aren't you, miss? How could you not think so? Say you haven't noticed the number of handsome gentlemen on this ship! I do not wish to be a nurse living alongside lazy Irish housemaids for long, you know.'

'Do you not enjoy your charges, Miss Christie?'

'Those little devils! It is well enough, for I tell them there is a black man who swallows up little children who do not listen to their nurses. Oh, but those Irish girls – the Sallys and Marys and Bridgets – they just stir up the children's spirits again.'

'Unfortunate,' said Rebecca.

'I shall not weep for long for them when I find a husband. This ship is full of such possibility! Think of the bachelors, businessmen and club men, and the young men with rich fathers, and the possibilities of love from one of them. I suppose one might even try slipping off the side into the waves to wait to be rescued.'

'Yes,' Rebecca said quietly. Her raven black hair had been loosened by the breeze and fell pleasantly over her face. 'One might also drown,' she said wryly.

'Oh, or being shipwrecked, just the two of you!' came the oblivious response. Christie chatted on, 'You're spoken of as one of the four prettiest maidens aboard. Mind, that's in spite of a too-high brow and the fact that you haven't a bit of style to speak of with your mourning clothes, which make you look so pale and strong-willed. Why not put a flower in your belt sometimes as a starter for any lover's casual flirtation? And you always have a book at your hip like some kind of tomboy. What of that charming young man you're travelling with? There are plenty of women who have designs on him, if you are too selective for his hand.'

'I am here to work,' said Rebecca, looking away so the girl would not see her cheeks colouring, her body betraying her when she most needed it to submit. 'I should like very much to prove myself capable of working as a self-supporting individual. That is all I seek from Mr. Osgood.'

'He dresses nicely and keeps his temper.'

'Well, yes, he does.'

'That is what matters.'

'He is much less ordinary and average than that,' Rebecca objected.

'What's your counsel?'

'What do you mean my counsel?'

'Yes, on impressing your Mr. Osgood!'

'He is not *my* . . . My counsel is that Mr. Osgood is occupied with his business affairs and not nonsense.'

'A pity!' replied her companion, disappointed by James Osgood's inverted priorities. 'I would have invited you to the wedding, you know.'

During their voyage, Rebecca would often meet Osgood in the ship's library to help compose letters to Dickens's publishing representatives in London or draft other documents. Though she could not dine at his table or take part in first-class pastimes, one pleasant afternoon she was sitting out on a deck chair reading the pages of *Drood*, wearing a wrap to protect herself against the wind. She had been joined by some girls who were knitting. In a nearby porthole, she noticed a reflection of the parlour, where Osgood was playing chess, a game which Rebecca had taught Daniel to fill his evenings at the boardinghouse in Boston after he had stopped drinking.

At first, feeling she should not spy, she tried returning her attention to her reading but could not help herself. She became fascinated at the idea of watching her employer without him knowing. She had to remind herself that she'd remained a bit disappointed towards Osgood, and as though a sort of punishment of him, she decided she should withhold her interest. But before long, she was so enamoured by the manoeuvres of the game that she concocted her own silent strategies. Osgood reached a critical turn, his hand frozen above the table, and she urged him mentally to move the knight to the back left of his opponent's board.

That will do it, Mr. Osgood! she thought to herself. She knew he would do nothing more than smile politely if he won, so as not to belittle the other player.

A moment later, after withdrawing his hand from several aborted moves, he chose the move she had counselled. She clapped her hands in delight, and two of the girls peered over their knitting with shaking heads.

Even after only a few days at sea, she felt herself to be in an entirely different world than Boston. The voyage did not remove Daniel from her mind. In his absence, she realised how much of his resilience and buoyancy had passed into her own ambitions for herself. His voice had become part of her inner life in a way she could not describe. The voyage made her feel temporarily at peace about his death, as though he were part of the endless expanse of sky and salt-water and warm breezes.

One warm morning, Osgood was walking along the upper deck in a general abstraction. The winds were picking up and the ship was shakier than it had been. Nausea gradually spread to a few new people each day. The ship's doctor passed out small draughts of morphine to calm the nerves. Passengers who were not sick had grown bored of chess and cards and of talking politics over cigars. Soon, not even the dinner bell interested them; only a whale sighting could temporarily stir the general sluggishness. But not Osgood – Osgood had avoided ennui entirely.

He remained industrious, well dressed and engrossed in his coming mission. While other men were now regularly unshaven, his moustache was trim and his face clean. Osgood saw this not just as habit but necessity. His face, though composed of pleasant enough features, was rather inconspicuous, not to say nondescript. In fact, it was not uncommon for a person who had met Osgood in one place – say, the Tremont Street office – to then, perhaps days later, meet with him in another setting – the bridge at the Public Garden – and evince not a shred of recognition. Sometimes a change of sunlight to gaslight, or a Saturday rather than a Tuesday, was known to produce the same confusion in those attempting to place a memory of the publisher's identity. This all would be made more problematic had Osgood ever changed the cut of a single hair, which the publisher did not dare to do. It might risk him waking up one morning and finding his home and position taken away from him.

Osgood had continued to study the pages of *The Mystery of Edwin Drood* he had brought with him. The book was different from the usual Dickens work and his most artistic endeavour since *A Tale of Two Cities*. It was the work of a ripe genius, restrained and taut, and would have been his masterpiece when finished, Osgood was convinced, and like any masterpiece equally beloved and misunderstood. Morbid and dark, it had a divided family of the fictionally named Cloisterham village and only a bleak hope for happiness for them. The characters were infused with such life that one could almost feel that they would step out of the pages and act out the remainder of the story without Dickens's pen to help. The looming question lurked at the end of the existing pages: Was Edwin Drood, the young hero, murdered? Or was he in hiding, waiting to return triumphantly?

Of course, there was no thinking of Drood's disappearance without thinking of Dickens's death. The two were welded together for all time now. Would learning more about one ease the sad reality of the other? This was the momentum of Osgood's thoughts as he roamed the deck when he lost his balance on a slippery board and, before he could grab the railing, fell down hard on his back.

After a moment of confusion, he realised he was being offered a hand. Or a head, to be precise – the gold head of a heavy walking cane. Osgood reached hesitantly for the ugly, fanged monster carving and started to pull himself to his feet. Osgood had seen this man, with the wide moustache and brown turban, who kept mostly to himself, grumbling occasional demands to a waiter or steward, waving this queer cane around. Osgood had heard him referred to as Herman, and thought he appeared to be Parsee, but knew nothing else of him.

'All right?' Herman asked in his gravelly voice.

Osgood lowered himself back down, feeling a pain run through his back.

'I'll send for the ship's surgeon,' Herman said, with a cold but polite tone.

By this point, a small circle of passengers from all steerages and several crew members had gathered at the spot of the fall. Rebecca saw the crowd forming and ran as fast as she could move her legs in her narrow dress. She had to squeeze through the other girls, who were making a show of their concern.

'Well, you are a goose!' said Christie. 'We were here first, miss,' said another girl from their steerage, a gaudy redhead.

'Miss Sand,' Osgood called out with relief. 'Very sorry for the spectacle. Will you help me?'

'Beg your pardon,' Rebecca said to the redhead and her freckled companion with more than a little pleasure as she pushed by them. The wind draped her plain black dress around her and showed in her simple form a beauty to rival any of the other more lavishly displayed and ribboned girls lined up behind her. She gave Osgood her arm. 'Mr. Osgood, how very unlucky!' she said sympathetically. 'Are you hurt?'

'Luck – which they say in business is dispersed at random – played no part in this fraud, my dear young lady,' came a voice from the perimeter of the circle of onlookers. It was the English businessman, Wakefield. The tea merchant was elegantly dressed in a traditional cape and checked trousers. He stopped to nod courteously to Rebecca, then continued making his way forward. 'My friend Osgood, victim!'

'Mr. Wakefield, you are mistaken. The spray from the ocean has been quite rough, you see, and I slipped in a puddle,' Osgood insisted.

'No. That is what *this* man would like you to think.' Wakefield turned sharply at the large man who had helped Osgood to his feet.

'Beg pardon?' Herman asked the impudent accuser, his hands resting on the cord tied around his tunic and knotted in four places.

'The spray *has* become quite vicious, it's very true,' Wakefield explained, 'which is why I was out walking instead of feeling sick in my stateroom. It was thus that I witnessed this man pouring water from a bucket into that corner. He appeared to be watching for someone to appear before doing it.'

'Do you mean he did this on purpose? Why would he do such a horrid thing?' asked Rebecca, turning to look at Herman. As she met the accused's eyes and innocent smile, a sudden, almost magnetic repulsion forced her to take a step back. The dark, malicious eyes gave her a rush of inexplicable fear and hatred.

Wakefield glanced at Rebecca. 'My little woman, you are very innocent! I am embarrassed to say we have sharpers in England who would target any good-natured gentleman. I travel frequently on this and other liners and have been robbed two times myself. I believe this man is what the police call a floorer, or a tripper.'

'What?' Osgood asked.

'Never mind!' Herman's face grew bright. He stuck a toothpick in his mouth and chewed restlessly. 'I know not what this bloke means by this, and I suggest he retreats.'

'Just a moment, please, my dear Mr. Wakefield,' said Osgood, the natural diplomat. 'This man did *help* me after my fall.'

'Let us consider why he would do that, what opportunity that might afford him,' Wakefield mused, squaring the lower part of his face by placing one finger on each curve of his dusty-coloured moustache.

Herman swatted his hand at Wakefield's head, knocking his hat high into the air. The breeze took the hat right down to Rebecca, who caught it.

'Search this man,' ordered the captain, a hairy, square-shaped man who had joined in the circle. He pointed at Herman, and the stewards seized him. They pulled out a watch and a calfskin pocketbook from Herman's tunic pocket.

'Are these yours, sir?' the captain asked Osgood.

'They are,' Osgood admitted with dismay.

'I will knock your damned guts out, and yours, too!' Herman growled to Osgood and then Wakefield.

'Threats will do nothing,' said Wakefield, though his hands trembled as he straightened the pin in his cravat. He accepted his hat back from Rebecca, bowing courteously again as a means of suppressing his trembling.

Two stewards rapidly wrestled Herman into submission and

secured the thief. Most of the women covered their faces with their handkerchiefs or cried out, but Rebecca, standing next to Osgood, kept watching him in a mesmerised stare. Herman looked across at Osgood. 'You louse! I'll feed your legs to the sharks, mark that!'

The voice was grating and deep, a baritone that made one wish one had never heard it.

'Go to the devil, villain!' said the captain. He turned to a steward standing near him. 'Take him below deck! The police in London will know how to deal with him.'

The ship's surgeon concluded that Osgood's injuries were superficial. The captain offered him a special tour of the ship, including the brig, where Osgood was surprised to see an array of strong cells befitting a battleship.

'The construction of all the major English liners are subsidised by the Royal Navy, you see. In return they are built so they can be converted into warships,' the captain explained. 'Cannons, prison cells and what-you-will.'

Herman, slouched on the floor in the corner of one cell, praying to the red-hot furnace outside the cell, glanced up at his visitors, then looked back at the furnace. To the evident satisfaction of the captain, the man appeared worn out. Yet Herman retained a slippery grin of the strangest type, as though everyone else aboard were in prison, and he was the one completely free. His feet were bound together by a chain, and his wrist chained to the wall, and rats ran back and forth over his legs. His turban had been removed and his head was shaved clean, except for coarse patches of hair at the temples. Osgood found – from fear or humility – that he could not look into the eye of his assailant.

As Osgood and the captain climbed up the stairs again, the prisoner began singing a children's rhyme.

> *In works of labour or of skill,*
> *I would be busy too:*
> *For Satan finds some mischief still*
> *For idle hands to do.*

Then there was a sound, like a rat squealing.

★ ★ ★

The days after the attack saw Osgood feted at the captain's table at supper and given a hero's greeting every time he met his fellow passengers. Coming on to the deck for a morning walk now attracted a procession of the single women. Rebecca would sit on her deck chair and watch this grudgingly from under her hat.

Her roommate, Christie, sat down next to her. 'What a picture of romance Mr. Osgood is!' she smiled at Rebecca, leaning in. 'He is more admired now than ever!'

Rebecca did her best to appear occupied by the book in her lap. 'I find nothing to smile about. He might have been hurt,' she said.

'Well, then just what is your idea of romance? Perhaps you haven't one, miss.'

Rebecca kept her eyes on her book and tried to ignore her. But, contrary to her own determination, she spoke. 'Till the judgement that yourself arise, you live in this, and dwell in lovers' eyes.'

Christie listened to the verse from the Shakespeare sonnet, then said, 'Beg pardon?'

'Romance is not an idea, Christie, but a moment. An unspoken glance when someone looks into your eyes and knows exactly who you are, what you need.'

The other girl sat up with a mischievous energy. 'Well, ain't that nice! Let us get a gentleman's opinion on the same question.'

'What?' said Rebecca, taken aback.

She turned her head and saw to her horror that Osgood was standing behind the chairs. She wondered with a slight shiver how long he had been there.

'Now, Mr. Osgood,' said the loquacious Christie, 'how does a real Boston gentleman like yourself define real romance?'

'Well,' Osgood said, blushing, 'self-sacrifice for one's beloved, I suppose I'd say.'

'How very endearing!' replied Christie. 'You mean such sentiment on behalf of the man, I guess, Mr. Osgood? Oh, it is much more charming. Don't you think, Miss Rebecca? Oh, how dreadfully you look, dear girl.'

Rebecca stood up and straightened her dress. 'The ship is shaky this morning,' she said.

'I'll walk you to your cabin, Miss Sand.' Osgood offered his arm with concern.

'Thank you, but I'll find my way, Mr. Osgood. I wanted to visit the ship's library.'

Rebecca left Osgood standing, while Christie continued to gaze at him, tossing her hair. 'Miss didn't need to have such a conniption fit, did she, Mr. Osgood?' Osgood gave her an awkward nod before hurrying away.

'You have become more popular with the ladies than the captain himself!' Wakefield said later as he and Osgood shared cigars in the main saloon.

'I shall fall on my head tomorrow again then,' Osgood said. His companion seeming alarmed at this proposal, Osgood recited to himself his rule not to try jokes.

'Well, I suspect with a young lady as you have singing second in your duet, the feminine attention should not turn your head too much.'

The publisher raised his eyebrows, 'You mean Miss Sand?'

'Do you have another beautiful girl in your trunk?' Wakefield laughed. 'I apologise, Mr. Osgood. Am I wrong to presume you have designs on the young woman? Do not tell me: she comes from another class of society than you, she is just a career woman, and so on. I am a philosophical person, as you'll learn, my American friend. It is my conviction that we make ourselves who we want to be and not chain ourselves to the notions of busybodies who wish to judge us. Neglect your friends and family, neglect your dress, go to the devil generally, but do not neglect love! Do not lose that siren to the next Tom or Dick who is not as cautious and proper!'

Osgood had a rare feeling in his throat: he was at a loss to respond appropriately. 'Miss Sand is an excellent bookkeeper, Mr. Wakefield. There is not another person in the firm whom I would trust as I do her.'

Wakefield nodded thoughtfully. He had a habit of caressing his own knee – sometimes kneading, sometimes tapping to an unheard but thoughtful rhythm. 'My father used to say that I *can* let my imagination run away. And when I do, all manners disappear. I apologise, I do.'

'To place trust in your confidence, Mr. Wakefield, she is a divorcée only in the last several years. By the laws of the Commonwealth of Massachusetts, she may not have romantic ties for another full year, or her divorce grant will be revoked and she will lose privileges for future marriage.' Osgood paused. 'I say this to point out that she is a most sensible person, by character and by necessity. She does not fancy excitement for its sake like many girls.'

After his time in the saloon, Osgood was surprised to notice Rebecca standing on deck looking out at the ocean.

'Is something wrong, Miss Sand?' Osgood asked, approaching her.

'Yes,' she said, turning to him with a forceful nod. 'I think so, Mr. Osgood. If you were a pickpocket on a ship, would you not wait until the end of the voyage to steal?'

'What?' Osgood asked, unprepared for the subject.

'Otherwise,' Rebecca went on confidently, 'yes, otherwise when someone reports the theft to the captain, the criminal would be trapped with the stolen goods.'

Osgood shrugged. 'Well, I suppose so. Mr. Wakefield commented that this type of crime is not uncommon in England nor on ships.'

'No. But this Parsee man, Herman, he hardly seems like the usual pickpocket, does he?' Rebecca asked. 'Think of Charles Dickens's own descriptions of that breed of criminal. They are quite young rascals, desperate and set on quick profit, inconspicuous. Certainly not like him. I should wonder if he is any less than six feet tall!'

A few days later, the weather was inclement, too soggy to be out on deck, while Osgood, despite his better instincts, sat in the ship's library brooding about Herman. He had found an English edition of *Oliver Twist*, published by Chapman & Hall, and had turned to the chapters describing Oliver's experiences with the circle of pickpockets. It was hard to return to the normal routine of shipboard life in the shadow of that strange assault and Rebecca's astute observations. Those burning orbs of the thief had remained seared in Osgood's mind.

Remembering the maze of halls from the captain's tour, he brought a candle from his stateroom and quietly retraced his steps through the dark halls to the brig. He did not fear for his safety, not with the prisoner chained and the iron bars between them. No, he feared more, perhaps, whatever it was Herman might reveal: some danger that Osgood could not yet anticipate. Prompted by Rebecca's questions, he had begun to wonder just what a man like Herman had been doing in Boston in the first place.

When he reached the lower level of the ship and found the row of jail cells, each one black with iron and metal, strewn with grime and dust, he stopped in front of Herman's. He raised the candle and gasped loudly. The cell was empty but for a dead rat, its head missing, and a set of dangling chains.

X

SGOOD STOOD IN PLACE FOR a moment, paralysed by fear and surprise, though he knew he must act quickly. Hesitation could put him in even greater peril – worse, it could endanger his friend Mr. Wakefield or even Rebecca! Herman might be anywhere on the ship, and if he could escape a prison cell built for war, he could also prove far more dangerous than a petty floorer.

Osgood dashed though the dark and climbed the stairs two at a time.

'What's the matter, sir?' asked a steward whom Osgood nearly knocked over.

Osgood rapidly conveyed the situation to the steward, and the captain and his staff soon gathered. They divided into groups to search the steamer in all quarters for Herman. Osgood and the rest of the passengers were left in the saloon with an armed sentry to ensure their safety. When the captain returned, hat in hand, rifle under his folded arm, wiping the sweat gathered from the expedition, he reported that Herman was nowhere on board.

'How is that possible, sir?' Rebecca demanded to know.

'We do not know, Miss Sand. He was seen yesterday morning when one of my stewards brought him his soup. He must have forced open the lock and escaped sometime during the night.'

'Escaped to where, captain?' Wakefield cried, both of his hands engaging in a fierce kneading of his knees.

'I do not know, Mr. Wakefield. Perhaps he saw another ship and decided to swim for it. The winds were choppy yesterday, though: it is unlikely he would have survived if he tried such a mad flight.

He has almost certainly perished in the depths, and will sleep soundly in Davy Jones's locker.'

Hearing this grim scenario, the passengers exhaled their excitement and by the time they returned to their staterooms were bored again. After a few days, thoughts of soon reaching England erased those of the escaped prisoner. Passengers packed up the contents of their staterooms into a few small valises and settled up surprisingly high wine bills with the stewards. Osgood likewise attempted to suppress the questions in his mind. Not Rebecca, though.

'It doesn't make sense, Mr. Osgood,' she insisted one afternoon in the library, tapping her fingers busily on the tabletop.

'What doesn't, Miss Sand?'

'The disappearance of the thief!'

Osgood, one hand locked behind his neck in his usual pose of concentration, looked up from his ledger abruptly but quickly resumed his preoccupied pose facing the window. 'You mustn't think too much on that subject, Miss Sand. You heard the captain say that the man perished. If we believed otherwise, we might as well believe in sea serpents. And surely they would have devoured the thief, if we believed in them!'

'What kind of a man drowns himself to escape charges of petty theft? What if . . . ?' Rebecca's voice trailed off there, replaced by her tapping fingers.

A few hours later, Osgood could be found pacing the deck alone as he had done the morning of Herman's trap. As they had sailed closer to England, he looked dreamily at the distant vessels with unknown destinies that sat high against the horizon. Osgood thought about the anxiety on Rebecca's face and knew what she had wanted to say earlier in the library: *What if Herman were still alive, what if he comes back for you?* He did his best to eject these thoughts by imagining what Fields would reply, holding his head erect and his beard thrust forward. *Remember the reason for this trip. It is to end Dickens's mystery, not to create your own. Otherwise, our enterprises can become helter-skelter, our lives out of our control.*

SECOND INSTALMENT

I know one little girl who, when she is happy, reads Nicholas Nickleby; when she is unhappy, reads Nicholas Nickleby; when she is tired, reads Nicholas Nickleby; when she is in bed, reads Nicholas Nickleby; when she has nothing to do, reads Nicholas Nickleby, and when she has finished the book reads Nicholas Nickleby over again.

William Thackeray

XI

TWO AND A HALF
YEARS EARLIER:
BOSTON, NOVEMBER 19, 1867

HEN IT WAS ANNOUNCED THAT tickets for the first of the novelist's public readings would be sold the next morning, a queue started to form at the street door of the publishing firm. James Osgood ordered Daniel Sand to carry out straw mattresses and blankets for those spending the night in the cold, windy street. Fields had interjected that if they really wanted a happy crowd, the shop boy ought to bring down beer.

By dawn the morning of the sale, the mass of people outside stretched a mile and a half along Tremont Street. Some had brought their own armchairs to sleep in.

The two partners, Fields and Osgood, were watching from a window that had been hastily barred for fear people might climb in for the tickets. They were astounded to see that not only were aristocratic gentlemen shoulder to shoulder with Irish workmen, but also that several Negroes could be seen amid the throng . . . and that three women had taken places in the rowdy line! This last fact was considered so touching by the men waiting in the arctic cold that after a vote, the first of the women was invited to take a position at the head. In honour of the rather English theme of the gathering, tea was brought out – though some of it was mixed with the contents of small black bottles.

In the line there were also the ticket speculators who would buy up seats and resell them at a profit. They had been expected, these enterprising vultures that populated America, but not so many.

One speculator, among the most aggressive about obtaining and hoarding tickets, was dressed like George Washington, complete with the wig and hat.

As the sale progressed, big bald-headed George Dolby, shuttling back and forth along the crowd, was handed a telegram. 'Sent from port at Halifax,' Mr. Dolby had said after first reading it silently. 'Announcing the *Cuba*. Dickens en route to Boston right now! The Chief will be on American soil before nightfall!' The last words were drowned by cheers.

That was hours ago. It was pitch black by now at the harbour, bitterly cold, and no sign of the *Cuba* yet. What a crowd! Pressmen roamed the wharves in packs, ready to describe the novelist's first steps back on American soil for the morning editions. The customs officer lent Fields the steamer *Hamblin* to search the bay farther out. He and Osgood were joined on the steamer by Dolby, who had come from London early along with several assistants. The Englishmen wrapped their coats tightly against the frigid air.

'*Cuba* in sight!' the lookout man barked.

They steamed ahead until they were alongside the larger ship. As they got close, they could see that it had become grounded by a mud bank. The party signalled for the gangway plank to be lowered between the ships. Bright rockets were bursting through the dark sky behind them in a grand display of welcome for the novelist.

The lookout, squinting, grumbled at Dolby, 'That don't look like no author at all. That looks like an old gentleman pirate!'

High above them, Charles Dickens himself stood on the deck of the steamer, his flashy vest and gold watch chains illuminated in the halo of the fiery display in the sky. Lithe and standing tall, looking taller from such a height than his five foot eight inches, he peered down with arms outstretched.

The Americans on the smaller ship could not help showing surprise to see that Dickens's head was uncovered. After shouting back and forth with the crew of the *Cuba*, they helped Dickens across the plank into the smaller boat where he grabbed two hands at a time in his greetings.

The author seemed equally pleased and discomfited to hear about the waiting crowd at the wharf. 'I see,' Dickens said, scratching at his grizzled imperial beard. 'So I'm to face the public right away?'

'Your ship's accident with the mud bank, my dear Dickens, may work to our advantage,' said Fields. 'We have chartered two carriages now waiting at the Long Wharf to take us directly to the hotel. As long as all eyes remain waiting for signs of the *Cuba*, you will arrive unnoticed and in peace at your hotel, with ample time for a light supper.'

But – as it happens when enough people are interested in a secret – the public picked up the trick. At the Parker House, the arriving party had to struggle through a waiting throng that had them cornered. 'Hats off in front!' yelled the ones in the back of the crowd.

It was not until the party had been brought inside the Parker House and sat down for supper that the atmosphere began to relax. Then Dickens noticed. He did not say anything, but his plate of mongrel goose scraped against the table as he pushed it away. The waiter had left the door to the private dining room open slightly in order to allow the public a peek at the famous man.

'Branagan!' Dolby whispered urgently to the young porter he'd brought from England, who got up, crossed the room, and slammed the door. He then gave a hard stare to the offending waiter and whispered to him. The waiter nodded nervously, in apology – or perhaps fear, for this Branagan was hale and strong.

Later that evening, Dickens was slouched in the sitting room of 338 as his bathtub filled. 'These people have not in the least changed in the last five and twenty years,' he was saying, falling fast into a sombre attitude. 'They are doing already what they were doing all those years ago, making me some object of novelty to gaze upon! Dolby, I should have kept my word.'

'When have you ever not, Chief?' asked his manager, indignant on his behalf.

'I swore to myself never to return to America again. There can only be bad things from coming here.' The last time Dickens had come, in 1842, he had planted himself in the middle of a public row by calling for American publishers to adopt international copyright law to stop the free reproduction of British books. Dickens was called greedy and mercenary and accused of coming to the country only to increase his wealth.

His manager now tried to placate the Chief by speaking in generous detail of the first ticket sale and of their great prospects. 'Line two miles away from the *ticccket boox!*' Dolby had long ago conquered a fussy stammer, but still there always seemed a rock in the path of his speech that he had to take care not to stumble over. To master it he had formed a strange habit: he would enunciate the most mundane word with the elaborateness of a regal pronouncement. Cash, telegraphic and ticket box sounded Shakespearean coming out of Dolby's prominent jowls.

'Look at these,' Dolby said. He removed several bundles as big as sofa cushions.

Dickens sucked in his tongue. 'Surely that must be the family wash,' he said.

'Our receipts, just from the first series! Mr. Kelly and I will begin wiring the money to Coutts in London in the morning.' Dickens weighed a pile in each hand as Dolby spoke. 'Remember, Chief, seven dollars to the pound.'

Dickens said, 'I knew you would see to it that the ticket sales were a slap-up success, good friend. Of that I never doubt.'

'You shall have plenty of peace. See that door over there? It's a private stairs in the rear of the hotel so you needn't be among the public when you don't wish it.'

'Surely, surely. Hot and cold bath, too,' Dickens commented as he wandered again, impressed at the well-appointed rooms and the brilliant flowers left there by Annie Fields that he now ran under his nose. 'Now Dolby, be sure to convert those greenbacks directly into gold. Don't ever trust American currency.'

'Never would, Chief!'

After bathing, Dickens took his seat at his desk. He removed his writing case, which held a variety of pencils and quill pens. He had a small red leather diary that he opened to a page towards the back to study it. Plucking up one of the many feathered writing instruments, he then sought out the inkwell provided by the hotel. Wetting the tip of the pen until it soaked black, he proceeded to compose a brief message. 'Dolby,' Dickens said, folding the paper when he was done, 'have this brought to the telegraph office, won't you? It is important.'

Dolby opened the door and snapped his fingers to call for Tom Branagan.

XII

OM BRANAGAN FELT THE MANAGER's eyes linger on him approvingly as he exited room 338 on his latest mission. Downstairs in the Parker's office, the telegraph operator adjusted his eyeglasses and held up the piece of paper to the lamp.

'From Mr. Dickens. "Safe and well, expect good letter full of hope." Is that all?' the operator asked, squinting as he read the cramped writing. The operator seemed disappointed to find no more sensational message to transmit from the world's most famous writer. 'I suppose you came all the way from dear old England to carry scraps of blotted paper up and down the stairs.'

'Thank you for your help. Good evening,' replied Branagan evenly.

As Branagan crossed through the loud barroom and climbed back to the third floor, he was thinking about quiet conversations he had overheard between Dickens and Dolby about Nelly Ternan, the young actress who resided back in England, and whether she would also join them in America. Branagan guessed that the seemingly trifling note was a secret way of instructing Miss Ternan, though he did not know whether it meant she should come or not. But Branagan could guess at that, too.

The crowds awaiting Dickens upon their arrival suggested there would be nothing quiet about a twenty-six-year-old actress joining Dickens, the married father of eight grown children whose mother had moved away from the family estate in England ten years earlier. Branagan did not believe Dickens would want the extra scrutiny. No, nothing ever seemed to stay quiet in America, and that had been the disappointment showing in Dickens's face at supper. Through the narrow gap of that open door Charles Dickens had seen the nation as if it were one enormous curious eyeball trained on him.

Tom Branagan was one of the four subordinates in Dickens's camp brought for the tour. The assistants shared two rooms on the same floor as Dickens, whose own spacious rooms adjoined George Dolby's. Tom shared his with Henry Scott, the novelist's dresser and tailor. Henry was the only person – with the exception of Dolby – allowed in Dickens's dressing rooms before and after public readings. Henry, a melancholy man, would dress the novelist and adjust his hair into the perfect image of the younger man seen in so many photos in the windows of so many bookstores: the dashing, carefree genius whose eyes seemed to penetrate through the world around him just like the novels that made him famous.

Henry liked to consider himself in a different class than the other assistants, and when not in Dickens's company would remain reserved. Henry always referred to the Irish porter as 'Tom Branagan', never using just his first or surname. There was also Richard Kelly, a ticket agent with much bluster but a delicate constitution who was still recovering from the rough passage aboard the *Cuba*. George, the gasman, adjusted the lighting at each theatre to Dickens's exacting requirements. Conversation with George was doomed because every time he saw a lighting configuration – such as those in the glowing marble lobby of Parker's – he would stop and mutter to himself a long list of potential improvements.

Tom, at twenty years old, was the youngest of the group. His father, who had immigrated to England from Ireland, had worked for Dolby for ten years as a driver in the town of Ross. Tom's father died after being kicked in the chest by a horse and Dolby, in a fit of compassion, agreed to engage Tom, who needed to help support his elderly mother and two unmarried sisters.

The young fellow was well built, cool and collected, the right traits for a decent porter. Tom had no mandate as specific as seeing to Dickens's dress, light or profits. A whistle, a snap of the fingers, a tapped foot – all were signals for Tom to do anything that was needed.

Not everyone approved of the decision to bring Tom to America.

For each of the trusted advisers in England originally consulted in planning Dickens's trip, there had been different notions about what might go wrong in America: Charles Dickens himself had been most worried about the Fenian Brotherhood, the radical Irishmen spread throughout the United States, particularly in Boston and New York, devoted to bringing down ruin upon England. They would relish the opportunity to assault a conspicuous Englishman like himself on American soil. George Dolby, meanwhile, worried about the American speculators ruining ticket sales by buying up excessive numbers of tickets. John Forster, who considered himself Dickens's closest friend and most selfless adviser . . . well, Mr. Forster worried. He worried that Dickens's presence could inspire anti-English riots like the ones against the Shakespearean actor William Macready in New York. Forster also thought, generally speaking, that it was unseemly for a man as great as Dickens – and in John Forster's eyes no man was greater – to be seen going to such lengths for no grander purpose than making a profit.

Dickens had not been shy swatting aside this point. 'Expenses in my life are so enormous,' he'd say, 'that I feel myself drawn towards America like the Loadstone rock, as Darnay in the *Tale of Two Cities* is to Paris. America is the golden campaigning ground.'

Forster knit his brow and kept it knit. What profits could be made in America, land of paupers and thieves? Even if there *were* money to be made, the Irish would find a way to steal the money right out of the American banks. If the bank managed to somehow keep the money, the bank would surely fail, like all American banks! 'Dickens should not go to America!' said Forster in a half shout. 'I am opposed to the alpha and omega of the idea as an unacceptable breach of dignity and wish to hear no more about it. In*tol*-er-able!'

When Forster was told about the subordinates chosen to travel with the novelist, he was further appalled an Irishman was among them. What if the seemingly harmless Paddy were a Fenian himself with a secret plan to attack? Neither Dickens nor Dolby could exactly prove Forster wrong about Tom Branagan but managed to convince him that Tom was more ordinary porter than revolutionary.

Tom, for his part, found it interesting to observe that it was the members of the public who loved Dickens that caused the most concern. Tom had helped keep the onlookers away when Dickens had arrived at the Parker House; he was not surprised by their presence but by their persistence. A young woman yanked out a piece of fringe from Dickens's heavy grey and black shawl; a man excited to touch the novelist took the opportunity to pull a clump of fur from his coat. A lady energetically jumped up and down and waved a few pages of her manuscript, which she pleaded with Dickens to read.

Tom looked into their faces. Did each think that Dickens would turn around and walk home with them arm in arm?

Tom knew one thing. He had never before in his life met a man to whom *women* would offer their seats in a public vehicle or ante-room – until he had met Charles Dickens.

On the second morning after Dickens's arrival at the Parker House there was an uproar on the third floor of the hotel where Dickens and his staff had their rooms. At first, Tom had only noticed that Henry Scott, his roommate, was leaning his head against the wall and crying.

'All right, Mr. Scott?' Tom asked, concerned.

Henry looked right at Tom, thankful to find a witness. He dropped his usual reticence and slumped into one of the plush armchairs. 'Baggage handlers? Baggage *smashers!*'

The trunks of Dickens's clothing from the *Cuba* had been delivered to the hotel crushed and dented. Tom sat down on the rug and helped Henry reorganise the clothes.

'Thank you, Tom Branagan,' Henry said, embarrassed. 'It's more outrageous than a man could bear when one's work is treated like this. Beastly country!'

As soon as the two men had restored sufficient order to the wardrobe, there was another disturbance from across the hall. George Dolby was braying and shouting. He stood with Dickens and the others in the hallway of the hotel passing around a copy of *Harper's Weekly*. Tom asked if they were all right.

'See for yourself, Branagan,' said Dolby, pronouncing his name with a most stately explosion of the tongue that conveyed a measure of censure. 'All right? Certainly not!'

In the magazine was a cartoon showing in grotesque caricature the figures of Dickens and Dolby barring the door of a room labelled 'Parker House' against hordes of Americans on the other side. The cowardly Mr. Dickens was crying out, 'Not at home!'

'I don't suppose this artist was actually present here,' Tom said after a moment of deliberation. 'This drawing shows Mr. Dickens hiding in his room from the onlookers, which was not the case.'

'Of course he wasn't hiding!' said Dolby, aghast.

Dickens stroked the slight iron grey streak in his beard and, punching his cheek out with his tongue as he did at uncomfortable times, looked up wearily from the cartoon. 'Weren't we? Didn't I come here to do just that: hide, then sneak out from my hole long enough to collect my profit?' The novelist sighed and limped into the room on his lame right leg, an old injury reawakened by the sea travel.

That night Tom woke up in the small hours. His eyes danced in the darkness of the hotel room to the mantel clock.

'Did you hear that, Scott?' he whispered across the room to Henry.

Henry Scott stirred in his bed.

'A noise,' Tom explained. 'Did you hear a noise?'

Henry's face was in his pillow. 'Go to sleep, Tom Branagan.'

Tom had been having trouble sleeping in the Parker House – there was something about its opulence that disoriented him. Tom was not certain he had actually heard a noise – or at least not a noise different from the usual ones from the busy streets of Boston outside – but he was glad to justify his uneasy wakefulness. The clock's ticking teased him out of bed.

He took a candle into the hallway wearing a pilot coat over his long white flannels. Passing Dickens's rooms, he noticed that the door to the novelist's bedroom was open.

It looked like it had been kicked open. The inside latch broken.

'Mr. Dickens?' Tom knocked.

Tom went inside. For a moment, a strange thought flashed through him: how wrong it would be for anyone to ever see Charles Dickens *sleeping*. But the bed was in disarray and empty, and the novelist nowhere in sight.

Tom ran through the novelist's parlour glancing around for other signs of struggle and pounded with his fist on the door that adjoined with Dolby's rooms. As he entered, Dolby was pulling his dressing gown around himself. 'What is it, Branagan? You'll wake the Chief!'

'Mr. Dolby,' Tom said, pointing. 'Dickens is missing.'

'What? Heavens,' Dolby began to stammer, barely able to order to send for the 'p-p-pol-l-lice!'

Just then Dickens himself strode in. 'What is going on in here?' he asked, alarmed. He'd entered from the back staircase that connected by the private door to his room.

'Chief!' Dolby cried, rushing over to the novelist at full speed and embracing him. 'Thank heavens! Is everything all right?'

'Surely, my good Dolby.' Dickens explained that thinking about the awful *Harper's* cartoon – and the shooting pain in his foot – had disrupted his sleep and he had decided to take a breather outside.

Dolby, tying the cord waist of his gown in a dignified fashion, turned to his assistant. 'You see, Branagan, all is quite well in here. The Chief went down the back!'

'But it is the front door that was forced open, and the latch broken,' Tom said.

Dickens suddenly looked concerned as they confirmed this by examining the door. 'Dolby, ring for a hotel clerk. No, don't! I don't want the whole staff to hear the bell. Fetch someone quietly.' Dickens hastily went to his desk and checked the centre drawer. He appeared relieved at finding it locked.

'Do you think someone has been in here, Mr. Branagan?' Dickens asked.

'Sir, I feel it is very likely.' After a few moments of examining the room, Tom noticed a scrap of paper on the bed.

Dolby returned to the room. 'I've sent Kelly downstairs. Is anything missing, Chief?'

Dickens had been surveying his belongings. 'Nothing of consequence. Except . . .'

'What is it?' Dolby asked.

'Well, strange to say, isn't it, you'll likely laugh. But I notice there is a pillow taken from my bed, Dolby.'

'A *pillow*, Chief?' Dolby asked. 'Branagan, what have you found?'

'A letter, sir. It is difficult to read the hand.'

I am your utmost favorite reader in all of these vulgar American states. I anticipate with delicious fervor holding your next book in my hands. Your next book will be your utmost best, I know without qualification, because you are . . .

Dolby and Dickens both burst into relieved laughter, interrupting Tom's reading.

'Mr. Dickens, Mr. Dolby. I hardly find this comical. Worrisome indeed,' Tom pleaded.

'Mr. Branagan, it wasn't a renegade soldier of the Fenian Brotherhood, at least!' Dickens said.

'Just some harmless fellow who worships at the feet of the Chief,' said Dolby. 'We shall never exhaust *them*. Let's leave it at that,' added Dolby.

Tom persisted. 'Someone forcibly entered the room and then stole from it. What if Mr. Dickens had been inside at the time? What if this "harmless fellow" comes back when Mr. Dickens is alone?'

'Stole? Did you say "stole"? A nothing, a mere pillow!' said Dolby, now almost jolly about the incident. 'Haven't you seen the hotel barroom? Why, you may liquor up with all creation. It is quite the place to give people the courage for such pranks.'

Henry Scott procured another pillow for the Chief and straightened his bedclothes. Tom relayed the story in truncated form to Richard Kelly, but the ticket agent, too, found the conclusion of the events a singular source of amusement. 'All that for a stone hard pillow!' Richard raved. 'The American republic!'

'Mr. Dolby, I would like to stay on watch outside of Mr. Dickens's door,' Tom said, turning to his employer.

'Out of the question! I'll tell you what you will do, Branagan,' Dolby replied grandiloquently with a wave of his hand. Dolby's hand travelled down to the end of his moustache as though yanking a bell pull, but before he could finish he was interrupted.

It was Dickens: 'If Mr. Branagan should like to wrestle with humanity outside my room, I give my blessing.'

'Thank you, sir,' Tom said, bowing to Dickens.

Tom kept the note, folding it into his pocket as he took his place of vigilance at the door.

XIII

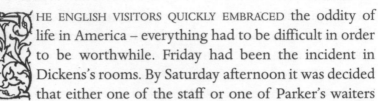

THE ENGLISH VISITORS QUICKLY EMBRACED the oddity of life in America – everything had to be difficult in order to be worthwhile. Friday had been the incident in Dickens's rooms. By Saturday afternoon it was decided that either one of the staff or one of Parker's waiters would be in front of Dickens's room at all times, and someone would always walk with him on his daily breathers. Dolby informed Tom Branagan of this procedure at Sunday's breakfast with a proprietary air, but Tom suspected that Dickens himself had requested the change. The novelist outwardly took a light approach to his own safety, yet he had seen something more serious in Dickens's eye.

At one point, Tom thought he had his man. He caught a slender man with a craggy face sneaking around Dickens's door. It turned out to be a speculator from New York who had taken rooms near Dickens's hoping to overhear the time and location of the next ticket sale.

When Dolby was away for tour business and Mr. Fields and Mr. Osgood occupied, Tom would accompany Dickens on his long walks.

At a shop window, Dickens would have only a few moments before a crowd would surround him. He was pleased with the bookstores in Boston celebrating his visit by filling their window displays with his photographic portraits and towering stacks of his novels, often displacing *Guardian Angel*, the new novel by Dr. Oliver Wendell Holmes, and the recently published literary sensation, Longfellow's *Dante*. The novelist also slowed down to see how enterprising cigar stores put Pickwick Snuff, Little Nell Cigars and a Christmas Game of Dickens (for Old and Young) out front.

'The ingenuity of the Hub of the Universe! That's an Americanism, you see,' he'd explain. 'The *hub* being the name in this country of the nave of a wheel. Little Nell *cigars*! Remember to tell Forster that for my biography.'

Dickens handed Tom his walking stick while he went in for a closer look. Tom, while waiting, nearly sliced his hand on a large screw that he had not noticed sticking out from the side of the handle.

When Dickens emerged happily smoking a Little Nell, Tom asked whether he should remove the screw so that Dickens would not accidentally injure himself.

'Heavens no, Branagan! Why, that is a most purposeful screw to strengthen it. You see, I sometimes find myself walking in the marshes,' he said as they crossed the street. 'Nearby the convicts perform their labours. In case one escapes, the tip of this cane can be used as a weapon. Come,' he said in a suddenly high-pitched voice, grabbing Tom's arm. 'Let us avoid Mr. Pumblechook, who is crossing the street to meet us.' Then, in a different voice, 'No, down this alley. Mr. Micawber is coming, let us get out of his way.'

Tom was already used to this. Dickens would often act out the roles of Pip, Ralph Nickleby, or Dick Swiveller to practise his readings while on his walks or in the hotel room. He'd sometimes take his after-breakfast constitutionals along Beacon Street, which was also called New Land, where there had still only been a bleak swamp on his last visit to Boston. With snowfalls alternating with rain, a thick, sloppy mud now coated the sidewalks. On this particular walk, as Dickens and Tom rounded the corner, a woman in a formal gown walking several paces behind paused, taking unusual care where she stepped. She leaned down gingerly, removing a piece of paper from a carpetbag. This she pressed against the gravel where the two men had stepped a few moments earlier. After allowing it to soak up the mud, she then lifted the paper. With a razor, she then sliced the paper around the edges of the novelist's boot print. *A Dickens print. A perfect Dickens print.*

All the while, the two men rushed ahead to find shelter from the rain, never noticing the woman or her ecstasy as she clutched her prized footprint.

★ ★ ★

The day of the first public reading was spent by the Dickens staff readying Tremont Temple. Dickens was testing the best place on the stage from which to read. Henry Scott was tiptoeing around him like a ballerina laying out Dickens's water and books on the reading table. George Allison was meticulously arranging gas burners that would throw just the right light on to just the right places on Dickens's face.

Dolby had chosen that hall over newer ones like the Boston Theater because the gradual rising floor meant all seats were good. Dickens had liked this idea. 'Exact equality for my hearers!' he'd said. He hated the notion of the wealthier being able to buy a better view and refused to allow the cost of the tickets to be raised above a democratic one dollar, even if it might have inhibited speculation to have done so.

Tom, meanwhile, was assigned to inspect the hall's entrances.

'Does all seem well?' Dolby enquired.

'You say there will be hundreds of people here, Mr. Dolby?'

'The largest audience ever assembled in Boston since they threw the cargoes of our tea ships into the harbour!' Dolby seemed agitated when Tom did not smile.

'This will be the first public appearance of Mr. Dickens here. I am concerned, to be candid, Mr. Dolby, that whoever was after him at the hotel will look for him here.'

'What are you talking about?' asked Dolby, shaking his head vigorously. 'That fellow? The Great Yankee Pillow Thief, you mean?'

Tom was amazed that the manager could have put the incident so far out of his mind. 'It is only possible, sir, and I fear without knowing what his intention was that night and what the man even looks like—'

'Enough! You're quite candid enough!' Dolby cried out. He chewed at his lip while examining his porter. 'It is a matter of pride for me, young Branagan, that I make a tour successful and, at the same time, pleasing to the Chief – not to rattle him and risk undermining his genius.'

Dickens, standing at his mahogany table at the platform to test the acoustics, glanced towards the spot of Dolby's outburst.

'Chief, you sound first rate from this spot!' said Dolby. 'I'll move to the other gallery and listen from there.' Then, turning back to Tom, he said quietly, 'Did you know when my predecessor died, it was the Chief himself who wrote the lines on his tombstone?'

'No,' returned Tom. Did Dolby plan on needing a tombstone soon?

Tom thought for a moment of walking right up to the platform and telling the Chief himself his concern. Perhaps Dolby sensed this, as he gave him new orders.

'Remember, Branagan, the special guest is to be seated before anyone else. If there is one thing you will learn from the Chief while in America, it is a consideration for others,' he said. The special guest Dolby referred to had earlier written a letter to Dickens saying she was paralysed and asking whether the doors to Tremont Temple could be opened for her early. Dickens had complimentary tickets sent to her and had instructed Dolby to make arrangements to ensure her comfort.

When the paralysed woman arrived, almost weeping with excitement, Tom lifted her inside. As he did, he could see the hundreds of people waiting outside the building for the doors to open. The tangle of carriages in the streets around the theatre had in fact nearly stopped the whole business of Boston. Those who didn't have tickets loitered around the building staring with resentment at the theatregoers pushing their way inside where Tom and police officers directed them to seats. At one point, there was a sudden sound like an explosion from one of the galleries.

Tom raced to the spot. The sound had come from a man who had sat on his neighbour's opera hat that had been left on the wrong seat, popping it and sending the crown into the brim. An argument between the two blue bloods ensued over who was to blame, then over the price of the hat, then moving to how the hatless gentleman was ever to hail a hackney coach later with his head uncovered like a tramp.

Dickens finally climbed the platform at fifteen minutes after eight, a dark suit chosen by Henry set off by a white and red flower on the lapel. A roar of applause, shouts of welcome, a waving sea of handkerchiefs, and Dickens bowed left, right, ahead. The only sounds that could quiet the audience were the novelist's first words:

'Ladies and Gentlemen, I shall have the honour and pleasure of reading you this evening some selections from my work . . .'

And so began the tour. Dickens would choose extended scenes from two different novels for each reading and act out a condensed, dramatic rendition of each. The characters came alive as he gave each one their own voice, manner and soul; he was author, character, actor. The performer never came to a full stop in the readings, making the next sentence always the most anticipated. Nor did he slow down or pause for emphasis on a moment of subtle wit or meaning, trusting instead in his audience. All the while, Tom guarded the doors. He kept Dolby's commands in his head, though he could not stop himself from wondering what the hotel intruder would look like and if he were present somewhere in the mass of faces.

At one reading, while Dickens performed Magwitch from *Great Expectations* running through the marsh, Tom was examining the rapt members of the audience at Tremont Temple when he heard a sound. Like an unintelligibly quick whisper – no, like a cat scratching on wood. He tried to identify the source, but it wasn't from a single place. It was on all sides. There were a few members of the audience scribbling rapidly with pencils – faster than he had ever seen *anyone* write.

Upon Tom reporting his intelligence at breakfast the following morning to Dolby, the manager escorted him to the publishing office down the street and asked if they might see Mr. Fields.

'Scribbling, you say?' Fields asked, hands wide on his hips. 'Men from the newspapers, perhaps?'

Tom said that he did not think so; the members of the press had been given seats by Dolby in the front rows, while these men and women were dispersed throughout the various galleries and in the standing-room area.

Osgood had walked into the Authors' Room while Tom was explaining what he saw. Hearing Tom's description, he shook his head. 'Why didn't we anticipate this? The *Bookaneers!*'

'Pray explain what you mean, Mr. Osgood,' said Dolby, who was sharing a sofa with Tom.

'As you know, for the purposes of these readings the Chief has condensed his novels, rather brilliantly so, to each fit one hour. You see, Mr. Dolby, other publishers no doubt hope to pirate "new editions", bagmen's editions, to erode our own authorised sales of his books. Harper, I am certain, is one of the culprits.'

'But a Bookaneer, Mr. Osgood?' asked Tom. 'What is it?'

Osgood considered how to explain to the porter. 'They are

literary pickpockets, of a sort, Mr. Branagan. The piratical publishers hire them to perform such tasks as stalking around the harbour for advance sheets coming from England, to come by through bribes or even theft. Though they may appear to be common ruffians, they are by constitution cool in demeanour and highly intelligent. It is said from a brief glance at a single page of sheets, they can identify an author and the value of an unpublished manuscript.'

'I suppose that is not such an extraordinary feat,' Dolby offered.

'A brief glance, Mr. Dolby,' Osgood continued, 'through a *spyglass*, from fifty feet away. Each are said to know three or four languages of the nations with the most popular authors today.'

'What draws them into such a shady line of work, if they possess such natural talents?' Dolby asked.

'They are well paid for their endeavours. Beyond that any guess of their motives is speculation. It is known that one of them, a woman called Kitten, served as a spy during the War of Rebellion and could signal entire paragraphs' worth of information to collaborators through lanterns and flags. Another of their nefarious herd is said to have learned lip reading from a deaf mute. Several of them are also expert shorthand writers in order to record overheard conversations between publishers that would be paid for by rivals – and it is whispered that some of the Bookaneers are responsible for writing the more vicious examples in the field of book criticism. I would bet our rivals sent several Bookaneers to the theatre in order to copy down what the Chief was improvising. Mayor Harper will stop at nothing to best us, and his brother Fletcher, whom they call the Major, counsels him into ever more conniving schemes.'

'I have noticed the Chief devise new lines – brilliant lines, I should say – in his reading from the trial of Pickwick,' Dolby added, nodding his head. 'It is like he is writing a new book in front of our eyes, which these pirates can now steal out of the air and profit from! What can we do, Mr. Osgood?'

'Your associate,' Osgood said, indicating Tom Branagan, 'could escort any of these pencil-wielding John Paul Joneses out to sea, to start.'

'Yes. But it is unlikely we can stop all of them, even with such a brawny young man on our side,' Fields pointed out. 'They have already seized some of the "new" text in their notebooks!'

'I have an idea.' This was spoken timidly from the back of the room. It was a lanky young lad who had been patching a crack in the wall from a fallen picture frame.

Fields frowned at the interruption, but Osgood waved the young man closer. 'My new shop boy, gentlemen. Daniel Sand.'

'If you'd permit me,' said Daniel. 'You gentlemen have what the pirates do not: I mean Mr. Dickens himself. With his personally condensed copies, you may publish special versions of the editions at once.'

'But we wish to sell our editions of his work already printed, my lad,' Fields objected. 'That is where the money is.'

Osgood smiled broadly. 'Mr. Fields, I believe Daniel has a good notion. We can sell *both*. New special editions, in paper covers, will be unique. Memorabilia for those who attend the readings and inexpensive gifts to their family and friends who could not get tickets to see Dickens. While the standard editions will still be sold for personal library collections. Excellent idea, Daniel.'

Rebecca, who was bringing a box of cigars for them to the Authors' Room, had paused at the door and glowed at Osgood's praise for her brother.

On the way out of the office building on that day, pleased at the resolution, Dolby purchased several papers from a newsboy. 'That Osgood is a genial man, Branagan, though with an almost grim smile,' he was saying. 'Don't you notice? He smiles as if he does not believe anything he beholds. Oh God! That I were but dead!' Dolby exclaimed upon opening one of the papers.

The article called 'Dickensiana' described a floral offering left for Dickens at his second Boston reading by a young woman. *Dickens does not live with his wife, it is said. This fact adds spice to this little story. The nice parties he gives are usually to several people largely of the female persuasion, all of whom were captivated by the Bozzian soup and sentences. Oh, Charles, at your age and with that bald head and that gray goatee!*

In a different paper, a cartoon showed a haughty Dickens on the streets of Boston with a young boy running up to him. The boy held a large letter H – the letter dropped from most words by the Cockney accent – and was shouting, 'Hello mister, look-a-here, you've dropped suthin'.' It was not the first paper to mock his modest Cockney origins.

'"At your age", dear heavens! That would put him in a red-hot fury for three days. On penalty of your life, don't let the Chief see them, Branagan!' Dolby stopped the next newsboy he could find and bought up every copy of the papers in his possession.

After a series of successful readings in Boston, the entire party took a nine-hour express train to New York, where it had been snowing heavily. Within a few days of their arrival, eighteen inches covered the ground, walls of white lining the sides of the streets. Dolby hired a sleigh for the Dickens party to use since the carriages could no longer get around. Dickens, whenever he left the Westminster Hotel, would resemble some kind of Old World emperor as he was pulled on the red sleigh, his lap piled high with buffalo robes to keep out the cold.

The *New York World* in an article about how Dickens desired privacy included his room number at the hotel. The article also noted rather disapprovingly Dickens did not use the mustard on the table once during his first dinner there. The *Herald* suggested that the scum of New York surround this visiting Homer of the slums and back alleys so that he could not slip out unnoticed as he had tried to do in Boston.

Tom arrived at the hotel with some of the late baggage and found Dickens and Dolby comforting an old woman who was sobbing tears of humiliation. The hotel detective stood over them.

Tom joined Richard Kelly, their ticket agent. 'What happened?' Tom whispered.

Kelly explained that she was a widow who was very dear to the hotel landlord and had brought flowers to Dickens's room. As she was exiting Dickens's room, another woman appeared in the hall and started pummelling the widow with her fists. By the time the victim's shouts brought Dickens and a hotel waiter running, the other woman was gone.

'Imagine a poor little white-haired widow – one of the Majesty's admirers – attacked!'

'Why would that other woman have done that?'

'Because she was a little off her head!' concluded Kelly.

Tom, preoccupied with what had happened, left Kelly's side and went back to the hall.

'I don't know,' he could hear the crying widow saying. 'She said

I had awful daring to go into the rooms of Charles Dickens without escort like I was your wife. She just kept hitting me, first with her carpetbag and then her fists. Oh, Mr. Dickens!'

Dickens replied, 'I am sorry for this. Queer it is that I should be perpetually having things happen that nobody else in the world would be made to believe.'

For the next series of sales, Dolby had a plan to combat the speculators. Each ticket would be stamped with a unique number before it was sold, defeating reported counterfeiting attempts. With ten thousand tickets for the next New York sale, and then eight thousand for Baltimore and six thousand for Washington, this required many days' work for Tom, Richard and Marshall Wild, an unassuming American ticket agent hired to help them. The labour of the stamping kept waking Dickens, so Dolby moved the group into the hallway where they had to sit on the floor. Next, Dolby instructed his staff that the first fifty men on line for the tickets – who were always mostly speculators or their agents – should be sold tickets only for the back rows of the theatre so that the speculators could not grab the best seats.

The papers, of course, printed reports of Dolby bullying the innocent New York citizens in his search for speculators and gleefully remarked that no 'Dolby ex machina' would solve the problem. 'Surely it is time that the Pudding-Headed Dolby' – preached the World – 'retired into the native gloom from which he has emerged!'

This time the sale was to be held in Brooklyn and on a bitter day, colder than any they experienced in Boston. At eight o'clock in the morning, their sleigh arrived after being conveyed by ferry across the river. Dolby stepped down to the street with his case of tickets, followed by Tom, Kelly and Wild.

'Good Lord,' Dolby swore to himself in a low whisper looking over the spectacle.

The line was three-quarters of a mile long. Later it would be reported by the newspapers, in the aftermath of the incident about to transpire, as three thousand people. They had chosen the Plymouth Church for the reading as the only building suitable for the expected size of the audience. The pulpit had to be taken down to make room for the gas lighting and the screen.

The ticket staff was hassled by the crowd as they went.

'We'll buy you right up, Dolby, sleigh and all!'

'So Charley has let you have the sleigh, has he, Dolby? How's he feeling this morning? Writing a new book for us?'

'Let me carry the ticket portmanteau for you, Pudding-Head! Tell Dickens to take my wife back with him to the mother island if he don't want his no more!'

There were policemen and detectives already present trying to hold back the crowd. One of the police officers made his way to Dolby and whispered to him. Dolby nodded and headed to the ticket office to prepare for the onslaught.

During the night the Réaumur thermometer had dropped below zero. The men who had lined up stretched out on straw mattresses, drank cheap whiskey, sang rowdy songs, built fires. Pocket pistols had been displayed to ward off latecomers hoping to steal spots.

The policemen had identified a large number of known speculators not only from New York but from Philadelphia, New Haven and Jersey City as well. The speculators' aides toasted to Dickens's health with bourbon whiskey and ate bread and meat they had been supplied in little bags by their employers. Included in the group was the speculator seen before, old in appearance yet quite energetic, in the outfit of George Washington. He was babbling about how Charles Dickens's visit was the most important affair in all American history. Coming from George Washington, this seemed rare praise.

'For we won't go home till morning, till daylight does appear!' The song started somewhere in the middle of the line and spread through the motley crowd. One fellow proposed a toast to the two men who had put their stamps on the civilisation of the nineteenth century, 'William Dickens and Charles Shakespeare. Let anyone deny it who dares!' he boomed.

Another man stepped out of the line and tapped Tom on the arm with his bamboo walking stick. 'You! What do you mean by this?'

'I beg your pardon,' Tom replied.

'You mean to fix me next to two God darned niggers?'

Tom looked at the line behind the man and saw two young men with the slightest tinge of brown in their faces.

'You will sit in the church, sir, exactly where your ticket indicates,' said Tom.

'You'd better promise to move me, boy, if I'm next to one of these two!'

'I am certain Mr. Dickens would not recognise that objection,' Tom said evenly, his muscles tensing in preparation to restrain the man if he had to. 'You may leave now if you'd like.'

The man, fuming and looking ready to pull out his hair, turned and walked away shouting epithets directed at Charles Dickens for holding open readings and Abraham Lincoln for freeing blacks to attend them. The two men in line both touched their hats in thanks to Tom.

Meanwhile, the police were extinguishing bonfires too close to the wooden houses along either side of the narrow street, eliciting a bluster of threats from the mob. Tom continued inspecting the line, struck by the endless representation of humanity. As had happened in Boston, the higher classes had employees or servants to hold their places through the night; as a result, around nine o'clock in the morning the composition of the line metamorphosed from caps to hats, from mittens to kid gloves and walking sticks.

Tom shifted attention to a woman who was staring inquisitively in his direction. Eyes cold and clear but dim. She stood outside the queue of people, almost as though she were undertaking the same sort of inspection as Tom's. She had a notebook and was writing pensively with a pencil stump, frowning in a way that seemed to indicate the permanent expression of her face. Was she another shorthand writer sent by the pirate publishers? The gazer flipped some pages to find a fresh one. One of her pages had a splotch of mud, or some sort of muddy footprint pasted on top.

'Do you wish to wait for tickets, ma'am?' Tom asked, approaching her and lifting his hat. 'We do permit women in the line, or you may ask someone to wait on your behalf.' Just then some rowdy men in the queue burst back into song.

> We'll sing, we'll dance, and be merry,
> And kiss the lasses dear.
> For we won't go home till morning,
> Till daylight does appear . . .

'Those horrid, vulgar, vulgar knaves,' the woman observed loudly of the ragged choir. She had removed a pearl-handled switchblade to sharpen the lead of her pencil. Tom noticed that for a small knife it had a smart blade. 'Not the sort that would ever appreciate, truly, a Charles Dickens. I heard some of those knaves and fools quoting passages to each other – quite wrongly. One said he was quoting *Nickleby*, but it was most obviously *Oliver Twist*! "Surprises, like misfortunes, seldom come alone."'

Something about her tugged at Tom's memory as he looked upon her. 'Have you attended a reading by Mr. Dickens before?' Tom asked.

'Have I? Come closer. What's your name, dear boy?'

Tom hesitated, then leaned in to the woman and told her. She had a manly demeanour but pretty features covered up by the wide black feathered hat that was in fashion. He guessed she was around her fortieth year but she had the self-assurance of a sixteen-year-old belle or a seventy-year-old matron.

'Indeed I have been to his readings!' she suddenly said in an even bigger shout. 'He adapts them for me, you know!' She paused, pursing her lips. 'He changes the books as he reads, doing all manner of wild improvising for me. Dickens, I mean,' she said after testing the length of Tom's silence. 'I daresay you think me very odd.'

'Ma'am?'

'You do!' she shouted. 'There's one of those horrid, vulgar Americans, you say to yourself. Well, yes, it's true, I'm not a nice girl. I am an incubus, really. I'm part English, too, you know. But you're – you're from the potato lands, aren't you? You dream of want and woe, with buttermilk in your blood.' Suddenly she jumped as if it startled by thunder. She pulled a watch from her carpetbag. 'I'm horrid late! I've just missed two appointments in the time we've spoken. Good-bye, au revoir.'

Tom moved on, suddenly realising what had struck him about her. It wasn't the woman exactly, though he *had* seen her before among the crowds that always formed around Dickens. It was the notebook he had noticed: the paper of which was the same peach-colour and size – *just the same*, Tom was certain – as the letter left in Dickens's hotel room that he still kept. He retrieved that letter from his coat. The writer had claimed to be Dickens's favourite reader in *all of these vulgar American states*, words similar to the ones the women had spoken. Tom turned back and saw she was heading away from the line.

'Ma'am,' Tom called out, and she began to walk more quickly. 'Hold there. Ma'am!'

Then Tom heard his own name being called from a distance. He tried to ignore it – if this woman was who he thought she was, this might be his chance to put to rest his questions about the incident at the hotel. Tom waded through the throng, keeping sight of the feathers of her hat swaying above the landscape of people.

'Branagan!' It was another shout, louder, and there was no ignoring it. 'B-B-Branagan!'

Tom looked over his shoulder and found that the previously small bursts of commotion in the line had erupted into a brawl. Combatants were thrashing each other hard with sticks from the bonfire and trampling over the fallen. In the middle of it all was a party of Brooklyn police and speculators. The police were swinging their batons against the sticks. Mr. George Washington staggered, his nose dripping blood and yanked-out strands of his white wig hanging from his ear. As the combat spread, several enterprising ticket seekers, faces bloodied, dragged their mattresses behind them and rushed to the front of the line for better spots.

Tom leaped into the heart of the fight, tackling one of the offenders, and liberated a policeman. A man screaming wildly swung a burning stick at Tom's head – Tom caught the stick in the middle, breaking it with his hand and then shoved the attacker into the snowbank. By this point, more police charged by with batons drawn, dragging rowdies away. Many wanted more than anything else just to keep their places in line by gripping the iron railing of the church fence as if their lives depended on it. To his astonishment, Tom noticed that several plainclothes detectives, instead of helping, used the disturbance to take their own prime positions in line.

The George Washington speculator was crying out in an outraged scream as he was being pulled away by his belt, 'Hand out honours to a Cockney foreigner for his trashy literary pamphlets that were never given to our own homegrown heroes – our own democrats like Washington himself! The literary war between the Old World and the New World has begun!'

'Branagan, all r-r-right over here?' Dolby rushed to his side, breathless, eyes wide at all the men knocked down around his porter. He studied Tom with a new respect.

Tom was inspecting his palm, which had been burned by the flaming stick and would need to be wrapped right away. 'What happened?' he asked Dolby.

'Disaster!' Dolby cried. With his stutter heavy from the fright, he explained they had begun the ticket sales by enforcing their new policy against the speculators. When it was understood that the first portion of the line were to receive tickets in the rear galleries, the hotheaded speculators protested and cursed vociferously, while the levelheaded ones bribed the men behind them to trade places. Those who were not speculators protested, as well. The various disruptions escalated into general mayhem up and down the line.

'Where were you?' Dolby said to Tom accusingly. 'They wanted to tear me to p-p-pieces!'

Tom looked over his shoulder, but knew that the woman with the notebook would be gone. There would be no point now in getting his employer's dander up. 'I apologise, Mr. Dolby. I was inspecting the bonfires.'

'You should have been at the ready.'

'I am sorry, sir.'

Dolby straightened out his suit and neckcloth, though he remained the model of dishevelment. 'Well, let's get on with it. There's at least two thousand dollars to be taken from this crowd, if there's a dollar! Isn't that the American way?'

After a set of readings in New York, the schedule required Dickens, Dolby and staff in Boston. Because the snow had closed the railroad, they waited around until Saturday in New York, where they were subjected to the papers' columns condemning the events at the Brooklyn ticket sales and blaming a 'hotheaded Irishman' employed by Dickens for starting the near riot. This fact was confirmed by an unimpeachable 'bewigged, buckled, three-corner hatted witness', the George Washington speculator who urged the police to arrest Tom at once. Meanwhile, Dickens had entered the depths of a worsening cold – 'English colds are nothing compared to those of this country,' he proclaimed gravely – but Dolby privately worried it was worse, perhaps influenza. Another long train ride now would not help. Dickens signalled Henry Scott to remove a flask from the travelling case as soon as they took their seats.

Henry, meanwhile, prayed for Dickens before each journey by rail.

'Is anything wrong, Henry?' Tom asked him once when he had first noticed this display.

'Staplehurst!' Henry replied gloomily.

'Staplehurst?'

'Yes, *only* that. If there were but no Staplehurst at all – no June the ninth – perhaps the Chief should not be such a sad man.'

'He still seems rather gay to me,' Tom noted, 'for what you call a sad man.'

'Don't you read the papers? Don't you know *anything* at all, Tom Branagan?'

He described how approximately two years earlier, on 9 June, 1865, Dickens had nearly been killed. A terrible train accident near the village of Staplehurst in Kent. The railway tracks covering a bridge had been removed for repair without alerting the oncoming trains. Dickens and his party were aboard the 'tidal train' from France, which, reaching the portion of missing track, careened off the bridge.

Dickens had lifted Nelly Ternan and her mother from their dangling first-class car to safety, and then the novelist climbed to the ravine below where he pulled out as many victims as he could. Despite his brave efforts, ten people died that day as the novelist watched helplessly. Dickens climbed back into the dangling train compartment twice during the ordeal. First to retrieve brandy for the suffering patients below. Then he realised however dangerous it was he had to climb back in again. Inside his coat was a new instalment of the novel he was writing, *Our Mutual Friend*, the pages of which were dirty but unharmed. Forever after, whenever the novelist stepped foot in a railway car, a steamer, even a hackney cab, he could not help but be reminded that *here could be our final passage on this earth*. Brandy helped nerve him on these occasions.

'Staplehurst,' Henry repeated, and finished his story with a silent prayer. 'Amen,' he said softly.

'Amen,' Tom echoed.

A stove heated the car they sat in on the way back to Boston, but it could not be said whether it made the compartment more comfortable or miserable when combined with the number of passengers and the rough motion. The nine-hour express route was slowed considerably by the rivers in Stonington and New London, both on the way through Connecticut. At each of these places the train navigated on to a ferry to cross the river, the passengers free to stay aboard or to explore the ship and eat at its restaurant. Dickens stayed on the train during these ferry rides, even when a nearby American war vessel unfurled a British flag and struck up a rendition of 'God Save the Queen' in his honour. Dickens watched from the window.

His spirits seemed especially restrained on this passage as he played a slow game of three-handed cribbage with Tom and Henry.

'I remember,' Dickens said with sudden excitement to nobody in particular, 'it was my first visit to America when – yes, that was when! – when I first practised the art of *mesmerism*! Strange to say the railways seem to have stood still while most other things in this country have been changing for the better. They were terrible then and terrible now.'

'Mesmerism, Chief?' Tom asked. 'You've done it yourself?'

'Ah, Branagan, spiritualism is nothing but a humbug, but the unfathomed ties between man and man are as real, and as dangerous, as this very train being planted on a rickety boat.' Dickens described how he used lessons from the famed English spiritualist John Elliotson to mesmerise his wife when in Pittsburgh in 1842. 'I admit to feeling some alarm when Catherine fell into a *magnetic* sleep in under six minutes, though I was excited enough by the slap-up success to repeat it the following evening. When I returned to England I tried it on Georgy – my children's auntie, my sister-in-law and my best and truest friend. Georgy, the sweetest soul, became almost violent over it.' Dickens laughed luminously at this memory but then was silent and spiritless again, perhaps at the thought of Catherine. He never would talk about Catherine, the mother of his eight children, even as he never really could talk about Nelly Ternan, and certainly would not stand for anyone else talking about either.

'Well, perhaps Mr. Scott has heard all this before,' he went on. 'What do you say to a trial of my mesmerism skills, Mr. Branagan?'

'On me?' Tom asked.

'Great fun, Chief!' Henry called out.

'Come, come,' said Dickens with a businesslike air. 'I have magnetised unbelievers before. I have the perfect conviction that I could magnetise a frying pan! You won't remember any of it when you wake, anyway.'

Tom sighed and submitted as Dickens passed his hand in front of Tom's eyes until they closed, then began to move his thumbs in a transverse motion across his face. Suddenly, he stopped, looking into

Tom's face with an odd twinkle in his eye. The train was rocking back and forth.

'Chief?' Henry asked.

Tom opened his eyes to find the novelist's nostrils were dilated and his eyes restless. Dickens was no longer trying to mesmerise him at all. The jolts of the train had pulled his mind somewhere else.

'Perhaps, Branagan, this isn't the time to—' Dickens clutched the arms of his seat and turned pale white. Beads of sweat formed across his forehead every time the train shook, and his lips were trembling as if he were the one under a spell. This state of suspended animation lasted several minutes before the novelist returned to life and took a long pull from his flask. The three dropped the project of mesmerism and returned to the cribbage game just where it had been left. Tom was baffled.

After getting out at their station, Henry Scott whispered to Tom, as his only explanation, 'You see? Staplehurst!'

This was the most anticipated event of the reading tour. Dickens was to give his reading of *A Christmas Carol* on Christmas Eve at Boston's Tremont Temple. More than three thousand dollars of tickets had been purchased for the performance in less than two hours. 'It is,' Dolby boasted with grandeur, when counting out the money from the sale back at Parker's, 'as though the Chief invented Christmas with the *Carol*.'

Tom had not told Dolby what he now believed about the hotel invader: that he had stood face to face with the culprit in Brooklyn, that it was a woman, and that he had spoken with her. That all but certainly it was the same woman who committed the bizarre assault in the hall of the Westminster Hotel on the poor widow. Not only that, but Tom now remembered where he had seen her before – it had been the night of Dickens's arrival to America, in the dense crowd in front of Parker's, waving some papers she was demanding the novelist read. Tom knew his evidence would hardly be convincing, and could imagine Dolby's response: *You think this lady, a lady you never saw in your life but once, followed us all the way to New York from Boston and back, and you think it because of her notebook?* Could there not be another woman interested in Dickens's readings with a notebook that size, could there not be hundreds of people with hundreds of notebooks?

The woman had been dressed like a gypsy the night of Dickens's arrival to the Parker House, with a bandanna handkerchief tied around her neck and a too-small blue jacket. In Brooklyn, she wore a fine silk dress, sash and shawl like an aristocrat. But what stuck out most in Tom's mind was the word she had called herself. An *incubus*. He had heard the fairy tales when he was a child from the other servants' children in the underground kitchen of Dolby's estate – incubus and succubus, the demon visitors and tormentors of unsuspecting mortals. But it was succubus that was the female class and incubus the male. What had she meant?

Plenty of speculators and reporters had been following them from city to city but with naked motivation. It was the element of the unknown about this woman that began to disturb and preoccupy Tom. That image: a line for tickets, people who wanted nothing more than to see Dickens, and a woman standing outside of it, looking on jealously at the people she did not feel were worthy to see the Master. There was a dazzling, enthralling, unwanted air about her.

Two minor emergencies occurred for their party back in Boston. First, the Chief could not find his pocket diary. The staff looked everywhere and could not turn it up. Dickens thought the last time he saw it was in New York in his hotel room. He insisted it didn't matter, since it was a record for 1867 and the year was about to end. He burned them at the end of each year, and this saved him the trouble.

Can she have taken it? Tom thought. *Is that what she was doing lurking around the halls at the Westminster?*

George Allison was the second emergency. He had fallen ill twice in the course of several days. It was discovered by the doctor at the Parker House that both times were preceded by a meal of bad partridge, who were often poisoned in the winter by berries when the bird's usual food supply was buried by snow. The substitute gasman, a nervous Bostonian, spent the afternoon of 24 December alongside the regular staff preparing the theatre for that evening. He had received elaborate instructions at George's bedside, as though

George were conveying his dying wishes. The newcomer was so eager to please Dickens he sprained his leg running up the stairs of the theatre.

This provided an illustration of Charles Dickens taking charge of an emergency, which he did in high spirits and with relish. He walked the injured man with Tom to a druggist, where he ordered a particular type of mountain tobacco.

'Why, Mr. Dickens, you are like a doctor yourself!' the gasman exclaimed his appreciation, his cheeks aglow that he had been blessed enough to sprain his leg in such company.

'When you travel as often as I do, my boy, with as many men, you haven't much choice. Why, you should see the variety of blue and black phials and liquids waiting in my medicine chest. Laudanum, ether, sal volatile, Dover's powders, Dr. Brinton's pills. Trust your Chief. We live among miracles. This will heal you, body and spirit.'

That evening, when doors opened for the Christmas Eve reading, the galleries seemed to fill all at once. The two thousand went after their places so voraciously that the attendants and police at the doors scarcely had a hat or coat in place, and the decorative hollies and festoons had their red berries shaken loose and squashed underfoot.

'That's something!' one of the policemen said to Tom as they tried to keep some order. 'Has it been like this for all the readings, or is this special for Christmas?'

'I suppose both,' Tom said.

'You're a Dubliner, aren't you?'

'My family is of Irish blood,' Tom agreed. 'I am English.'

'I can tell by your accent you're a Dubliner. Not that I pay any mind to it, you know. We have nearly forty of them on our force, you know. Say,' said the officer knowingly, 'you weren't that same Paddy who started the riot at Dickens's ticket sale in Brooklyn as I read about?'

'You've read the wrong papers,' Tom said.

'No hard feelings, friend. Making conversation. Now, my wife, she adores your Mr. Dickens. I say, "Spend hard-earned money on something useful, just what we need another book in the house to sit on the shelf and take up space and be feasted on by the rats." She don't listen, says what do I know, only book I've read is the Good Book. 'Tis true. 'Tis the best book there is. You a married fellow?'

As Tom turned around to answer, his eyes passing over a group of people walking by, he blinked in surprise: the same woman he had chased in New York. The incubus, this time, garbed once again in the clothes of a beggar.

'Don't know if you're married or not, fellow?' the policeman demanded. Then he laughed to himself. 'But I understand Mr. Dickens doesn't know if *he* is, either. The man should be ashamed, if you ask me – I read he carried on with his own wife's sister. Shame!'

'Did you see that lady just now?' Tom asked.

'Lady?' the policeman responded. 'There are a thousand people that just rambled in!'

The man was right – Tom had lost her in the surging mass. But he also knew this – she was in the theatre, and he would have an hour to find her before the doors opened at intermission.

Tom began to stalk through the sloping aisles as the audience members climbed over each other into their seats. He was stopped by someone grabbing his arm – Dolby. The manager was standing with a short, well-dressed man surveying up and down the theatre.

Tom had to think quickly. He did not want to lie but he knew Dolby would not accept the truth; he'd probably give Tom his walking papers on the spot.

'The police are watching the doors, Mr. Dolby. I thought I should look for some of the known pirates we've seen here before.'

Dolby nodded his encouragement. 'Well done, Branagan. After the New Year, Mr. Osgood says the new condensed editions will put the freebooters out of business.'

Tom wished to be free of the manager, but Dolby didn't move. Instead, he took Tom's arm with one hand and the other man's arm with the other.

'Why, gentlemen, Mr. Aldrich was telling Osgood and myself the other day, the great Mr. Dickens, he was saying, the great Dickens has eyes when he is on the stage that are unlike any before in his experience, swift and kind, seeing what the Lord has done and what he intends. Eyes like exclamation points. This, you see, Mr. Leypoldt,' he said to the other man, 'this is why we work so hard. You may explain this to your readers who have admired the performances. Because of the advances in transportation over the last years, the reading public has been allowed to know Dickens not only as an author but as a man with a voice, mannerisms, facial expressions. They have been able to come to know him as a person as had never happened before in the history of literature. We do our work for *this*!'

Dolby, glowing with pride, continued with his soliloquy to the reporter, but Tom, no longer listening, was searching the rows for any clue to the location and intentions of the incubus. By the time Dolby had released his grip on Tom's arm, the lights flickered and then went out, except for a dramatic silver splash on the platform, where Dickens emerged in front of the plain screen amid a deafening welcome of cheers and several rounds of applause.

'Ladies and gentleman,' Dickens said, 'I am to have the pleasure of reading to you first, tonight, *A Christmas Carol* in four staves. Stave One: Marley's Ghost. Marley was dead to begin with. There is no doubt whatever about that. The register of his burial was signed by the clergyman, the clerk, the undertaker and the chief mourner. Scrooge signed it. And Scrooge's name was good upon exchange for anything he chose to put his hand to! Old Marley was as dead as a doornail.'

Tom felt his survey was hopeless in the dark galleries. His only chance was to wait until the lights were on again at intermission. If she were here to make some kind of trouble like she had done with the widow at the hotel, Tom would be on his toes. He would be ready. And if she tried to escape, Tom would call out to the policemen positioned at all the doors to stop her. There was no way she could get out.

Tom's darting eyes caught a quick motion in one of the aisle seats. It was another blasted shorthand writer, a rapid-fire pencil blazing away in the hands of rakish Esquire, the Bookaneer. With no time for niceties, Tom reached in, grabbed the pencil and cracked it in half. Esquire protested at the unlawful seizure of his property. Tom obliged, dropping the two halves into the man's hat on the floor. Another of the piratical species sitting across the way, the former substitute soldier Molasses, paused his own shorthand writing, putting his pencil between his jagged teeth to applaud his rival's misfortune. On his way past, Tom slapped Molasses on the back. The pencil broke between the Bookaneer's teeth and landed in his lap.

Dickens, meanwhile, continued.

The scene: Christmas Eve. Dickens, acting the part of Scrooge, turned in pantomime to his poor clerk, snarling, *'You'll want all Christmas day tomorrow, I suppose?'* Then all at once he was the simple clerk, a shining timid smile, saying, *'If quite convenient, sir. It's only once a year, sir.'*

'Branagan!'

'A poor excuse for picking a man's pocket every twenty-fifth of December!'

'Branagan!'

Tom heard the familiar urgent whisper and located Dolby at the front of the theatre. He looked white, as white as one of the ghosts in the Chief's story. The manager mouthed some words that Tom could not follow and gestured. Tom moved closer to the foot of the stage and his jaw dropped.

Dickens was lighted twelve feet above the platform by a large iron batten with gaslights suspended by strong galvanised wire. This cast a dramatic shadow on the dark crimson screen that stood behind the reader. The replacement gasman had mistakenly arranged the copper wires directly over the gas jets, causing the wires to become red hot. If the gas were to burn through, the iron batten would fall and could not only land on Dickens but tumble down into the audience.

If the emergency were announced, the crowd would panic and rush away all at once, not only raising the risks of knocking against equipment that could induce the wires to snap but also trampling women and children along the way. Even if the iron batten tumbled down and somehow missed the audience members in the front stall of the theatre, a fire could start and swallow up the whole place in a matter of minutes. There was no question about it: Dickens had to keep reading as though nothing were wrong.

Tom looked back at Dolby and nodded his understanding. With the new gasman in his hobbled condition, there was no hope of him helping. Tom went to the far wing of the stage and found the extra wire. As he readied this, there was a commotion at the stairs that led to one of the balconied galleries. Tom, looking at the iron batten and then back at the stairs, sprinted towards the disturbance. Could it be *her* about to charge at Dickens with her knife? But it was a man who came down, shaking both of his fists.

The man grabbed Tom's coat sleeve as though desperate for assistance. 'Who the deuce is that man on the platform reading?'

'Charles Dickens,' Tom replied.

'But that ain't the real Charles Dickens, the man whose books I've been reading all these years?'

'Yes!'

'Well, all I've got to say about it then is, that he knows no more about Mister Scrooge than a cow does of pleatin' a shirt, not my ideas of Scrooge, anyhow.'

'*I know him! Marley's ghost!*' Dickens bit his fingernails just as Scrooge did in the story. He rubbed his eyes and stared at the apparition. The muscles in his face tightened, his face seeming to contort into that of an old man.

Tom raced to the far wing, climbing up the back stairs until reaching the cupola above the ceiling of the hall. Around him were glass panels on the walls giving views of the entire city and all the way to the harbour islands. Rows of square ventilators lined the cupola to continually expel the heat and air from below. Tom lay on the floor and lowered his head and arms through a network of gas piping that separated the cupola from the hall. He could see Dolby standing all the way down below, urging on Tom's mission.

'*Mercy! Dreadful apparition, why do you trouble me?*' Scrooge was demanding.

A young woman with bright red hair and a bright red dress in the front row, her gaze roaming to the iron gas fixture, audibly gasped. Dickens, pausing, looked over to her and gestured for her with a slight movement of his hand to remain calm. So the Chief had seen! He, too, knew they must prevent a panic; and this pretty girl who probably went through great pains for months to claim a seat right at the foot of her favourite author in the world, suddenly had to trust this same author with her life.

From a seat in the middle, another woman shrieked. Tom shuddered at the helplessness of his position and the realisation that they were about to witness a mass panic – but then saw it was a young woman in mourning crêpe, who was grieved hearing about Tiny Tim. An usher escorted the sobbing young mother from her seat gently.

Tom, meanwhile, stretched his arm down over the batten to turn the gas flame lower. Next, looking down to signal Dolby to be in position in case anything dropped, Tom supported the batten with one hand while he meticulously wound the wire roll around another part of the iron structure and began fastening the other end to a hook in the ceiling left there from some earlier performance. Rounds of laughter came in waves from the audience. Dickens took a sip of water from the glass at the side of his reading desk. As Tom attached the wire, his head and arms just barely sticking out from the ceiling in view of the audience – they might have noticed him, had they not been enraptured by Dickens – he looked out into the crowd and immediately saw.

In the back of the second gallery of seats. The incubus he sought! She was rummaging inside her carpetbag. Was she looking at Tom? Had she seen him looking at her from high above?

Tom's heart raced.

'Go on! Finish!' Dolby called up in a throaty whisper of despair. 'Hurry, Branagan! Hurry!'

Tom wanted to be done more than Dolby could have known. Tom had nearly finished his work above when he realised: Dickens was at the end of his *Christmas Carol* reading. That meant intermission. The doors would open: and the incubus, who possibly had already seen him spot her, would be free to escape.

'*And to Tiny Tim, who did* not *die . . .*' (a roll of cheers like thunder) '*And so, as Tiny Tim observed, God bless us, every one!*'

A large object flew on to the platform and tumbled towards the speaker. Tom flinched. A bouquet of roses in every colour.

His repair complete, Tom moved to go back down and found that his arm was lodged between two pipes. It would not budge. Below, Dickens closed his book and the audience broke into rapturous applause. Dickens bowed and left the stage.

Grimacing, Tom yanked his arm hard, cutting it on both sides on the old pipes as it pulled out. Righting himself, he hurried to the narrow stairs and descended as quickly as he could. The men and women rose from the seats as one – some to applaud, others to start towards the doors to get air, smoke or exercise their legs before the second hour of reading. There was a blur of colour as a woman vaulted herself on to the platform – no, not one, but four or five women, reaching their hands out to grab the geranium petals that had drifted down from Dickens's buttonhole during the reading.

Dolby came over to the side of the platform with a congratulatory smile directed towards Tom and a warmly extended hand, but Tom would not stop. As soon as he reached the hall, he broke into a blinding run up the steep floor of the theatre, past the first gallery, to the second, and nearly leaping over two rows of seats he grabbed the woman's shoulders in a near embrace.

'You were the one who came into Mr. Dickens's room at Parker's?' Tom demanded.

She met Tom's accusatory gaze with her powerful stare. Then she smiled, and in a loud, irreverent voice, said, 'You do think me odd!'

Tom could see the woman's carpetbag was stuffed with papers. He removed a few sheets. They were identical in size and type to the note he had found at Dickens's bed.

'It was you.'

She surrendered a slim smile. 'You can see what nobody else does. Not my husband. You understand it. He needs me, the *Chief*, the Chief needs me. These others aren't fit for the likes of him at all.'

Tom was startled most of all by that one casual word: Chief. Boz, the Great Enchanter, the Inimitable, all were Dickens's nicknames with the worshipful public. But no one outside their circle called Dickens the Chief. How close had she been?

Suddenly her eyes turned dark and she sneered at him as though he had just spit on her. 'You are the meanest and most unkind man.' Now she actually did spit at his face, with a look of disgust. 'I have so many lots of friends, they are all more than kind to me and nobody who meets me forgets me. The Prince of Wales is a great, great friend and protector! The Chief shall be *beloved* again.' This last phrase she chanted to herself in eerily perfect imitation of Tom's light Irish brogue.

Tom now noticed that on the wooden back of the seat in front of hers, there were carvings. They were deep and had to be done with a knife. Words and phrases, quotes from Dickens's novels, ran into each other in mostly illegible patterns. The word Tom could make out by moving his fingers over the chair was 'beloved'.

A crowd of spectators had begun to surround them by this point. Tom was digging through her carpetbag for the pearl-handled blade he had seen her holding in Brooklyn but stopped when he found a small pistol instead.

'It's not easy to love a man with the fire of genius,' she said confidentially, nodding towards the pistol. 'His voice stays in my ears even when I don't want to hear it. "You have no idea what it is to have anybody wonderful fond of you," says he, "unless you have been got down and rolled upon by the lonely feelings."'

'Branagan?' Dolby cried, swimming upstream through the crowd. 'Branagan, what is the meaning of this? People are pointing. Who is this woman? What are you doing, put that away! You'll cause a riot!'

The policeman who had stood guard with Tom earlier at the door also fought through the crowd with two officers behind him. Suddenly, they pushed Tom away.

'Stand aside!' one of them said.

'Officer,' Tom replied, 'this woman entered Mr. Dickens's hotel room at the Parker House, I'd be bound she's the one who assaulted a widow in New York. She means him harm – there is a gun in there!'

The pistol was pulled from her bag by one of the policemen.

She nodded. 'That *is* mine, officer. Protection. In case anyone had in mind to steal my tickets for the reading. Now this is a spiteful-looking bald man, isn't it?' she said looking at Dolby. 'Who are you?'

'You must take this woman away from Dickens immediately, officers,' Tom said.

'Thunder!' the policeman said with an astounded gasp at the situation, for a moment not knowing how to react. 'Very sorry, Mrs. Barton,' he finally said, taking off his hat. He turned back to Tom. 'You are a saucy Dubliner after all. Just like the newspapers said about your actions in Brooklyn. Haven't you any notion who this *lady* is?' he said, placing his emphasis on the word as a correction to a mere *woman*. 'I hope for your sake she does not allege an assault.'

'See here!' Tom said, charging back towards her. 'What does her name matter?'

'Mind our orders, Paddy boy, or I'll have to write to your mother to take you back home to look after the pigs.' The officer stepped in front of her to block Tom. 'Stay away from her or we shall have to lock you up!'

'No need for that officer, no need at all,' said Dolby, taking Tom by the hand and lowering his voice to a whisper to hide the scene from any reporters. 'A mere mistake on the good man's part. He'll return to the hotel for the remainder of the reading.'

'Mr. Dolby!' Tom began to protest.

'Branagan!' Dolby growled. 'Be silent now!'

'Oh, dear, all of that fuss over me.' Mrs. Barton said calmly. The police officer gave her the pistol. She took it, smiling eerily, and stored it in her strange carpetbag. 'That Thomas is a sweet, sweet boy.

He reminds me of a poem by . . . well, I can't remember by who. One of the tragic ones. There are too many poets these days.'

Dolby dragged Tom Branagan away through the aisles and tried to pull the porter's gaze away from the woman.

'Au revoir, Thomas,' she said with a wave. 'As Mr. Weller says, "I came to look after you, my darlin'!"'

'Keep Dickens away from her!' Tom called back helplessly to the policemen, his voice echoing up the high auditorium. 'Keep Dickens away!'

THIRD INSTALMENT

XIV

KENT, ENGLAND, JUNE 30, 1870

AMES R. OSGOOD AND HIS bookkeeper Rebecca Sand found no welcoming party or waving of handkerchiefs for them when the steamer reached the port in Liverpool. Osgood had expected that John Forster, Dickens's executor, or Frederic Chapman, Dickens's English publisher, might send a coach to meet them at the docks after receiving word from Fields of the visit. Instead, Mr. Wakefield, their business-minded companion from aboard the ship, seeing they were stranded and on their own, gallantly arranged their transportation to Higham station in the Kent countryside. He warned Osgood to receive a rate from their driver before hiring it or they'd face extortion. Before they boarded the carriage, Wakefield also recommended they find lodging at an inn called the Falstaff, 'a fine little establishment – also the only one!'

In the ancient country town of Rochester, within the quaint and narrow streets Dickens seemed to be everywhere. On passing the church cemetery, the first tombstone one saw read Dorrit – there, Osgood surmised, Dickens might have first thought out *Little Dorrit*'s story of greed and imprisonment. A sign above a shop on the High Street spelled out BARNABY – and somewhere to match perhaps, there was 'Rudge'.

Osgood thought about Dickens's popularity. People had gone to church to pray for Little Nell, they had cried for Paul Dombey as though for their own son, they cheered – how they cheered at Tremont Temple – when Tiny Tim was saved. His books became real for everyone who read them, whether the humble labourer in the Strand or the patrician in Mayfair. That is why even those who never in their life read any novels, would read his.

Their carriage slowly mounted a steep green hill to the summit where there stood an inviting white building bathed in rustic summer charm. The faded sign of the house was painted with Shakespeare's obese character of jolly Falstaff with Prince Hal; and a scene of Falstaff stuck inside a laundry basket while the Merry Wives laughed. The inn was located on rolling meadows directly opposite from the wooden entrance gates to the grand Dickens estate, known by the name Gadshill Place.

They were greeted on the steps by the landlord of the inn, whose appearance made them stop in their tracks. Solidly built, though not quite fat, he was dressed in large, brightly coloured Elizabethan garments padded for good measure. His puffed-up velvet cap carried a small bird's worth of wilted feathers. He said to call him either Falstaff or 'Sir John' and held a goblet of beer ready to toast any trifle in his sights.

'You may eat us out of house and home and still be welcome,' he said. 'That is the motto of the Falstaff Inn!'

'I wonder if all English landlords wear such costumes,' Rebecca whispered to Osgood as the landlord and a lad transported their trunks.

'Come, Sir Falstaff will show you to your rooms!' exclaimed the very merry landlord.

The next morning, John Forster, having received word of their arrival, met them in the coffee room while they recovered from their Atlantic voyage over eggs, broiled ham, and coffee. Though wearing an expensively tailored suit of the London style, Forster was himself a more genuine Falstaffian figure, with a globular body, slow movements and the face of a spoiled child. Unlike the innkeeper there was no gaiety about this Falstaff.

'And this would be Mrs. Osgood?' Forster asked, extending his hand.

Osgood rushed to correct him, explaining her position as book-keeper.

'Ah, I see,' Forster replied gravely, removing his hand from hers hastily and then sitting at the table. 'Then you are in mourning for a husband,' he declared oracularly of her dark outfit.

'For my brother, actually, sir. My brother Daniel.'

Forster knit his brow in consternation, not at the potential of embarrassing the young lady but at his being wrong twice. 'Hail to

America, I suppose, to have blushing young girls trail along at your side as bookkeepers! A fine thing that.'

At this point, one of the waiters came over and whispered into Forster's ear, 'That's against the rules in the coffee room, sir.'

Forster took the cigar he was half-smoking and half-chewing out of his mouth and looked at it as if he had never seen it before. Then he rose to his feet and shouted, 'Leave the room, rascal! How dare you, sir, interfere with me! Clear out, and bring this gentleman and lady some cakes with their breakfasts!' With the waiter taking flight, the visitor resumed his place.

'No cakes for me, though, Mr. Osgood, as I have already break-fasted, thank you,' Forster said, without having been offered any. 'I wake at five every morning before even my footboy for taking your morning meal at once aids the labours of digestion and staves off sickness. Now, on to the little matter of your business, shall we?'

After Osgood explained their wish to examine Dickens's private belongings, Forster curtly said he would return to Gadshill and discuss the matter with its residents. He returned across the road to the Dickens estate shortly thereafter. An hour later, Osgood and Rebecca received a note on black-bordered mourning paper that they were welcome to Gadshill at their convenience.

'Perhaps I should stay here at the inn,' Rebecca suggested as she finished writing a note back accepting the offer. 'Mr. Forster seemed rather, well, ungenial towards me.'

Osgood did not want to make her self-conscious, though she was correct. 'He is ungenial in general. Remember, he was one of Mr. Dickens's closest friends. His spirits cannot be whole, after such a loss,' he said. 'Come, Miss Sand. With a bit of luck we may secure our information and have some leisure time to do something very English around London, too, before we leave.'

On the outside, the redbrick Dickens family home was austere but still welcoming – stone steps leading up to a spacious portico where the large clan would once have gathered. Towering oaks formed the boundaries around the property where boys used to run and play, which gave way to wilderness beyond the gardens and now-empty cricket fields that the master of the house had made available to the townspeople for matches.

Walking through the fields felt like a walk through the legends of the novelist's life. Charles Dickens had written about first seeing the house when he was a very young child but still old enough to be aware of how poor his own family was. Before his troubles with debt that brought him to prison, John Dickens would take his queer small boy to look at Gadshill from the street. *If you were to be persevering and work hard, and mind the study of your books, you might some day come to live in it,* he'd say to the boy, though the father himself was not persevering and never worked hard.

Two big Newfoundland dogs, a mastiff and a St. Bernard raced around from the side of the house. A tinge of disappointment seemed to pass through each animal's body upon seeing Osgood and Rebecca. One canine in particular, the largest among them, tilted his handsome head slowly with a devastated air that was heartbreaking. The head gardener called out and the dogs bounded as a pack back to the stable yard, then listlessly tiptoed into a cool tunnel, which led to the other side of the road.

Considerably less life awaited them inside Gadshill. The house, in fact, was being drained of it before their eyes. Some workmen were removing paintings and sculptures from the walls and tables; other sombre-faced intruders in silk vests and linen suits were examining the furniture and prodding each object and fixture. The atmosphere was completed by a melancholy rendition of Chopin on piano floating on the air.

A workman lifted an oval portrait of a little girl as Forster led Osgood and Rebecca through the entrance hall to the threshold of the drawing room.

'You cannot visit Gadshill,' he suddenly announced with a gouty frown that was even less friendly than his demeanour at breakfast.

'What do you mean, Mr. Forster?' Osgood asked.

'Do you not see it with your own eyes, Mr. Osgood? Gadshill is *no more* – not how it was. A blasted auction of his possessions takes place next week and they are dismantling everything in sight,' Forster said, angrily waving his arms. Then he turned and cast a hard gaze at the better dressed invaders. 'These other men, who are arranging the remains of the place with artificial homeyness, are the representatives of a different auction firm that will sell the very house you stand in to the high bidder. In*tol*-er-able, every bit!' Whenever the executor spoke, it was as if he had memorised the words beforehand, and now were reciting them to an investigating commission out to put an old enemy out of public office.

'Must every single thing in the house be sold, Mr. Forster?' Rebecca asked with genuine sadness.

'Don't tell *me*, young lady! Absolutely everything to the last door-nail, don't I know it!' Forster cried out accusingly, as if Rebecca herself had just decreed the destiny of the place. 'The Dickens family is very large,' his voice dampened into a loud whisper, 'and his many sons, like him in no aspect but his name, lead expensive, wasteful lives. Of his two daughters, one is married to an invalid painter who is Wilkie Collins's brother – which is worst, I don't know, to paint, or to be crippled, or have Wilkie Collins as a relative? The other girl, though passing comely, has never married. No, without the income of future books, Gadshill cannot stay as it was.' He looked out over the meadows outside and waited for Osgood and Rebecca to do the same before continuing. 'The land out there shall be remembered for three things. First, for Sir Falstaff robbing travellers with Prince Harry and the local vagabonds. Second, for Chaucer's pilgrims who passed along the way to Canterbury. And, third, for the most popular novelist that ever lived. Of the first item, your buffoon of an innkeeper has made a mockery already for the sake of profit. I shall always say "William", the man's rightful Christian name, if only to gall him. Pray there not come a day where some cheap landlord dress like one of Mr. Dickens's characters, or I should as soon have my eyes torn out by the old raven Mr. Dickens used to keep as his pet.'

Osgood thought it an opportune time to interject with a question, but Forster put an imperial hand on his shoulder and steered him.

'There: that watercolour the workman is bringing through now from the dining room. That, Mr. Osgood and Miss Sand – is that the name, little dear? – that is a painting of the steamer *Britannia* that Mr. Dickens sailed on in his *first* trip to America, the fourth of January, 1842. That will be discussed in chapter nineteen of my *Life of Dickens*. Hold that up higher, you, men, don't let that frame's corner damage the wall!'

Osgood felt a sharpness, a recrimination in the word *America*.

'I hope you'd agree that Mr. Dickens's second tour of America,' Osgood said, 'was a verifiable success.'

Forster laughed grimly and wrung his hands out as if squeezing out wet laundry. 'Monstrous thought! Your tour left Mr. Dickens ill, hobbled in his foot, drained of all life with which he parted from our shores! I fully opposed his going, as I said at the time to that gold-hungry gorilla Dolby. If American readers had not taken Mr. Dickens's books without paying any authors' fees for so many years, if they had made us part of your copyright laws, he oughtn't ever needed the extra income. To think of everyone prancing around calling Mr. Dickens "Chief" like he was an Indian savage—!'

'Charles liked to be called Chief, if I recall,' a female voice interrupted. 'With the many things to make us sad, we can at least be happy he still had enough vigour for travel.'

The voice from above belonged to an elegant and slender woman a few steps past forty years old coming from upstairs.

'May I present to you, Miss Georgina Hogarth,' muttered Forster indifferently to their guests. 'My fellow executor to the house and all its possessions.'

'Please call me Aunt Georgy. Everyone at Gadshill does,' she said in a soothing tone that overthrew Forster's shrillness.

Osgood knew her by name to be Dickens's sister-in-law. Even after Catherine, Charles Dickens's wife, moved away from Gadshill, Aunt Georgy was the novelist's confidante and housekeeper, and a mother to her two nieces and six nephews. The separation between Dickens and Catherine was never an official divorce – the novelist of domestic harmony could not afford so permanent a stain on the public record. Dickens's novels celebrated the family and the ideals of loyalty and forgiveness. The audience expected him to be an exemplar for the same.

Dickens and Georgy became so close that other members of the Hogarth family, furious that she had supported Charles, were even said to have repeated wicked slanders that he'd seduced her. It did not help allay the whispers that the lovely Georgy never married.

Osgood recalled that *Harper's* magazine had been only too pleased to sell copies by importing the rumours about Dickens and Georgy back to America. *To make the affair still more notorious, a young lady, Mrs. Dickens's sister, has undertaken to 'keep house' for Dickens*, the magazine had commented when Catherine had moved away more than ten years before. *The whole affair is very repugnant to our idea of matrimonial constancy.*

'Thank you both. I can see well enough you are quite occupied without our intrusion,' said Osgood.

'In truth, Mr. Osgood, we only wish there were more guests who were not dreadful auctioneers or house seekers tramping up and down the stairs.' Aunt Georgy had a ready smile that brought to mind a picture of the lively household as it used to be. 'Shall we?'

In the drawing room, a matronly and attractive young woman approximately of Osgood's age sat caressing the keys of the rosewood piano. She wore a fashionable mourning dress, weighed down by elaborate mourning jewels, and played with an abstracted air.

Osgood, momentarily distracted by the music and its performer, introduced their mission to his hosts. 'Our firm is set to publish *The Mystery of Edwin Drood* in America. Yet back home we are surrounded by literary pirates, who will use the impunity that comes with Mr. Dickens's decease to plunder the text for themselves.'

'Typical Americans!' Forster intoned. 'Greed comes in abundance in Yankee-doodle-dom.'

'There is plenty of it here, too, Mr. Forster,' Georgy chided Dickens's friend.

'Because of the peculiarity of our laws,' continued Osgood, 'we will be in a rather bad way if the pirates issue their cheap copies. We had relied upon expectations of a success for our firm – and of course for royalties to Mr. Dickens, mandated by our morals though not by our laws. These would go to you and your family now,' he said, turning to Georgy. 'That shall never be able to come to pass if Dickens's wishes that we are his exclusive publisher vanish with his death.'

At this point in the interview, a small white blur, which turned out on closer inspection to be a Pomeranian dog, flew across the room and landed at Osgood's feet. She gave a sharp bark for Osgood, but when he reached down, she shook her muzzle and barked at him with recrimination. The piano-playing woman came to a discordant stop and lifted her wide skirts as she rushed over. The musician, throwing back her mourning veil to show her face, was presented as Mamie Dickens, the novelist's first daughter, the one Forster had dismissed as comely and unmarried.

'I am very sorry for her behaviour, Mr. Osgood,' Mamie said shyly. 'That is Mrs. Bouncer, she is a sweet creature but truly like Mephistopheles' little dog when she is angry. Like a true well-mannered young woman of England, she does not ever tolerate a man reaching for her. She likes to be petted by a man's foot instead.'

Mrs. Bouncer went round and round Osgood with an asthmatic

barking. Osgood exchanged a quick glance with Rebecca, who seemed to want to laugh but suppressed the urge. Osgood unfastened his shoe and, Mrs. Bouncer immediately flopping over, scratched the dog's stomach with his foot.

'Oh, isn't that lovely!' Mamie exclaimed as she bit her bottom lip with emotion. 'That is everything she has been missing. Oh, no – must that go, too?' she said, spinning around, distracted. A workman was wrapping a pink tazza taken from the mantelpiece. 'I did always admire it when I was a little girl. Can I stop that terrible work person, Auntie?' she whispered.

'I'm very sorry, Mamie, you know we can only afford to keep what is necessary.'

Osgood passed a look of sympathy at Mamie. Rebecca watched Osgood as he watched the piteous young Miss Dickens. For a few moments, the three were as captive and uncertain as figures in a sketch.

'We were hoping,' Osgood said, returning to their topic, 'there might be more pages that have been found here for *The Mystery of Edwin Drood*, beyond the six instalments that Mr. Forster has sent us in Boston.'

Georgy shook her head sadly. 'I am afraid there are not. The ink on the final slips of paper of the sixth instalment was still drying at his desk when he had his collapse. I saw it myself.'

'Perhaps there are memorandums or fragments? Or private corre-spondences about his plan for the rest of the novel that could satisfy a reader's natural curiosity.'

'It might have been possible,' Georgy replied. 'But Mr. Dickens burned his letters periodically and asked his friends to do the same. He had a great horror of the improper uses often made of the letters of celebrated people. I can recall years ago when he had a bonfire and the boys roasted onions on the ashes of letters of great men like Tennyson, Thackeray, Carlyle.'

'Tell me, Mr. Osgood,' Forster interrupted with a strange, contemptuous expression, 'what good would notes on the book do you, even if there were any, without Charles Dickens to write the chapters themselves?'

'All the good in the world, Mr. Forster!' Osgood answered, adeptly bounding over Forster's negative tone. 'If we could publish a special edition that exclusively reveals to American readers how Mr. Dickens's mystery was *truly* to be ended, we could overtake our swindling competition. But we have only a brief time to spend in England to find answers – or it shall be for naught. The pirates will have their hands on the rest of the known instalments on the first of next month, and shall print the book to sell everywhere under the sun.'

'What do you mean, Osgood?' Forster leaned over with a distrustful scowl. He gripped the arms of the chair with his massive hands as though without such restraint he might fly at Osgood's throat. 'Incredible! What do you mean when you said "how it was truly to be ended"?'

Osgood and Rebecca exchanged curious glances at the executor's heated reaction. 'I mean, sir, how the mystery of the novel was to come out in the end.'

'Well, you don't have to tell me! That's clear enough, I think! John Jasper, the audacious villain of the book, leading his secret life of depravity, has cruelly killed his innocent nephew Edwin Drood. Isn't that most obvious to anyone with two eyes?'

'It certainly seems like it at the end of the sixth instalment, yes,' Osgood agreed. 'Yet our senior partner Mr. Fields has pointed out that Dickens might have had some other surprises behind the scenes for his reader in the subsequent six parts. Mr. Dickens did say in a letter to our offices that the book would be "curious and new".'

Forster shook his head. 'Jasper was to confess his crime – *this* was the "curious and new" notion of it. Why, Dickens told me himself.'

'Mr. Dickens told you?' asked Osgood.

Forster crossed his arms square over his chest and pushed out his thick lips in displeasure. 'Perhaps I did not express my relationship with Mr. Dickens very clearly to you, Mr. Osgood. The annals of our friendship, perhaps, were not as celebrated across the ocean as they are here. I do not flatter myself to say that Mr. Dickens and I were on the closest terms, and though I am afraid he was not as open to counsel in regard to points of personal conduct, he confided nearly every detail of his books to me.'

'Well, he told *me* nothing about how the novel would end, even though I asked days before he died,' Georgina said, looking at Forster with suspicion.

'You asked him, too, Aunt Georgy?' Rebecca asked.

'Yes, dear. After I heard the instalments read aloud to us as he wrote them, I said to him, "Charles, I hope you have not really killed poor Edwin Drood!" He answered, "Georgy, I call my book the *mystery*, not the *history*, of Edwin Drood" – but he would not say more.'

'Monstrous!' Forster exclaimed, his broad brow now creased and snarled. 'I wring my hands! Preposterous! That could mean anything, Miss Hogarth! Couldn't it?'

Georgy ignored the objection. 'Mr. Osgood, Miss Sand. If you would like to look at the papers on his desks for yourselves, you are quite free to do so. In the summer months, he liked to write in our Swiss chalet. That is where he was working on his last day before coming inside the house and collapsing. A second desk stands in his library. I have not had the strength to do anything more than to keep his desks and drawers orderly.'

'Thank you, Aunt Georgy,' Osgood said.

'If you find anything that would help, we shall rejoice with you,' said Georgy.

Forster refolded his stumpy arms at the sentiment.

Osgood and Rebecca, led by an undergardener, crossed under the high road by the brick tunnel where the four big dogs lounged. A separate Swiss-style wooden chalet stood hidden by shrubbery and trees. In this small wooden sanctuary, they climbed a winding staircase to the top room.

The removed quiet of Dickens's chalet was untouched by the auction preparations. On the walls of the summer study were five tall mirrors that reflected the trees and corn fields all the way down to the river in the distance and its faraway sails. The shadows of the clouds seemed to drift across the room.

'I can see why Mr. Dickens prized this place to write, away from everything else,' Rebecca commented when they entered.

At an open window stood an expensive telescope. Osgood pressed his eye against its lens. Deep in the meadows by the hop fields was a tall, hatless man with wild hair who somehow seemed to be looking right into their window. Osgood shifted the telescope to the hilltop and found the Falstaff Inn and could see its proprietor out by the stables. As he combed the mane of one of the horses, the landlord pinched his eyes as though in a fit of dreamy melancholy. It seemed every corner of the world around Gadshill had been made bleak by Dickens's death.

The register on the desk was still on 8 June, the day Dickens had last sat and wrote. Also crowding the desk were several quill pens and inkwells, a memorandum slate, various trinkets including two bronze frogs, and a stack of slips of blue stationery covered with writing in blue ink.

'This is it,' Osgood said with awe of the latter object, sitting on the dusty chair. 'The first six instalments of *The Mystery of Edwin Drood* in his own hand, with corrections from the printer in the margins.' He gently fingered the edges of the pages. Dickens's hand-writing, not always neat, was strong and dynamic. It did not seem to be written to be read by anyone other than the writer – printers and compositors be damned. Usually when Osgood saw the working space of one of his authors, the revelation was purely mechanical, like visiting the dusty floor of a factory. It had become too common, in fact, that when he finally met an author he had held in high esteem, the result was disappointment in the ordinariness of the person behind the words. But with Dickens there had always been a magical feeling, as though Osgood were not the seasoned publisher of Boston but once again a college lad from Maine or that shop boy on his first day in the Old Corner in an India rubber apron streaked with ink. To this day, even now with Dickens gone, he was still excited to be Dickens's publisher.

'Are you ready?' Osgood asked, inhaling it all. 'Let us begin, Miss Sand.'

Time for the researchers over the next few days was broken up by short respites and occasional interruptions from the outside world. The most notable one came as they continued the next morning. They had by this point found a few small gems in the vast spread of materials. Osgood had discovered an early page of Dickens's notes that listed titles before the novelist had settled on *The Mystery of Edwin Drood*: *Flight and Pursuit, One Object in Life, Dead? or Alive?*. He had been dictating these to Rebecca before he stopped in midsentence.

'Mr. Osgood?'

'My apology, Miss Sand. My eye was drawn away by that. Rather grotesque little thing, isn't it?' On the chimney piece, there sat a light yellow plaster figure. It depicted an Oriental man with a jaunty fez smoking from a pipe, sitting cross-legged on a settee. Osgood picked it up and held it out at arm's length as he examined it. It was heavier than it looked.

Just then, a man rushed up the stairs of the chalet and into the study. The intruder wore a ragged suit and wild uncovered hair over a sunburned face. It was the same man the publisher had seen through the telescope walking through the hop fields the day before. His mouth was agape as though in some kind of sudden terror, and he grabbed Osgood's arm.

'Do you need some help, sir?' Osgood said.

The man studied the publisher with searching eyes. He held out his other hand to Osgood and kept it outstretched.

Cautiously, Osgood put his own hand up to shake. The stranger grabbed it with both hands and pressed hard. Rebecca gasped.

'Yes, I see it! You are. You are. You are ready for it!' the man sputtered out when one of the Gadshill servants burst in.

'Come on now.' The moustachioed servant removed the invader by the ear like a misbehaving child. 'Come on, old fellow. That's enough of that beastly behaviour. They are at some important work. Very sorry, sir, miss. I'll see to it he won't bother you again.'

Later that afternoon, Osgood took the one-hour train into London while Rebecca continued their research. Using the map from his guide-book, he reached the offices of Chapman & Hall, Dickens's English publisher. The day of their arrival, Osgood had sent a messenger with his card and a note asking for an interview but had yet to receive a reply. Osgood did not have the luxury of waiting if their stay in England was to succeed in time.

But there would be more waiting at the busy Piccadilly offices of the publishing firm. Today was Magazine Day, when every publisher, printer, binder and bookseller in London scrambled to release the latest journals and periodicals to readers. In the case of Chapman & Hall, this meant the latest serial instalment of *The Mystery of Edwin Drood*. Messenger boys stuffed their sacks with pale green-covered pamphlets of the instalment to deliver all across the city and to the country towns to book stands and stalls, shouting instructions at each other. On the first of the next month, the next Magazine Day, the final instalment in the London publisher's hands would be printed and sold to the hungry public – and the pirates back in America would have all they needed.

Osgood, as he watched the mayhem of clerks and messengers,

noticed that the mere mention of the name Mr. Chapman, the head partner, caused bowed heads and darting eyes among the man's employees. He had been kept sitting in the anteroom for an hour when broad-shouldered Chapman appeared in a sporty outfit.

'Terribly sorry, old boy,' he said after Osgood presented himself. 'Must run to the country to go shooting with some capital people – terrific bores, really, but capital – will you call another time?'

Osgood gave one more long look at Chapman's office and staff before starting back, with a rising feeling of futility, to Rochester. Taking a buggy from Higham station, Osgood found reliable Rebecca still hard at work in the Gadshill chalet.

After another two hours, the men from Christie's auction firm came in to finally break up the quiet of the chalet. The workers snatched up the Oriental statue and the other saleable effects inside Dickens's sanctum. The men were accompanied dutifully by Aunt Georgy, who gave them instructions.

Georgy shook her head in dignified frustration as they did their work. 'I suppose it is impossible to try to pretend things haven't changed forever. How empty the world feels now!'

'Where will you go once you sell Gadshill, Aunt Georgy?' Rebecca asked.

'Mamie and I must look for a small house in London, though my mind frets at the long, bitter winters in the city.'

'I believe you and Mr. Dickens will always be part of this land, no matter what,' Osgood said. 'No matter where you go.'

Georgy looked hard at Osgood. 'I must confess that my role as executrix is new for me – not in managing the children's careers, for that has been my life's devotion. But in reading documents and contracts.'

'I can imagine the strain,' Osgood replied.

'I've learned too quickly it is rare to meet a man of business who can wear an honest face. Forgive me, but I wonder if I might trouble you while you stay in Rochester. Would you consider looking over Mr. Dickens's will if I left a copy with the Falstaff?'

'It would be my honour and pleasure,' Osgood said, standing up and bowing, 'to repay your kindness.'

'Thank you. It will put me at ease to have an hour of time to ask someone questions – someone other than Mr. Forster, to be perfectly candid. I feel, for one thing, such an infant around him! As if I had no power of free will of my own when he is near.'

They became quiet when a heavy tread ascended the stairs. Then came the burly form of Forster, who yelled after the departing auction men to remember the value of what they had in their unworthy hands.

'Superfluous creatures,' Forster concluded, turning to the desk, where his eyes landed on the stack of blue sheets. He rubbed his hands together. 'Ah, there it is! All of the manuscripts of Mr. Dickens's books, you see, Mr. Osgood, were left by order of his will to be given into my care.'

Forster, with two careful, trembling hands, grasped both sides of the manuscript of *Drood* and picked it up. His reverence was touching, if excessive.

'This is the last of them in the house, I think?' Forster asked Aunt Georgy.

'It is the last of his manuscripts here,' Georgy said, sighing. 'The last anywhere.'

With the manuscript safely lodged in his case, Forster's eye now darted across the desk to a particular quill pen. It was a long goose's feather, white and wavy, the nib stained in dried blue ink.

'That's the one, isn't it?' he asked.

Georgy nodded.

Rebecca asked what it was.

'That is the pen with which he wrote *The Mystery of Edwin Drood*, Miss Sand,' answered Georgy. 'Charles liked to use a single pen for a single book – there was a purity about it that way. He did not want the book's spirit mixed up in trifling bills and sundry cheques. With this, he finished the novel's sixth instalment, just before coming into the house.'

Osgood asked if he could see the pen. He picked it up and turned it over in his hand, then gripped it as if on its own it might finish the final six parts of *Drood*.

'Shall I,' Forster began, licking his plump cracked lips, 'keep it at my office?'

Georgy cleared her throat.

'Just for now,' Forster clarified, clearing his own throat as an answer to her gesture. 'Until you decide what you shall do with it,

Miss Hogarth. Then you may – well, you may throw the thing into the Thames if you wish!'

'Keep it for the time being,' Georgy agreed, at which point Forster eagerly plucked the *Drood* pen from Osgood's hand, deposited it into his case and fled down the stairs without bidding any farewells.

XV

N THE MORNING, OSGOOD AND Rebecca had planned to separate, Osgood to try again at Chapman & Hall in London and Rebecca to continue the labours at Gadshill. At the last moment, Osgood called Rebecca back to the Falstaff's wagon. He looked at her with a curious air. 'I think you ought to come to London with me this morning, Miss Sand. If Mr. Chapman does concede to see me, I should like you to take down notes.'

Rebecca hesitated. 'This shall be my first time in London!' she exclaimed, then held in her excitement with her typically neutral air. 'I shall get my pencil case.'

'Good thing,' Osgood said. 'Your eyes could use a respite from reading over Mr. Dickens's papers, I'm certain.'

After arriving at Charing Cross station in the Strand, Osgood and Rebecca, in the shadows of theatres and shops, walked through the astounding number of street performers and merchant booths on every corner, which made Boston seem quiet by comparison. Rebecca's eyes danced at the sights. The shouting pedlars held up repaired shoes, tools, fruit, puppies, birds – anything that could be offered for a few shillings. The variety of accents and dialects made every English pedlar's vocal promotions seem yet another different language to the American ear.

'Do you notice something strange about the pedlars?' Osgood asked Rebecca.

'The sheer noise they create,' she replied. 'It is quite an astonishing thing.'

As they spoke, they passed a Punch and Judy show. The wooden marionettes pranced across the small stage, Judy hitting Punch over the head with a cudgel. 'I'll pay yer for a throwin' the child out the winder!' shouted puppet Judy at her puppet spouse.

'Look again,' Osgood said. 'There is something stranger than the noise, Miss Sand, and that is that London businessmen do not seem to notice the roar of the streets at all! To live in London, one must possess an iron concentration. That is how it remains the richest city in the world. Here we are,' Osgood said, pointing to a handsome brick building ahead displaying the Chapman & Hall sign in the window.

This time when Chapman marched through the anteroom, he paused and took a few small steps backwards upon seeing the guests on the sofa. The ruddy-skinned English publisher, with his strapping deportment and sleek dark hair combed into a flashy split across his wide head, looked the part of a sportsman and man of leisure, far more than that of a bookman.

'Say, visitors I see,' said Chapman, though his eyes were fixed not on both visitors, but on Rebecca's slender form. Finally, he resigned himself to also noticing the gentleman.

'Frederic Chapman,' Chapman announced himself, extending a hand.

'James Osgood. We met yesterday,' Osgood reminded him.

Chapman squinted at the visitor. 'I remember your face vividly. The American publisher. Now, this little woman is . . .'

'My bookkeeper, Miss Sand,' Osgood presented her.

He took her hand gingerly in his. 'You are most welcome into our humble firm, my dear. Say, you will come in with us to my office for my interview with Mr. Osgood, won't you?'

Osgood and Rebecca followed a clerk who followed Chapman in the procession into his private office. The room displayed some expensive books but a greater number of dead, stuffed animals: a rabbit, a fox, a deer. The frightful artefacts emitted a stale, bleak odour and each one seemed to stare in dumb loyalty only at Mr. Chapman wherever he moved. The office had a large bay window; however, instead of looking out on to London, it overlooked the offices and rooms of Chapman & Hall. Periodically, Chapman would turn his head to make sure his employees were hard at work. One of his harried clerks delivered a bottle of port to the meeting with a bow that was more like a spontaneous wobbling of the knees.

'Ah, excellent. I presume you and Mr. Fields have a wine cellar back in Boston,' Chapman commented as two glasses were filled.

'Subscription lists and packing supplies fill our cellar.'

'We have an extensive one. A game larder, too. Thinking of adding a billiard room – next time we'll play. It is always a pleasure to see a colleague from the other side of the water.'

'Mr. Chapman, I suppose you have already thoroughly investigated what else might remain of *The Mystery of Edwin Drood*. We would benefit greatly if you'd share whatever intelligence you have gained.'

'Investigated? Why, Mr. Osgood, you speak like one of the detectives in all the new novels. You tickle my belly with your American notions.'

'I don't mean to,' Osgood returned seriously.

'No?' Chapman asked, disappointed. 'But what would be investigated about it?'

Osgood, flabbergasted, said, 'Whether Mr. Dickens left any clues, any indications about where his story was to go.'

Chapman interrupted with a satisfyingly hearty laugh, proving the alleged tickling. 'See here, Osgood, old boy,' he said, 'you are a laugh in the real American fashion, aren't you? Why, I'm perfectly content with what we have of *Drood*. Six excellent instalments.'

'They are superb, I agree. But if I understand correctly, you paid quite a sum for the book,' Osgood said incredulously.

'Seventy-five hundred pounds! The highest sum ever paid to an author for a new book.' This he pointed out boastfully in Rebecca's direction.

'I would think your firm would wish to do whatever were possible to protect your investment,' Osgood said.

'I will tell you how I see it. Every reader who picks up the book, finding it unfinished, can spend their time guessing what the ending should be. And they'll tell their friends to buy a copy and do the same, so it can be argued.'

'In America, its unfinished state will bait all the freebooters, as they are called,' Osgood said.

'That scoundrel Major Harper and his ilk,' Chapman said, tipping his glass high and ingesting his port with a predatory swiftness as he glanced up at the congregation of animal heads. His hunting eyes, always roving, paused back on Osgood. 'That's the thing you're worried about, isn't it?' he finally added. He leaned in towards Rebecca – not exactly unfriendly to Osgood's predicament but entirely lacking in interest relative to the pretty bookkeeper sitting across. 'Say, I suppose your employer fought bravely in your War of Rebellion, didn't he? Lucky. Why, here we haven't any wars to speak of lately – small ones, but nothing worth suiting up for. Nothing to show oneself to the world as a man or to impress the ladies.'

'I see, Mr. Chapman,' Rebecca replied, refusing to shrink from the intensity of his attention.

'Remind me which battles you fought in, then, old boy?' Chapman asked, turning to Osgood.

'Actually,' Osgood said, 'I had suffered the bad effects of rheumatism when I was younger, Mr. Chapman.'

'Shame!'

'I am all better now. However, it prevented any notion of being a soldier.'

'Still, sir, Mr. Osgood helped publish those books and poems,' Rebecca interjected, 'that contributed to the enthusiasm and commitment of the Union to persevere in the cause.'

'What a pity not to have soldiered!' Chapman responded. 'You have my sympathy, Osgood.'

'Thank you, Mr. Chapman. About *Drood*,' Osgood said pointedly, changing the path of his persuasion. 'Think of the value of our being able to better understand Dickens's final work. For the sake of literature.'

It seemed by the twinkle in his eye and the draw of his mouth that Chapman might start another laughing fit. Instead, his impressive frame bounded to his window and he put a fingertip against the glass. 'Why, you sound like some of the young clerks out there. I can't tell them apart most of the time, they're rather indistinct, don't you think, Miss Sand?'

'I suppose I do not know, Mr. Chapman,' Rebecca began. 'They seem dedicated to their work.'

'You!' Chapman's strong brow curled up on itself and he leaned out the door where some clerks were packing up a shipment of books into boxes.

A clerk nervously stepped inside the office. The other clerks all stopped what they were doing and waited on their colleague's fate.

'Say, clerk, can't you go more quickly than that packing the books?' Chapman demanded.

'Sir,' answered the clerk, 'quite sorry, it's the smell that slows us down.'

'The smell!' Chapman repeated with an indignation suggesting he had been accused of personally originating the odour. He unleashed a series of furious expletives describing the clerk's incompetence. When the publisher finished, the clerk meekly explained that Chapman's latest addition to the larder room, a haunch of venison, had become too malodorous in the summer heat.

Chapman, putting up his nose as a test, relented, nodding. 'All right. Put the venison on a four-wheeler, and I'll take it home for dinner,' he ordered.

Chapman had punctuated his insults by lighting a cigar, while the clerk was waiting for dismissal. When Chapman turned back to the young man again he looked on him as though he did not know where he had come from.

'You don't look very well!' Chapman remarked to the young man.

'Sir?'

'Not at all well. Pale, even. Say, can you drink a glass of port?'

'I think so.'

'Good. Tell them to send you up a couple of bottles from the basement.' The clerk fled.

'This office runs like a clock,' Chapman said with impatient sarcasm to his visitors. 'Now, you were – you were commenting about literature.' He picked up a bundle of papers. 'You see this poetry book? Quite lovely. What they call literature. This, I will save in the closet to burn in my hearth in the winter. Why? Because poetry doesn't pay. Never has paid, never will. No use for it, you see, Miss Sand.'

'Why, Mr. Chapman, I quite adore novels,' Rebecca said, sitting more erect and looking right at their host. 'But in our saddest or happiest time, when we are all alone, what would we do without poetry to speak to us?'

Chapman poured another glass of port for himself. 'A fiver is plenty to give for any poem, especially as all poets are hard up. Five pounds would buy the best any of them could do. No, no, it's adventure, out-of-air expeditions, that people want to read these days, with the wretched state of the trade. Ouida, Edmund Yates, Hawley Smart, your American rye-and-Indian novels, that's the new literature that people will remember – God bless Dickens, with all his social causes and sympathies, but we must forget the past and move forward. Yes, we must not look back.'

Outside the office, in the deep shadows of the back alley, the slight clerk who had been reprimanded by Chapman, his head buzzing with port, climbed on to the back of a wagon. He tried to drag the massive, smelly venison haunch up by a rope. He struggled and puffed until a stronger hand easily slid it up from the ground.

'Thanky, gov'n'r!' said the clerk. 'Blast this venison. Blast venison, generally.'

The man who had helped him was cloaked in the shadows. He now tossed a coin in the air, which the clerk clumsily caught to his chest with both hands.

'Why, shouldn't *I* pay *you*, gov'n'r?'

'You hear what your boss was saying to Mr. Osgood?' asked the stranger.

'That American?' The clerk thought about it, then nodded.

'Then there's more of this for you. Come.' He held out his hand to help the clerk step down from the wagon, though as it emerged from the shadow, it was clear that it was not a hand at all. It was a gold beasty head at the top of a walking stick. Its glittering black eyes shined out like holes bored through the shadows.

'Come. It won't bite,' the dark stranger said.

'Why'd you want to know about Mr. Osgood, anyway?' the clerk asked as he took hold of the cane and stepped down from the wagon.

'Let's say I'm a-learning the book trade.'

XVI

ACK AT THE DICKENS FAMILY home of Gadshill, Osgood and Rebecca had turned to the books and documents in the library. Osgood observed the library with a publisher's jealous interest in another man's books. There was a row of Wilkie Collins volumes and an English edition of Poe's poetry – as well as many editions from Fields, Osgood & Co.

The walls between the shelves danced with famous illustrations by Cruikshank, 'Phiz', Fildes, and other artists who had decorated Dickens's novels. Oliver Twist staggers as a bullet lands in his arm from the smoking pistol of Giles from around the corner . . . from the same novel Bill Sikes prepares to murder poor Nancy . . . In a cavernous cell from *A Tale of Two Cities* in the Bastille, death and doom lingers . . . True-hearted Rosa confides at a quiet table to her upright guardian, Mr. Grewgious, that she suspects Edwin Drood's uncle, John Jasper, of grave mischief . . .

Multiple books were found on the subject of mesmerism, and Rebecca noticed that Dickens had written notes in the margins of a few of them. One was titled, intriguingly, *Footfalls on the Boundary of Another World*.

'He read these books carefully,' said Rebecca, respecting the heavily used pages with a gentle touch.

'What is it about?' Osgood asked as he was walking along the columns of books.

'I am not certain,' Rebecca replied. 'Enquiries into the super-natural.'

She read a passage. *The enquirer may grope and stumble, seeing but as through a glass darkly. Death, that has delivered so many millions from misery, will dispel his doubts and resolve his difficulties. Death, the unriddler, will draw aside the curtain and let in the explaining light. That which is feebly commenced in this phase of existence will be far better prosecuted in another.*

'That sounds like a humbug,' Osgood remarked. 'Let us see what else he had.' At one of the other bookcases he tried to dislodge several books before realising they were not actually books at all.

'Mr. Dickens had these imitation book backs produced,' said a servant who had just entered the room, the same moustachioed man who had firmly ejected the intruder in the chalet. He put a tray of cakes on the table with a bow, then went to Osgood's side. 'This is a hidden door, you see, Mr. Osgood, so that Mr. Dickens could enter the library conveniently from the next room. As ingenious at home as in his writing!' The servant pushed the shelf lined with the false books out on to the billiard room, where games and cigars waited for Gadshill's male guests of years gone by.

'Ingenious!' Osgood agreed, enchanted by the device. He read with a smile some of the titles of the false book titles Dickens had concocted. His favourites were *A History of a Short Chancery Suit* in twenty-one volumes; *Five Minutes in China* in three volumes; four volumes of *The Gunpowder Magazine;* and *Cat's Lives*, a nine-volume set, which made him think of lazy Mr. Puss curled into a cosy lump on a seat cushion in Boston.

'I should like very much to publish some of these myself!' Osgood said.

'Mr. Osgood! I should think you have quite enough to occupy yourself at 124 Tremont,' said the servant knowingly.

'How did . . .' Osgood began to ask, at hearing the address of his firm back in Boston. He turned to look more carefully at the servant. 'Why, is it you, dear Henry Scott? It is you, Scott!' He scrutinised the familiar face, so altered by the passage of two difficult years and the long, handlebar moustache carefully combed upwards at either tip. A big difference in appearance was Gadshill livery, a loose-fitting white overall with cape and top boots.

'Yes, Mr. Osgood,' he said. 'Perhaps you recall, Miss Sand, that I accompanied Mr. Dickens and Mr. Dolby on their travels through

America, as the Chief's personal dresser – and I daresay his most trusted man. You'll remember it was the time when all that had happened with Tom Branagan! Well, just before we were away on the tour, the Chief's top house man here at Gad's, his servant – or "domestic", as your American help prefer to be called – was found by Scotland Yard to have been stealing money from the cash box. A man who had worked for the Chief for twenty-five years and was paid generously for it! I am glad to say the Chief came to have enough regard to give me the station with a post for my wife, after we returned from America. Five years to the day.'

'Pardon?'

'His death, Mr. Osgood. It was precisely five years after the railway accident at Staplehurst. When he fell ill, I wandered to his calendar and I could not help think to myself, an ill wind that blows nobody good.'

As Henry bowed to depart, Osgood pleaded that he stay. 'Mr. Scott, what can you tell me about what happened in the chalet yesterday with that man?'

'I am mightily sorry again for that,' Henry said adding another and lower bow. 'I suppose a mad beast must have a sober driver, as the saying is. Why, if the poor Chief were present in spirit *or* in body, or in some middle way, he would not have his guests so harassed. And if there is one man clever enough to come to us in spirit, it is the Chief! Don't you think so, Miss Sand?'

Rebecca had an unwavering air about her that made every man seek her approbation for their ideas.

'I was just looking at his reading into spiritual topics, in fact, Mr. Scott,' said Rebecca.

'I'm curious what troubled that man,' Osgood interrupted.

'Ah, you might name anything and that likely qualifies as troubling that beastly sun-scorched loafer!' Henry explained that Dickens sometimes ministered mesmerism as therapy to troubled or sick individuals. He would lie them down on the floor or the couch and place them in a magnetic slumber until he woke them trembling and cold. There was a blind lady who credited Dickens's use of a magnetic treatment on her with regaining her sight. 'This man, though, he was a special case,' noted Henry.

The man, a poor farmer, had been told by London doctors months earlier that he had an incurable illness. Having heard about Dickens's special skills he begged at the novelist's doorstep for treatment through spiritual and moral mesmerism. Dickens had been less active with his mesmeric power in recent years but relented and began the magnetic therapy for the man.

'Had it worked, Mr. Scott?' Rebecca asked.

'Well, perhaps it did work on him, Miss Sand – but the wrong way,' said Henry.

'What do you mean?' asked Osgood.

'One of the cooks told me that the farmer's illness was better, but his mental condition had become feeble during those mesmerism sessions. Now the poor tramp still lurks around, just like those dumb dogs out in the stables, as if the Chief is hiding in the woods somewhere with Falstaff's thieves and Chaucer's pilgrims, waiting to come back.' This Henry said in a tone more unconsciously sympathetic to the tramp than he knew.

With eyes red from reading and copying, Osgood and Rebecca decided to return to the inn at the end of the day. Forster was waiting on the Gad's porch.

'Will there be more of your expedition in the morning?' asked the executor, as if genuinely interested, instead of just groping for information.

'After three days, we can find little in the way of clues other than a list of titles, some scribbled notes on the book, and some rejected pages, Mr. Forster,' Osgood admitted. 'I fear we've exhausted your materials here.'

Forster nodded with barely concealed satisfaction, then hastily forged an expression of disappointment. 'I suppose you shall return to Boston.'

'Not yet,' Osgood answered.

'Oh?' Forster said.

'If there is nothing to find inside Dickens's rooms, perhaps there is some clue outside them – somewhere.'

Forster's pupils dilated with interest, and he picked up a pen and a slip of paper. 'You are an enterprising American, and I well know enterprising Americans detest wasting their time. Your search, I am afraid, Mr. Osgood, can merely be that: a waste. This address is where you can find me when I'm back in London, where I serve as lunacy commissioner, should you need me. Mr. Dickens was too good a man to attempt to mislead readers who trusted him: the end of *The Mystery of Edwin Drood* would have been just as it appears – a devious, jealous man who meant to snuff out an innocent youth and did – there is nothing more. Any other idea on the matter is pure stuff!'

XVII

EMPHATICALLY DIRECT THAT I be buried in an inexpensive, unostentatious and strictly private manner, that no public announcement be made of the time or place of my burial, that at the utmost not more than three plain mourning coaches be employed, and that those who attend my funeral wear no scarf, cloak, black bow, long hatband or other such revolting absurdity. I direct that my name be inscribed in plain English letters on my tomb without the addition of 'Mr.' or 'Esquire'. I conjure my friends on no account to make me the subject of any monument, memorial or testimonial whatever. I rest my claims to the remembrance of my country upon my published works, and to the remembrance of my friends upon their experience of me; in addition thereto I commit my soul to the mercy of God through our Lord and Saviour Jesus Christ.*

Osgood reviewed the will's language with Georgina Hogarth at the Falstaff Inn coffee room and offered opinions about her obligations in relation to Forster. The document created an admirably complicated distribution of responsibilities and burdens. Forster controlled all the manuscripts of Dickens's published works. But to Georgy, the document bequeathed all the private papers in the house as well as all decisions related to jewellery and the familiar objects from Dickens's writing desk, like the quill pen temporarily pocketed by Forster.

'Mr. Forster,' Georgy said to Osgood, 'sees his duty as reminding the world that Charles should be worshipped. That is why Charles is buried in Poets' Corner rather than in our humble village, as he would have wished. If Mr. Forster could have moved Dickens's pen for him over the lines of this will, he would have.'

That afternoon, following the one-hour train ride from Higham to London, Osgood and Rebecca entered the most awe-inducing man-made spot in England, Westminster Abbey. Both Osgood and his bookkeeper automatically leaned their heads back to the remarkable ceiling far above, where the expanse of pillars crossed like the tips of forest trees meeting each other in the morning sky. The light streaming into the Abbey was stained red from the ornamented rose-coloured glass windows surrounding them.

In the south transept, the American visitors found the marble slab that covered the coffin of Charles Dickens. The grand monument at Poets' Corner inside the famous cathedral was surrounded by the tombs of the greatest writers. Dickens's itself was overlooked by statues of Addison and Shakespeare and a bust of Thackeray. Though little else from his instructions had been followed, the inlaid words on the tomb read as Dickens's will had requested.

Charles Dickens
Born 7th February 1812
Died 9th June 1870

Hordes of people filed in to leave verses and flowers over the novelist's slab, and the remains of yesterday's offerings had begun to wither in the warm air of the Abbey.

As they stood there, a flower was tossed past Osgood and Rebecca on to the Dickens grave. The bloom had large, extensive petals of a wild purple hue. The publisher looked over his shoulder and saw a man in a wide-brimmed hat shading most of an angular, red face turning to leave.

'Did you see that man?' Osgood asked Rebecca.

'Who?' she replied.

Osgood had seen the face before. 'I believe it was the man from the chalet – that queer mesmerism patient.'

Just then, a caravan of other Dickens mourners had appeared in the Abbey. They had come all the way from Dublin to see Dickens's final resting place, they explained to Osgood enthusiastically, as if he were the keeper. They crowded Poets' Corner, pushing Osgood to one side, and the mesmerism patient, in the meantime, had vanished.

Not sure where to turn next, Osgood and Rebecca walked the streets of London.

There was already a line of dead ends besides their search through Gadshill. They had heard there was a London resident named Emma James who claimed to have the entire manuscript of *The Mystery of Edwin Drood*. James turned out to be a spiritual medium who was dictating the final six instalments of *The Mystery of Edwin Drood* from the 'spirit-pen' of Charles Dickens and was soon to begin Dickens's next ghostly novel, entitled *The Life and Adventures of Bockley Wickleheap*. Other rumours – for example, that Wilkie Collins, Dickens's fellow popular novelist and occasional collaborator, had been hired to complete his friend's work – quickly proved just as fruitless. They had also heard that at an audience with the royal court a few months before his death, Dickens had offered to tell Queen Victoria the ending.

'Mr. Osgood?' Rebecca said. 'You seem ill at ease.'

'Perhaps I am somewhat overheated today. Let us pay a call on Mr. Forster at his office, he may know something about Dickens and the queen.'

Osgood did not want to be discouraging to Rebecca by saying more. He dreaded the possibility of returning to Boston to tell J. T. Fields that *The Mystery of Edwin Drood* was never to be unravelled – that Drood was to remain lost in every way. That Fields, Osgood & Co., bearing the financial loss, could soon follow.

Protect our authors: Fields's mandate above all else. That is what Osgood thought about as they walked. His efforts in England were not only for the financial life of the company and all its employees, it was for the authors, too – Longfellow, Lowell, Holmes, Stowe, Emerson and others. If the publishing house plummeted from its current financial precipice, how would the orphaned authors fare? Yes, those writers were beloved, but would the breed of publisher represented by Major Harper care about that? Without Fields and Osgood to protect them, would they be buried by obscurity, like Edgar Poe or the once promising Herman Melville? The true future of publishing was not publishers as manufacturers, as Harper foresaw, but publishers as the authors' partners – the joining of the upper and lower half of the title page.

Osgood thought about all this responsibility that had landed on his shoulders. He actually had wanted to be a poet at one time: to think of it made him laugh inside! A young Osgood, top student, reciting the class poem at Standish Academy. He'd watched a dozen of his classmates leave to chase gold in California that October, but it was the quiet halls of college instead of the wild hills of California for him. Phi Beta Kappa at Bowdoin, class secretary, member of the Pecunians club, but friends with the rival Athenians. He had always been expected to be successful by everyone around him. It had been a worthy sacrifice of his own artistic ambitions to take up the cause of those artists and geniuses who otherwise might flounder.

With these thoughts pressing him down, they arrived at the government building which housed the Lunacy Commission, where Forster held a post. Osgood and Rebecca were greeted by a government assistant. Osgood explained that they wished to speak with Mr. Forster.

'Are you from America?' asked the assistant, brows raised with interest.

'Yes, we are,' Osgood said.

'Americans!' the assistant smiled. 'Well,' he said with renewed seriousness, 'I am afraid we do not have any spittoons in the anteroom.'

'That is well enough,' Osgood said politely, 'as we do not have any tobacco.'

'No?' the assistant asked, surprised, then looked at Rebecca's mouth to confirm that she, too, was not currently masticating tobacco. 'If you can wait for a moment?' The assistant returned with an address written down on a piece of paper. 'Mr. Forster left the office some hours ago. I believe you can find him here. I have written detailed directions, for Americans never can find their way around London.'

'Thank you, we shall look there,' Osgood said.

The summer day had grown hotter and sloppier. London with its crowds of holiday strollers and industrious businessmen was much less comfortable than Gadshill with its sloping fields and generous overhangs of vegetation.

After going in what seemed to be a few circles, Osgood looked at the street sign at the corner and compared it with the paper written by the assistant. 'Blackfriars Road, west side of St. George's Circus – this is where he told us to find Mr. Forster.' They were at a massive pentagon-shaped building that shaded the entire street. Osgood leaned against a stone pillar at the portico to pat his forehead and neck with his handkerchief. As he did, they could hear a loud exchange of words floating their way as if through a trumpet:

'It is quite a phenomenon in the history of friendships, that of this uncle and nephew.'

The man's voice was followed by a feminine one, which said, 'Uncle and nephew?'

'Yes, that is the relationship,' answered the man. 'But they never refer to it. Mr. Jasper will never hear of "uncle" or "nephew". It is always Jack and Ned, I believe.'

Responded the woman, 'Yes, and while nobody else in the world, I fancy, would dare to call Mr. Jasper "Jack", nobody but Mr. Jasper ever calls Edwin Drood "Ned".'

Osgood and Rebecca stood listening in disbelief.

'There,' Rebecca pointed excitedly.

Osgood wheeled around with a start. A placard along the side of the massive theatre building heralded its upcoming productions for the Surrey Theatre season: *Up in the World*, *The Ticket of Leave Man*, and . . . *The Mystery of Edwin Drood*. Dickens's play adapted by Mr. Walter Stephens and boasting, on its poster, 'New and Elaborate Scenery!' and 'a Powerful and unprecedented cast of characters that will hold audience in thrilling excitement!' with 'Charles Dickens's last book! Now *complete!*'

'Now complete,' Osgood and Rebecca read out loud.

After entering the lobby and climbing an enormous staircase, they found themselves inside a more massive auditorium than ever seen in Boston or New York. It was constructed in the shape of a horseshoe. Fifty feet skyward, an astonishing gold dome ornamented with delicate designs covered the whole space. At the base of the dome were Venetian red panels with the names of the nation's great dramatists: Shakespeare, Jonson, Goldsmith, Byron, Jerrold . . .

A confusion of people on the stage pulled away Osgood's attentions. The actors and actresses of this production of *Drood* were now shifting from rehearsing Septimus Crisparkle's conversation with the newcomer to the village, Helena Landless, to a different scene occurring in an opium room. But apparently they could not locate the actor playing the part of the Chinese opium purveyor.

Behind the stage, Osgood found a man who was standing dramatically still while a young woman was adjusting a garish cravat around his neck. As she worked on him, he studied the inside of his mouth and shook out his long dark hair in an oversize mirror. He had a large head, something of a phrenological masterpiece, with a delicate body that seemed to strain to support its upper portion. When the man stopped mouthing *as* and *os*, Osgood presented himself, and asked for the person in charge.

'You mean the executor of Mr. Dickens, do you?' said the man. 'He was here to peep and eavesdrop at rehearsal but already flew away, I believe, like a giant very fat eagle.'

'John Forster authorised this play, then,' Osgood said softly. 'And are you an actor, sir?'

The man opened and closed his strong jaw several times in an attempt to overcome his amazement at the question. 'Am I an . . . Arthur Grunwald, sir,' he said, extending a proud hand. 'Groon-woul-d, sir,' he corrected him with a French enunciation before Osgood could say it.

'Armand Duval in Dumas's *Dame aux Camélias* at the St. James last season,' the girl fixing his cravat said discreetly while Grunwald pretended he could not hear his list of accomplishments. 'Falstaff at the Lyceum's *Henry IV*. And you must have seen Mr. Groon-woul-d's engagement as Hamlet at the Princess. Her Majesty attended four times.'

'I am afraid I am not in London quite as often as the queen,' Osgood said.

'Well, sir!' said Grunwald. 'I see what you are thinking – Groon-woul-d is a sight too slender and handsome to play the goodly portly knight with any manner of realism. Not so! I was praised for my Falstaff to the sky. I possess the role of Edwin Drood in this drama. Your friend Forster thinks because he authorised our production, he may oversee me, too! Tell me, where is Stephens?'

'Who?'

'Our playwright! Walter Stephens! Did you not say you were his publisher, hardly a minute ago? Have you forgotten, is your mind even as dull as that? Or are you an impostor, a dealer seeking my autographs to sell?'

Osgood explained that he was the publisher of the late Charles Dickens rather than of the writer adapting the novel for the stage. Grunwald calmed himself again.

'All of Dickens's fame.' Grunwald lamented this into the mirror. On close examination, the actor was ten years too old to play Drood, though his skin had an ageing artist's artificial glow of youth and romance to it. 'So much fame, and it goes for nothing since he had not the most important thing.'

'What's that?' Osgood asked.

'To be happy in your children. Now, have you brought another wishful actress to us? I'm afraid she won't do. Next!'

'Beg your pardon,' said Osgood, 'this is my bookkeeper, Miss Rebecca Sand.' Rebecca stepped forward and curtsied to the actor.

'Good thing. You would not get many roles, my dear, by walking around in all black as if you were in mourning, not without a more buxom upper form.'

'Thank you for the advice,' said Rebecca sharply, 'but I *am* in mourning.'

'Grunwald, there you are,' said Walter Stephens, coming over from behind the stage in long strides. 'I'm sorry, I do not think I've been acquainted with your friends,' he said indicating Osgood.

'Not my friend, Stephens. He was your publisher, until a moment ago.'

Stephens confusedly looked Osgood up and down, just as Grunwald was called to the stage to perform a scene. It was one in which he (as Edwin Drood) and Rosa, the beautiful young woman to whom he was betrothed, amicably discuss secretly abandoning their unwanted union. Jasper, the opium fiend who loves Rosa, meanwhile stands plotting on the other side of the stage the removal of his nephew Drood.

Osgood introduced himself to Stephens the playwright, who took the publisher's arm and led him towards the stage. Rebecca followed, staring excitedly at the complex machinery behind the scenes of the theatre.

'What brings the two of you to England?' Stephens asked.

'Actually, the same *Mystery of Edwin Drood* that has consumed your own attentions of late, Mr. Stephens.'

'We were quite robbed of its progress by the death of Mr. Dickens.'

'Then, I hope I may take the liberty of asking, how shall you convert it into a complete drama, without the ending?'

Stephens smiled. 'You see, I have written an ending myself, Mr. Osgood! Yes, the life of the drama writer is not as luxurious as that of the novelists you publish. We must work with what is before us with great respect, but never so much respect that we fail to fulfil our task of pleasing an audience. When we read, we use our brains, but when we watch a performance, we use our eyes – much more trivial organs.

'Now, I fear I must attend to many matters at the moment. Shall you and your companion do us the honour of being our guests in our nicest box?' asked Stephens.

Osgood and Rebecca sat in on the day's rehearsal. They were of course particularly interested to see Stephens's original ending for the story. Dickens, in his final instalments, had introduced the mysterious Dick Datchery, a visitor to the fictional village of Cloisterham, who acts as investigator in the case of the young Drood's disappearance after others have pointed an accusing finger at Neville Landless, Edwin Drood's rival. Datchery has other suspicions. But in Stephens's rendition, Datchery – with his flowing white hair covering his face – was revealed to be the feisty young Neville himself in disguise. Neville was to use his disguise as Datchery to confront John Jasper, Drood's uncle, with evidence that would cause the guilt-ridden Jasper to take his own life with an overdose of opium.

Osgood and Rebecca prepared to leave during the fourth attempt at staging this scene when Grunwald interrupted the other players.

'Where is Stephens? Ah, Stephens, what is this? What of the revised version of this act?'

'This *is* the revised version, Grunwald. Now, if you'd please remember you are too dead and your body incinerated by this point in the story to have such a corporeal presence on stage.'

Grunwald threw his manuscript pages into the air. 'The hell with it! Hang the whole lot of you and dash your brains out! Perhaps you ought to find a different damned Edwin Drood!'

Stephens screamed back. 'There are ladies present, sir, and Americans, who should not appreciate the vulgarity of your tongue!'

'Vulgar?' This Grunwald asked before he flew at Stephens with his fists up. Stephens pulled the actor's thick hair.

The manager ushered off the playwright and actor and instructed them to finish murdering each other away from the stage.

Osgood noticed two workmen walking towards the stairs to smoke. 'I see Mr. Grunwald and Mr. Stephens were having words,' Osgood said to them.

'Aye, gov'n'r?'

'Do you know the meaning of it?' asked the publisher.

One of the workmen laughed at the foolishness of the question. 'We should. They have the same ticklish row every day. Art Grunwald thinks it as clear as the blue sky above that Charles Dickens meant Edwin Drood to *survive* and come back at the end of the story to seek revenge on the man what tried to kill him. Mister Stephens thinks it most obvious Drood is dead and rotting in the quicklime.'

'What do *you* think?' asked Osgood.

'*I* think Grunwald thinks he's too good an actor to stay out of sight in the scene docks for the final act. I wish Dickens didn't die, I vow it deeply 'fore God – then we wouldn't have to hear their bickering.'

XVIII

SGOOD WAS PACING BACK AND forth in the parlour at the Falstaff. Rebecca had just moments before read him a note from one of the queen's ministers informing them that Her Majesty had not pursued Dickens's offer to tell her the ending of *Drood*, thinking it more proper for her to be as surprised as her subjects by the instalments.

'I half wish I could believe in the medium who keeps company with Dickens's ghost,' Osgood remarked.

'Perhaps Mr. Dickens himself may have believed,' Rebecca replied with a smile. 'It seems he was taken with spiritualism. I wonder if we ought not study it for ourselves.'

'Surely you don't think highly of such practices, Miss Sand?'

'We might find a window into his private mind when writing the novel.'

Osgood sat in a chair and rested his head in his hands. 'If a medium can inform us right now how to make a quarter of a million dollars in a quarter of a year, I shall become the most enthusiastic of her devotees. We cannot afford to waste any more time.'

'You are a born sceptic,' Rebecca said, dropping the topic but clearly hurt that Osgood dismissed her suggestion so quickly.

'I should think so. I have no fondness for phenomena, Miss Sand. I very much dislike the trouble of wondering. Forget the mesmerism, but think of the mesmerism patient. Do you remember what Henry Scott said about him?' he asked.

'Yes,' answered Rebecca. 'That he was a farmer who sought Dickens's help.'

'Scott said that the man was a regular visitor to Gadshill during the last months of Dickens's life to receive those "spiritual" sessions. If this poor fellow was such a frequent visitor to Dickens's study,' Osgood continued, 'might he have heard clues as to the novelist's plan for the end of the book?'

'Mr. Osgood, you'd be placing credence in the words of a man with a shattered constitution,' Rebecca pointed out. 'You saw how he behaved at the chalet.'

'I feel the paths before us narrowing, Miss Sand. With Forster having authorised the theatre production of *The Mystery of Edwin Drood*, it is in the interest of his reputation and his purse that if there are other clues waiting to be discovered, they be revealed only if they happened to match the ending written by Walter Stephens. Likewise, even if Wilkie Collins has no intention of finishing his friend's last novel, that rumour may give some member of the Dickens family the idea of finding someone else for the task. With every last floorboard and ornament from Gadshill to be auctioned any day, the family is eager for income. We are without any allies here in our search, Miss Sand.'

'But if you find the patient, how will you convince him to speak sensibly?'

'What is it Henry Scott said? A mad beast needs a sober driver.'

Rebecca enquired with Henry Scott at Gadshill, who questioned the other servants and determined that the mesmerism patient had not been there since their encounter with him in the chalet. There were bets among the staff on whether the fellow had given up or died. But Rebecca suggested that if the patient had been at Westminster Abbey the day that she and Osgood visited, it might be one of his regular stops.

Osgood, agreeing, returned to Poets' Corner. When he visited Dickens's grave again, he found the same peculiar purple flower. From then on, Osgood went to the Abbey at intervals waiting for this other man to show. 'It is only a matter of time, I'm certain,' he'd say to Rebecca.

On one visit in particular, Osgood and Rebecca passed through the gates together at the same time as Mamie Dickens, holding her little dog in her bag and linked to another young woman on her arm. Mamie wiped away her tears and smiled sweetly at the sight of Osgood and Rebecca.

The woman on Mamie's arm was small and perky, having a strong resemblance to Charles Dickens around her face. She wore an old-fashioned muslin kerchief on her head from which red ringlets dropped, decorated with distinctly non-mourning double hollyhocks. Her lace cape only barely kept her little shoulders concealed and her neck and throat were almost entirely exposed.

She was presented to Osgood and Rebecca as Katie Collins, the younger of the two Dickens girls.

'Oh, be proper, Katie!' Mamie scolded her sister, pulling her sister's cape over her shoulders. 'In a church, too!'

'Proper! Now you sound like old Beadle Forster. Sometimes I wonder whether I got married to make dear father happy when our household had little other than sadness. Or did I marry because I knew father and his Beadle despised my husband?'

'Katie Collins!'

'Intolerable and stuff!' Katie imitated Forster's voice and then rubbed her hands together like he would.

'Tell me,' Osgood said. 'Do you know who the man was who had come to him at Gadshill for treatment in the last few months, a tall man with a military air and long white hair?'

Mamie nodded. 'I think I have seen the man you mean at the house. He was a very persistent and dedicated follower of father's methods. Even when father was delayed for their appointments, he would sit outside the study for hours.'

'Do you know his name?' Osgood asked.

'I am afraid I don't,' Mamie said, with a sigh. 'Father was a mesmerism fanatic of no mean order and believed it a remedy for any illness. I know of many cases, my own among the number, in which he used his power in this way with perfect success. He was always interested in the curious influence exercised by one person-ality over another.'

'Now, Sir Osgood,' Katie, bored with the exchange, examined the publisher flirtatiously. 'Where were *you* when a girl was to find a husband?'

Rebecca seemed as embarrassed at the question as Osgood. Katie raised an eyebrow to show she had noticed this.

'Miss Sand,' sharp-tongued Katie said, 'do you not think Mamie should look just smashing in a bridal gown on the arm of a man like this?'

'I suppose so, ma'am,' Rebecca replied demurely.

'You are the sort of girl who thinks well of weddings, Miss Sand?' Katie pressed.

'I don't think much of weddings at all,' Rebecca replied.

Mamie interrupted the awkward moment. 'Mr. Osgood and Miss Sand have come all the way here for business, Katie, and to find out more about *The Mystery of Edwin Drood.*'

'What a bore business is,' said Katie, snapping her fingers. 'Oh, very well. Do you really want to find your way through the tangled maze and arrive at the heart of the mystery? If you want to know about *Drood*'s ending, simply buy me a new ribbon for my hair! We are auctioning all mine.'

'Oh, don't always tease everyone, Katie!' Mamie cried.

'I'll tell them then,' Katie said while coyly wrapping one of her red ringlets around her finger. 'Drood will be dead or alive; Rosa will marry Tartar or become a nun; Dick Datchery will find Drood's body or find Drood playing cribbage in a cellar with Rosa's guardian Grewgious. I don't know the first thing about it! And that is the answer to the riddle.'

'What do you mean?' Osgood asked.

'The old Beadle, faithful little Aunt Georgy, my wayward brothers, none of those dear creatures know how it was to end because Father *didn't wish* them to know – he didn't wish *anyone* in the universe to know except himself, Mr. Osgood. It was a game for him, you see. He always loved to surprise us and was completely thorough when he had set his mind on it.'

Back at the Falstaff Inn that same evening, 'Sir Falstaff' brought tea to Osgood as he sat contemplatively by the fireplace downstairs. Rebecca had retired to her room to read. Sir Falstaff's mind seemed to wander and the tray slipped, shattering the pot and cup.

'I apologise, Mr. Osgood,' the landlord said after the shards had been swept away and the spilled tea mopped by his sister. He seemed saddened by something other than the broken porcelain.

Osgood followed the landlord's gaze and found its focal point. It was one of the leafy purple flowers left at the Abbey: Osgood had taken it with the intention of asking one of the street vendors that sold plants to identify it for him.

'This is an ugly thing, isn't it, Sir Falstaff? I'm sorry for gracing your table with such a shockingly nasty weed,' he said. 'Are you unwell? Shall I fetch some ice water?'

The trembling man waved him away. 'Mr. Osgood, did you not know? That . . . that is an opium poppy! It feels like I have been struck in the heart by a bludgeon.'

'I did not know!' Osgood said apologetically, though he still could not comprehend the proprietor's reaction.

The landlord gazed with a doomed expression into the small fire, and removed his cap and folded it over his lap. 'You couldn't have known, Mr. Osgood. Many years ago, I learned to hate that vile plant. My son had only twenty summers to his name *and* his faculties of judgement, and it was to the evil seduction of that plant that we buried him. The house was so empty without him. That is why, after he was gone, I moved here with my sister from our home in town to manage this snug little inn: to give other people pleasure when you have lost all of your own is a small miracle.'

Osgood crumpled the flower into the pocket of his vest as casually as possible. Poor Sir Falstaff did not move at all, his expressionless face hanging low.

'But what's this? Enough of that solemn manner.' The landlord suddenly rose from his chair, putting his hat and cheer back on. 'Yes, enough of that, how about some ale to pluck us up?'

The next day, Osgood again took the noisy train to Charing Cross. Osgood planned to attend the auction at which the belongings from the Gadshill estate were to be sold to benefit the Dickens family.

He had left himself enough time to reach the auction house on King Street well before the announced start at 'one o'clock precisely'. Besides, thought Osgood, it was the day of the annual Eton and Harrow cricket match, which would clog the streets. His sense of frustration had seemed to mount by the hour. He had less and less faith that the mesmerism patient would show himself again, but the opium poppy had made him think of the Oriental statue of the opium smoker from Dickens's summer study. Was that what Dickens had gazed upon when writing the scenes of opium smoking in *The Mystery of Edwin Drood*? Was that object the source of his ideas? If so, Osgood wanted another chance to examine it carefully.

The large auction room at Christie, Manson & Woods was a historic institution in London, and dusty and grimy enough to prove it. To Osgood's surprise, the hot room was overfilled by noon. Nor was it only the usual lofty collectors, mercenary dealers and commission agents: shoulder to shoulder with men and women of society in fine summer linen, the room contained multitudes of people in the plainer garb of the working classes. Looking around, it seemed every character from every Dickens novel, aristocrat and common, pompous and inconspicuous, had come to life and come straight to Christie's with their purses open.

Osgood saw that he could not swim upstream through the eager crowd to either of the green cloth-covered tables closest to the auctioneer. Instead, he found a vacant chair near the auction clerk's table.

Osgood circled two items in his catalogue. His neighbours in the chairs around him peered at each other jealously, certain each was there exclusively for whatever object among Dickens's personal effects they had already set their heart on. Osgood's eyes also met those of Arthur Grunwald, the actor from the Surrey, who nodded to him dramatically as though one of them were to die today or at least tomorrow. He wore a wide scarf even though it was hot and sticky.

One of the first items brought between the two tables was the picture of the *Britannia* from Gadshill.

'Depicting the vessel in which Mr. Dickens first went to America. Engraved in the popular edition of *American Notes . . .*' intoned Mr. Woods, the auctioneer, from his rostrum.

Competition was fierce. 'Eighty guineas!' 'Ninety!' 'Ninety-five guineas!' 'One hundred guineas, one hundred and five!' 'Going, going . . . *gone!*'

Mr. Woods's hammer came down. The first few dozen lots were portraits and paintings priced out of the range of the amateur bidder. Then Mr. Woods announced they would move to the 'decorative objects late the property of the gentleman deceased'. In this class of object, the general Dickens fanatic could be far more competitive. Mr. Woods's well-bred face, in fact, seemed to betray his utter amazement at how high the numbers could go for worthless tidbits that simply had been touched by one man's fingers. Elaborately dressed women lifted their opera glasses and leaned side to side for better views.

The assistant displayed a gong with a beater that Dickens had used to gather his family together at Gadshill.

As a battle ensued up to thirty guineas, Osgood's neighbour behind him whispered squeakily, 'He was always fond of gongs.' Osgood, not certain how to respond, smiled politely. 'Oh, yes,' the squeaky man continued insistently, a handkerchief pressed to his right cheek, responding to an objection Osgood had not made. 'Don't you remember the weak-eyed young man and the gong at Dr. Blimber's in *Dombey and Son*?'

By this point, Grunwald had secured a pair of watercolours depicting Little Nell's house and grave from *The Old Curiosity Shop*. As the actor stood to go, he stopped at Osgood's row. He was followed step for step by the same young woman that was fixing his cravat at the Surrey.

'There you are, Osgood, sitting with your hands in your pockets,' he said, shaking out his black mane. 'Did you see what happened?'

'Yes, congratulations on your purchase, Mr. Grunwald.'

'Not a purchase. A victory. I knocked these down from the hands of those mischievous dealers through fortitude and decisiveness. I did not depict Hamlet at the Princess without learning something of courage. People have misunderstood Hamlet for centuries, you know – it is not he who is indecisive; he has perfectly fine resolve: it is the critics that cannot make up their mind about him! Good afternoon, Mr. Osgood.'

Before leaving the room, Grunwald passed a look over the entire auction house as though he had outsmarted not just a few dealers but every person there.

At last: 'Lot seventy-nine, a tazza, pink, with ormolu foot, formerly upon Gadshill's drawing room mantel.'

Osgood entered the fray, crossing over the actual value of three pounds and elevating each dealer and admirer's number until reaching seven pounds fifteen. That price won the day.

He received his ticket from the clerk, who wrote down the sale price. The publisher proceeded down the aisle into the next room where, in return for his payment, he was handed the pretty glass bowl pulled from a box of other household items. Returning to his seat, Osgood found the sale at its highest pitch of excitement yet.

Grip! Grip! Grip! was called out from all sides. Front and centre was a glass case holding a stuffed raven called Grip that had been Dickens's favourite pet and the prototype for a talkative bird of the same name in his novel, *Barnaby Rudge*. The cacophony of spirited voices quoted their favourite Grip sayings from that novel. The bidding was ferocious, and the hammer did not fall before 120 pounds were pledged.

A wild round of applause followed, and 'Name!' was called out for as a way of honouring the purchaser. 'Mr. George Nottage, of Cheapside!' the man complied heartily.

'What's the matter?' Osgood asked his confidant when the audience began to moan and hiss.

'Nottage,' his neighbour replied, 'he's the owner of the Stereo-scopic Company. Why, he'll simply use the bird to make stereoscopic photographs to sell for profit!'

Osgood realised what an oddity it was: at an auction house, a crowd of moralists who in the name of Charles Dickens sneered at profit. After a few more sets of lots, they had finally come to the next item circled in his catalogue: the plaster statue of a Turk seated smoking opium. The grotesque he had seen in the Swiss chalet at Gadshill by Dickens's writing desk that could hold clues they'd be able to use. But the auctioneer skipped to the subsequent items. As Woods described them, Osgood stood up and raised his hand.

'I beg your pardon, Mr. Woods, but I believe you have forgotten lot eighty-five. The Turk –'

'Lot eighty-six . . .'

'But, respectfully, sir,' Osgood continued, 'eighty-five is supposed . . .'

Osgood's sweaty neighbour was pulling at his sleeve, his squeaky voice more high-pitched than ever. 'If you don't be quiet . . .'

Down smashed the hammer. 'Eighty-*six*!' Woods pronounced with divine authority, as though the number eighty-five had been gener-ally eliminated from genteel arithmetic, '*Night* and *Morning*, a pair of reliefs after Thorwaldsen in gilt frames!'

Osgood sat back down defeated. The gatherers had begun to mutter inquisitively about the skipped lot but were soon placated by watching an entertaining squabble between two dealers over the framed reliefs. Osgood regretfully prepared to leave with the tazza in hand.

There was a stocky man with hands deep in his pockets inching his way through the mob of people. He was looking down at his feet, but at intervals, Osgood noticed, he would look directly at the publisher. It must have been Osgood's imagination, fuelled by his displeasure at the auctioneer's omission. But then Osgood turned to look over his other shoulder. The exit was blocked by a larger, scowling man with a face like a whetstone, gazing right at Osgood. He began to move closer.

For a few more seconds, Osgood kept dismissing the idea that these two men were as threatening as they appeared. Telling himself to be rational, he decided to perform a test. As he rose to his feet slowly, they both paused, looked at one another, then resumed their paths towards him more aggressively, like two ends of a vice. The stocky onlooker was no longer hiding his gaze. Meanwhile, Osgood was penned in everywhere else by the immense population of Dickensites packed in the room.

Then a hand was on Osgood's shoulder.

'Beg pardon,' Osgood said in firm protest. 'Is there something wrong, sir?'

'We'd like to take you upstairs,' the stocky man replied.

'Who are you?' asked Osgood. 'I insist on knowing what you gentlemen want before I go with you.'

Giving no reply, the man pulled Osgood up by the arm and began to drag him towards the exit behind the auctioneer.

Osgood threw his hand up.

'Do you bid, sir?' Woods asked Osgood, clearing his throat nervously.

The auctioneer's assistant was holding up a sad little salt cellar that had thus far attracted little notice. 'Ten shillings value, sir,' Woods said.

'What bid are we at?' Osgood asked loudly.

'Nine shillings, sir.'

'Ten guineas,' Osgood said, then raised his own bid: 'Ten and a half!'

The crowd gasped at the remarkable amount for the salt dish. This suggested that the rest of the crowd had overlooked its worth and other bids bounced around the auction hall, until Osgood finished it at eighteen and a half guineas. The spectators exploded into cheers to commemorate the extravagant purchase. Osgood threw his hat into the air. This sent the audience into paroxysms of excitement and everyone around the room stood and applauded. In the meantime, he used the attention and the confusion to slide from the man's grasp.

But the man was behind him in a flash and the crowd was still too thick to get around.

In a remarkable deliverance, before he knew what had happened, Osgood was hoisted on two men's shoulders. Jumping down, he nearly tumbled right over the head of the other pursuer while desperately clutching his newly purchased glass tazza. Osgood balanced the tazza safely under his arm and ran, escaping the crowd only to lose his balance, tripping as he crossed over the threshold into the anteroom. The tazza went flying.

'No!' Osgood cried, caught in the helpless moment of waiting for it to shatter.

A man stepped out of the shadows and caught the tazza before it could hit the floor.

Osgood exhaled in relief. The tazza had survived. The man who looked up from underneath his wide-brimmed hat had intelligent, dashing eyes. A floppy purple flower leaned out from his buttonhole.

'They're still behind you!' he said. 'Follow me.'

XIX

HIS RESCUER LED OSGOOD THROUGH a back corridor of Christie's into a basement and out the street door. The two men came out into a small lane that led them into the cover of the boisterous London crowds.

'Whatever did you do to make them so keenly interested in you?' asked the man, after they looked around and decided they had not been followed.

'I honestly don't know,' Osgood answered. 'I enquired to the auctioneer about that item they had left out – item eighty-five. It's here in the catalogue. I had noticed it at Gadshill that day you were there – I even saw it being wrapped up by the auction workers the next day.' Osgood handed him the catalogue.

The man nodded as they walked across the busy square of brick and mortar buildings. Every passerby in London, even the poorest newsboy, had a flower in his coat, though no one else boasted an opium poppy. 'If you saw this plaster statue taken out of the house, and it was printed in the catalogue, we know it made it to the auction rooms. Why would they skip over it, then? There is only one strong likelihood to suspect. That it was stolen from Christie's rooms after the catalogue was printed but without enough time to correct it – shortly *before* the one o'clock auction, then. That explains why they were after you.'

'Do you mean they thought *I* was the one who stole the statue?' Osgood exclaimed.

'Unlikely enough! But you were calling attention to the fact it was missing. Think of it through their eyes. If a theft from Christie's auction house were to be reported in the papers, all the finest dealers in London would hear of it. They'd note, too, that it occurred from a prize sale like Dickens's. How many customers would be lost to rival auction houses?'

Osgood thought it over. He recalled that Mr. Wakefield from the *Samaria* had mentioned using Christie's for his tea business and decided he would write to Wakefield asking him to enquire into what had happened to the statue. For now, Osgood studied the steady gait and bearing of the man who had acted so unaccountably strange in the chalet at Gadshill.

'I have wanted to speak to you, sir,' Osgood said cautiously.

'I know it,' said his walking companion without breaking stride.

'You do?'

'You have looked for me at the Abbey.'

'You saw us going back there then? You have been following us!' Osgood exclaimed.

'No, that is without making the least investigation. There is much to know by simply opening the eyes, though, my friend.'

'How then?' Osgood asked, genuinely curious but also as a test of the man's sanity.

'First, I saw you keenly interested in my flower when we were both at Poets' Corner together.'

'The opium poppy.'

He nodded. 'Then, on another day, I had seen that one of my flowers had been removed. I surmised it was likely the same person who observed it attentively on the first occasion: you.'

'I suppose that makes some sense.'

'Have you received any responses about me from your letters to the mesmerism experts?'

'What?' Osgood's jaw dropped. 'But I left my bookkeeper at the inn writing those letters of enquiry as we speak! I instructed her to do this only this morning, thinking that without Mr. Dickens you may have sought those services elsewhere. How did you possibly know about that?'

'Oh, I didn't! I merely surmised it as well, which is a rather more convenient way of obtaining information than actually knowing it.'

Osgood was impressed. 'Have you seen another mesmerist?'

'Mr. Dickens cured me quite thoroughly, I have no need.'

'Sir, I owe you my thanks today for what transpired at the auction house. My name is James Ripley Osgood.'

The man turned towards the publisher with a military air. His lank white hair was combed with perfect care this time, although his clothes were dishevelled and loose. His sun-scarred features were handsome, large and chiselled. It did not surprise Osgood that Dickens would have accepted the farmer into his home – his pride in helping the working poor had been almost as strong as his pride in his writing, for he remembered his own humble childhood.

'I fancy you are ready, Ripley,' the man said with an enigmatic, crooked toothed smile upon adopting an immediate nickname for the publisher.

'You said the same thing at the chalet. But ready for what?'

'Why, to find the truth about Edwin Drood.'

Osgood took care not to show excitement or even surprise at the startling pronouncement. 'May I take the liberty of having your name, sir?' Osgood replied.

'I apologise – I was in one of my unnatural spells when you saw me at Gadshill and not acting right. I did not present myself. What you must think!' He shook his head in self-recrimination. 'My name is Dick Datchery. Now that you know who I am, we may talk openly.'

XX

EBECCA HAD RECEIVED WORD FROM a messenger with a note to wait for Osgood in the coffee room of the Falstaff. When he arrived, she sat patiently as he hung his hat and his light coat on the peg and put his satchel and a paper-wrapped package carefully on the table. He looked to be in a state of quiet excitement and anticipation. He poured out the whole story of the auction, his escape, and what had been revealed by his meeting with the mesmerism patient.

'Then he *is* a madman,' Rebecca declared, throwing up her hands. 'I suppose that decides it. He'll be no help in remembering anything he heard from Mr. Dickens.'

Osgood made a noncommittal gesture.

'Mr. Osgood,' she pursued, 'is it not the case – did you not just explain to me for a quarter hour that this poor farmer believes himself Dick Datchery, a character from an unfinished novel?'

Osgood crossed his arms over his chest. 'What would the novel's state of completion matter in terms of his sanity, Miss Sand?'

Rebecca looked at her employer with a decidedly practical air, but her usually even voice wavered with emotion. 'It would be somewhat more reasonable to believe oneself a character in a book that is finished. At least, one would know if one's fate is dire or grand.'

Osgood smiled at her chagrin. 'Miss Sand, I admit your scepticism is well founded, of course. This man calling himself Datchery has suffered a type of mental strain, as we saw with our own eyes at Gadshill. He does not seem to remember anything about a time before he began the sessions, or where he came from. But what if – just think of this – what if the mesmerism sessions performed by Dickens had some unintended effect on an already-shattered constitution, one that could prove to be to our benefit? What if in the process of mesmerism, Dickens transferred, by some profound exposure, the skills of investigation displayed by the fictional character of Datchery on to this man. The man even spoke like Dick Datchery! Look at these.'

Rebecca watched dubiously as Osgood removed from his satchel some books he said he had purchased in Paternoster Row on his way back to the hotel. Each tome examined an element of spiritualism or mesmerism. 'These books speak of the fluid of life passing through us. The ability to chase away pain and repair nerves through magnetic forces—'

Rebecca, incredulous at hearing this terminology from her employer, put the cup she had just raised to her lips down with a bang.

'What's wrong, Miss Sand?'

'Some of these are the same titles from Gadshill's library.'

'Yes, they are!'

'Mr. Osgood, you didn't wish me to examine those books at the Gadshill library. You said then that you do not believe one whit in phenomena.'

'Nor have I changed my mind. But Mamie Dickens and her sister Katie confirmed at the Abbey how much Charles Dickens believed in it. Mamie even testified that the mesmerism worked on her. If Dickens, intentionally or accidentally, exposed this man to more information about the novel, even if he doesn't consciously know it, this may be our chance – the best chance to quit England with more knowledge than when we entered it. This man's mind – however disordered – may carry inside it the last strands of *The Mystery of Edwin Drood*.'

'What do you propose?'

'To treat him as Datchery. Let him continue the investigation. He wishes to meet tonight at the Abbey. He promises to take me to a secret location he says will provide the answers we seek.'

Rebecca's eyes narrowed on the package at the table.

'Have a look,' Osgood said proudly. 'This is what I purchased at the auction, before I was chased out for asking about the statue.'

She unwrapped the edge of the paper. 'The glass tazza from the mantelpiece at Gadshill!'

'I wanted Miss Dickens to have it back. I thought it would be a small token of our gratitude to the family.'

Rebecca's heart beat at the kindness of the gesture, but her feelings were conflicted and her mouth felt dry. 'That is,' she swallowed, 'very gentlemanly of you.'

'Thank you, Miss Sand. I must prepare for my outing. This sort of suit would be a phenomenon where we must go tonight, says Datchery,' he cited his new acquaintance approvingly. 'I'm afraid I didn't bring anything quite appropriate. But you've been shaking your head so much your bonnet strings are coming loose.'

'Have I?' she returned innocently. 'It is only the idea of not knowing where it is you will be going. With a man of an unstable, and potentially shattered mental state, as guide, in a city unfamiliar to you. Consider!'

Osgood nodded. 'I thought of consulting with Scotland Yard to secure a police escort, yet it would likely drive away the very man who can guide me. I am a publisher, Miss Sand. I know what it means. It means I must find a way, very often, to believe in people who believe in something else – something I often may not be inclined towards in the least. A story, a philosophy – a reality different from one I have known or will ever know.'

As Osgood readied himself for his expedition, Rebecca sat and stared into the leaves of her tea as though they, too, were endowed with the spiritual or prophetic attributes her employer seemed to want to find in his new acquaintance. She could not help somehow feeling stranded by the decision and how he had come to it.

Osgood returned in a suit only a little less formal. 'I am afraid I shall still stand out,' he said, smiling. 'We have a letter from Fields today, by the way,' Osgood went on, branching away from the topic with a comfortable businesslike tone. He put a troubled hand at the back of his neck. 'Houghton and his man Mifflin, they are like two halves of a scissor, you know. They have formed a journal to compete with our juvenile magazine and are pouring money into it. And the Major announces the Harper brothers will open an office in Boston, no doubt in order to try to drive us into deeper trouble! Harper is not wrong. I cannot shield myself from business realities, not if I want to continue what Mr. Fields has built. And to show that I can be a publisher of the same calibre, that I can find the next Dickens. Miss Sand, I must try everything I can think of.'

'You must,' she said.

'Yet you disagree,' Osgood said. Seeing her hesitate, he said, 'Please, speak freely to me about this, Miss Sand.'

'Why did you ask me to come to Chapman & Hall with you the other day, Mr. Osgood?'

He pretended not to understand. 'I thought we might need to copy documents – if he had given us any to see. What does that have to do with this?'

'Pardon my saying, but it seemed to me like I was present there only to be, well, womanly.'

Osgood looked like he wanted to move on, but Rebecca's strong gaze would not let the topic go away. 'It was true,' he answered finally, 'that I had noticed on my previous visit to their firm that there were no female employees there and thought Mr. Chapman just the type of strutting man to speak more easily in front of a pretty woman. You did say you wanted to help by coming to England.'

The colour in Rebecca's cheeks flushed carelessly by his untimely compliment. 'Not by being pretty.'

'You're right, I shouldn't have done that with Chapman, not without explaining myself to you, at least. Still, I must notice that you are upset all out of proportion about this.'

'Perhaps I am not as talented as Mrs. Collins at speaking bluntly, making suggestions of marriage upon first meetings,' Rebecca said, standing with hands on her hips.

'Miss Sand . . .' Osgood said, nervously flustered in a way that upset her even more. 'This whole conversation is unfathomable to me.'

Rebecca knew that signalled the end of the exchange and that she should not speak to her employer any further in this manner. But her gaze kept shifting to the glass tazza, her distorted reflection urging her on like an inner demon.

'I can see why Mamie would be far more persuasive than I can be,' she added. 'She should be a good match for any man. She is a Dickens.'

'Miss Sand!' Osgood exhaled impatiently. 'I've brought you here to help me, and to help you after Daniel's death. Perhaps this whole idea of your accompanying me was a mistake. To think I had designs on Mamie Dickens because of who she is – I'm not looking for a Dickens!' It seemed like there was another sentence waiting on his tongue but he swallowed it down.

Osgood, consulting his watch, exited and his footsteps could be heard rushing down the stairs of the inn. Rebecca stood there scared. Scared of what had just passed between them, scared of what their failure might mean for her future in Boston, scared of what could befall Osgood in the dark corners of London.

XXI

BENGAL, INDIA, JULY 1870

HE OPIUM *DACOIT* HAD BEEN captured. Now he had to be interrogated for more information relating to the crime – including the whereabouts of the stolen opium. Outside the room where this was to take place, Mason and Turner, of the Bengal Mounted Police, tried to be patient.

'I'm surprised he'd be found holed near his family village,' Mason said. 'An obvious place for an escaped thief to hide!'

Turner sneered. 'Not obvious enough, was it, Mason? We wasted a whole afternoon encamped in the mountains waiting for him, while Dickens tripped over him like a lucky fool.'

'Do you think the inspector from the Special Police will have some luck in there? Turner?'

'A lucky fool. That's Frank Dickens!'

'Are you innocent of that opium *dacoity*?'

The thief nodded.

'I understand that is what you have been explaining to our mounted officers,' said the special inspector. 'Yet you are a registered *dacoit*. Lie down there, my son.'

The thief lay on the *chabutra*, the inspector offering a gentle hand to position him so that his feet were on the higher edge of the platform, his head the lower. He trembled in fear at what he knew was coming.

'The *budna*, please,' the inspector said to his assistant. Then he frowned at the prisoner as if apologising for some minor personal rudeness.

★ ★ ★

'I hear he's mute as an Egyptian Sphinx.'

'Don't mumble,' Turner grunted in response, then added: 'He's no mute.'

'He's barely said a word since he was arrested,' Mason pointed out. 'That's what I meant. Even when they flogged him something awful. You think he'd dare to, after seeing how we captured his friend, with your carbine and my sword? 'Course he had to jump through the train window – lost his head, that one.'

Turner grunted.

'Dickens says.'

'What?'

'Superintendent Dickens says the thief's scared. That he's hiding more than the theft.'

'Dickens doesn't – that damned stuttering scamp!' Turner replied. 'He's the one who called in the inspector. I could have done the duty just fine – give me a whip and a rod on any dark-skinned heathen where you will, don't need no Special Police at all.' Turner pushed his chair away and paced down the hall.

'Turner? Where are you going? We're still to collect the prisoner when the inspector's finished.'

The inspector held the *budna*, a copper vessel with an elongated spout, over the prisoner. He slowly poured water on to the upper lip of his subject. The water ran down the small cracks of his lips and collected in pools around his nostrils sending the man into spasms of drowning.

Mason stood from his chair, trembling. 'You hear him shouting, Turner? It chills your blood.'

Turner wheeled back around and looked into the small square window on the door where the screams emerged – suddenly, he looked frightened. 'What do you think he'll say, Mason?'

The thief's eyes filled with tears and looked as if they might burst.

'Sit up now,' said the still-smiling inspector, handing the copper vessel to his assistant.

It took a few minutes for the thief to find his breath again. 'Take me to the baboo! Please!' he said as soon as he could form the words. 'I shall confess all, your honour, and tell of my other thefts, but no more, for God's sake! Take me to him!'

'At once, my son.' Gently the inspector helped the prisoner to his feet. 'And will you tell us where you've hidden the opium?' he added.

'Yes! Yes!' said the thief.

As the thief was interrogated, Frank Dickens was seeking different answers, answers he did not believe the thief could provide. For these, he needed to journey to the village where the thief's partner in the crime, the notorious Narain, had lived.

This was no pleasant journey. The natives held two sets of poles, front and back, of the palanquin, or *palki*, on their shoulders as they ran. Inside the *palki*, tossed inside a thin blanket, was the wearied traveller. Frank tried to sleep as the natives chanted to the Kali goddess for their strength. *When will they be rid of their gods and goddesses?* wondered Frank as he swayed inside the rickety structure. It was not the night heat nor the bearers' primitive singing that kept him from sleeping as the journey continued through the night but the foul odour of the slow flame of dirty rags and rotten oil that lighted the way for the *palki* at the front of the vessel.

A while later, they had stopped. Frank stirred, realising he had fallen asleep and wondered what he had been dreaming. In India, he never seemed to remember his dreams. It was morning and Superintendent Frank Dickens had reached the distant Bengalee village of his destination. There was no magistrate or native official to greet him, for he deliberately had not made his sojourn known in advance.

On the road towards a crumbling temple in the distance, the fertile fields teemed with the reddish purple opium poppy. The poppy replaced most of the food crops, and left the surrounding land dry and brittle.

Crossing the opium fields, his police uniform sparkling from its brass on this sunny morning, he saw the *ryots*, or peasant farmers, men, women, children. They were scraping residue from the opium poppies with an iron *sittooha* into an earthen pot. Later, the drug would be packed for shipment into balls by natives in long rows at

British-controlled warehouses. Frank felt a wave of nausea run through him as he passed the pungent poppies. A *ryot* looked up from his hoe and suddenly dropped it and ran. Dickens found the patch of land he'd been working and saw that the crop here was in fact rice. He frowned. The opium was mandated, the rice illegal.

The British government paid the *ryots* to grow the poppy instead of other crops, but they also ordered it, when they had to, by the point of bayonets.

This was one of the poorest villages, Dickens knew, fraught constantly with the threat of famine because of the loss of their natural agriculture. Three years earlier, during the Orissa famine, starvation spread quickly across villages like this. Parents, it was said among the policemen and English officials, had eaten their own children. The government did not want the opium cultivation to get a bad reputation with the moralists back home in England, and so the army delivered as much food as they could to the poorest villages. Still, more than five hundred thousand acres in Bengal at any time were dedicated to the opium poppy, and no amount of rations could make up for the loss of agriculture.

The adjacent river, once bustling with trade to and from Calcutta, trickled quietly now that the English had finished building the railroads for faster transport of opium and spices. Instead of the commerce of the past, men, women and children now bathed and played there. Elders prayed and chatted as the children splashed about. Everyone in the village went outside at this early hour because later it would be even hotter.

Asking for directions from a group of near-naked natives, Frank, stopping to wipe his brow and take water, reached a mud hut in a narrow lane. On the side of the house was a pile of dried plants, dead animals and rubbish. An even stronger odour attacked him from higher up. Stuck to the walls of the house, clumps of cow dung were being heated in the sun and dried for use as fuel. Under the veranda, a striking young woman, bareheaded and barefoot, was preparing food. She had not lit a fire – a sign she was in mourning. A naked toddler held on to both of her legs for balance. Flies were swarming around the woman, the child, the grain, the ghee.

'You are the widow Narain?' Frank Dickens asked, stepping forward.

She nodded.

'It was my officers, some weeks ago, in the Bagirhaut province, that had him in custody after he and some partners stole opium.'

'We are a very poor village, sir,' the widow remarked, without any shade of apology in her strong voice. 'He worked the fields until there were too many workers and no land left to work.'

The hut was surprisingly clean. Frank saw the articles of farming, a rough plough, a broken sickle, hanging from the roof, long in disuse. In the bedroom there was the bed, made of string and wood, and a single book on Hindoo gods in an indentation in the wall that had room for several more volumes. Using the bed as a sofa, Frank sat down and skimmed through the pages of the Hindoo book.

Returning to the widow, who was now nursing her child, he asked whether the book had belonged to her husband.

She nodded.

'He read often?'

'He was never without books.'

After receiving directions to the bookseller where she had sold other books, Frank walked across the village and found the stall at the quiet end of the busy bazaar.

'The widow Narain has sold you some of her husband's books, I believe. Tracts on Hindoo mythology and religion. Do you remember this?'

The bookseller lowered his spectacles at the Englishman. 'Indeed!'

'And you still have these in your stall?'

'I believe I do, good sir. But all the books are mixed together.'

'I will purchase all of the books on those subjects that you have.'

After his return journey in the wretched *palki*, that evening Frank met the inspector who had questioned the captured fugitive.

'Oh, yes, Superintendent, he has confessed it all to the magistrate of his village. Not as tolerant of physical discomfort as the Thuggees I used to interview in past years, these ordinary *dacoits*.'

'You believe he has told the truth?' asked Dickens.

'I do, yet . . .'

'What is it, Inspector?'

'Only that although he has told the truth, it seems to me there's more he's not saying, as though afraid, afraid in a different way than I can make him on the *chabutra*. The thief may have a secret he has yet kept from us. Your man Turner has been trying to find out what has happened all day. He is rather worked up over the affair.'

Dickens ignored this. 'The thief has told you where we will find the stolen opium?'

'I warned him not to play games. He's drawn a map.'

'Recovering the opium shall be our first order of business. Then I shall see to his secret and to Officer Turner's.'

XXII

LONDON, LATE AT NIGHT, 1870

———————◆◆———————

'DATCHERY' WAS AT THE ABBEY that night waiting. Madman or not, he could be trusted to be where he said he would, thought Osgood. Punctually mad. Datchery – for Osgood had no other name for the man than that preposterous one – took the publisher by the arm and they began to walk the damp streets. A sharp afternoon rain had driven people indoors. But as the two men gradually plunged deeper into the eastern districts of London there was more life; if the rest of London quieted when darkness fell, this place was just waking up. Contrasted with the frail, sputtering lamps of the streets, the public houses and dram shops provided blazing illumination through their windows. Bright signs advertised telegraph services to India to reach family or sailors; posters offered new watches and hats. Sailors were presented ways to spend every penny to their names before shipping off again.

It drizzled to a deviously slow rhythm as the two men continued on their journey. Murky liquid rushed through the gutter becoming something altogether different from water by the time the drain swallowed it. The men left wide streets for labyrinthine courts, lanes, byways and alleys. There was Bloody Bridge, below which the water looked more like mud, named for the number of people who would regularly choose that spot to scuttle themselves.

'Is this near where you live?' Osgood asked.

'No, no,' said Datchery. 'I live nowhere.'

'Come!' Osgood objected to the absurdity.

'I mean I'm as poor as Job's turkey, so I keep to rented rooms and lodging houses, mostly, so they will not find me.'

'So *who* will not find you, Mr. Datchery?' Osgood demanded,

but the topic was pushed aside by Datchery's impervious disposition and the vague and inhuman moans and cries circling
around them. Osgood tried a different question: 'How far will we
go?'

'When we are somewhere we should stop, we will,' said Datchery.
'Though I am the guide, it is not I who guides us.'

'Then who does?' Osgood asked, knowing there wouldn't be an
answer forthcoming, probably because none existed.

Sick men and women lay huddled in the corners. Agents from
the charity homes picked up wanderers, mostly women with infants,
some with three babies balanced in their arms. Osgood knew Dickens
had taken this sort of walk – expeditions to every lost corner of
London to observe and record its multitudes. Like the geologist,
Dickens had built his books by digging up every layer of life underneath the city.

There were times when Datchery's expression would flatten and
become dull – or when his eyes seemed clearer, sharper tools than
just a moment before.

They were inside the roughest part of London Osgood had ever
seen. In fact, the publisher's only comfort was in observing the fact
that none of the cursing crowds of humanity – who, by all appearances, would have spent their daylight hours either on ships or as
thieves – had approached them yet. Some offered sarcastic 'good
nights' from windows or open doorways. Then Osgood noticed that
his guide was carrying a large club. In fact, it was more complex than
a club. At the top, it had a spike and a hook coming out from the
side.

Datchery, noticing Osgood's interest, said, 'Without this, we'd be
stripped to our shirtsleeves by now, dear Ripley. Dearest Ripley! This
is Tiger Bay, and we are coming to Palmer's Folly!' The names themselves sounded like warnings.

There was a cul-de-sac at a narrow court, entered under a crumbling
archway, that ended at a three-storey building of blackened brick with
a black door and sightless windows. On either side of it stood a public
house and a thieves' lodging house. As the two men walked, each
step produced a brittle cracking. It took Osgood a few minutes to
realise their path was littered with the bones of animals and fish. In
front of the public house was a wretched column of people of both

sexes and all races, trying to push past each other for a better view of the steps.

The demonstration on the steps was being performed by a man called the Fire King. He offered, for the reward of small bills, to prove his power of resisting every species of heat. 'Supernatural powers!' he promised the crowd.

To the cheers and applause of his spellbound followers, Fire King swallowed as many spoonfuls of boiling oil as were matched by donations, and he immersed his hands in a pot of 'molten lava'. Next, the King entered the open doors to the public house and – for a steeper fee, gladly supplied by the philanthropically minded crowd – he inserted himself into the public house's oven along with a piece of meat and came out only when the meat (a raw steak he'd held up for the crowd) was finished.

The two pilgrims to this region did not remain outside long enough to see the grotesque human cooking experiment, however, for Datchery had walked up to the black door and knocked. A man stretched out on a crusty, ragged couch granted them admission into a corridor, after which they ascended a narrow stairs where every board groaned at their steps; perhaps out of disrepair, perhaps to warn the inhabitants above. The building smelled of mould and what? It was an odour that was heavy, drowsy. They made a wrong turn into a room where there sat a piano and a small audience before it; everyone turned to look at them and would not move a muscle until they were gone. Barmaids and ballet girls sat next to or on top of sailors and clerks. One man in the audience seemed to be balancing a dagger in his teeth.

Osgood could only imagine what demonstration would happen after they left, as he never heard any piano music while in the building.

They continued upwards through the smoke and mist. 'Here,' Datchery said with eerie finality. 'Take care, Mr. Osgood, every door in life can lead into an undiscovered kingdom or an inescapable trap.'

The door opened into darkness and smoke.

'No weapons!' This was the greeting, in a gravelly voice that seemed to belong to a woman.

Datchery put his club down in the hall outside the door.

Only after some slight, slow commotion was a candle lit. The small room showed itself crammed with people, most coiled together on a collapsed bed. Several were asleep and several more looked as though they could fall asleep at any moment. At the foot of the bed sat a gaunt, careworn woman with silver hair holding a long, thin piece of bamboo.

'Remember, pay up, dearies, won't ye?' she greeted the newcomers. 'Yahee from across the court is in quod for a month for begging. He don't mix well as me, anyhow!'

Over a small flame she was mixing together a black treacly substance. Sprawled on the bed was a Chinese man in a deep trance, and a Lascar sailor with an open shirt mumbling to himself – both with glossy, vacant eyes. Across the Lascar's mouth, drool escaped from between rotten teeth and ran down the craterlike sores on his lips. Rags and bedclothes hung from a string to dry in the smoke. The smoke! As the woman held out the bamboo pipe, Osgood recognised the reeking smell as opium.

Osgood thought about the narratives of Coleridge and De Quincey, both of whom, like almost everyone else including Osgood, had taken opiates from the pharmacist to quell rheumatism and other physical ailments. But the writers had indulged heavily enough to experience a swirl of ecstasy and fatigue that were opium's powerful effects on the brain. As De Quincey wrote in a series of published confessions, before it became the motto of thousands, 'Happiness might now be bought for a penny, and carried in the waistcoat pocket.' Osgood thought, too, about the accusation of the police against Daniel Sand that he had left so far away in Boston, that Daniel had given up everything for the thrill and ease of opiate entertainment.

'Sally's is better than Yahee's brand – you'll pay accordingly, won't ye, dearie?' the manager of the establishment repeated. 'Have a whiff. After payment, of course.'

As she recited her slogans, a petite young woman on the other side of Sally's grisly bed slid to the floor with a moan.

'Is she unwell?' asked Osgood. Sally explained that the young woman was in a peaceful dream state and would be better than if she were in the terrible, unclean groghouse where the girl's mother used to take her.

Then Osgood realised. He could suddenly name the feeling he had experienced upon entering the building. It was a word he would have never guessed. *Familiarity*.

Witnessing this squalor was like seeing photographs of scenes from *The Mystery of Edwin Drood*! It recalled the very first scene of the book, where the devious John Jasper takes refuge in his opium dreams as he prepares to begin his villainous plans against his nephew Drood; and Princess Puffer, the old woman stirring the opium, questions her visitor. It was just as they performed the novel's scenes at the Surrey, too.

Here's another ready for ye, dearie. Ye'll remember like a good soul, won't ye, that the market price is dreffle high just now?

Osgood's hope had been proven right! Datchery, consciously or not, must have absorbed something about the writing of the novel if he knew of this place. Then, a less settling feeling touched his nerves as he looked back at Datchery, standing behind him. Datchery and Sally were eyeing each other with the familiarity of a suitor and his former love.

A sudden and unexpected movement pulled away Osgood's attention: four white mice had scurried across a dirty shelf and over the occupants of the bed. Sally assured them they were very tame pets and, after a few clumsy attempts, managed to light another candle as if to demonstrate the highly civilised nature of a two-candle colony. The light revealed a ladder running up into a hole in the ceiling. In the time they had been standing there, a Malaysian sailor had left the room and a Chinese beggar had entered, left, and entered again. Sally spoke to the beggar – apparently her usual plea for advance purchase of her opium, but now in Chinese. She also berated a ship's cook from Bengal, whom she called Booboo, who was apparently not only a drug purchaser, but her lodger and servant.

There was repetition in the operation. After being given a shilling from a customer, the dealer would toast a thick black lump, which she had been mixing slowly with a pin, over the flame of a broken lamp. When it was hot enough, the black mixture was inserted into the cup of the bamboo pipe, which was just an old glass ink bottle with a hole pierced in its side. The customer would then suck the end of the whistling pipe until the opium had been used up – usually after only a minute at the longest.

As Sally prepared the concoction, she gave a hard stare at Osgood – impatient with the lack of payment. Even one of the half-sleeping opium eaters now seemed to take a curious interest in the well-dressed publisher. Osgood, meanwhile, under the wet rags at his feet, noticed a small booklet or pamphlet among other soiled papers. Though the lighting was too dark to make out the details, the booklet's battered cover looked like he had seen it before.

'Well, dearies,' Sally the opium manager said, scowling a little, 'is there something more ye want here, if it isn't any whiffs?' The Lascar meanwhile had now managed to stand and was also gazing at them.

Osgood felt a second wave of nausea from the newly thickened fumes. As he kneeled down to take a breath in the clearer air near the floor, he also slipped the booklet into his pocket. Datchery asked if he was all right.

'Some air,' Osgood responded, woozy from bending over. He found the door and climbed down one flight of stairs to an open window at the landing. Leaning his head out, he closed his eyes, still burning from the smoke. He realised when he opened them again that his vision was blurry from painful tears, and he tried to dry his eyes with a handkerchief. The air felt soothing on his face – though it was hot, it seemed like an ocean breeze compared with that cauldron upstairs.

He now removed the booklet from his pocket, and his suspicion was confirmed. He was holding the latest instalment of *The Mystery of Edwin Drood*, the same instalment he had seen shipped out of Chapman & Hall on Magazine Day.

'*Drood!*' he said to himself. How in the land had it come to be here, too? Charles Dickens truly was read in every corner of the earth.

Returning up the stairs, gripping the handrail very firmly, Osgood felt his vision blur again as he neared the dark opium room. The entrance now seemed to be one solid block of smoke. He felt blind as he took two steps inside and then stumbled over something. Looking down as he plunged forward, he realised he had just tripped over Datchery, sprawled out on the floor. Osgood was caught and pushed against the wall, where he was held erect by the Lascar sailor who threw a fist into Osgood's stomach.

'Stop! Ripley!' This cry came from Datchery, who pulled himself up from the floor and stumbled towards Osgood's attacker. Datchery wrestled with the Lascar, but Booboo, the Bengalee, shook him away and threw him back to the floor, where Datchery landed on his head and was knocked out cold.

Osgood, blinded by tears and blood, tried to feel his way out of the room, but the Lascar grabbed him and pitched into him with his fists, again and again, left then right, crushing him against the wall. Then the Lascar ripped open Osgood's waistcoat and frisked his pockets. Osgood could hear Booboo squatting on the floor similarly ransacking the unconscious Datchery.

As his body slumped down, Osgood felt himself slam against the wall and his head hitting it hard. Then, suddenly, it all came to a halt. Screams. The Lascar collapsed, his head rolling limply on the side of his neck. Booboo seemed to fly across the room splattering blood as he did. Sally had scrambled to the ladder and scurried like one of her mice up its rungs out of sight. Then Osgood was grabbed by both of his arms by someone new.

Through the blur, Osgood thought he could see the figure who'd seized him.

'Impossible!'

He knew this assailant. How could he be here! The giant figure loomed over him, grasped the top of his arm roughly. Seconds later, Osgood hit the floor and everything around him went black.

The next thing Osgood could remember, he awoke covered by darkness. His clothes were dripping wet and tattered. Strangely, he felt a state of dreamy peacefulness, the call of sleep, the crash of oceans, still starry skies – these pulled at him. The air had turned thickly blue, and he reached out to touch it.

Then a vague thought pierced the peace. Danger: he had to reach for the word – although it should have been self-evident. *He* was in *danger*. A snake, black and yellow and then all yellow, slithered by, nearly touching him; it spoke, or someone else spoke, now ten, fifteen, fifty voices could be heard at once trying to drown him in an incoherent chorus.

He thought about Rebecca, who had warned him . . . Rebecca who had been loyal and believed he could succeed in their mission . . . Rebecca whom he knew now that he had loved from the first time he saw her. He felt like crying – he felt as though this would relieve some of his bleak frustration – to produce tears but he could not manage. Without rising – for that seemed beyond his means – he looked for any sign of Datchery.

His eyes wanted to close but he felt if he allowed them, he would not be able to open them again. Struggling, his eyes won and Osgood tumbled backwards into the dark.

The sewer hunter stepped carefully into the lowest section of the tunnel. Unlike most sewer hunters, Steve Williams had been able to secure the expensive leather boots that went up to the knee. This gave him a giant help as he waded through the bubbling offal and mud that filled the two thousand miles of brick sewers under London.

Armed with a long iron pole, with a flat hoe at the end, Steve dug through a crevice where something was lodged. He opened the slide on his lantern, which hung from his belt, so he could see more clearly through the dim, noxious air.

'God bless!' he said to himself, reaching out his arm and pulling up two silver table knives. 'God bless, silver!' he exclaimed, stuffing them in his pocket. This, along with the gold milk jug found a day before, gave Steve an ancient air of heroic triumph. He noticed a bulge in the muddy floor near the drain out to the east end. Poking the lumpy mud with his pole, a flurry of rats the size of small cats rushed past him. Steve stepped forward two boots' lengths and coughed. He did not cough at the awful air, punctuated by the waste of the butchers thrown into the drains, which he was used to after three years hunting in sewers, but at the sight of another dead body washed up in the tunnels. Though their treasure seeking was illegal, the police were permissive of the sewer hunters as long as they reported dead bodies and human remains. This one wore a nice suit.

But on closer inspection, he found that the prostrate man was not dead. He was even breathing.

'Now come along, fellow, how'd you get in this place?' Steve called out, pulling up the man's arm. 'Get along, you beasts!' he said. There were massive rats clinging to the man's arms, legs, head and body and chirping at a deafening volume. 'Get along!' Steve used his pole to knock off the rats and fight off others trying to climb on his discovery. He removed a pouch and forced a powdery substance into the man's mouth.

'Take these Epsom salts – take some of this. It will draw the blood from your head.'

Rising to his feet, finally, hugging his sides in pain, the man stumbled forward and found himself falling down again into the filth.

'Rebecca! Tell her!' he cried out.

'What do you mean? What is all this choke-pear?' answered Steve.

'Stop him! I saw him! You must . . . !'

'Who? Who ever did you see, gov'n'r?'

'Herman,' Osgood groaned. 'It was always Herman!'

FOURTH INSTALMENT

XXIII

BOSTON, DECEMBER 24, 1867

ACK AT THE PARKER HOUSE, in the parlour of George Dolby's hotel room, Tom Branagan sat in a state of dejection. Dolby had put him in a worn oak chair that faced the fireplace, which was overrun with Christmas stockings and mistletoe; it was a hard punishment to be forced to watch the ashes fall one by one into the grate when there was too much to do. Tom's mind was on the woman who had caused all this. His insides burned hot, not with anger so much as with desire for the truth. Suddenly every detail he could remember about her took on significance. Suddenly the coming new year became portentous.

Dolby was walking up and down the room, and James Osgood, there to dutifully represent the outrage of the Boston publishing firm sponsoring the tour, was sitting diagonally across from Tom. Christmas gifts left at the hotel for Dickens – which could not all fit in the novelist's own rooms – were in careless piles under the furniture.

Tom's attention snapped back to the present. Dolby was shouting, 'I know not what to say. Did I not – remind me now, perhaps my own memory fails me – did I not instruct you specific-ally to forget about playing hide-and-seek with that hotel intruder after it happened? I cannot but conclude I erred in trusting you, boy, was swayed by my duty to your father. Is this your Celtic excitability displaying itself?'

'Mr. Dolby, please understand . . .' Tom tried to interrupt.

'You are fortunate Mr. Fields has as much political influence as he does, and that he chose to use it in your favour, Mr. Branagan,' Osgood chimed in.

Dolby went on listing his grievances. 'You accost a lady – a blue blood lady of society – at the theatre, cause a commotion, *and* draw attention away from the grand success of Mr. Dickens. And, if it were not bad enough, all on Christmas Eve! The Chief has enough of a burden right now with his influenza and being away from his family during the holiday season. And what will the press make of it if they get a hold of it!'

'Your thoughtless actions have risked tainting the entire reading tour to the public eye, Mr. Branagan,' Osgood said. 'The future reputation of our publishing house is at stake.'

Tom shook his head. 'That woman is a danger. I know it in my heart and my bones. She should not have been released, and we must urge the police to locate her!'

'A woman,' Dolby cried. 'You want Charles Dickens to look like he is afraid of a woman! That *woman*, by the by, is named Louisa Parr Barton – her husband is a renowned diplomat and great scholar of European history. She comes from an American branch of the Lockley family of Bath.'

'Does that prove she is sane or well meaning?' Tom asked.

'You're right,' Osgood replied. 'Understand, Mr. Branagan – Mrs. Barton is known for her eccentricities and is unwelcome in many homes of society in Boston and New York owing to her strange behaviour. Mr. Barton, it is said by some, married her chiefly for the connection to her family name, and she never could master housekeeping or be a proper mistress to her servants. Others say Barton was passionately in love with her. Whatever the truth, he spends most of the time travelling. It is rumoured he would have received the appointment as our ambassador in London if not for her behaviour. Ever since she slapped the Prince of Wales in the face upon being introduced to him, she is forbidden from joining Mr. Barton's trips.'

'That is why she is able to do as she pleases here,' Tom said.

Osgood nodded. 'With her husband away, she is alone and free with her strange habits and money. She is harmless.'

'She struck an old woman at the Westminster Hotel!' Tom said.

'We cannot prove that. Don't you see what thin ground you stand on, Branagan?' Dolby replied. 'What compelled you?'

'Perhaps I speak above my position, but I've acted on my instinct,' Tom replied.

Dolby shook his head again. 'You speak *and* you acted above your position, Branagan. The Boston police hadn't any choice but to let her go.'

'What about the fact that she broke into Mr. Dickens's room, Mr. Dolby?'

'Well, what *if* it was her, Branagan? We may box her ears, have the police court fine her but not jail her, as she never threatened the Chief nor took any of his belongings. Save a hotel pillow, for which the most severe magistrate would order this Boston Brahmin to pay a dollar!'

'I think she might have been the one to take the Chief's pocket diary,' Tom said.

'And your evidence?' Dolby asked, pausing for an answer that didn't come. 'Thought not. What would she want with an old diary, anyway?'

'To learn private details,' Tom persisted. 'Mr. Dolby, I am only trying to see to the protection of the Chief.'

'Who asked you to do so?' Dolby asked.

'You instructed me to serve him,' Tom answered.

'Well, you've taken it too far,' Dolby said. 'And you won't do it any longer.'

Osgood, taking a long drink of punch, shook his head sadly and added a comment with a thoughtful air. 'You say you act upon instinct. Men like Mr. Dolby and myself act upon what is right and proper, what is within the rules. What is safe for people who put their trust in us. If we could, Mr. Branagan, we would be tempted to send you back to England. But that would bring attention in the newspapers.'

'Instead,' Dolby broke in with the voice of a disciplining father, 'you are from this point on to act strictly a porter, as you were hired. You are to stay in the hotel, unless instructed otherwise, and carry out chores when asked. When we've returned to Ross, I shall decide on your future – if I hadn't paid three guineas for your livery, I'd give you walking papers now.'

Tom, deflating, gazed at the marble fireplace. 'And the Chief? Does he agree with this?'

'Pray worry about your own condition! The Chief will be just fine under our care, thank you, Mr. Branagan,' Dolby said haughtily.

'Indeed,' Osgood added. 'We'll make sure Mr. Dickens is busy enough while we finish dealing with the authorities, so there is no more attention paid to your fears. In fact, I have already recruited Oliver Wendell Holmes to show him the sights of Boston. If anyone can numb a man into distraction, it is Dr. Holmes.'

After Dolby walked Osgood out, he was stopped back in front of his door by a waiter.

'Mr. Dolby? There is a gentleman downstairs to see you – urgent business.'

'It's ten o'clock at night on Christmas Eve,' Dolby remarked, taking his watch from his coat. 'Ten and a half, actually, and I have been running about the city tending to business since six this morning. Did the caller send up a card?'

'No, sir. He said the words *very urgent*, though. I should say from the way he looked that he was *indeed* urgent.'

Urgency indeed. It was probably another stranger who *needed* tickets to sold out readings for his blind, deaf and mute sisters and aunts and wives. 'Very important American writers', whose names Dolby and Osgood had never heard before, wrote pleading for a single free pass, front row, to properly honour Dickens's visit to their city, plus five more for their friends, if you please.

Downstairs at the bar, Dolby searched the faces for his mystery caller. One man stood out. His arms stiffly folded across his chest. A fat, boyish face, but grizzled with scars and grey columns in his beard. He was short but had a robust, qualifying as stocky, build with an imposing presence. The man waved to Dolby.

'I'm afraid, my friend,' Dolby began an amiable but aloof speech, 'our tickets for the next readings have been sold already. You may try again for the next series which we have added to accommodate more hearers.'

The man passed him a pile of documents and a badge.

'I'm not looking for tickets, Mr. Dolby. Or . . . not unless I must *confiscate* them along with every piece of property in your possession.' He smiled humourlessly.

Dolby examined the documents. Income-tax papers. The badge gave the name of Simon Pennock, tax collector.

'I understand you have been seen with paper *bags* piled with greenbacks from your ticket sales, Mr. Dolby,' Pennock said in the same tone he might have chosen if the bags had been human bones. The tax collector's chair was in front of an anthracite coal fire, which outlined the man in a disturbing haze of dark blue that served to distress Dolby further.

'Mr. Pennock, it is my understanding of your country's law that "occasional lectures" – that is the language in the act of Congress – by foreigners on your soil are exempt from taxation.'

'You've misunderstood the law. Not that it's my duty to explain it. You should begin payments to me from your proceeds now, Dolby, five per cent precisely, to avoid more unpleasant business than you've had.'

'I assure you we haven't had any unpleasant business, sir.'

Pennock stared hard. 'You are having it right now, Mr. Dolby.'

Dolby looked around the barroom as though he would find help. Instead, he saw a man who was in a sealskin cap and peacoat, the unbuttoned coat revealing the corner of another Treasury Department badge. Dolby did not like the idea that he had been watched by these men taking in his money from the ticket offices, and most of all he hated that he was outnumbered. He wished Tom were there with him, at least. Not that Dolby thought that government agents would attack him, yet with Tom, younger and sturdier, he thought he would have mustered more self-confidence.

'Even if you are correct in your assessment of this claim, Mr. Pennock,' Dolby began to reply.

'I am,' Pennock, interrupting, said flatly. 'You will pay ten thousand, in gold or greenbacks, or you, each one of you – your beloved Boz included – will be locked away as a hostage before your steamer leaves the shore.'

'Even if I were to agree to five per cent as a just claim,' Dolby said, trying hard not to appear irate. 'Even so, I have sent in the receipts from our sales to England already. The money is banked. I couldn't pay you if I had to.'

'There are alternative solutions.' Pennock waved to the man in the sealskin cap, who moved towards the door. 'Mr. Dolby, you are not the only theatrical manager with whom I have business. I understand Mr. Dickens is a man who likes things in good order. I suggest you deliver your payments before the final readings in New York, or you shall bring Mr. Dickens into some hot water that he won't soon be out of, and shall make him regret stepping foot on American soil. Good night.'

The next morning, while Dickens had enjoyed his usual breakfast at the Fieldses' of a rasher of bacon and an egg with tea, Osgood had asked whether there was anything else the novelist had wanted to see in Boston that had been overlooked. When Osgood pressed the question rather insistently, Dickens had said he was curious about the site of the extraordinary murder of George Parkman at the Medical College. Dr. Oliver Wendell Holmes, who'd joined them for breakfast, and who had up until then been boring Dickens with his incessant talk, happened to be a professor there and immediately offered an expedition.

'Careful now, careful, Mr. Dickens . . .' Dr. Holmes cautioned. They'd arrived at the site and were descending to an underground chamber beneath the Medical College. 'Another two steps down.'

The two men raised their lanterns. Around them in the grim chamber, shelves and medical jars glimmered with anatomical broth. Dickens picked up one to study by the light. 'Pieces of sour mortality,' he commented. 'Like the forty robbers in Ali Baba after being scalded to death!'

'It is all terribly morbid!' Holmes said as Dickens returned the jar to the shelf with the others. 'Our Mr. Fields would insist this is no subject for after breakfast. Quite terrible!'

'Was it not my idea for you to take me here, Dr. Holmes? I could not leave Boston without seeing this.'

'Perhaps it was your idea, Mr. Dickens,' admitted Holmes. 'But you mustn't blame yourself. There's never use in that. My Wendy – Wendell Junior – he would sneer at me for spending time on "trivialities" like this when every hour could be in hot pursuit of dollars.'

Dickens laughed. 'Count yourself lucky, my dear Dr. Holmes. Until Babbage's calculating machine shall be completed, the bills my boys acquire every day could never be added up! I think they have the curse of limpness upon them. I cannot get my hat on some days, I tell you, with how my hair stands up. You are blessed not to know what it is to look around the table and see reflected from every seat of it some expression of inadaptability, horribly remembered from your own father. Now, is this the spot – is this it?'

Holmes nodded.

'To be in such a grim place gives that sensation of cold and boiling water alternating down your back.'

'Right here, unseen by any outside eyes, the unthinkable . . .' said Holmes.

Dr. Holmes, poet and medical school professor, savoured the chance to be the storyteller. It was in this underground laboratory, Holmes said, that the crime had been committed one chilly November day. That afternoon in 1849, George Parkman, a tall and gangling man, entered the grounds of the Medical College to visit John Webster, professor of chemistry and Holmes's colleague. That was the last time Parkman had been seen alive.

The Medical College's janitor, Littlefield, had been present when Parkman came into the building. Littlefield had heard Parkman whisper sternly to Webster, 'Something must be done,' as if there had been some argument between the two men. Littlefield climbed upstairs to Dr. Holmes's lab to help clean up after a lecture and did not give Parkman any further thought that afternoon.

'After days without any word of him, Parkman's family was in a state, as you can imagine, my dear Dickens. When it became known that he was last seen here, the janitor Littlefield, a stranger to most men of our society, found himself the object of suspicious eyes, including my own!'

It was a quiet Wednesday the week of Thanksgiving, when Littlefield noticed Webster was in his lab, doors bolted. The janitor, determined to defend his good name, had his own suspicions and watched through the keyhole as the professor hurried around in urgent activity. When Littlefield brushed his hand on the brick wall, he almost cried out. It was scalding hot.

The janitor waited for Webster to go out for the evening. He then bored a hole from the basement up into the same vault where Holmes and Dickens now stood. When Littlefield pulled himself through to the vault, he saw it. A human body, or part of one, on a hook. Hours later, the police would search more of the lab and find the charred bones of a chopped-up body in the furnace.

'Nobody in the Medical School has ever used this laboratory again, even though we are sorely out of space and it has been fifteen years and more since the body smoked and burned. You see, superstitions run deep even in men of science – nay, especially in men of science.'

Dickens listened to the doctor's story intently. 'Yet if there is a single place in Boston that has innocent reason to be awash in bones, this Medical College is it,' he commented.

'The defence attorney argued that! There are bones and bodies everywhere you step here. But it was the false teeth,' Holmes said. 'That's what did in poor Webster. The dentist who had made them up for Parkman said he could recognise them anywhere. The broken jaw with the false teeth found by this furnace was the most un-impeachable witness ever seen in court.'

'The most clever criminals are constantly detected through some small defect in their calculations,' noted Dickens.

'Poor Webster. To see a man just before he is hanged is really to see a ghost!'

'Surely, surely,' Dickens mused. 'I have often thought how restricted one's conversation must become with a man to be hanged in half an hour. You could not say, if it rains, "We shall have fine weather tomorrow!" for what would that be to him? For my part, I think I should confine my remarks to the times of Julius Caesar and King Alfred!'

Dickens fell into a fit of coughing while the two men laughed and wrapped himself tighter in his mangy coat. After months of assault from the American worshippers acquiring souvenirs snatching at the fur covering, he looked like a shedding animal.

'Well enough now, Mr. Dickens?' Dr. Holmes said gently. Word had spread of Dickens's illnesses since the author landed in America and that weakness for Dickens was a private matter. Dickens had obviously become more exhausted every reading he performed, and his foot grew lamer every day.

'Yes, no doubt of it!' exclaimed Holmes. 'Fields will become warm at me if I don't return you to the comfort of his hearth to rest for your next reading.'

'You can almost smell it,' muttered Dickens.

'My dear Dickens?'

'The burned flesh in the air. Let us stay just a few moments longer.'

XXIV

S THE TOUR'S ORBIT PUSHED farther from New York and Boston, reaching Philadelphia, Baltimore, Washington, Hartford and Providence, George Dolby and his harried ticket agents frequently travelled ahead of the rest of the party to arrange sales and lay the way.

Tom, in the meantime, never protested Dolby's restrictions on his duties. He was more preoccupied with the fact that Louisa Parr Barton had been allowed to walk free without questioning or a proper search of her carpetbag. At least Dickens's travelling to small, outlying towns would make it hard for the phantom incubus to follow, for she seemed a creature of the city. During Tom's duties, carrying baggage between train stations and hotels, he would keep his eyes open, which was more than anyone else was doing. He had been taught by his father in Ross that it was not the duties one was given but how one performed them that mattered.

At Syracuse, the inn was a grim place that looked like it had been built the day before, as did the whole town, and they were served what seemed like an old pig for breakfast. Henry Scott sat down in the public room and wept while George attempted to recruit an emergency militia to clean the hallway on their floor.

Between Rochester and Albany, the whole country seemed to be under water from a furious storm that had displaced the ice and snow overnight. They had to stay the night in a desolate region that went by the name Utica. Even the telegraph poles had been knocked over and were floating like the masts from shipwrecks, so no communication was possible with the next reading hall.

Once they were near enough to Albany, they took paddleboats through the flooded expanse to get to their next hotel. Broken bridges and fences drifted across their paths alongside blocks of floating ice.

Tom was worried about Dickens as the boat struggled through. As they had crossed the United States, Tom had seen on many occasions a repetition of Dickens's sudden fits of dread while in a railway car or a ferry, or anything that the novelist had no power to stop in case of emergency. In their familiarity the fits were no longer startling but still created a distressing picture of internal terror. It was not unusual for Dickens to call out 'Slower, please' to a coach driver several times until they were proceeding at the pace of a walk.

As they floated along the seemingly endless expanse of water, Dickens took out his chronometer watch to see whether they would be able to keep to their schedule. It was possible that the audience of ticket holders would not be able to reach the theatre, but to Dickens that was not what was important: punctuality to him was a matter of principle and self-mastery. He shook his watch.

'It is remarkable, men,' he said. 'My watch always kept perfect time and could be entirely depended upon, but since the moment of my railway calamity three years ago it has not gone quite correctly. The Staplehurst experience tells more and more, instead of less and less. There is a vague sense of dread that I have no power to check that comes and passes, but I cannot prevent its coming. Hold, what is that?' Dickens asked their guide, a superintendent of works. There was an entire train floating in the water ahead of them.

'Freight train, caught in the flood. Cattle and sheep. Men got out of it, but the livestock will have to perish, s'pose. Start eating each other in a couple of days, s'pose.'

Dickens turned to him with a hard glare.

'That's what dumb animals do, Mr. Dickens, when starved,' the superintendent continued nervously.

Dickens stared over at the abandoned train bobbing up and down in the filthy rain water. As they passed, they could hear cries and moans from inside; it sounded like human misery. 'They won't perish,' he said quietly, then moved to the head of the tiny boat. 'Not a single one of them. Paddle back. That way.'

'But, sir, my instructions are strictly to get you to Albany in time for . . .' the guide started to protest.

'You didn't say something, did you?' Dickens asked with fire in his eyes.

'S'pose I didn't, sir,' he replied after taking a hint from the expressions of the staff in their boat.

'The Albanians can wait for us,' Dickens said. 'Everyone paddle to that freight train, and no half measures! We're going to emulate Noah today!' After the work of several hours, they released the sheep and cows to swim across to land, and pulled the weaker ones up the shore high enough for them to rest until they brought food. All along, though it began to snow and hail, Dickens cheered and spurred on the men and animals with such enthusiasm that even the guide added a bounce to his step in the rescue of an emaciated calf.

Their misadventures brought them to Albany. Dickens sat before the fire at the hotel holding his hat out at the heat. It was almost a solid cake of ice, as was his beard. He tried to loosen his necktie but it was frozen into his collar.

As the new year began, most of their staff fell terribly ill. Tom was one of the few who had remained in good health, with Dickens increasingly dependent on him as the writer's own health continued to waver between hearty and weak. At one reading, ticket holders there to hear *Nickleby* and *Mr. Bob Sawyer's Party* were given notices: *Mr. Charles Dickens begs indulgence for a severe cold but hopes its effects may not be perceptible after a few minutes' reading.* The first clause was composed by Dolby and a doctor; the second was the Chief's. Besides his small breakfasts, Dickens had begun limiting himself to an egg beaten up in sherry before a reading and another at intermission, which Henry would have mixed and ready in the dressing rooms.

By this time, Osgood had finished implementing his shop boy Daniel's idea of 'special' condensed versions of the readings, thin volumes which Fields, Osgood & Co. sold for twenty-five cents at the front of the theatres.

'We need not worry about chasing away the Bookaneers from our readings, Mr. Branagan,' Osgood had told him when he and Fields came to see the group off at the railway station. 'Mr. Sand's idea has worked exactly as we planned.'

'That lad will be on his way to clerk in no time!' Fields had said, congratulating Osgood on the innovation. 'He's like another shop boy I can recall.'

On the way to Philadelphia, Tom was obliged to play cards with the Chief while Henry Scott dozed, keeping his legs locked together so that his boot would not be out at the moment some rude American spat his tobacco. Dickens, as usual when on a train, had his flask open beside him. Every few minutes, Henry's head would drop to one side and he would straighten up with great propriety as though he had been wide awake.

'No one ever likes to sleep in public like that,' Dickens said to Tom. 'As a practice, I never do it myself. A contest of cribbage is good to keep you active and awake. It brings out the mettle.'

Dickens, perhaps finding Tom too quiet, seemed content to speak for both of them as they played. 'How much has changed in this country it is impossible to say. The last trip I had to Philadelphia, twenty-five years ago, I remember nearly the whole city showed up at my hotel for interviews. Every Tom, Dick, Harry and Edgar – Edgar Poe, that is. Never was a king or emperor on earth so followed by crowds as I was in Philadelphia.'

'Edgar Poe, you say, Chief?' Henry asked, his dropped head having suddenly jolted him into consciousness. The dresser was sufficiently impressed whenever he heard any person's name that he recognised as famous, especially one who had died. 'Poe wrote morbid and weird tales,' Henry said as a didactic aside to Tom. 'Then he died.'

'He was also a poet,' said Dickens, 'as he reminded me many times. I spoke with him some about my poor raven Grip, who died eating part of our wooden stairs. We also talked about the tragic copyright situation for authors who did not reap a farthing while scoundrel publishers grew rich with spurious editions. Poe was writing tales of "ratiocination" then – of mystery – as was I. Then I spoke to Poe of – yes, I can recall exactly, as if it were yesterday – of William Godwin's *Caleb Williams*, a work we both admired.'

'That novel I read in a single day,' Henry said happily.

Dickens continued. 'I told Poe what I knew about its strange construction – that Godwin had written the hunting down of Caleb first. Only later did he decide how to account for it, and he wrote the first half of the book afterwards. Poe said that he himself wrote his stories of ratiocination backwards. He wanted more than anything for me to see him as a common spirit so that I might find him an English publisher, which I later tried but failed to do with Fred Chapman. Nobody knew much of Poe then and to print American writers was a risky venture. He was certain Europeans could appreciate him better than the Americans. Poor Poe took fire at me after that, a miserable creature.' Dickens seemed immediately sorry to have said that. 'He was a disappointed man, you know, in great poverty. It may be my mood, or my anxiety, or I know not what else that makes me think of him now.'

Two readings in Philadelphia were followed by four in Washington and then two in Baltimore. At the first Washington stop, congressmen and the ambassadors of almost every country attended, as did a stray dog that passed by the police guards and began howling during the reading. President Johnson attended all of the Washington readings, and invited Dickens and Dolby to the White House on the novelist's birthday, although Dickens's illnesses had grown worse. Dickens was certain, after the visit, that Andrew Johnson would manage well despite talk of his undoing for trying to push reconciliation with the Southern states through an unfriendly Congress. 'That is a man who must be killed to be got out of the way,' Dickens commented to Dolby afterwards.

Dolby soon left Washington for Providence to arrange ticket sales there while the others went on to Baltimore before returning to Philadelphia. On one of the longer train rides, the whole group exhausted, Dickens stirred from a deep, uncomfortable sleep.

'What are you smiling at, my lad?' he asked Tom, who was sitting across from him.

'You've been asleep,' Tom said, his pleasant smile remaining in place.

Dickens thought about it. 'I have, sir! And I suppose you're going to tell me that *you* haven't closed an eye.'

At Baltimore, seemingly spurred by his own harsh words on the train to Philadelphia, Dickens located Maria Clemm, Edgar Poe's mother-in-law who was living by the charity of the state.

'This was the very same building where he died,' the old woman said when she was brought to the courtyard of the Church Home where he sat waiting with Tom. 'It was a hospital then. Were you a friend of Eddie's? Do *you* know what happened?' she asked absently. The attendant had already explained who he was, but she had forgotten.

'I am a brother writer. Every author, my dear Mrs. Clemm, every poet and every editor, has known his despair,' said Dickens gingerly. He entreated her to accept $150 for her care.

Dolby reunited with the party again in Philadelphia on the night of the farewell reading there. The manager had stopped directing calculated glances of anger at Tom over the Christmas Eve debacle; instead, he just ignored him. Dolby had enough to agitate him now. The advertisement circular for the Hartford engagement had been printed to say that the reading would last two *minutes* and that the audience members should arrive at least ten *hours* early to claim their seats.

Dickens only laughed, but was surprised to see Dolby so angry about the circular.

'My dear Dolby,' Dickens said, gesturing towards a chair. 'You seem to be at your wits' end today. Don't be too serious about the papers. Why, depending on what American paper you read, my eyes are blue, red and grey, and the next day I'm proven a Freemason. You know, I used to suffer intensely from reading reviews of my books before I made a solemn compact with myself that I simply would not read them, and I have never broken this rule. I am unquestionably the happier for it – and certainly lose no wisdom.'

The manager shook his head sombrely and sat down. 'The papers can use me up all they like, Chief. Let them, the pudding-head business and all the rest! I did not wish to worry you, but I received a visit from an agent from the Treasury Department, claiming we owe five per cent on all proceeds in America.'

'Five per cent!' Dickens exclaimed. 'Is the fellow correct?'

'No! But he threatens to confiscate our tickets and any property we have and to take us prisoners if we try to leave the country. I have written some letters to lawyers in New York, but they have been slow in replying.'

'Fancy that!' Dickens tried to keep his tone light. 'Well, we made friends in Washington, didn't we?'

'We had nearly every member of the political class at your readings!'

'I'd wager they would happily use their influence to swat away this pest, don't you think? Take a trip back there.'

Dolby went back to Washington for a day as instructed. He dined with the chief commissioner of Internal Revenue of the federal government, who confirmed that Dickens's readings were considered occasional and, as such, exempt.

'We will always have rogue collectors, a rowdy element here and there in this bureau,' the commissioner said to Dolby apologetically when writing out a letter at the table. 'Why, Congress had to even investigate the tendency of some of our men to make, well, ungentle-manly demands of some of the new women bookkeepers in Trea-sury. Keep my letter with you, Mr. Dolby. It should stop the mischief. Many of the collectors in the eastern states, you see, are Irish, and suffer greatly from Anglophobia. We hope to enlighten them yet with visits like yours from our English cousins.'

Returning immediately to Boston, to a Saturday dinner planned for Dickens and Dolby at the Fieldses', felt like being home again when compared to their recent itinerant lives.

They took a long walk around Boston before the meal. The amiable Mr. Osgood pointed out places of interest. So much was being built. The Sears Building, at the moment formless piles of stone and dust and scaffold, was said to be on its way to be a grand palace of offices and shops of seven storeys. 'There,' Osgood said, pointing to it, 'that shall be Boston's first steam elevator when this building is finished. You see, they say that is where it will go.' A space had been left in the middle of the construction on each floor, at the very bottom of which was an engine room with a steam pump connected to a series of pipes extending to the top of the building. There was an elabo-rately decorated elevator car, like a small parlour room, resting on its side by the building.

'Before long, they say,' Osgood commented, 'nobody will use stairs at all and we shall save the lives of fifty persons a year who die by falling down stairwells. I only wonder whether things in Boston have begun to change too rapidly to comprehend them. We will all move up and down by steam power.'

'Any politician with that platform has my vote,' said Dolby, who was openly spiteful of walking as much as was required by Boston and Dickens.

Joining the dinner at the Fieldses' that evening was Ralph Waldo Emerson, who had come from Concord. Unlike most of the Cambridge literary delegates – Longfellow, Lowell, Holmes – Emerson seemed only half interested in Dickens as a man, and even less in Dickens as a writer. Yet the Concord Sage could not help laughing at Dickens's singing an old Irish ballad ('Chrush ke lan ne chouskin!') over punch that Dickens made for the group; Emerson's laughing, in spite of his best philosophies, looked as if it must hurt.

There were several other grim faces at dinner that, like some imperceptible force, spread a dark cloud over the levity. The faces belonged to high-level Massachusetts politicians who insisted that after President Johnson's rash dismissal of the secretary of war, impeachment had become all but certain. The leaders of Congress were in secret meetings through the night. Chaos was in the air.

XXV

⸻

THE NATIONAL POLITICAL CRISIS PREDICTED at the dinner came to pass that Monday – articles of impeachment against Andrew Johnson were issued for high crimes and misdemeanours for his defiance of Congress during reconstruction of the Union – and the public fell into a fervour. The lines at the ticket office that day were thinly populated – even most of the speculators were gone! Observing the public distraction and considering Dickens's health, Dolby cancelled the next Boston reading series.

The staff did all they could to entertain Dickens during the quiet period. Dolby and Osgood raced each other in a walking match dreamed up by Dickens, which also gave Dickens an excuse to call for a grand dinner party. 'That Osgood!' Dolby commented to Henry, who helped him prepare for the contest by fitting him with seamless socks. 'Hardly ten stone and a half, my luck, I daresay he can move faster than me in any weather, much less in snow and ice. With his rheumatic smile all along. Mark my words, he is faster and stronger than he appears – in racing and otherwise. Confound that Johnson for being impeached!' Soon Dolby and Osgood were both leaving town to address the changes to the schedule. Tom and Henry Scott were left at the Parker House with Dickens. Compared with the rest of their time in America, these days at Parker's without any readings were absurdly slow. The weather and Dickens's health confined the novelist to his rooms for the most part. He was weakened by his sneezing and coughing and most of all by missing Gadshill.

When he was not at his desk writing, Dickens would talk with anyone who was nearby, waiter, staff or hotel guest. Tom was asked to bring the latest telegraphed reports to Dickens's rooms whenever they arrived from Dolby and Osgood. Another time, Dickens had received a letter from home that sent him into a melancholy mood. When Tom came to take mail for the last post of the day, Dickens was still staring at the letter.

'Surely not John Thompson!' Dickens exclaimed.

'Chief?'

'Thompson is one of my men at Gadshill. The police discovered he was stealing money from my office cash box. After all these years! Why, I trusted him with my babies – I mean my manuscripts, delivering them here and there. What I am to do with, or for, the miserable man, God knows!'

'I'm very sorry, Chief.'

'Tell me,' the Chief said, 'my good Branagan, do you read my books?'

Tom paused with surprise. Usually Dickens talked near but not really to him. He also remembered Dolby's words about their mission to keep Dickens content.

Dickens laughed at his hesitation. 'Oh, you may tell the truth, Mr. Branagan! One more blasted "Dickensite" and I may tip over from the weight. Nothing terrifies a writer like meeting his reader for the first time.'

'I do not often read novels, sir.'

'Sir? I want only strangers calling me "sir", and in truth I'd prefer strangers not to call me anything at all. Do you know why I am called Chief?'

'No.'

'Dolby never felt comfortable calling me Charles or Dickens. Well, I had at least been able to convince him to call me Boz.' Dickens continued his story, saying that one afternoon during a reading tour of Chester, Dolby had come to find Dickens in front of a fire with a Turkish fez and a bright muffler around his neck because cold air was coming into the room at the Queen's Hotel.

How do you feel? Dolby had asked, concerned.

Dickens had grumbled to this: *Like something good to eat being kept cool in a larder. How do I look?*

Like an old chief, Dolby had answered, *but without the pipe.*

'That is where it comes from. I respect Dolby more than I can say, for he overcame the same defect of speech that my India boy – that is my third son, Frank, now in Bengal with the police – had suffered with as a child from his severe want of application. Now, no novels at all, you say?'

Tom had forgotten the earlier subject. 'Novels and romances pretend,' he commented.

'They lie, you mean to say?'

'Yes,' Tom replied. 'They pretend to be what they are not.'

'The books do pretend, Mr. Branagan. Surely. But that is not all. Novels are filled with lies, but squeezed in between is even more that is true – without what you may call the lies, the pages would be too light for the truth, you see? The writer of books always puts himself in, his *real* self, but you must be careful of not taking him for his next-door neighbour.'

'It is still only imagination. Isn't it?'

'Let me show you something. Suppose this wineglass on the table were a character.' Tom nodded at the demonstration. 'Good. Now, fancy it a man, imbue it with certain qualities, and soon fine filmy webs of thoughts spin and weave around it until it assumes form and beauty and becomes instinct with life. From there, the writing comes of itself until those two words, sorrowfully penned at last, stare at me, in capitals: THE END. But if I don't strike while the iron is hot – by iron I mean myself – I drift off again.'

Tom was not certain he fully understood, but he said he saw what Dickens meant.

'Do you?' asked Dickens. 'That was a quick change of heart, Branagan. You're a slap-up man of good sense, I think. I'd rather you be honest with me next time, I'd always much rather that, whatever dear Dolby tells you.'

Taking Dickens's instruction to be honest to heart, Tom's thoughts turned to what was really on his mind since the cancellation of the readings. If Mrs. Barton had been attending all of Dickens's readings in Boston, as Tom suspected, she would have been disappointed, bitterly, by their cancellation. She would have felt personally insulted. If every other person in the country was too distracted by the impeachment to notice, she would not be – she might not even know there was an impeachment.

That night, Tom woke to the usual fire engines clanging outside. He had been dreaming when the noises pulled him out of his sleep.

He shook out his head as he sat in bed with his old flannels hanging on him. How strange the dream had been. The scene was a terrible railway accident like the one at Staplehurst where Dickens had nearly perished. Only Tom was in the novelist's place in this vision, and lowered himself down rocky ledge by rocky ledge to the bloodstained ravine where people screamed. Sheep and cattle, too, glided by his face as he tried to pull the victims to the shore of the river, only they were all dead, human and animal. Above, the first compartment of the train dangled over the broken bridge, raining loose pages of all Dickens's books into the river below.

Tom thought about this terrifying dream as he splashed his face with water from the wash basin and rubbed his eyes. His fingertips felt raw and cold against his skin. It was then he had an urgent premonition. Since tomorrow they would be leaving Boston, if Louisa Barton were going to act, it would be tonight. If she was not already at the Parker House, she would be. Tom *knew* it to be so.

Perhaps he was emboldened by the fact that Dolby and Osgood were not there to reprimand him. Tom dressed hastily and went down the hall to Dickens's door, where a hotel waiter sat guarding the entrance.

'What is it now?' asked the waiter, stirring spasmodically from a half sleep. He brushed Tom's hand off of his arm. 'I'm dead beat tonight, fellow.'

'I need to speak with Mr. Dickens.'

'I doubt he desires an audience with anyone at this hour! Especially some Paddy porter! Come back in the morning.'

'You've had too much at the bar.' Tom waited, his eyes remaining fixed on the waiter.

'Very well,' the waiter huffed. He knocked on the door to the room and said there was a caller. Would Dickens allow him to enter?

'I'll be damned if I will!' came the novelist's reply from behind the door.

The waiter grinned triumphantly. Tom stood for a few more moments then, relenting, began to walk away. Just before opening the door to his own room, he heard sounds of a struggle – someone being strangled, a woman screaming out – coming from inside Dickens's room. The waiter at the door looked paralysed with fear. Tom ran back and dashed through Dickens's door.

There was Dickens in his velvet dressing gown, alone, standing before the massive mirror, his face wildly contorted and his hands squeezing a blanket as though it were his enemy's throat.

'Branagan! Come in,' he said cheerfully.

'Chief, I thought I heard . . .' Tom began, doubting his own senses.

'Ah, yes,' Dickens replied, laughing and then coughing. 'I was just practising a new short reading I've made – very different from the others. I have adapted and cut about the text with great care. Close the door there, if you would, and you'll hear some of it.'

The reading from *Oliver Twist*, one of the earliest novels of his career, told of Bill Sikes, the criminal, beating and killing his lover Nancy for betraying him by helping orphan Oliver's cause. Dickens acted this out step by step with vigour and violence that all brought out the inevitability of death. Tom felt a chill through his body as he seemed to watch the honest prostitute die before his eyes.

When it was done, Dickens fell back into an armchair and rolled his head in a circle to the left and right. 'Nobody has seen it yet,' he said excitedly when he had his breath back. 'I told Dolby, Fields and Osgood about it at dinner. I have been trying it secretly, but I get something so horrible out of it I am afraid to do it in public.'

'It was petrifying, Chief. If any one woman in the audience screams, there could be an outbreak of hysteria.'

'I know it.'

'I suppose you can't sleep well with that on your mind,' Tom wondered.

'I can't sleep anyway! I have been coughing badly for three hours now and have not closed my eyes. Laudanum is the only thing that has done me good, but even soporifics fail me tonight. I have tried allopathy, homeopathy, cold things, warm things, sweet things, bitter things, stimulants, narcotics.'

Dickens pulled out the opiate mixture made from the various phials in his travelling medicine case and took another bitter spoonful. His previous energy had drained from him in the way it did when an actor went behind the back curtain after a scene. There was a sense that a combination of exhaustion and narcotics had taken a full hold of him.

'I hope to get sword in hand again soon,' said Dickens wearily. 'I am as restless, Branagan, as if I were behind bars in the zoological gardens. If I had any to spare, I would wear a part of my mane away by rubbing it against the windows of my cage.'

'Chief, you asked me before to be honest,' said Tom.

'Did I?' Dickens asked, sucking at his tongue. 'What do you say?

Perform the new scene or not? I thought it was one of my finest. Though perhaps I should not commit murder in America, it may be too much for this country's sensibilities.'

Tom had to raise his voice to be heard over the other man's regular bouts of coughing. 'Mr. Dickens, not that. I am concerned about Louisa Barton, the woman who came into your room once before, and has attended your readings regularly, following us to New York and assaulting that widow, possibly stealing your diary: I believe that lady could be looking for you here tonight.'

'Even with the Argus-eyed guardian at my door?' Dickens asked sarcastically. 'You have a reason to think so tonight in particular, Mr. Branagan, I take it.'

'The last series of Boston readings have been cancelled – I'll be bound she would have attended, and I know not what the result on her mental state would be after being denied this. This is the last night – she will try *something* to find you and get what she has wanted from you.'

'Which is what?'

Tom's confidence waned. 'I don't know.'

'Have you finished?' Dickens asked angrily.

'I have said what I feel.'

'Your infernal caution will be your ruin one of these days!' said Dickens, releasing a loud sigh, and sat at his desk. Tom knew his words had not been persuasive enough, even to his own ears, but was surprised at Dickens's furore. He readied himself to leave the room.

'Wait. Very well, Branagan.'

'Chief?' Tom asked. He turned around and saw Dickens wiping a tear from his eye.

'Forgive me. I know you are right. Before I left England, you see, I received various letters warning me of danger by my coming to America. Anti-Dickens feeling, Anti-English feeling, New York rowdyism, and I don't know what else. As I had already decided to come here, upon my soul I resolved to say no word about it to anyone, not even Dolby, especially not that old beadle, Forster, who thought my soul would evaporate the moment he was Godspeeding me!'

'Then you thought the measures I have urged on Mr. Dolby were needed?'

'That was why I agreed that you watch my door that night. Imagine being a man who needs a bodyguard as though from phantom goblins and ghouls! I wonder was Milton visited by angels or by devils when he wrote – and who is it that appears to me?

'I know you have taken pains to understand it, my good Branagan,' Dickens continued. 'You have seen for yourself how I am beset, waylaid, mashed, bruised and pounded by the crowds. Never have I known less of myself in all my life than in these United States of America. My boy, if I greeted you in poor spirits when you knocked at the door, I assure you I repent it. A character not under my own control takes over when I practise a reading. Now, what do you suggest we do? If I am to begin something, I begin it at once.'

Tom had not yet concocted a plan. He thought quickly. 'Chief, I would just as soon to catch this lady red-handed so she can never again bother you.'

'Please God! What do you say we do, then?' the novelist asked impatiently. 'Much better to die, doing, Branagan, than to wait. I have always felt of myself that I must die in harness one day.'

Tom's improvised proposition was this: Tom must take Dickens's place in his bed. Dickens would quietly slip into the adjoining suite of rooms usually occupied by George Dolby. If the intruder made her way inside as she had their first week in Boston, expecting the novelist, she would find Tom waiting instead. And if Mrs. Barton did not show up, they could toast the Chief's safety on their way out of the city.

Dickens contemplated this and quickly assented. He first gathered up some personal belongings from the bureau and the desk drawers and placed them in a calf-leather case.

'Do you believe in the wisdom of dreams, Branagan?' the writer asked as he did.

Tom thought of his strange Staplehurst dream. 'Do you mean whether I believe they tell us what is to come?'

'Surely, surely. Or what has come to pass already. I dreamed once of my dear friend Jerrold, the dramatist. In the dream, he handed me something he wrote, though it was not in his own hand, and he was anxious that I should read it for my own safety. I looked, but could not make out a word of it! I woke in great perplexity, with its strange character quite fresh in my sight. The next day, to my astonishment, I learned Jerrold had died.'

Tom searched for a response. Dickens bowed his head slightly as though he had just finished another dramatic reading. Tom worried what Dickens's fascination with the dream meant for his own health and well-being.

'I have come to be fond of you, Tom. Do not abandon saying your private prayers, as you likely do – I never have myself, and I know the comfort of it. If I should live to publish more, I'd want you to read my books, whether or not you can make out that they have anything to do with your own life. Will you do it?'

'Yes,' Tom said.

'Good, you will be a reader I am proud of.'

When he was finished gathering his belongings, Dickens entered Dolby's rooms and closed the door behind him. Tom waited with a racing heart. At every creak or shuffle or murmur in the hotel walls, Tom imagined the intruder bursting inside and the ensuing capture. He could not help but also imagine the fury that Dolby would exhibit were the manager by some chance to return early to Boston. He imagined Dolby telling the overly proper Mr. Osgood about it, and predictable Osgood telling his partner Mr. Fields, and furious Fields sending for the police to come back in force and this time to lock Tom up.

As the night passed on uneventfully, Tom began to think he'd been wrong and that Louisa Barton was not to make an appearance. He had scared the tired novelist enough for one night. He knocked lightly on the door adjoining to Dolby's rooms where Dickens was sleeping.

'Chief,' Tom whispered. He opened the door slightly. 'Chief, I think we have given this a sufficient trial. Do you wish to reclaim your bed?'

There was nobody inside. The bed had been slept in, but the bedclothes were only slightly disturbed. It was not unlikely he had gone out for another breather. Unless Louisa Barton had shown up as Tom had expected.

Tom went into the hallway to question the waiter who had been guarding Dickens's door, but the waiter was nowhere to be seen either. Descending the stairs, he found a night clerk and sent for the fugitive waiter, who came from the barroom with a glass of brandy in his hand.

'What are you doing in the bar?' Tom said to him.

The waiter studied Tom with offence. 'You a temperance man now?'

'It's three in the morning. Why aren't you on guard at Mr. Dickens's room upstairs?'

'There's nothing to guard, is why. Mr. Dickens left.'

'When?' Tom asked.

'Not a half hour ago. Said he wanted to get out for a little exercise. Went out the back stairs.'

Tom knew at once how foolish he had been. He had never persuaded Dickens about the danger of the intruder at all! Dolby's enraged voice now shouted in Tom's mind and had one thing to say: *You lost the Chief, you lost Charles Dickens!*

Outside, Tom found a hotel janitor who had seen Dickens leave through the back entrance, signal for a hackney cab and drive away. The janitor said that the coach drove north with Dickens inside. Tom began to walk towards the river looking for any signs of the novelist or his hired cab. The streets were nearly empty this early. A rickety wagon drove by hauling bread. Tom pulled himself on to the baker's open wagon, where he crouched so the stacks of rolls blocked him from the driver's view. After jumping back to the street and surveying his surroundings, Tom gave up his search as fruitless.

Then he heard an unexpected sound in the morning stillness – a groan. The noises came a few paces down from the riverbank. Tom followed the sounds and found a red-haired man face down in the rocky, icy bank. Likely a local drunkard who had lost his step. Tom pulled the man on to higher land and could see that he had been battered, his clothes shredded in spots in some kind of assault. His head was uncovered and there was no hat nearby.

'What happened?' Tom asked, loosening the man's clothing around his chest.

The man moaned more, trying to say a word. 'Coach!'

'I'll call for help.'

Before Tom could move, the man grabbed his collar determined to make himself understood. Through his laboured breathing and dizzy spells, the man was able to communicate that he had been driving his coach when he saw a woman gesturing for help. She was holding her ankle as though in great pain. When the man stepped down from the box and started for her, she ran past him, took his hat, and leaped on to the driver's box, grabbing the reins. He scrambled back towards the carriage, but she whipped the horses into a frenzy, trampling him. She then stepped down and pushed the staggering man tumbling over the embankment.

Tom could see through the ice and black mud that the man was wearing the outfit of a hackney cab driver. 'Did you have a passenger in the carriage?' he asked.

The driver nodded.

'Who? Was it Charles Dickens?'

Coughing overcame the driver, and he sprayed out blood.

'Can you stand?' The attempt failing, Tom put one arm under the half-frozen man's neck and one under his legs and lifted him with a great heave. He carried him to the street.

Just then, a brougham carriage came roaring back in the direction of the hotel. Tom tried to signal for help, but it careened wildly past at a breakneck speed, far faster than the legal limit of a slow trot. It passed too rapidly for Tom to see anything but the driver's hat and to observe that there were no passengers to be seen. But the cabman that Tom was holding stretched his hand out at the sight of the vehicle.

'Stay calm, fellow,' Tom said.

Bracing his legs to carry his load farther up the road, Tom found the driver of a truck watering his two blanketed horses at a hitching post.

'This man needs help immediately. Take him to the hospital,' instructed Tom, laying his burden down gently. Then Tom began untying one of the truckman's horses, saying, 'I need to borrow her.'

The confused truckman was too startled to object, and Tom climbed up on to the horse without a saddle and kicked her into a launching gallop.

Tom was soon in the immediate wake of the speeding carriage that had passed them. When he was even with the rear of the carriage, Tom breathed in deeply and leaped off the horse, grabbing the back of the chaise. With one hand hanging from the top of the chaise, Tom swung around, unlatched the door, and threw himself inside. The chaise was *not* empty. There was Dickens on the floor.

The Chief was sprawled out, out of view of the window. His head rested on a pillow – the stolen hotel pillow from Parker's!

This moment had been dreamed up all along.

There was Louisa Barton's carpetbag full of bundles of ragged manuscript pages. Tom took up the title page. *A New Book of Job by*

Charles John Huffam Dickens was scrawled out in a cramped hand. Also in the bag were slippers, curlers, a mirror, pomatum and rope.

'Chief, it's Tom Branagan. Are you hurt?' Tom whispered and shook him.

'Slow, slow please,' Dickens mumbled in reply.

Tom realised that Dickens was not bound or constrained physically. But Dickens's extreme torpor was the same that had come over him when in any fast conveyance.

Just then, the horses came to an abrupt halt, the carriage lifting in the air.

Dickens began to try to speak, but Tom signalled for quiet. The novelist was insensible and confused – plus Tom was not armed but knew Louisa Barton could be. If the kidnapper saw him there, she could become desperate.

The brougham carriage had two rows of seats facing each other and space beneath each of the rows for luggage. Hearing the driver step down from her seat, Tom slid to the floor and rolled beneath one of the seats into the luggage space. He grabbed Dickens's walking stick and pulled it against his body where it couldn't be seen.

'Here we are,' said Louisa theatrically, as she opened the door. Her abundant hair was half stuffed under the stolen driver's cap, which she now removed and threw aside. 'Chief, you'll need to wake yourself now. You'll want to be spirited, *spirited and energetic* as always you are, to show what you're all about. This will beat the other readings for those groundlings hollow, hollow, hollow!'

With considerable strength, the woman dragged Dickens under her arms and out of the side door. Tom, meanwhile, rolled over to the other side of the carriage and popped that door open so he could observe them. They were in the massive shadow of Tremont Temple.

The assailant was walking Dickens gently towards the theatre with one hand, carrying her pearl-handled switchblade in the other. She had on a pink sash and dazzling flame red gown, with dead geraniums dropping down from tousled hair.

Tom waited until they had entered the theatre and then he went up the stairs to the main hall. He knew the building inside and out from the readings and knew that inside he'd have the best chance of separating Dickens from her long enough to get him free. He considered going for a policeman, but they'd surely be resistant to his story:

particularly the part about the attacker being a woman from the upper classes of the city named Louisa Parr Barton.

Tom went through the side entrance where he had previously guarded against people trying to sneak into the readings. Now it was Tom doing the sneaking. He silently climbed the stairs to the balcony, peering over the railings to survey the scene. Louisa had placed Dickens, who had revived but was still in a state of confusion, on the platform in front of the podium. She sat at his feet on the platform with her wide gown flowing around her, like the ghostly image of a schoolgirl. The blade dangled in her hand.

Her intention was clear as it was bizarre: Dickens was to do a reading of her manuscript. Poor Chief. The lines on his face looked like they had deepened since he had arrived in America; without George's lighting and Henry's choice of a fashionable hat, straggly hair hung from his bald head down over his cheeks. He was a shadow of himself.

Dickens fumbled through her manuscript pages, and began to read. 'They slain the servants with the edge of their swords – I only have escaped to tell the vulgar people that God is upon our city.' Louisa appeared to be enraptured with her words coming from her idol's mouth.

Tom raised himself just above the iron railings. He caught Dickens's eye and Dickens, without betraying Tom's presence, nodded. Dickens raised his voice and began to read her strange and discordant text louder, allowing Tom to descend the stairs and make his way along the side of the auditorium unheard.

But he reached a point where he could go no further without risking detection. Dickens, recognising Tom's dilemma, thrust aside the woman's pages and began to speak in an earthy growl. '*Let it be! There's enough light for wot I've got to do . . .*'

It was Bill Sikes and the murder scene from *Oliver Twist*! Dickens's teeth were clenched with fury, completely transforming into the savage killer – he looked right at Louisa Barton. He held his hand down to her as though he would seize her by the wrist.

She trembled with a thrill of fear. Her face flushed a fiery red.

'*You were watched to-night, you she-devil. Every word you said was heard!*'

The dramatic performance mesmerised Louisa, and Tom success-fully crept to the side of the platform unseen. He could see her hand clenched the knife so tightly her knuckles were turning white. Tom could take her by surprise by coming through the dressing room on to the platform, but if he had to struggle, he feared Dickens's proximity to her weapon.

As he debated his best chance, Louisa seemed to sense something wrong. Her head whipped around.

'Why, you!' she screamed violently, as though infused with Bill Sikes's venom. She caught him with her hypnotic glare and cut the air with her blade. 'You can't be here!'

Before Tom could move, she jumped up and put her knife to the soft flesh of Dickens's throat. 'Keep reading!' she commanded him.

'*Every word you said was heard . . .*' Dickens tremulously repeated Sikes's warning.

'Yes, that's it – keep going,' she said to Dickens, and then to Tom, said, 'Now you leave!'

Tom, eyes locked on the switchblade, backed away through the middle aisle. 'I'm going, Mrs. Barton,' Tom said. 'You see, I'm going.'

Then a different idea came to him, and he dropped into a seat with a loud thump. Tom dug himself into the cushion and reclined.

She looked back from Dickens to Tom but then, as though deciding she never wanted to leave the writer's side again, she said, 'You're spiteful because we were never friends. Fine, stay! You wouldn't understand what you're about to see!'

Tom put his boots up on to the chair in front of him. 'I think I do.'

Then understanding dawned and her mouth opened wide. 'That's why, you're sitting – that seat's *mine*!'

Tom was sinking deep into the seat from which she had watched the Christmas Eve reading, where she had carved a string of words about Dickens. Unloosed with rage, she ran through the aisle towards him, her knife held out.

'Run, Chief! Quickly!' Tom called out to Dickens.

'I won't!' Dickens cried.

'Chief, run!' Tom repeated, but to his astonishment Dickens did not move. 'Fetch the police!'

To this urgency, Dickens thankfully seemed to assent. First, he threw up the pages of Louisa's manuscript in the air and then darted out of the theatre.

'No!' she cried, watching her book's pages flutter in all directions.

Tom used her distraction to swing the hook of Dickens's walking stick at her hand, the jutting-out screw landing right on her knuckles and creating a deep gash. Her switchblade went flying into the air. Tom staggered backwards when she pulled up a pistol from her pocket, then pounced forward and knocked her down. They both rushed to where it landed and struggled over it. Tom drew his fist back but knew even in the rush of the moment that he could not strike a woman. She wrestled her hand free and threw her fist into his jaw again and again with surprising strength.

'There is an actress,' Tom said to her, fending off her blow with his arm. Even as he spoke, he could not help feeling as though he were betraying the Chief. He unconsciously switched to a whisper. 'There is a young actress back in England whom the Chief loves. That is why he and his wife separated, not because of you.'

'No, you've invented it all!' Louisa wailed.

'The Chief told me, he told me himself. He's come here to earn enough money to buy her anything she wants – to buy her the crown jewels and the Tower of London and Buckingham Palace if that's what she desires!'

'No, he came for me!'

But the poisonous words had worked. Her face contorted into confusion, she began to sob and her grasp loosened. Tom wrapped her in his arms. Within minutes, Dickens returned with several policemen and citizens who had heard his call.

When she saw Dickens again, it was as though life returned to Louisa. She began softly singing to herself like a child. In a sudden movement, she pulled away from Tom's grip and drew a razor from inside the lining of her shoe.

'No!' Tom cried. 'Chief, watch out!' He jumped in front of Dickens.

She stabbed the razor into her own neck and began to slice her flesh from right to left, dropping into a puddle of her own blood.

One of the policemen ran for a doctor and another kneeled beside the woman and tried to staunch the terrible gash in her neck with her sash. Dickens, watching in shock, fell to her side and dislodged the razor from her hand. She was trying to speak again but gurgled blood instead. Her arms flailed wildly until her hand sat on top of Dickens's, at once growing calm and still.

'Chief . . . our next book . . . what . . . ?' she said, spitting shiny geysers of blood on to her chin, unable to go on.

Dickens leaned in to the woman's ear and whispered something. Tom could not hear what was said, but a strange and shrewd grin rose upon Louisa Barton's face, and as her life was slipping, she began to giggle hoarsely. Dickens, dismayed, backed away and allowed the police and a newly arrived doctor to attend her.

Tom said to the dazed Dickens, 'Chief, what is it you said to her?'

Dickens nearly fell headlong into his protector's arms from exhaustion and relief, leaning on him bodily. 'Never mind that. One of our devils is at peace, Branagan.'

XXVI

THE NEW YORK PRESS HAD arranged to give a celebratory dinner to the novelist before his departure, to be held at the famed Delmonico's restaurant. He was suffering again from severe swelling in his right foot – erysipelas, according to a local doctor – and only upon application of special lotions from the best drug store and painful bandaging, hidden by a borrowed gout stocking sewed over in black silk by Henry Scott, did the writer go out. Dickens said, as he ground his teeth, that he did not want the pressmen to telegraph England about the extent of his maladies.

'Points of difference there have been, points of difference there probably always will be, between the two great peoples,' Dickens said after the many toasts to his health at the long table. 'But if I know anything of Englishmen – and they give me credit for knowing something – if I know anything of my countrymen, gentlemen, the English heart is stirred by the flutter of your stars and stripes as it is stirred by no other flag that flies except its own. I beg to bid you farewell, and I shall often remember you as I see you now, equally by my winter fireside at Gadshill, and in the green English summer. In the words of Peggotty from *Copperfield*, "My future life lies over the sea." God bless you, and God bless the land in which I leave you' – Dickens paused there, a tear in his eye – 'forevermore.'

All two hundred pressmen, having finished with their special literary menus of *timbales à la Dickens, agneau farci à la Walter Scott* and *côtelettes à la Fenimore Cooper*, stood to cheer. The restaurant band played 'God Save the Queen'.

'I feel like erecting a statue to your stamina, my dear Dickens,'

Fields said into his author's ear as he shook his hand and helped him away.

'No,' the Chief said sombrely, 'don't. Take down one of the old ones instead.'

After hearing about his heroics in Boston, Dolby had given many hearty congratulations to Tom, very nearly apologising to him for having doubted. He insisted Tom search for Louisa's accomplices.

'There were none,' Tom said.

'Impossible! That little lady . . .' Dolby replied, still flabbergasted by it all.

'Obsession of a strong-hearted woman, Mr. Dolby, can be more dangerous than ten men.'

On their final night in America, Dolby confided to Tom about a remaining worry: the threats of the tax collector who had accosted him at the hotel. Dolby asked Tom to help watch out for any trouble.

The warning of the tax agent, whether bluster or not, had stuck in the manager's mind. *You will pay, or you, each one of you*, Agent Pennock had said to him, *your beloved Boz included, will be locked away as a hostage before your steamer leaves the shore.* Would the novelist, in his weakening health, survive imprisonment if it came to that? A squalid place like the debtors' prison he had seen his father endure in Marshalsea in his youth?

'I shall have the letter from the Treasury chief on my person at all times, in case,' Dolby said.

'Then there shouldn't be any trouble, I'd think,' Tom responded.

'I hope not,' said Dolby. 'But it seems many Americans prefer not to respect authority.'

It was only when they boarded the *Russia* the next morning without incident that Dolby finally smiled for the first time in what seemed weeks. The porters pulled up not only their luggage but the many gifts of portraits, bouquets, books, cigars and wine.

While the ship was still anchored in the harbour boarding passengers, they sat down to a lunch of some hot soup in the saloon of the ship. Yet before a bit had been taken, there was a commotion on deck. Dolby found several passengers pointing out a police vessel coming in their direction.

As Dolby made his way down the stairs to investigate, the manager faced two men in dark suits and sealskin caps on board, though the police vessel had not yet reached them. They both unbuttoned their coats and revealed shiny brass Treasury Department badges. Dolby, sucking in his breath, removed the letter of protection from the commissioner of Internal Revenue.

The agent who had visited him before, Simon Pennock, emerged to take the letter and read it. He slowly looked up from it and met Dolby's eye. Then he tore the letter and ground the pieces into the floor with his boot toe. 'That is what I think of that.'

'Sir!' Dolby said. 'That is the official word of the chief of your department. Your superior! He assures me that neither Mr. Dickens nor myself is liable for any tax in this country.'

Pennock sneered an ugly sneer. 'Let me make this case clear to your frozen British brain. We don't care a miserable damn for the opinion of the chief of my department, as you call him. With the president under impeachment, there *is* no government, no department. Only justice and injustice, and we stand before you now as judges.'

'Mr. Dickens would be the last man in the world to evade a claim upon him if it were just!' Dolby thought to try his last tactic. 'Is it Irish blood that makes you hate Mr. Dickens, Agent Pennock?'

'I haven't a drop of it in this body, sir,' the collector said.

'Then why harass us so? Are you driven so mad by base greed?'

'You look for greed?' Pennock asked. 'Look no further than your boss, sir. Who comes here for money and deification and wishes to give nothing, not even friendship, in return. Perhaps Mr. Dickens should have taken better care to be courteous to the citizens of this country!'

'Courteous? That man has exhausted himself, has made himself sick b-b-b . . .' – Dolby struggled with his words – 'bringing joy to Americans. What do you m-m-mean?'

'Hold your tongue if it's too oily to talk, Dolby! My dear brother is a fine gentleman of Boston, one of the greybeards among the city aldermen. He has read every book by Mr. Dickens for twenty years. Yet, when he left his card at the Parker House with a letter of introduction upon Mr. Dickens's arrival, the response was a note declining – not even in Dickens's own hand, nay, he could not take the time for that – because your sultan was busy resting. I do not call that courtesy! I call it an insult! I say let the great Boz drink from the dregs of the cup he serves to others!' With that he summoned more of his men up the stairs.

'Halt,' Tom, entering from above, said to two of the men. 'State your business.'

'None of yours, likely, Paddy!' said the rougher looking of the pair.

'They mean to arrest Mr. Dickens and myself,' Dolby said shakily to Tom.

Tom, without hesitation, stepped in front of Dolby and addressed the tax men. 'Take me instead and let them go. I will stay behind until this is sorted out.'

The rougher sealskin pushed Tom hard in the chest, sending him tumbling down. He stopped himself from cracking his skull open at the last moment by catching the railing.

Pennock removed a pistol from his pocket. 'We'll deal with Dolby – and then with Mr. Dickens.'

There had been no chance at escape – the rogue agents meant business. Suddenly, the sounds of heavy boots came from behind Dolby. Four detectives from the police boat, which had just arrived, appeared, their coats also unbuttoned on their badges. They surrounded Dolby, and demanded to know the sealskin caps' business.

'Halloa! We're the Treasury Department,' answered one of the tax agents.

'Treasury Department? Too late. New York police here and *we've* got him and Boz for what they owe the *city* of New York.' Two of the detectives took Dolby's arms. Another grabbed Tom Branagan. As a cacophonous shouting match erupted over which arrest took priority, the bell sounded from above alerting those going ashore to return to the ferry.

'We have our police boat alongside,' one of the detectives said. 'But since it appears you boarded at the dock, I'd disembark with the others before you lose your passage, unless you fellows plan to see much of Liverpool.'

Pennock and his unhappy agents yielded, rushing back to deck and jumping on to the last ferry taking away the passengers' visitors and servants. When they were gone, the detectives said to each other, 'Shall we put them in shackles now or on our boat?'

'Let's round up Dickens first, so there's no escape.'

'Get your stick ready, then.'

'Imagine! What the pressmen would have done with seeing the Inimitable Dickens in irons!'

Suddenly, the four men laughed. Dolby, amazed at this change in demeanour, stared at them.

A detective removed his hat and smiled. 'Very sorry, sir. Our chief of police is quite an admirer of your Mr. Dickens. When he heard something about the tax collector's plan, he sent us to scare them off. Now we should be returning to our own boat presently and let you be on your way. But perhaps old Boz can spare an autograph or two for our boss?'

Dolby and Tom looked at one another in amazement.

Before they made their way back to the police boat, the policemen were carrying with them armfuls of autographs. Cannons from nearby tugs fired to say good-bye. After endless cheering and many farewells from the ferry and from the shore, Dickens, standing on the rail, put his hat on to the top of his cane and waved it high at the crowd.

Tom stood close behind him on deck, just in case his boot slipped. From his vantage point, he could see Dickens's eyes tearing up.

'Perhaps you will come back to America again, Chief,' Tom suggested.

'Surely,' Dickens agreed. 'Maybe, though, I've left just enough of myself here already.'

FIFTH INSTALMENT

XXVII

LONDON, ENGLAND, JULY 16, 1870

———————•———————

OR FIVE DAYS AFTER OSGOOD'S assault by the opium fiends, Rebecca tended to her employer at the Falstaff Inn, where he slept almost continuously. There were frequent visitations by the local Rochester doctor. Datchery had come, too, looking distraught and weepy at the sight of Osgood's condition. In his waking moments, the publisher tried to breathe but mostly coughed.

'No blood expelled when coughing,' Dr. Steele observed to Rebecca a day after the attack. 'The fractures are likely on the surface of the ribs, and the lungs unhindered. I do not like to apply physic or leeches in such cases if there isn't inflammation.'

'Thank God for that,' Rebecca said.

'He must be bathed with cold water regularly. You seem to have had some experience as a nurse before, miss.'

'Will he recover fully, Doctor?' asked Rebecca urgently.

'The chloroform and brandy *should* cleanse his body, I assure you that, miss. If he's one of the lucky ones.'

When Osgood's mind felt clearer, he still could hardly describe what had happened in the early morning at the opium rooms that had ended with two of the opium fiends dead and mutilated. Rebecca was sitting at a writing desk composing a letter to Fields with the latest news, and Datchery was half asleep in an armchair when Osgood woke again.

'It was Herman!' Osgood groaned as he had done when found by the sewer hunter. His ribs were wrapped in a broad bandage that went twice around his body, constraining his movements and respiration. Bites from the sewer rats had swelled around his face and neck in giant red patches.

'Are you very certain it was him, Mr. Osgood?' Rebecca asked, coming over to his bedside.

Osgood gripped his forehead with both hands. 'No. I'm not certain at all, Miss Sand. We know he couldn't have survived the ocean, after all! And who would have stopped him from doing worse to me, if he was there to see me dead? It must have been a vision from the opium, like the snakes and the voices. I had fallen under its spell.'

'We shall find out what it was that happened, I promise you that!' cried Datchery. 'My dear Ripley, my dear Miss Rebecca, I certainly promise you that!' He took one of Osgood's hands and reached for Rebecca's, but Rebecca stepped away distrustfully. 'They say you'll be sick as a horse for a while, old fellow. Only tell me you'll live a day longer and I'll be tripping on the light fantastic!'

Though his head remained bandaged, Datchery's own injuries were more superficial than Osgood's. He had not seen anything that had happened after his own attack, and had not seen any sign of Herman before he was knocked out by the fiends. As they had with Osgood, someone had dragged him unconscious into the streets. Rebecca wanted nothing to do with the man who had brought Osgood to a low point and had before that caused them to argue in what was now a shameful memory.

Datchery said, 'Miss Rebecca, I wish to help. I can help, you know. Let the idea ripen in your mind.'

'I think you have helped enough,' she said. 'And you may refer to my employer as Mr. Osgood, if you please.'

Datchery chewed his lip in frustration, then turned to the patient in bed and then back to Rebecca. 'Perhaps there are some things I must say that shall help you trust me as your employer has so quickly learned to do.'

'Ah, Mr. "Datchery", is it?' This was Dr. Steele coming into the room. 'May I have a private word with you?'

Datchery, looking over the drowsy face of Osgood above the blankets, nodded and left the room. To Rebecca's great relief, the visitor did not come back that afternoon.

The next time Osgood woke, he asked for the suit of clothes he had been wearing during the attack, now hanging in the wardrobe. Searching the pockets, he removed the green pamphlet he had taken from that filthy floor.

'Edwin Drood! Look.'

There it was. The cover was a kaleidoscope of illustrated scenes from Dickens's novel. The pamphlet was in fact the fifth instalment published of the serial of *The Mystery of Edwin Drood*. Dr. Steele, just arriving for another inspection, came over to the bed when he saw Osgood had stirred. This doctor, a lanky and studious man, had become a tyrant over Osgood's care. He commanded that light only be allowed through the window blinds at short intervals.

'I have asked that Mr. Datchery to leave Mr. Osgood in peace,' Dr. Steele explained to Rebecca. 'He only seems to agitate him, I can assure you.'

'I think so too,' Rebecca said firmly.

The doctor now discouraged Osgood from studying the booklet that apparently also agitated him. Rebecca consented to remove the object from the patient, though she pondered the terrific coincidence of the item having appeared in such a place. Had Osgood's misfortunes in the low streets really been due to the region's usual dangers or somehow connected to their singular mission in England? She opened the booklet and noticed the pages looked like they had been read, perhaps multiple times. She placed the instalment in a drawer.

'I do not understand,' Osgood sighed as the doctor unwrapped his dressings and applied fresh bandages. 'I do not see how the opiates I breathed could have had such a strong effect on me.'

'Oh, you are quite right,' Dr. Steele said conclusively. 'On their own, the fumes could not do such harm. I hope the lady present will not be too embarrassed,' he said as a caution, and waited for Rebecca to turn away. When she did not, he folded up Osgood's flannel sleeve and revealed what he had seen in his examination.

'I do not understand,' Rebecca protested.

'There,' Dr. Steele said, 'a single puncture wound in Mr. Osgood's arm – from a hypodermic syringe. You see it?'

The doctor continued with detached interest. 'Someone inserted into your tissue a very high dosage of the narcotic, sir. That is why it has required a long time to be ejected from your body.'

Rebecca felt herself shaking. Osgood sat bolt upright. They caught each other in a mutual moment of unreserved shock. They had come halfway around the world, in part in an effort to leave Daniel's tragedy behind and yet came round to face the same poisonous injection marking in Osgood's own skin as Daniel had suffered. Everything seemed to be brought into a single line of sinister action, though why and where it had all started was more of a mystery than ever.

Rebecca knew that if Dr. Steele believed any conversation over-excited the patient he would intervene to end it. So she waited, pretending to the best of her ability that the puncture wound was the least interesting sight ever witnessed. The doctor soon moved into the next room, giving long-winded instructions to a messenger boy to secure more phials of medicine from the town druggist.

'Mr. Osgood, is it the same as what you saw on . . . on Daniel's body?' Rebecca asked in as calm a whisper as she could manage, so the doctor could not hear them from outside the door. 'You mustn't hold anything from me. It is, isn't it?'

'Yes,' Osgood whispered in return.

'What could it mean?'

'We have faced the same adversary since the morning of Daniel's death.'

'But who?'

'I don't know.' Then Osgood whispered half brokenhearted and half triumphant, 'It wasn't Daniel who injected himself with opium. We know that now for certain. He was poisoned, Miss Sand, just as I was!'

'Do you believe that?'

'It must be! Dickens himself could not write such a discovery as coincidence! This knocks the wind out of the whole thing. We must seek a clearer view of everything: of Daniel, of the opium fiends, of *Drood*. Miss Sand,' he added with an abrupt urgency. 'Miss Sand, some paper!'

Rebecca brought him hotel stationery and a lead pencil and a book to rest them on.

Osgood wrote on the stationery, crossing words out then trying again until he got it:

> *It is God's.*
> *Itisgod's.*
> *ItsOsgoods. It's Osgood's.*

Daniel Sand didn't exclaim a sentiment of religious peace, but the words carried a beautiful meaning nonetheless. 'Look,' he said. 'Bendall was wrong. Daniel didn't leave out a final word before he died. Daniel didn't want me to be angry, even at the edge of life. He never failed the firm at all.'

When Dr. Steele came back to complete his examination, the darkness of the room hid the hot tears in Rebecca's eyes.

It had not only been Osgood's physical but his legal standing that had been in jeopardy the balmy morning of the attack. When he had first partially recovered his senses, he had found himself carried out of the sewer tunnels by two toshers, the sewer hunters, to a police station house. He could not explain to the constables how he had come to be there.

Moreover, Osgood's state at the time – his now-tattered and wet clothing, his slurred speech and senses, and the harsh smell of burned narcotics and rubbish – subjected him to reproach by the officials as if he were another bothersome tosher. When he described what had happened, other constables were dispatched and the dead bodies of a Lascar sailor and a Bengalee known as Booboo by local residents were found in the squalid rooms described by Osgood.

'That is not good for us,' the station sergeant said to Osgood. 'Not good for you, sir. Your story is not complete.'

'Because I know not what has happened to me, sir!' Osgood protested.

'Then who would?' the sergeant demanded.

Only the arrival of a respected London man of business, Marcus Wakefield, had saved him from being charged as a public nuisance. Mr. Wakefield had been alerted about the presence of an unknown American brought to the station house because Osgood had had Wakefield's calling card on his suit when he was found.

'You know this poor soul, sir?' the sergeant asked sceptically. 'Or perhaps he *stole* your card from your possession.'

Osgood was stretched out on a bench, mangled with pain and delirium.

Wakefield slammed his fist against the table. 'This is outrageous! Release him straight away, gentlemen. I crossed the ocean with him – his name is Osgood, James Osgood. He is no vagrant at all but a respected publisher from Boston who preferred a cabin on the sunny side of a steamship. You have a gentleman in your custody. It was my understanding he was to be residing in the country near Rochester conducting his business.'

The sergeant looked Osgood up and down. 'I have never met a

publisher that would choose to dress and, shall I mention, stink like that, sir! We shall have to write a report.'

'Write your report, then let him free.'

Wakefield used his influence to expedite Osgood's liberty and then sent a message to Rebecca summoning her to Higham station, where Wakefield met her with Osgood so the injured man could be transported back to the Falstaff Inn to recover. When they met at the station, Wakefield asked to speak with Rebecca alone.

'May I walk with you, my dear?' said Wakefield.

Rebecca held out her arm for their visitor as they walked through the station.

'My dear, I would continue with you to the Falstaff but I am afraid I must return to London at once on business,' he said apologetically.

'You have been very kind to bring him all the way back to Kent, Mr. Wakefield,' she replied.

He shrugged. 'I confess that although I am horribly alarmed by Mr. Osgood's surprising state and these circumstances, I take solace in the pleasure I feel to be in your company again,' he said. 'And are you well, my dear?'

'As well as I can be, thank you, Mr. Wakefield,' Rebecca said politely. 'I only wish I had not permitted Mr. Osgood to go to such a place with that awful Mr. Datchery.'

'I am afraid the tender woman, though she must try, cannot prevent the less cautious sex from our imprudent pursuits, Miss Sand,' said Wakefield, smiling. 'Mr. Osgood, it seems, has discovered, too late for his health, that all of London is not a picnic. Women's instincts are often right. Mr. Osgood had sent me a note about some matter with a plaster statue at Christie's auction house that he suspected had gone missing. I enquired about it with an associate – apparently this statue your employer was interested in was dropped by a careless workman at the auction house and, embarrassed, they did not want to reveal it. I hope you insist on him suspending these wild activities in such dark corners, whatever they may have been.'

Rebecca shook her head. 'I do not know that anyone in the whole world could sway him now. Perhaps not even Mr. Fields.'

Wakefield sighed worriedly but with a note of admiration. 'He is a man of inner resources, I can see that, and confess it is like looking in a mirror. I did not know being a publisher carried with it such adventures! I suggest you keep a most watchful eye on him from now on, my dear Miss Sand. I have friends up and down the city. Send for me at the slightest worry. As a businessman, I fear I know too well that whatever flame of ambition fires Mr. Osgood's heart, it will not soon be extinguished unless his goal is attained.'

'Our united thanks,' she said tentatively, as the interview seemed to be at its end.

Wakefield took Rebecca's hand and slowly put his lips against it. 'I hope that is not too bold, my dear,' he said. 'You are truly the pink of perfection, a rare type of woman not found enough among the conceited peacocks of London. Mr. Osgood is fortunate for your loyalty.'

Taken by a peculiar sensation of vulnerability and freedom, she found herself at a loss for words.

'Mr. Osgood told me about your having been married before,' Wakefield went on in a gentle tone. 'But the laws are different in England. You need not give a thought to that ever again, if you wished.'

'Mr. Osgood told you of my being divorced?' Rebecca asked in surprise.

'Yes, when we were on board the *Samaria*,' he said. Sensing her confusion, he added, 'He wished merely to protect you, Miss Sand. I believe he could see my instant and sincere affection for you and wanted to prevent any impropriety. Is my interest in your life so surprising, my dear, as the expression on your face makes it appear?'

The bells of the carriage readying to drive the patient to the Falstaff Inn jingled.

'I must go help him, Mr. Wakefield,' Rebecca said.

Each day the publisher awoke from his sleep with a little more physical stamina and more pronounced mental restlessness. The fractures in his ribs, though still painful, were healing at pace. Dr. Steele had given urgent orders to Osgood to keep his torso in bandages and restrict heavy breathing or exertion at risk of causing grave permanent injury to his lungs. One morning, as he cleared Osgood's breakfast, the landlord of the inn placed a fresh vase of flowers on the washstand.

'That is kind of you, Sir Falstaff,' said Rebecca, who sat by Osgood's side and bathed his forehead.

'Many apologies if I interject trivial business upon the patient's health,' the landlord said with a tentative air. 'I am afraid I require your signature on some papers, Mr. Osgood, to extend your stay beyond our original arrangement, owing to the circumstances.'

'Of course,' Osgood said.

As Osgood was examining the bill of charges which he rested on top of a pillow, he paused. Above the landlord's stationery was Sir John Falstaff's given name, William Stocker Trood. *Trood*: Osgood mouthed the word to himself.

'Anything wrong, my dear Mr. Osgood?' asked the landlord.

'I was only noting your surname's resemblance to the title of Mr. Dickens's last book.'

'Ah! Poor Mr. Dickens, how he is missed around here, I cannot say! I have to confess, Mr. Osgood, that *this*' – here the landlord stopped and pulled at his old-fashioned baggy coat and neckcloth – 'I mean these costumes and my trying to be like the fat knight, Falstaff. This is because of him.'

'Because of Dickens?'

He nodded. 'For many years people have come to Rochester from all over the world in order to get a glimpse of Mr. Dickens's home and perhaps even of the man himself! Americans would come round and leave their card hoping to be invited into Gadshill, in the meantime coming for bread and wine at our fireside. At other times, the Dickens family would have too many guests and they would use us for additional lodging. The location of our little place has meant that we could always command decent fees for our beds and meals. Now that he is gone and the family leaving, well, I have had to think of other ways to attract sightseers. As my sister says, God protect us if we must rest our small claims on my Falstaff impersonation! "The better part of valour is discretion; in the which better part, I have saved my life." I tried to memorise some lines, but you will notice I have nothing of the theatre about me.'

After finishing with their business, the Falstaff landlord bowed and began to exit.

'Mr. Osgood? What is it? What's the matter?' Rebecca asked when she saw the colour drain from his face all at once.

'His son, his son died . . .' Osgood murmured before trailing off.

'What?' Rebecca asked, confused and worried about his state of mind. 'Whose son?'

Flashes of all the connections between the small town of Rochester and Dickens's books raced through Osgood's mind. Dickens had taken names, characters and stories from the country life outside his study window. The novels of Rudge and Dorrit had intimations of their stories in the byways of Rochester, what about the story of poor Drood? Osgood spoke more to himself than Rebecca. 'He became sad at seeing the opium poppy on the table downstairs and said opium had to do with his son's death . . . but I never thought of . . .'

Suddenly, the publisher jumped down from the bed, knees wobbling as his legs strove for balance. With one arm wrapped around himself, he struggled to drag his beaten body into the hallway.

'Mr. Trood! Your son!'

The landlord's face went snowy white, his self-appointed role of the jolly host vanishing again. 'Perhaps we have had enough conversation today,' he said sharply. He saw Osgood was waiting for more. He looked up and down the stairs. 'I cannot talk of it here. Are you well enough to come into town, Mr. Osgood? If you walk with me, I'll promise you a story.'

Osgood insisted. 'Your son, sir, what was your son's name?'

The landlord took in a gulp of air to regain his voice. 'It was Edward. Edward Trood,' he said. 'He would have been around your age, had he never disappeared.'

XXVIII

—◆—

EDWARD TROOD'S FINAL DISAPPEARANCE BEFORE his murder did not arouse much concern because it was not the first time.

Edward had had a difficult early life. He was always small for his age, and was born with a clubbed right foot. The other boys of the village showed no mercy in their torments. Then the stealing began. Small amounts of change at first, extra food from the cupboards, articles of clothing. Some of it, as far as his parents could determine, were offerings by the boy to his peers on threat of violent retribution. But sometimes they would find a missing object – a family candlestick, for instance – buried in the garden, as though in the crippled boy's gnawing imagination it would sprout and grow.

It was worse than all of this. Worse because the boy was by all outward appearances quite *good*. In the presence of strangers, even most times in the presence of his family, Eddie was polite, keen to keep his manners and his dress orderly. He was genuinely kind and amiable when in good spirits.

When William and his wife asked for counsel about their son from the town minister, they would be greeted by benevolent laughter. Edward? What trouble could be fancied in little, complying, polite, well-mannered Eddie Trood? The parents tried to force themselves into the same attitude. Our Eddie? Boyish mischief, that's all that plagued him. There would be long periods of quiet where Edward, a good scholar according to his teachers (some said exceptional), behaved at home and in his school and managed to avoid trouble from his tormentors.

Then he'd steal again – this time from the small hotel where

William and his wife both worked doing cooking and housekeeping. Edward forced open the ancient landlord's locked drawer and removed a purse containing several pounds. And – the true horror – Edward had committed the theft in plain sight of his mother! He brushed right by her as though he didn't know her from a housemaid.

That evening, Eddie had appeared back at home with a sullen but guiltless demeanour.

'My poor wife could hardly utter a word,' William Trood said, taking in a very deep breath like a dying man as he retold the story. Osgood and Rebecca sat next to him on the pew of the empty but sublime Rochester Cathedral, which was filled with ancient light and atmosphere, where the landlord had insisted they go to speak. He had refused to say another word at the Falstaff, as though there were too many ghosts there eavesdropping. Here, the story could be told under God's protection.

'I said to him, "Edward, my son. Eddie. You have not done what your mother thought you did, you would not, would you?" And he looked right at me, he looked into my eyes, Mr. Osgood, like this . . .'

It was another minute before Trood could finish his line of thought, saying Edward had admitted to the deed.

'I didn't see no harm in it,' added Edward. Then Edward's eyes filled up and he fell to the floor weeping and kicking. The tears had held William in check momentarily.

But William Trood knew he had no choice. He banished the fifteen-year-old from their house and from his family.

William's wife became utterly fragile with depression and dropped into the grave. She had been ill for years, but still William blamed her final turn on the dark influence of their son. William's spinster sister Elizabeth moved in with him to help him manage the Falstaff. Hearing of her nephew's actions, the very first thing Elizabeth said was, 'Like Nathan!'

That was the last she said of it. Elizabeth forbad any mention of Nathan Trood under the roof of the Falstaff Inn.

Nathan Trood was William's older brother. Nathan, in his formative years, had displayed all the mischief of his future nephew, Eddie, without any of the sympathetic and sad aspects, without the excuse of being a cripple. Sullen, lazy, mocking, nasty: that was Nathan Trood from the time he was old enough to speak, and old enough to speak meant old enough to lie. William's father, who had taken his family from Scotland to Kent, used to say Nathan was a mere nasty shadow of a real boy, a coarse creature with a bright red nose from too much crying that could not be stopped even when he was dosed with the strongest powders. Edward had only met his uncle Nathan once while a boy. Nathan, who lived in London ever since he had run away as a youth, had appeared – without invitation – at Edward's sixth birthday celebration, a simple gathering with some townsfolk and two specially made puddings.

That very moment: Nathan flashing his rotted, yellow teeth while pinching the boy's cheeks and rustling his hair. That was the moment William blamed, deep down in his soul, for turning Eddie for ever – as though some magic dust laced with death had passed from the man's breath into the child's heart. The long-estranged Nathan, by all accounts, had transformed into an even more nefarious man than he had been a boy. It was said he frequently visited dimly lit rooms in the darkest corners of London filled with opium smokers who hailed from China and other heathen lands. He consorted with scoundrels, prostitutes, smugglers, thieves and derelicts – and in them he found his income and his avenues of pleasure.

After mourning his wife's death and his son's betrayals, William had tried his best to forget banished Edward. But how to forget a man's only son? The task was impossible; attempting it was itself too painful and left William feeling clouded by sentiment and self-recrimination. All Rochester whispered about the lost cripple. William knew it. Kentish townspeople shared stories of other people's failures like they were singing carols house-to-house at Christmastime. Then William, through the whispers, heard something new: Edward, after his banishment from home, had sought sanctuary with Nathan, who had happily taken in the errant nephew he had not seen for almost ten years. Nathan's revenge on a family that never accepted him had come to pass.

In time Nathan was said to have treated Edward as though he were his own son. He brought him to meet his friends and associates. The physical suffering caused by Edward's clubbed foot was soothed by the opium-eating habit taught by Nathan.

Not to say the relationship between uncle and nephew was purely harmonious. Edward (William would hear much later, when it was all done) actually behaved on the whole quite well with his uncle, forgoing any tendencies of rebellion he had cultivated in Rochester – perhaps because he knew consequences would be severe with Nathan. Yet Nathan's generous instincts towards his nephew only appeared in bursts, to be regularly replaced by scowls, threats and demeaning insults. There were persistent rumours of a young lady in London that had set Edward's heart aflame, and Nathan's ire having been provoked by the younger man's prospects at happiness. Whatever caused the breach between the two, Edward soon disappeared. After much searching by a number of his new friends, it was discovered that he had gone abroad without telling a soul. It was said that in the course of these adventures, like so many other English boys his age, he sailed through Hong Kong and other exotic ports. When he returned to London eight months later he was welcomed home by his uncle.

Still, the young sailor and his uncle descended into a dangerous routine of perpetual indolence and indulgence in opium. Nathan seemed by his gaunt appearance and alternately drowsy and combustible manner to have become decidedly more dissatisfied in the last year. Even his wretched neighbours wanted nothing to do with Nathan. Then, Edward disappeared again.

'Who would think anything of it, less than a year after the last time he left voluntarily to go out to sea?' William asked. 'I was told later that no one in their dingy quarter had any concerns. Not even his uncle Nathan. *Especially* not his uncle Nathan.'

In fact, new whispers had started (for they also exist in London, only with a harsher undertone than in Rochester). It was said that Nathan and Edward had an ugly row about an opium enterprise that involved friends of Nathan's. These whispers told that Nathan had murdered Edward, or had paid some other men to have Edward killed, and that with the aid of his villainous compatriots they disposed of the young man's body where it could never be found. Whatever had happened this time, the fact was Edward never came back.

Nathan, increasingly sickly, soon after died in debt and in misery. William was sent for as the nearest relation and was charged with disposing of the small house in a dingy quarter of London. The house was the picture of disorder – to William's surprise, Nathan, who had thrown away his whole family so long ago, had apparently never thrown away anything else. Rats and other vermin overran the place. In the hopes of selling the old house to liberate himself of the burden,

William and a hired workman made some small structural renovations and repairs.

They were removing the rotting foundation of a wall when it happened. A sheet of canvas unravelled from above and a full skeleton of human bones fell on top of them. The skeleton, William knew instantly, was that of his son Edward Trood. The rumours were true.

'Imagine, if you can, Mr. Osgood and Miss Sand, your child's bones raining down upon your head! There is no horror that could compare to that, my last embrace with my boy. Even though we had parted ways in red anger, I confess that as the years had passed, more and more I had imagined seeing my dear son, Eddie, at my fireside again. I had merely fancied him in my imagination away at sea – sometimes I do still, and surrender to my tears when nobody is watching.'

He tried to catch his breath again in spurts.

'Oh, Mr. Trood,' Rebecca said with sympathy, 'it is your right to grieve. I lost my brother without saying good-bye, and now I must say good-bye to him every day.'

Giving up hope of a strong demeanour before his tenants, the grateful landlord began to weep on Rebecca's shoulder. When he had recovered himself, he led his guests outside behind the Cathedral.

'What did the police say when you found his bones?' Osgood enquired.

Trood stopped in the burial yard, at his family plot. 'Mr. Osgood, I never sent for them. Nor do I regret that decision.'

'But why?'

The landlord sat on the ground like a child, placing one trembling hand on the humble tablet for his wife and the other on his son's. 'I had lost my boy. Now was I to have my dead brother – however much I despised him – tossed around the columns of the newspapers as his murderer? I would not have been able to bear all of it. I would not have been able to live any longer with the Trood name. Perhaps that is why I have preferred to become of one form with my inn and the picture of the luckless Sir Falstaff. There are reasons murder is not always found out, and they are not always for cunning. The reason might be the fatigue among those who have been deadened on the inside. I buried Eddie quietly right here and told people he had suffered an accident at sea. The workman who had been with me in the excavation vowed to keep the circumstances of the discovery in his confidence, though I knew that would only go so far. Legends and fables sprouted – some told with more truth in them than others. I did not want to hear the stories, but I needed to. There was the story, as I say, that Eddie had stumbled on some kind of opium smuggling operation and was killed because of it. Eddie's terrible end at the hands of Nathan or other fiends became a topic for the Rochester busybodies to stir up.'

'And Mr. Dickens?' asked Osgood eagerly.

'What do you mean?' the landlord asked back blankly.

'Why, his final, uncompleted book – surely you realised when you saw the story, even incomplete in serial form . . .' Osgood did not know how to finish his sentence.

'The name, you mean,' the landlord of the Falstaff interrupted.

'*The Mystery of Edwin Drood*. Yes, the name, the plot of the story – did it not strike you as remarkable?'

'Mr. Dickens was a man of genius. In his novels, he'd often employ names and stories he heard for his purposes. Why, just down the road is the old redbrick mansion where "Miss Havisham" lived in her solitary gown as imagined inside his pages, and elsewhere you can ingest beef and beer where Richard Watts did the same courtesy of Mr. Dickens's imagination. I myself had been far too occupied with trying to save the inn to read more than a few instalments published of his last work. I had thought to read it all when it was published in its entirety as a book, that is, before the great Mr. Dickens died last month. And when he died, and the state of our inn was put in jeopardy because of it, I could not spare the time. In truth, I have little desire for sensational stories about the tragedy of my son other than the one I own inside. I held his skull in my hands, Mr. Osgood. It was cracked on top. I need to read no more of his death than that story written into my boy's bones!'

After returning to the Falstaff, Osgood immediately arranged to depart for London with Rebecca in order to make further enquiries into the remarkable tale of Edward Trood. This was against the strident orders of Dr. Steele, who Osgood thought might try to place him in a straitjacket to prevent his leaving. Steele warned the publisher that the rheumatic bouts that had plagued him through his youth could return if he did not wait for a full recovery, but Osgood would not change his mind. Osgood also left word with the Falstaff to direct any letters to their new address at the St. James Hotel, Piccadilly, and to send Datchery there at once if he came to call on him.

Osgood, gathering some of his belongings into the hall of the inn, also found himself facing a looking glass for the first time he could remember since his assault. Seeing his reflection, both of his hands involuntarily moved to his face and then slid down his cheeks to his neck as though to hold his head in place. He blinked. Where had the boyish appearance gone, the innocent visage he had always cursed and cherished? In its place was a ghost-pale, almost gaunt countenance, with a complex web of tired lines, crevices and dark shadows around his eyes. His hair was brittle and flat. He had either crossed towards a premature death mask or from a soft boyhood to a hardened manhood; he could not say which. There was an inspiriting element of his appearance, though. He no longer was inconspicuous or exchangeable with other young Boston Brahmin businessmen. This was James R. Osgood, however battered, there was no mistake about it.

Only then did he realise, confirming a suspicion by walking back into his room, that the looking glass previously there had been removed. He considered whether it could have been the dictatorial Dr. Steele or Rebecca – motivated by control if the former or affection if the latter. He reflected for a moment while standing at the threshold of his room and decided not to ask her about it.

'What about your gift, Mr. Osgood?' It was Rebecca, holding the pink glass tazza from the auction.

'Perhaps we ought to leave it with Mr. Trood to bring to Miss Dickens,' Osgood answered.

'It may be better presented in person. We have an hour before the next train leaves for London.'

'You would not . . .' Osgood said. 'That is to say, you would have no objections to calling on Miss Dickens?'

Rebecca shook her head. 'I'd think it a fine idea, Mr. Osgood.'

They went across the road to Gadshill but found it even more desolate than it had been. The front door was open and nobody was there to bring in visitors. Nearly every object was gone now since the Christie's auction. Piles of luggage filled the front corridor and the library. At first, Osgood and Rebecca did not even see Henry Scott, who was curled up in the corner of the library sandwiched between two trunks of clothing weeping. His fine white livery was streaked with tear stains.

'Oh, Mr. Scott, are you all right?' Rebecca asked, kneeling beside him and placing a hand on his shoulder.

Henry tried but failed to speak through his sobbing, communicating in broken syllables like an island savage that they were to leave Gadshill by the morning. Soon, a woman covered in a long black veil, and a flowing black dress with a short jacket with ruffled hem and a grand bustle in the back – mourning in the style of Queen Victoria for her Albert – descended the stairs.

'Other events have delayed my presentation of this, Miss Dickens,' Osgood said to her, holding out the tazza.

'We read in the *Telegraph* that this sold for seven pounds odd, but it did not say to whom!' Mamie Dickens answered, amazed.

'It did not seem fitting that anyone but you should have it.'

'It is uncommonly kind of you both!' She lifted her veil and wiped her eyes. 'Oh, how my sister would laugh at me to see me cry over a little bowl! I shall leave Gadshill tomorrow but shall bring this with me wherever we go in the world.' Putting the tazza back on the mantelpiece, she took one of Osgood's hands and one of Rebecca's.

'I hold my father,' she said softly, 'in my heart of hearts as a man apart from all other men, as one apart from all other human beings. I wish never to marry and have to change my name. So I can always be a Dickens. Do you think that so strange, Miss Sand?'

'How lucky you are to have been cherished by a man loved by all the world.'

'Good-bye and God bless you both,' Mamie said, squeezing her visitors' hands once more.

Aunt Georgy walked in alongside an unexpected man, who bowed coldly at the visitors.

'Dr. Steele!' Osgood said. 'I am afraid you shall not persuade me to remain in Rochester.'

'That is not why I am here,' said the doctor coldly.

'Nobody is sick, I hope, Aunt Georgy?' Osgood asked.

'I should have thought you would have been on your way to London already, Mr. Osgood,' Dr. Steele said disapprovingly.

'Dr. Steele has come to settle our bills before we leave,' Georgy said. 'I am afraid we haven't had time since . . . since the good doctor tried everything to revive poor Charles.' With these words, the matron of the house glanced towards the dining room. 'Unfortunately, we have not yet received the funds from the auction. I do appreciate Dr. Steele's patience.'

'Your servant,' the doctor said, bowing, though not exactly promising patience.

'You treated Mr. Dickens after he collapsed?'

'I can assure you I did, Mr. Osgood,' the doctor said. 'I see that in addition to disobeying my directions for your own health, you have added to Miss Dickens's grief. Perhaps it is best for both of you to leave Gadshill.'

Mamie had gone to sit in a quiet corner with the tazza to hide the fact that she was crying.

'Dr. Steele, perhaps—' Georgy started to object to his command.

But the imperious medical man gave her a steely-eyed look that combined a doctor's strict prescription and a collector's reminder of an overdue bill. Even the strong-willed voice of Georgina Hogarth was silenced.

'Good-bye, then, Mr. Osgood,' Steele said, vengeful over his disobedience.

'Good-bye,' Osgood replied.

'Wait.' Here was Henry, upright and with dried eyes. 'I have not seen Miss Dickens smile like that in some time. If she weeps, it is in the joy of the small swatch of memories you and Miss Sand returned to her. Come, Mr. Osgood, let me show you two something before you go, if you have a few moments.' These words of the servant's were meant squarely for Dr. Steele, but were spoken to Osgood.

As Dr. Steele glared at them, Osgood and Rebecca followed Henry out of the room. 'There have been very few people allowed in here since June the ninth,' said Henry, stepping across the threshold of the dining room with his eyes closed. 'That is the place where he died.' It was a green velvet sofa with a stylish curving back.

'Were you in the room, Mr. Scott?' asked Osgood.

Henry nodded. 'Yes, and I shall not fear to speak of it. Grief pent up will burst the heart, as the saying is.' His eyes became wide as he described the scene of Dickens's death. 'The Chief collapsed on the floor of the room when sitting down to eat after working all day on *The Mystery of Edwin Drood*. Messengers rushed to town to retrieve Dr. Steele, while I helped carry a sofa from upstairs into the dining room, and then assisted Aunt Georgy in lifting him. He was mumbling.'

'Mr. Scott,' Osgood interrupted. 'Did you hear anything that Mr. Dickens said when he did speak?'

'No. It could not be made out at all. Well, except one word I could hear.'

'What was that?' Osgood asked.

'A name. Forster. The poor Chief was calling for John Forster to be by his side. I daresay that shall be Mr. Forster's proudest moment. I know it would be mine had it been my name on his lips.'

As Dickens had continued to worsen, Henry was asked by Georgy to begin heating bricks at the furnace. 'When I returned to this room, the sombre doctors had cut away the Chief's coat and shirt. To see it! The room was crowded now – Miss Dickens and Mrs. Collins had hurried here from a dinner in London. Hours passed, and still he remained in an unconscious sleep. How I wished for another instruction to heat bricks or any such errand! I looked in on the scarlet geraniums in the conservatory and swept the tiles around them. Those were Dickens's favourites and I wanted the area clear for when the Chief woke up. He could look out and smell the conservatory's sweet fragrance through the open window.'

Amidst it all, there arrived a fair-haired, pretty and tightly cloaked young woman, a woman who everyone knew about even if they were not meant to. But the master of the house did not stir under the frightened gaze of her bright blue eyes, either. Deep into the night, the same stillness persisted. An even more sombre doctor from London joined the others in the dining room. Pale and rattled, the London doctor pronounced brain haemorrhage.

'The poor Chief, he would never be moved from this sofa again.'

Henry bowed with a regretful frown that he could say no more.

'Thank you, Mr. Scott,' said Osgood. 'I know it must be a painful thing to recount.'

'On the contrary. It is my finest honour to have been here.'

The train into London could not move fast enough for the two travellers. A few hours after their arrival in London, Datchery had received the message from the landlord of the Falstaff and met them at their Piccadilly hotel. Osgood could not go to Scotland Yard without betraying William Trood's trust, but the eccentric Datchery, mesmerised or not, could investigate unfettered. Osgood poured out all the information about Edward Trood and his connections to his uncle's opium merchant friends.

'Remarkable!' Datchery said, his long slender frame pacing the floor up and down. He looked as though he might break into a laugh. 'Why, Ripley, I believe you have turned a corner in the investigation!'

Osgood snapped his fingers. 'If it's true, it all fits together now, my dear Datchery, doesn't it? When Dickens said there was something "curious and new", this is what he meant – he was opening the case of a real murder mystery. It was different from anything he had done before, different from anything Wilkie Collins or other novelists had written. Think of how one of the first chapters of *Drood* begins.'

Osgood had read the instalments so many times, he could recite it from memory, but he removed the first instalment from his trunk to point it out to Datchery. 'For sufficient reasons which this narrative will itself unfold,' he read from the first sentence of chapter 3, 'as it advances, a fictitious name must be bestowed upon the old Cathedral town. Let it stand in these pages as Cloisterham.'

'Indeed!' Datchery called out.

'The reason for the alias Cloisterham to stand in for Rochester,' Osgood said, 'is that a real crime was about to be revealed, and a real criminal unveiled.'

Datchery nodded vigorously. 'And when *The Mystery of Edwin Drood* began to be published in serial, every eye was on it, and every eye in the world of these opium pushers and smugglers could see in it the story of poor Edward Trood. Think of it: Nathan Trood is dead, but if he had help in the murder of his nephew, someone would fear exposure.'

'Except that William never involved the police. Edward's murderer may have felt comfortable for these long years,' Osgood said.

'Indeed. But if Dickens's novel revealed new clues, it could lead the police to the discovery of the facts of the actual case and to the other killers of Edward Trood!' Datchery interrupted himself by putting up a hand for silence. He pointed towards the door, where there was a slight shuffling noise.

'Miss Rebecca?' Datchery whispered.

'No, I do not think it can be her . . . Miss Sand is out making arrangements for credit at the bank in London for our stay,' Osgood said in a quiet voice. 'The money we brought with us has melted away. She will be out another hour at least.'

Datchery motioned for Osgood to move aside and indicated that someone was eavesdropping on them. Then he grabbed the iron poker from the hearth. He stealthily made his way across the length of the well-furnished room and opened the door slowly. A strong hand shot out and grabbed Datchery's wrist, twisting it until the poker fell to the floor.

'Good God!' Datchery cried out, tumbling backwards. Struck with a quick fist in the jaw, he staggered and fell.

'Help! Call for help!' Datchery moaned while attempting to drag himself away.

'No need for that, Mr. Osgood,' said the attacker.

Osgood had reached for the bell pull but being addressed by name stopped and stared at the newcomer with amazement.

The young man stepping towards him removed his cape and cap to reveal the figure of Tom Branagan. *Tom Branagan!* A man whom Osgood had not seen in more than two years – since the end of Dickens's American tour – now plunging through Osgood's hotel door in a brazen assault!

Branagan, who no longer looked to be the lad he was in America, but a powerfully built man, retrieved some rope from the curtains and began tying Datchery's hands together.

'Mr. Branagan!' Osgood exclaimed. 'What is this about?'

'What do you want from me?' Datchery moaned pitiably.

Branagan, eyes dark with anger, stood over Datchery and held him down with the heel of his boot on the soft middle of his neck. 'In the name of Charles Dickens, the time has come for answers.'

XXIX

SGOOD LOWERED HIMSELF ON TO THE rug next to Datchery. The publisher could not fathom the sudden upheaval. He turned over in his thoughts what had occurred to try to make sense of it: the near fatal visit to the opium rooms, the revelations of William Trood about his son, Tom Branagan's sudden appearance out of nowhere at the London hotel and senseless attack on his companion.

'Branagan!' Osgood cried. 'What have you done? What are you doing here?' Taking Datchery's hand, Osgood attempted to restore his senses. He untied the curtain rope that Tom had used to bind him.

'I wouldn't do that, Mr. Osgood,' Tom said.

'Mr. Branagan, please soak a cloth with cold water from that nightstand. My good Datchery, this is some kind of preposterous misunderstanding. I knew this man briefly as a porter when Mr. Dickens had come to America.'

'It is not I who misunderstand, Mr. Osgood,' said Tom. 'I am a porter no more.'

'Then explain yourself at once, if you dare!' Osgood shouted to the handsome younger man. He had tried to restrain his anger but could not once he saw Tom's unrepentant demeanour. 'This is what you'd still call acting upon your instinct, I suppose?'

Tom closed the door to the hall. 'This man is a fraud and a double dealer. He is not who he says he is.'

'I know he is not Dick Datchery, of course – Datchery is a character in a Dickens novel! I fear you are out of your depth. This man is unwell and under no fault of his own has fallen under a powerful magnetic spell initiated by Mr. Dickens before his death – one that has allowed us unique insights into an important case through his talents as investigator.'

By this time, Datchery had risen to his feet and was steadying himself along the wall until he could be lowered into a chair.

Tom said, 'Why not ask him to explain for himself?'

'I don't know what you mean by browbeating me, laddie,' Datchery protested, rubbing his bloody jaw but trying to approximate a smile. 'You mistake me.'

'If you will not divulge the truth, so be it. I will. Mr. Osgood, this wretch, disguised in George Washington costume, acted as a speculator and a rioter during the whole of the Chief's tour of America – set on sabotage and ruin for the reading tour's financial success.'

The accused's eyes narrowed with anger and he lumbered towards Tom. 'I shall not stand here and be insulted!'

Tom threw a long punch into Datchery's stomach. Then he drew a pistol from his pocket and pointed it at the man doubled over in pain.

Osgood stood immoveable at the sight of the weapon.

'Datchery, clear out,' Osgood said with an attempt at calm. 'Datchery! Go now before you're hurt more seriously,' he repeated. But the man wasn't moving, just looking between Tom and Osgood.

'I will put a ball through you if you lie one more time to him, sir,' Tom said, pistol pointed steady as a rock.

'Datchery, go!' Osgood cried. 'Branagan, be still! This man has been a friend to me.' But when Osgood looked over his shoulder at the subject of his words, he saw a strange blank stare that contradicted him.

'Not . . . Datchery,' said the man, pronouncing the words between a confessional exhale, and his accent softening into a product more of the streets of New York than of the English countryside. He looked at them with a weary eye like the ancient mariner's. 'It is Rogers. Jack Rogers. Now you know my name. Pocket your pistol and strike me no more, Mr. Branagan, so that I may have my say.'

Jack Rogers looked down at his feet for most of his account.

'I did not mean to harm either of you and have grown to respect you, Mr. Osgood, more than I ever expected of a man of bustle and business, for your perseverance, your genuineness. I daresay you've become so tall with accomplishment, you stand in your own light, and don't see how much more of you there is. I hope after hearing my position, you shall understand.'

In his early life, Rogers had been an actor in the second-rate theatres of New York. He came from a modest family of small means, with an unfriendly disposition to his choice of work. His skills on the stage tended mostly towards broadly comedic work and violent adventure. Once, while he rehearsed for a play involving a long sword duel, there was a fall from the stage and the blade of his sword struck the theatre manager's son, whom no effort of the doctors over the subsequent hours could save. Rogers was devastated by the horrible accident and banished from the theatre. After Rogers had spent irregular bouts of hard employment in the ailing American economy, in the year 1844 the mayor of New York, one James Harper, founder of the Harper & Brothers publishing house, initiated the first police force for that city. These posts were considered undesirable, and it was difficult to fill the rolls. Rogers, having no other work, volunteered.

Harper's Police became a powerful army inside a city that was combustible with political and ethnic rivalries and corruption. The following year the Republican mayor was defeated and the police put in other hands, but the Harpers quietly maintained close ties to the policemen. Soon ex-mayor Harper privately employed Rogers, who had become known for a certain forcefulness of character and alert cleverness and an ability to resolve the enigmatic. When James, still known as the Mayor, or one of the other brothers comprising their publishing enterprise – the Colonel (John), the Captain (Wesley) and the Major, the youngest (Fletcher) – needed assistance, particularly of a secretive nature, Rogers would be discreetly sent for.

One instance of this occurred when Charles Dickens announced in the summer of 1867 that Fields, Osgood & Co. were henceforth to be his exclusive publisher in America. The Harpers envied and feared the income that could be collected by their rivals in Boston. They sent Rogers and one or two other agents to cause disruptions in the ticket sales for the author's American tour, hoping that the newspapers would portray the Boston publisher as incompetent, cheap and greedy. As part of this scheme of disruption, Rogers, in the guise of a speculator in memorable George Washington wig and hat, spread accusations to the newspapers of Tom Branagan's having sparked the violence at one of those sales. The Harpers, meanwhile, ordered their weekly magazine to print mean-spirited and inflammatory cartoons and columns about Dickens as quickly as they could be invented, just as Fletcher had done in attacks against the wretches, corrupt and immigrant-friendly, who controlled the Tammany political operation.

'You need not glare with moral judgement, gentlemen,' Rogers said, shaking his head in deep sadness. 'I know my actions to be deceitful! Many years ago, after my accident on the stage, I suffered constantly from sleeplessness. I would not have survived without laudanum from my doctor. But soon I found I could not go a few days without the drug in my system, I would yield, vowing to myself it was the last. A mere hour without it and my insides would feel torn and shrivelled, I would walk about in humiliation and melancholy. Laudanum no longer sufficed, I sought crude opium as if it were the most succulent meal, served by a voluptuous siren in the heart of a violent maelstrom. The opium was my panacea. I took a dose at ten o'clock and another at four and a half o'clock. For hours after taking a fresh dose, I felt invincible and energetic, with an intellectual and physical capacity beyond the mere human. I was Atlas with the world teetering on my shoulders. And so I remained the drug's perpetual slave, and to get more I would have crossed barefoot over hot coals or swam up to my neck in my own blood. Under its influence, my stomach and bowels felt twisted and my head screamed. I took more to try to harden myself, and I entered a dangerous overdose.

'The Major knew I was in turmoil. "Well!" said he, removing his spectacles with his usual dramatic gesture. "You know me to be a blunt man, Rogers, and a good Methodist, so I ask directly: will you survive your own habits and continue to serve this firm?"

'"To be equally blunt myself," said I, "I think I shall not, Major. Death would be a gift."

'"Well, then I shall help! Let us not surrender so easily to any enemy!"'

The Major arranged for Rogers to reside at an asylum for inebriates, headed by a doctor who insisted that opium was not a vice but a disease like other known diseases. The secluded life there cleared Rogers's blood of the poison.

'That was six months ago. Upon my word, I have never again brought opium into my flesh. But upon leaving that sanctum, free of the vile poppy, I found myself a slave to a new and imperious master: the Major. For the last few years, as the Major had gained more control of the publishing house from his more reasonable brothers, I squinted at his methods and manipulations. Yet the asylum that saved my life had been expensive, and I could not sever my ties with the house of Harper until this debt was paid.'

After the completion of Dickens's American tour, upon hearing intelligence that Dickens was at work on a novel of mystery, the Major and the Mayor Harpers wished to uncover the details of the new novel's plot in advance.

'Because I could employ any accent under the sun from my days as an actor, they chose to send me here to England to perpetrate the ruse. I was to get inside Dickens's sanctum. I made enquiries around Kent and found that Dickens ministered to friends and strangers alike who fell ill, with techniques of mesmerism and animal magnetism. And I knew by reputation that he was particularly sensitive to those suffering in poverty, a friend and champion of the working man.

'I determined to pose as a sick English farmer requiring Mr. Dickens's care to gain admission into his study and glean some hint as to the future of *Drood* before anyone else.'

'Did you find anything about it?' Osgood asked.

'The great man could keep his secrets!' Rogers threw up his hands. 'Each time, Dickens would lay me down on his sofa, pass his hands and fingers in a pattern across my head, and then, when he had been convinced I was asleep, he chanted to suggest better healing to the inner places of my brain. Finally, he would blow softly on my forehead until he thought I had just awakened. I guessed that if I should seem to have been severely mesmerised into believing myself one of the figures *in his novel*, he would be more likely to unwittingly expose revelations concerning it.'

'So that is when you chose to play Dick Datchery?' asked Tom.

'Yes. Datchery is introduced in mysterious fashion in one of the later chapters of *Edwin Drood*. Before it had been printed, I overheard this chapter one afternoon while waiting in the library at Gadshill when Mr. Dickens was in the next room reading aloud to some of his family and friends, something he did as he composed each instalment. I fancied from whatever poor science I have observed reading novels in my lifetime, that with the fate of that character of Datchery there resided the fate of the whole *Mystery*. And my ruse worked! To a limit.'

Rogers recounted the tricks he employed to play the role of

Datchery at Gadshill, including writing down on slips of paper and on the inside of his hat band every word he heard put into the character's mouth by Dickens and employing that exact language whenever possible. This authenticity seemed to have aroused the novelist's interest, yet their mesmeric sessions still dealt exclusively with the treatment of the patient's health and the master could not be coaxed into holding forth on the topic of his novel.

Rogers naturally took every opportunity when he was alone – when Dickens would excuse himself from the study to attend to one of his pets or to greet a caller – to secretly examine the contents of any papers on the desk or in an open drawer. He found some evidence that the opium smokers appearing in *Drood* had been inspired by the occupants of a notorious room in a court called Palmer's Folly, which Dickens had visited on a police-guided tour of London.

Soon after, Dickens's health had worsened and before long the sessions were suspended for Rogers and the other small circle of mesmerism patients who came to Gadshill. Upon learning of Dickens's death the first week in June, Rogers wired his employers back at Franklin Square in New York, presuming his mission complete. He was instead ordered by the Harpers to remain for a few weeks and to make himself a nuisance around Gadshill so that he might observe any dealings about *Drood* in that time. Because of the five-year wait since Dickens's last novel, *Drood* would mean hundreds of thousands of dollars of potential profits to whoever could publish it first in America. The Major would not take his eye off this goal.

Only days later, Rogers received an entirely new and unexpected order; he was advised of intelligence that Mr. J. R. Osgood was on his way to England in all likelihood with the aim of finding missing pieces of Dickens's final novel. Rogers was to stop Osgood from doing so, in order for Harpers' pirating of the novel to proceed unhindered.

'I confess this heavily, wearily, Ripley. I have since come to know you are a decent and good man, who cares for employees under his charge, as I have seen you do with Miss Rebecca,' Rogers continued. 'But do understand one thing, if only one thing about me, and I shall one day die content knowing you did not dismiss me wholeheartedly.'

'I wonder what you could possibly say for yourself,' Osgood replied sadly.

'Merely this: I am no artist. No genius like the people who occupy your life, perhaps like you yourself. Whether you think of yourself as one or not, you have the bravery of the artist inside you. But *this* is the worldly work I know and have practised since trained as one of Harper's Police. I had tried to work in a bank before that, but I flattened out at it because I did not like how the other men looked at me. We were the first policemen in the city of New York, and we were hated – people stoned us. We had to be armed with a "hook and bill" for each one of us – the peculiar club with the spiked top you saw when we went into the dark corner of London. The public thought we were there to serve as spies and, strangely, this fear made us *into* spies. Disguises, investigations, secret service, any dealings underhanded and scrubby, this has been *my* art, *my* lot. I meant to set you out on a wild goose chase by leading you into the opium room, knowing you would recognise it as the prototype for Dickens's book and be distracted. If I succeeded in this task, I could finally free myself from Major Harper's grip and return to the stage, where I was once happy and made others happy as your firm's books do. One day I shall have a houseful of children, and shall wish to be respected and loved by them. I did not intend any harm to come to you, dear Ripley!'

'But you did have every intention to mislead me, as you admit!'

'I ask not for forgiveness for the deception but do beg that you believe my purpose in owning it to you. I desire to help you.'

'Ha!' Osgood responded.

'Ripley, I, too, was attacked by those opium pushers!'

'Which was your own sorry fault, sir,' Tom said in reproach. 'Your careless doing.'

'To a point, yes, Mr. Branagan. But the violence done to us was only the hint of some far larger sinister movement. Ripley, I believe you to be in grave danger even as we speak.'

'From you as much as from anyone else,' Osgood said.

'You have had more say than you deserve now. Have a chair and be comfortable while I send for a police coach,' Tom added.

Rogers shook his head. 'No. You need my help, gentlemen – your survival may depend on it! Perhaps my own as well, though it may mean nothing to you now!' A glance passed between the two other men that showed no sign of wavering. Rogers, becoming more panicked, now pleaded shamelessly. 'My dear Ripley, can't you trust me again? I promise to repay my debt to you for what I have done.'

Osgood directed a heated look at his former companion. 'You have earned my trust and sympathy through a bundle of lies. You plotted to disrupt our American tour with Dickens, to lay blame on Mr. Branagan where there was none, to distract my mission here, all under the nefarious orders of those Harpy brothers. I have no doubt Major Harper holds the strings of your current plea, as well. Any minute he will pull you down and set up Judy, or the devil, or some other wooden grotesque to try to lead us astray. Remove yourself from our sight now, while you have your liberty, if Mr. Branagan allows it.'

Tom took a step back and waved the man to the door. Rogers made no argument this time. 'Thank heavens for you, Ripley,' he said. He quietly turned and, hat under his arm, scurried out of the room.

Tom Branagan's appearance – and the pistol he had brandished – had been as much a shock to Osgood as the revelation of Rogers's true identity. Once they confirmed that Rogers had left the premises of the hotel, and Rebecca had returned from the bank, Tom set out to tell them of his own winding path that had reunited them. Returning to England after Dickens's reading tour, Tom had continued to be employed in a domestic capacity in the town of Ross at George Dolby's estate. But he tired of the monotony of caring for the Dolby children's much-adored ponies and driving around Mrs. Dolby, who had taken full advantage of their greatly increased wealth since the American tour. Dolby, for his part, had been hardened by what he called the American bullying, and spent their money extravagantly and carelessly, especially after his second son died at only a few days old. Tom occasionally met with Dickens at Dolby's, including at George Dolby Jr.'s christening, but the novelist, though friendly to him, never spoke of the dangerous events of the late American tour.

Tom showed Osgood and Rebecca a pearl-handled switchblade he kept in his pocket. 'This was her knife that I took out of her hand. I realised I still had it after we left the country and found it among my clothing. I tried to throw it away, but found I could not. I think about her sometimes when I see it, and I think about what could have happened to the Chief.'

'You should be proud of what you did,' Osgood said.

'I was certain she would die, you know,' Tom said. 'You would have been, too, Mr. Osgood, had you seen the blood. The Chief must have thought so, he seemed so sad when he saw her, he even whispered something in her ear to soothe her, though I could not hear what it was. But the truth is that few women attempting suicide in that fashion ever possess the strength to cut their own skin deep enough after they begin. Many survive, as she did, though forever diminished inside and out. Their images from that day will always be with me – Louisa Barton's as much as Charles Dickens's.'

Dulled by his time in Ross and haunted by what had happened in those last hours in Boston, Tom applied to the police at Scotland Yard and waited several months, when a vacancy opened for a night constable third class, the lowest and most endangered tier of the English police. He served his beats from 10 p.m. at night until 6 a.m. This was the only position usually open to an Irishman, though the fact that he could read and write well brought him quick promotion to the place of police constable first class.

Because the Irish were assigned divisional beats in the poorest sections of London, Tom had been one of the constables on patrol alerted to the commotion in the Palmer's Folly court on the night of Osgood's attack. He had been fixing a coal hole that had come dangerously loose in a nearby street. Upon reaching the scene of activity, Tom witnessed Rogers fleeing, his head bloodied and injured, and recognised him.

'I knew him as the man who, in his Washington wig and old-fashioned three-cornered hat, started the riot at the ticket sale in Brooklyn that I was blamed for. His appearance in London was remarkable to me, as you'd imagine. I decided to shadow him so that I could discover more and I found out that he was boarding under an assumed name in an out-of-the-way lodging house. I followed him for several more days, discovering that he had been wiring telegraphs and sending letters back to New York. When I saw him enter this hotel, I examined the guest ledger and was freshly amazed to find your name among the occupants here, Mr. Osgood. I suspected that he had been operating some design of nefarious nature ever since our time in America, but I didn't know if he was a confidence man of some kind, a thief, a brazen murderer.'

'That is why you brought your pistol,' Osgood said.

Tom nodded, putting his pistol aside with a relieved smile. 'To be honest, it's lucky that I didn't have to use it. They have issued them to the department because of the Fenian attacks on the government and on the prisons. Because I'm of Irish blood, I have been assigned to infiltrate what's left of the Fenian groups. But the department has only held sporadic training with the pistols, and I have yet to be instructed in them.'

Osgood, in his turn, shared with Tom a full and detailed account of their adventures on the *Samaria* with Herman and their experiences in England.

Tom pulled the curtains around the room closed as he listened.

'Mr. Branagan, what's wrong?' Rebecca asked. 'Do you think someone is watching?'

Tom leaned both arms on the mantelpiece. In the two years since the American tour, he had grown a full beard and his arms and chest had become more prominent. Any Renaissance sculptor would have been grateful for him as a model.

'The cane you described with the strange gold head that the man called Herman possessed – did you see it up close?' Tom asked.

Osgood nodded. 'It was a sort of dragon.'

'Do you remember if it had teeth?'

'Yes,' said Osgood, 'sharp as razor blades. How did you know?'

'Herman,' Tom repeated the name to himself. 'We must move in secret from now on.'

'You know who that monster is then who attacked Mr. Osgood on the ship?' Rebecca asked.

'The marks on the necks and chests of the bodies of the dead opium fiends – they were almost like fang marks. The police did not know what to think of them.'

'Made by his cane!' Osgood cried. 'The beast's head!'

'If you encountered the same man on your steamship, then this was no random attack,' said Tom.

'Then I did not imagine him at the opium room.' Osgood said with a gasp. Even as he said this, Herman's stony visage entered his mind. 'He really was there, Miss Sand; you were right, he was never a mere pickpocket! If he was the one who injected me with opium, it must have been him who did the same to poor Daniel. It was Herman that intervened in the attack, killing the Lascar and the Bengalee. He is the devil we must confront to unravel all this! Can the police find him, Branagan?'

'Scotland Yard will not treat the death of two wretched opium eaters seriously. But I don't know if we will have to find him,' Tom said mysteriously.

'What do you mean, Mr. Branagan?' Rebecca asked.

'If I am correct, Miss Sand, the challenge will not be to find him. It will be to avoid him long enough to learn which way this fatal wind blows.'

Yahee was an opium dealer but not only that. He was said to be the first one of his craft in London, the one to show all the others how to mix and smoke the black ooze. Known by many East Londoners as Jack Chinaman, Yahee occasionally irritated the wrong member of the London police, and when he did, he would usually be put in the cage for begging or some other trifle, since opium itself was not illegal. He was pleasantly surprised when, after the latest incarceration, he was released from prison two weeks early; at first, he thought his internal sense of the calendar had been altered while he was locked away, but he was told the prison was too crowded to feed every ill-mannered Chinaman.

The newly liberated opium mixer walked on the night of his release through the long, narrow tar-stained streets towards the dismal slum region of the docks. The air smelled of rubbish mixed with the odours of coffee and tobacco from the big brick warehouses lining the streets. As he came closer to where he kept his rooms, Yahee was stopped by an unfamiliar man in a police cape and hat.

'Keep distance, bobbie,' Yahee mumbled, pushing him aside. 'Free man here!'

'You're free because of me, Yahee,' the constable said, the words slowing Yahee's steps. The wind was dispersing the fog and revealed a clearer view of the policeman. 'I was the one to arrange it and I can undo it. I suspect you heard about what happened at Opium Sal's rooms to two of her hirelings, a Lascar and Bengalee.'

'No,' Yahee said dumbly. 'What?'

Tom took a step closer. 'I think you probably know.'

'Yahee hear of it,' the man said, breaking quickly under Tom's knowing glare. 'They murdered, yes, I hear of it in quod.'

'Correct. And I wonder if you could have been behind it,' said Tom.

'No chance, stupid bobbie! Yahee in prison when happened!'

the Chinese man said angrily, spitting on Tom's boot. 'They try to rob wrong man, I hear. You try to make Yahee guilty! Go chase pickpocket!'

'Sally is your competition. How can we be certain you didn't arrange for her men to be attacked while you were in prison?' Tom asked.

'Unfair! Unfair, you Charlie!'

Tom didn't argue the point. He knew what he was doing was unfair – he knew Yahee had nothing to do with what had happened in Palmer's Folly. But he also knew that the small number of Chinese in London were looked upon with ready suspicion, especially an opium pusher like Yahee. Tom's threat to him was credible, and that made Yahee the perfect candidate.

Yahee, understanding something more was at hand, said, 'Why you want Yahee?'

Tom leaned in. 'I want to know about Herman.' This last word he whispered.

Yahee opened and closed his mouth as though ridding himself of a sour taste, waved this idea into the air and spouted out an impressive line of curses in Chinese as he began to hurry away. 'No, no! No Ironhead! I talk of Ironhead Herman, I die! You die!'

Tom drew his baton and blocked Yahee from moving. Yahee's fear of Herman was painted across his face and in that moment Tom knew he had him trapped. 'You *will* tell me everything you know of the man you call Ironhead, and I will never breathe your name to anyone. Or I lock you up – and spread the word that you told me about Herman.'

'Nah, you just plain bobbie! No one believe you!'

Yahee turned and scurried the other away but his path was blocked by another man. Osgood, who had been waiting in the shadows, stepped forward.

'They might not believe a constable,' Osgood said, 'but they will be ready to believe the American businessman who was attacked.'

Yahee looked around in fright. 'Why do this to Yahee?'

'We won't talk in the open, Yahee,' Tom said. 'We will go inside the jail. I am a constable, not a detective – nobody will notice anything but a beggar being taken in, and then taken out when we're done. Is it a bargain or not, Jack Chinaman?'

Yahee spat, this time on Tom's shoulder. 'Bargain no! No jail! Yahee not go back in there! Herman eyes everywhere inside the cage!'

'Very well,' Tom conceded. 'We'll go to your rooms, then.'

'To the devil with you! Yahee sooner die than be seen there with you!'

'Then we'll go to a place where nobody can see.'

The Thames Tunnel had been built with great ambition and fanfare and no thought of failure. The massive passage would, for a two pence fee, allow pedestrians and carriages a convenient and pleasant crossing under the city's main waterway. But this would be the third attempt to tunnel underneath the Thames, and though more ambitious, it had been no more successful than the first two.

The gigantic construction undertaking was fraught with problems. Accidents and escalating expenses plagued the eighteen years of work on the tunnel; ten lives, mostly miners', had been taken through mishaps and mismanagement, falls, floods, gas explosions; surviving miners had gone on strike; after a brief period of excitement upon its finally being opened to the public, the massive tunnel was soon abandoned by Londoners. Investors lost their shares. Even the prostitutes and cadgers who frequented it grew tired of the leaks, the dangerous disrepair, the long and treacherous walk down the dizzying staircase to the tunnels eighty feet below the ground. It waited in limbo as one of the railroad companies negotiated its purchase for a line to Brighton. Its entrance by now surrounded by dilapidated warehouses, the Thames Tunnel became a mercifully forgotten embarrassment.

It was here, underneath the metropolis, in these desolate trails to nowhere, that Yahee stood with Tom Branagan and Osgood. They had descended the winding stairs to the lowest level of the abandoned subterranean underworld.

'This is only what people say,' Yahee qualified himself before beginning, leaning against the cold, sweaty stone as the three listened to the harsh churning of water pumps. 'No more than that.'

'Tell us,' ordered Tom, trying to refrain from breathing in too much of the putrid air.

Yahee looked around, his eyes following up on the slightest noise. He put up his nose and winced. 'Do not like here. People die building. Devil here.'

Tom did not argue, simply nodded a promise of safety. 'Tell us what you know, and you can go. Tell us about Herman.'

What people said, according to Yahee's broken English, was that a boy named Hormazd had been part of the Cama family of Parsee opium traders who carried the drug in shipments from India to the Chinese ports.

'Parsees best opium traders in world. Fast and most fierce. Hormazd whole family traders – whole family slaughtered by Ah'ling, pirate chieftain.'

This chieftain took Hormazd captive, and put him with an assortment of European sailors taken from other merchant vessels. Young Hormazd had lived on an opium clipper since he was ten years old and was kept alive by the pirates to use his strength in labour. Hormazd prayed in his native Zend language towards the sun in the morning and evening. Living among the brutal Chinese pirates, Hormazd and the other captives were beaten with bamboo rods whenever they fatigued or failed to heed their superiors.

The captives were forced to aid the pirate *lorcha*, a swift and light vessel, in the attack of several smaller Chinese ships. The pirates were brutal in their attacks. When the captain of a captured vessel refused to cooperate in telling them where opium or precious metals were hidden, the pirates would cut open the captain's skin and drink his blood to terrorise him further.

The captives had to chew tobacco to prevent nausea at the sight of the horrors the pirates perpetrated on their way to treasures. All except Hormazd. The boy seemed to absorb rather than repel the grotesque lessons of the pirates. Though he did not forget how he had come to be there and never wavered in his hatred for his captors, he did not seem to cherish any particular notions of right and wrong. This friendless Parsee, knowing nothing else but his own strength and misfortunes, operated like a dumb animal, with no consciousness of the master's moral demerits.

The pirates lived in a vile state of humanity. To them, a delicacy every bit equal to guavas or oysters was a boiled rat cut into slices or raw caterpillars over rice served with a foul-tasting bright blue liquor they mixed.

One muggy afternoon, which happened to fall on Hormazd Cama's fourteenth birthday, he and some of the European captives had been taken on the *lorcha* away from the rest of the pirate fleet to a far-off strait for target practice. A malicious member of the pirate crew was beating Hormazd on his back and arms for some real or imagined infraction. Something flickered in the boy's eye, and in a swift series of motions, Hormazd had broken the pirate's neck. Some of the European captives were witnesses.

'You must escape,' said a young Englishman who had taken a particular interest in the singular Parsee boy. 'They will kill you and cut off your head if you don't! We will help if you take us with you, Herman.' The British and American prisoners had called him Herman, their best approximation of his Parsee name.

Realising that there would be consequences for his murder of the pirate, Hormazd stiffened and nodded. 'Please help,' he said.

'Nah, don't count me in,' said a Scotch prisoner. 'I won't risk my hide because of this fire worshipper's heathen impulses! A fellow who refuses even to smoke, and with that Hindoo wrap on his head!'

Hormazd took a step towards the Scotchman. The English prisoner stepped between them. 'Would you like to fight him?' he asked the Scotch sailor, who demurred. 'The man you see is neither a Hindoo nor a Mohammedan,' the Englishman went on, 'but a Parsee, a follower of Zoroaster and an ally of British power in India. Respect him, my friend, and we will help each other.'

Rolling the body of the murdered pirate into the water, Hormazd and the European captives were able to procure a small arsenal of weapons from the *lorcha*'s stores without being observed and then slipped into an open whaleboat. Before long, they had been spotted by the pirates' lookout aboard the *lorcha* and were fired upon with grapeshot. Lying down flat in the boat, Hormazd used a rifle to kill more than half of the twenty pirates on the deck.

Hormazd insisted on turning back to reboard the *lorcha*.

'Insanity! We have a clear path to escape!' the Scotchman in the whale boat protested. 'We're almost out of ammunition.'

'We have enough,' Hormazd said flatly. 'In ancient times, my people were driven from our land. In battle we scatter the heads of our foes – no Parsee ever turns his back though a millstone were dashed at his head.' Several of the pirates who'd escaped his fire because they were below deck, he said, had been responsible for the slaughter of his family and shipmates, and he would not leave them to prosper. Hormazd alone climbed up the netting on the side of the *lorcha*. After a quarter of an hour, Hormazd returned holding the head of one of the pirates. On the shore, he placed the head on a stake facing the water for Ah'ling to find. Then he strapped the body of a Chinese pirate to each yard arm, and Hormazd and the Englishman piloted the *lorcha* away.

When they reached Canton, they were congratulated by a chief mandarin on disabling one of the most nefarious pirate crews terrorising innocent fishermen and traders. The men were showered by the mandarin with drink, jewels and silver. On their way through the streets of Canton to the English settlement, a thief tried to take Hormazd's booty by smashing him across the head with a steel bar. Hormazd did not even flinch or turn around. Instead, he grasped the bar and flung the man to the ground, breaking the thief's arm in two places.

This was witnessed by many of the locals, who whispered of it, and from that day forward began to speak of a ghostly figure from foreign lands they called Ironhead.

The thief, who had fled by foot, dropped a bag filled with riches he'd plundered from other victims. Among these was a pure gold idol, a head of a Kylin with onyx for eyes – the Kylin, a mythological single-horned beast believed to bring good fortune and punish wicked men with fire and destruction. When it walked on land it left behind no footprints; when it walked on water it caused no ripple. Hormazd knew none of this then but, regardless, was drawn to it the empathetic way an ordinary man might be drawn to a starving dog. At the English settlement he paid to have the Kylin head attached to a walking stick and kept it with him when he sailed to London from Canton.

With his new riches and his great fortitude, Hormazd, it was said, began to build his own London-based opium smuggling business. Ships would procure opium taken from India, away from the official channels of the colonial government, which was strictly controlled by the English, and smuggle the drug into English and American ports without the burden of tariffs and inspection for adulteration. However, the Englishman who had been a captive with Hormazd among the pirates and had helped him to escape soon unwittingly discovered some of the secrets of his operations.

'Who was this Englishman?' Osgood interrupted the teller urgently.

'A son of Han,' said Yahee. 'Young man, name Edward Trood.'

'What do you mean, a son of Han?' Tom asked.

Yahee explained that Eddie Trood was a quick-witted though reserved young man who had learned Chinese so well in his travels that he had been kept alive by the pirates to do translations. He was called a son of Han, as if he were a Chinaman himself, by the natives, and a true rarity, for the Chinese government had banned the teaching of their language to foreigners, wishing to control Chinese merchants' dealings with Europeans and to curb the sale of opium to the Chinese people.

Back in London, where Eddie had also returned, Herman soon discovered that Eddie possessed great knowledge of the workings of Herman's operation. Herman and Imam, a Turkish opium trader also involved in the worldwide scheme, sought out Eddie's uncle, a minor opium pusher in London, who quickly and cowardly gave up his nephew. Eddie had been doomed, Yahee said with a glum chuckle, 'because he crossed Ironhead Herman'.

Opium eaters whispered to dealers who whispered to traders. The youth's body was rumoured to be buried in a wall of the uncle's home, and when Yahee and all the others heard the whispers, nobody ever dared try to infiltrate Herman's operation again.

Yahee stopped his story in the middle of a thought. He craned his head back and looked into the gloom of the tunnel.

'What is it, Yahee?' Osgood asked.

Yahee shivered. There was a creak from somewhere in the tunnel, a series of loud bangs following after.

A fevered look passed over Yahee's face and he broke into a run to the stairs. 'Herman! Herman here!' he shouted.

'No,' Tom said. 'It's just a broken water pipe. Yahee, nobody's in here!'

Yahee darted up the steep, winding steps at full and reckless speed. Tom first and then Osgood chased after him, pleading with him as they went to slow down. The opium dealer screamed of Ironhead Herman coming to kill them all.

'Yahee, stop!' Tom cried.

A rusted section of the railing gave way, plummeting twenty feet down to the bottom of the tunnel. Yahee slipped and hung on only by his fingertips to the broken railing.

Tom cried out for Yahee to be still. He heaved and pulled him up. As he secured him, the man fell limp and motionless in Tom's arms.

'Is he all right?' Osgood asked, holding his sides and panting as he reached the spot.

'He's fainted,' Tom said. 'Help me lie him down.' They carried Yahee to the next landing as his body shook and he mumbled in Cantonese.

They sat on the landing and waited for Yahee to recover.

'Herman nearly killed him,' Osgood commented after getting his breath back, 'and he wasn't even here. What are we up against, Branagan?'

Dividing up after leaving Yahee in a hired coach, Osgood hurried to the Piccadilly hotel and Tom went straight to the police station. When Tom returned to the hotel, where Osgood had shared their intelligence with Rebecca, he showed them a telegram cable. It was from Gadshill and composed of only five words:

Constable Tom Branagan. Yes. No.

'He still cannot simply address me as "Tom",' he said, shaking his head. 'This is from Henry Scott in Rochester.'

'What does this mean?' Osgood asked.

'If you are right to think that Herman assaulted Daniel in Boston,' Tom said, 'and then went with you on your passage on the *Samaria*, I've wondered why Herman would have been following an American publisher to learn more about an English novel. I suspected that if Herman was trying to get information from you, and from Daniel before that, about *The Mystery of Edwin Drood*, he must have already tried other channels of information in England. These confirm my suspicion. See for yourself.'

Tom placed a pile of documents from the London police in front of Osgood on the table.

Osgood examined them. 'A break-in at Chapman & Hall – Dickens's English publisher. Another break-in of the same sort at Clowes, the printer. Both the week of June ninth, the date of Dickens's death. In each instance, it appears nothing was stolen.'

'Nothing stolen,' Tom said, 'because what Herman was looking for – information about Dickens's ending – wasn't there. As nothing was taken, the police quickly dropped any inquiry into the incidents. That's why I sent a cable to Henry Scott asking for an immediate reply to two questions: Was Gadshill broken into after the Chief's death? And was anything taken? You hold his answers in that cable: yes and no.'

'Why should Herman have been following me, then?' Osgood asked.

'That we do not know, Mr. Osgood. But I think Herman actually may have been *protecting* you at the opium rooms,' Tom said. 'The fiends were likely merely trying to rob you, a foreigner in an expensive suit – a certain target. Herman needed you to continue your search, needed you alive and well enough to keep going. He even left you near the sewer drains, where there are always sewer hunters.'

'He thinks I know how to find the ending!' Osgood said. 'And if it's all true, there's something worse . . .' He sat down to ponder this and put his head in both hands.

'What is it, Mr. Osgood?' Rebecca asked.

'Don't you see, Miss Sand? The Parsee, trained in his skills of terror and murder by the worst pirates in the world, has torn England to pieces with his bare hands looking for something, anything, on *Drood*. And he would not be following me if he'd had any success. What if . . .' Osgood stopped himself, then found the courage to admit: 'What if it means there really is nothing to find?'

'Perhaps it's just a matter of our looking in the wrong places,' said Rebecca bravely.

'Yes,' Tom said with the spark of genuine insight, then slammed his hand on a table. 'Yes, Miss Sand! But not only that. Not only the wrong place, but the *wrong time*.'

'What do you mean, Mr. Branagan?' Rebecca asked.

'I was just remembering. When we were in America with Mr. Dickens, our party was on the train to go to the Philadelphia readings, and the Chief began speaking rather wistfully of Edgar Poe. He said that when he saw Poe the last time he'd been to Philadelphia, they'd spoken of *Caleb Williams*. Who was the author of that novel?'

'William Godwin,' Osgood said.

'Thank you. Mr. Dickens said that he told Poe how Godwin wrote the last part of the book first and then started on the first part. And Poe said he, too, wrote his mystery tales *backwards*. What if Mr. Dickens, when he set out to write his great mystery, didn't begin at the beginning?'

Osgood, lifting his head, sat back in his chair and considered this in silence. 'When Mr. Dickens collapsed in Gadshill,' Osgood said abstractedly, 'he had that afternoon reached precisely the end of the *first half* of the book. It was almost as if his body surrendered, knowing he was finished with his labour, although to us it hardly seemed so.'

Tom nodded and said, 'What if he wrote the second half of *The Mystery of Edwin Drood* first, and then the first half once he was back here?'

'What if he wrote the book *backwards*? What if he wrote the ending first?' Osgood asked rhetorically.

'Yet none of our efforts,' interrupted Rebecca, 'have suggested where the rest of the book would be stored if he really did write it.'

'Perhaps he would have tried to leave a clue with someone, to tell someone before he died where it was,' Tom mused.

'Dickens's last words,' Osgood said excitedly. 'He was calling for him!'

'Calling for whom?' Rebecca asked.

'Henry Scott told us, do you remember? The last thing Dickens was heard to say by the servants was "Forster"! Dickens had something left to tell his biographer!'

But to their great frustration, John Forster, whom Osgood and Tom found sitting in his office in the Lunacy Commission at Whitehall, shook his head with a baleful expression. He rolled his big black eyes coolly as they peppered him with their questions. He took out his gold watch, rubbed its face with his fingers, shook it as if shaking a bottle, and cringed busily.

'Friends, I am very busy – very, very busy. My afternoon has been taken up by a visit from Arthur Grunwald, the actor – a damneder ass I never encountered in the course of my whole life! He wishes to change the entire play of *Drood* we've already prepared to open. I really *must* finish my day's work.'

'You are certain that Mr. Dickens did not try to tell you anything else related to *Drood* when you arrived at Gadshill?' Osgood asked, trying to return him to the more urgent topic.

Forster wrung his hands outstretched. 'I wring my hands at this.'

'I see that you do,' said Osgood. 'We must know what he told you.'

'Mr. Osgood,' Forster continued, 'Mr. Dickens was insensible by the time I arrived. If he was saying anything, he could not be understood by human ears.'

'Like in a dream,' Tom added musingly.

The other two men looked at him quizzically.

'The Chief told me of a dream he had once,' Tom explained. 'In it, he was given a manuscript filled with words and was told it would save his life, but when he looked down at it he could not read it.'

'He never told me about such a dream . . . Why is it *you* are so interested in the matter of his final mumblings, Mr. Branagan?' Forster demanded.

'Mr. Forster, if I may,' Tom began. 'Why do you think Mr. Dickens called your name in his delirium?'

'Why did . . . Incredible question!' he roared back. The novelist's biographer began speechifying about his lifelong friendship and their unquestionable intimacy. 'All of that, most certainly, occurred to him, as he still clutched this,' Forster continued, picking up the white goose-feather pen he had brought from Gadshill. 'I suppose you will want this now.'

'Me?' Osgood asked, surprised at the offer.

Forster nodded his head. 'Oh, didn't I say? I suppose it fled my mind. You see, Miss Hogarth was charged with giving away the objects of Mr. Dickens's writing table. She has decided to give this pen – on which is the ink dried from his very final written words – to you.'

'But why?' Osgood asked.

'I asked the same thing! She appears to admire your . . . what shall we call it? Your fortitude for looking for more about *Drood*, however foolish. I thought perhaps you would leave England before we could find you. But since you have come . . .' Forster held it out reluctantly.

Osgood took up the quill pen. 'Thank you,' Osgood said, addressed more to the absent Georgy than to Forster. 'I shall treasure it.'

'One more question, if you please, Mr. Forster,' said Tom. 'When did you get new bolts on this door?'

'What?' Forster asked, for the first time since Osgood's arrival in England speaking in a quiet pitch. 'How do you know they're – why do you think they're new at all, sir?'

'Mr. Branagan is a police constable, Mr. Forster,' Osgood answered for him. 'He sees enough locks in his line to know the difference at a glance, I'd wager.'

'Very well, I suppose you think that is a great achievement. It was in the days after Mr. Dickens's decease, I believe,' Forster said. 'I came here and found that someone had been inside and rifled through my papers related to Dickens. They were all in one place, you see, for I keep my belongings well organised.'

'Was anything taken?' Tom asked.

'No. It was probably some ruffian looking for something of value to sell for drink. But there was one document in particular that seemed to have been, well, wrestled with, shall we say. It was yours, in fact,' he said, nodding to Osgood.

'What do you mean, Mr. Forster?' asked Osgood.

'I mean the telegram from your publishing firm asking that all remaining pages of *The Mystery of Edwin Drood* be immediately sent to Boston.'

He removed a wrinkled telegram from a file. *Urgent. Send on all there is of Drood to Boston at once.*

'I have a very particular system of organisation for my Dickens collection,' Forster continued. 'This was placed back but in the wrong spot.'

Osgood and Tom exchanged a quick glance with one another. 'That telegram is how Herman must have gotten the idea to go to Boston in the first place,' Osgood said. 'He believed Forster might have sent us what he could not find here. '

'Monstrous whispering!' Forster called out. 'What is that you're saying, gentlemen?'

'I beg your pardon, Mr. Forster,' Osgood said. 'Only speaking to myself. A bad habit.'

'A wretched one,' Forster bettered him.

'Mr. Forster, besides you and Miss Hogarth, can you think of anyone else that Mr. Dickens may have given confidential business information to in his final months?' Tom asked.

This was the absolute wrong question to ask Forster, unless one's purpose was to evoke a litany of his usual curses and lamentations about the world's lack of understanding of Forster's special intimacy with Dickens. Forster even removed Dickens's will and pointed to a clause.

'Do you see what this line says about me, Mr. Branagan?' Forster asked. 'Perhaps you need spectacles, sir, for it says "My dear and trusty friend". It was there that he left me this chronometer watch, which never fails to remind me of all the work that still must be done in this world to make it worthy of a man like Charles Dickens!' He then shook the instrument. 'Not that I shall ever know what o'clock it is with this blasted timepiece.'

Osgood looked distracted as Forster lectured. The publisher's eye rested on the will. 'I wonder, Mr. Forster,' said Osgood coolly, 'if you would allow Mr. Branagan and myself a moment in private?'

The commissioner's face became red. 'Leave my own office? Incredible!'

'Just for a moment, if you please. It is quite important,' Osgood said. 'Then we shall leave you in peace.' Forster finally agreed, apparently in hopes of ridding himself of his visitors. Osgood's hand reached for Dickens's will. But before stepping outside, Forster swung around and pocketed the document.

Osgood looked up at Tom and said, 'We cannot trust him about this.'

'What do you mean?' Tom asked.

'The will, I have my own copy from Aunt Georgy,' Osgood said, removing the document from his coat. 'Dash the thought for having never occurred to me! You see, Miss Hogarth asked me to review it with her. The will bequeaths Forster "such manuscripts of my published works as may be in my possession at the time of my decease". But all that is *unpublished* at the time of Dickens's death, goes to Georgina Hogarth. If the last six instalments of the novel do indeed exist, at the moment of Dickens's death they'd fall under *her* control by order of his will.'

'Control over Dickens is the one thing in the world I'd guess Mr. Forster won't relinquish,' Tom said. 'Do you believe he is hiding something from us?'

Forster began knocking insistently on his office door and declaring they were to have exactly half a minute more. Osgood fastened Forster's new door lock, leading to more severe exclamations.

'Not necessarily hiding,' Osgood said more quietly to Tom, 'but if he knows more about the ending of the novel or who Dickens may have confided in, he will not tell us. Not if it means making it appear that Dickens trusted any person on earth more than himself to direct his legacy.'

'Stuff! Come out or I send for the police!' Forster boomed out.

Osgood frowned and unlocked the door.

Forster, exuding rage, blinked several times at Osgood and leaned in towards him. 'Now, tell me, Mr. Osgood, did you really imagine you, a commonplace publisher, and your little girl bookkeeper could find more of *Drood* that I couldn't? Did you really imagine you could have accomplished any such thing? What it is you wanted from it, anyway? To be the nine days' talk of the trade? To be made as rich as a Jew, perhaps? You're not still caught in that fool's quest, are you?'

'I shall continue on, sir,' Osgood said without hesitation. 'I recall Mr. Dickens's words. There is nothing to do but close up the ranks, march on, and fight it out.'

'Then you hadn't heard?' Forster asked.

'What do you mean?' Tom asked Forster.

'I mean *this*,' Forster said. He removed a wrinkled slip of paper. 'Read for yourself.'

Osgood picked it up and examined it.

*8 June 1870. My dearest friend, I fear, with my illnesses wors-
ening each day, I shall reach no further than the end of the sixth
number of my* Drood. *What hopes I had for a unique ending, I
need not tell you! Will this truly be my last? I fancy it would have
been my best one, had I had the time to finish.*

It was signed, *Charles Dickens*.

'This is the date he collapsed. Where did this come from?' Osgood asked. 'Why did you never show this to me?'

'I received it only yesterday,' Forster explained. 'It was found lodged in a box of watercolour paintings at Christie's auction house, care-lessly put there by the auction house labourers. Clearly, he did not have time to post it before he collapsed.'

'This can't be,' Osgood said to himself, to the satisfaction of Forster.

'It does not say who it was addressed to,' Tom commented.

'Who else would it be?' Forster asked proudly. '"My dearest friend", who else do you think it would be but me? We have not yet made this note public, but we will. I am sorry this was not discovered earlier, it would have saved you, Miss Sand, and Mr. Branagan valuable time pursuing nonsense. Now,' he said, with a greedy smack of his lips, 'may I have my office?'

Osgood handed him the letter. 'Of course, Mr. Forster.'

'Think of it like this,' said Forster. 'You do not leave empty handed, my dear Mr. Osgood. You have Mr. Dickens's last pen – and how many people can boast such a rare forget-me-not?'

Fifteen minutes later, Osgood and Tom were back inside the rooms at the Piccadilly hotel. Osgood was already packing his things into his trunk. Tom had tried every form of argument to convince Osgood to continue their enquiries.

'Mr. Osgood,' Tom said, 'you cannot yield now. There is still too much not understood. You may still be in danger from Herman!'

'We haven't any choice,' said Osgood, half resigned and half reluctant. 'Once Forster makes his letter public, Herman will leave us alone, anyway. He'll know the truth by then, that he has no reason to fear, even as we have no reason to hope.'

'Perhaps the Chief had a motive to mislead Mr. Forster – knowing that Forster would try to manipulate the ending of the novel how he'd want it,' urged Tom.

Osgood shook his head. 'I don't think so. Our search has been utter folly, as Forster warned us it would from the first hour. There is nothing lost or secret in what Dickens left behind – nothing waiting to rescue us from our troubles. The book is no more, it died with him. I made a mistake. I, James Osgood, was carried away on an error of judgement, and now I must eat my words! I wanted to believe it, I wanted to believe that a man who called himself Datchery could help. Because of my stubbornness, because I wanted there to be something to find, all I have done here is waste time and give a head start to the literary pirates who even now prepare their editions back in America.' He turned to his bookkeeper. 'Miss Sand, make arrangements for our immediate passage back to Boston, and send a cable to Mr. Fields at the office informing him.'

'Yes, Mr. Osgood,' Rebecca said dutifully, each step taking her back to the normality and routine daily life of Boston.

Osgood looked over the room and at his two companions as Rebecca prepared a cable and Tom continued to try to persuade him. Osgood knew that to yield and go home was the proper, rational, *responsible* decision – really, the only decision he, James Ripley Osgood, could possibly make without some countervailing mandate from the heavens.

'We are too late to do anything for ourselves, in any case,' Osgood said. 'The Harpers will soon be able to publish all that was left of *Edwin Drood*. We will have to bear the loss and move on. Our rivals will see we are vulnerable. Fields will need us both in Boston to do what we can.'

Tom stepped in front of Osgood and held up his hand. 'Mr. Osgood, I give you my hand – I give you my word with it – that if you wish to try longer to investigate I shall be standing by your side.'

Osgood, with a small smile, took Tom's hand in both of his as Jack Rogers had done in their first encounter in the Gadshill chalet, but shook his head in a final refusal. 'Thank you for all you have done to aid us, Tom. Godspeed to you.'

'Godspeed, Mr. Osgood,' Tom said, sighing. 'I am only sorry your time here has to end like this. Mr. Dickens – and you – deserved something more.'

'To have gained your friendship has been worth all of it,' Osgood replied.

XXX

NEW YORK CITY, JULY 16, 1870

———————◆———————

HILE OSGOOD WAS HASTILY CLOSING their business in London and preparing for departure, there was a conversation involving him inside one of the more luxurious coaches crammed into the thundering roar of Broadway in New York City. Out of its window, a tall hat and long muttonchops belonging to a grizzled head appeared and the face between them inclined into a snarl at the tight traffic.

'So tell me, where in hell is that gump now?' Fletcher Harper, ducking back into the carriage, removing his tall black hat from his curly brown head, bellowed as his span of horses clopped to an irritable stop behind an omnibus.

'I'm sure I don't know, Uncle,' said his riding companion. 'But father trusted him.'

'Oh! I know he did,' the Major said with his usual tone of bemused bitterness. 'It is a big mistake, Philip. Take the next right turn away from this mess!' He stretched his neck out the window, installing his hat once again for the moment, and yelled to the driver.

'What mistake?' asked the companion, Philip Harper, son of Fletcher's late brother James, and now chief of the financial department, after his uncle had returned his neck and head inside the vehicle.

'Come! Trusting a man not named Harper. You will learn to avoid the practice before long, Philip, as this world goes. Your father always put too much faith in his Harper's Police to solve our problems. And now because of it here we are, and Jack Rogers has ceased communication. For all we know, that blackguard may have changed allegiances to another publisher for a higher fee – if he learned any secrets in England about Dickens, he may be using them against us, perhaps with the help of Osgood, with an eye on tendering a greater profit.'

The Major's counsel on trusting only individuals with the name Harper could have been noted as quite sustainable when entering the daunting fortressed offices at Franklin Square. There were multiple Fletchers – Josephs, Johns, this eager Philip, a lone Abner, sons of the original brothers – in varied roles managing the periodicals and production, with a line of grandsons already coming up as shop boys.

Franklin Square was Harvard and Yale for them. 'When my flame expires,' the Major would say to each of them as a kind of introductory address, 'let true hands pass on an unextinguished torch from sire to son!' This saying was also roughly the translation of the publishing house's Latin motto on the insignia of a flaming torch.

The Major, as he was entering, was told by a tremulous clerk that his expected visitors were waiting in the counting room.

'They are . . . impatiently waiting, I should say, Major,' said the clerk.

'Let them wait, it shall increase their hunger for my gold. And Mr. Leypoldt?' asked the Major.

'He sent a message and is to come at three,' the clerk replied. 'And Mr. Nast is waiting in your private office with a new Tweed drawing.'

'Good!' the Major replied.

'That's Mr. Leypoldt from the publishing journal, Uncle?' asked Philip.

'Yes, and we shall pour into him as many bottles of champagne as it takes to persuade him to sing the praises of Harper & Brothers in his columns. First, we have a different type of business. A more precarious kind.'

'Shall I leave you now?' Philip Harper asked his uncle discreetly.

'Don't think of it! You are to learn *everything* connected to our business, Philip, just as Fletcher Junior will,' the Major said, clamping down on his arm and pulling him along. 'Now, you see our friend up there?'

Philip followed the Major's gaze to a bust poised above the doorway to the main offices.

'Benjamin Franklin, isn't it, Uncle Fletcher?' asked Philip of the judgemental bust.

'Correct. Not only one of our nation's founding geniuses but a printer and publisher, too. To this craft he applied his industry and thrift. You see, he knew that to form the soul of America, one must control the presses. The basis of our firm is character, not capital, just as it was with him. Remember that, and you shall truly be a part of Harper & Brothers.'

In the great open office of the upper floor, the senior of the two Harpers guided them to a rectangular space closed in by a railing. Near the far wall was a circle of sofas and chairs meant for authors and other distinguished visitors to the firm, but on this day they hosted a different sort of occupant. In various positions of repose and sublime agitation, there were gathered four of the most striking and diverse individual human beings ever seen together in any publishing office.

Philip stopped in midstride and gave an anxious, gawky smile. 'Why, Uncle Fletcher! Are those—'

'The Bookaneers!' the Major finished his exclamation in a hoary whisper. 'The best of the lot, anyway, and all in one place this time.'

There was the smooth, chocolate-coloured Esquire, in his high-fashion silks and velvet and thick boots, looking an odd combination of actor and workman and balancing a walking stick on his lap; Molasses, with the particoloured growth undulating down his jaw and chin and dirty neckcloth; the lone woman of the group, called Kitten, also known by other mysterious appellations, who was unageing and ageless – those blue eyes might have been through twenty or forty summers, depending on what angle and light flattered them; and breathing in heavy, laboured contortions while sitting next to her, the seven-foot-tall man named Baby, a former circus giant, masticating a quid of tobacco between his monumental teeth.

'Uncle Fletcher,' said the young apprentice, 'those people are the scum of the land!'

'Well!' the Major replied, smiling with genuine amusement at his green nephew. 'If we cannot find Jack Rogers, it shall be near impossible to know what that James Osgood has been up to, and what he and Fields have in store for the last Dickens book. We are good Methodists, boy, but we cannot sit with our hands in our pockets waiting for our destiny. We must arm ourselves against the successes of our rivals, Philip. These scum, as you call them, might have been ordinary readers, writers, or publishers, but instead have become shadows of each, and as such can do what we cannot, can go where we cannot. You shall learn that you cannot count on a domestic cat, when what are called for are the arts of a Bengal tiger.'

When they had greeted the motley crew, the Major passed a slow glance over each of them before beginning.

'I hope you enjoyed the drinkables and eatables I asked one of our girls to provide for you.' The platter had been emptied already.

'I didn't get any,' Molasses grumbled.

'Sorry,' Kitten said to the others, fanning herself with a napkin, 'I arrived early and had missed breakfast.'

The publisher continued. 'I wished to have this consultation with you, my friends, because we are in a period of great excitement in the book trade.'

'Why all four of us?' asked Baby.

'It's uncommon!' shouted Molasses, passing a hand through his rainbow-streaked beard.

'Come! You shall find I speak plainly, Mr. Molasses,' said the Major agreeably. 'I am not unaware that the usual course of your profession renders yourselves rivals. Yet there is money enough here at Harper & Brothers to pay fine ransoms for all the latest literary treasures coming from the Old World, without wasting time scratching at each other's eyes.'

Esquire, the Negro dance master, bowed. 'I, for one, voice my approbation, sir. Why not encourage cooperation, gentlemen? And Kitty. But who's on the list we're looking out for?'

Harper rattled off his current list: 'George Eliot, Bulwer-Lytton, Tennyson, Trollope and – Esquire, you speak French, I presume?'

'Not only do I speak in French, Major, I dance and dream French,' replied the dark-skinned Bookaneer in his native tongue. Molasses rolled his eyes and knocked off Esquire's fashionable cap from his head as Harper continued.

'I'd wager there's not a language you know the name of that I don't speak, mister,' Kitten chimed in.

'Good,' said Harper. 'Because the town talk is a new play from Paris is about to cause a sensation – one the New York theatres would shell out hard cash for us to translate in advance. Keep your spyglasses trained for it, all of you, at the ports of Boston, New York, Philadelphia.'

Then the Major took from his frock coat several silver coins and placed them on the table. 'These are burning a hole in my pocket,' he said, his deep-set blue eyes blinking excitedly. 'One for each of you, to whet your taste.'

Kitten rose and put her coin into her bosom with a decidedly un-impressed expression. 'How much for a top manuscript, Major Harper?'

'My dear?' the Major asked. She didn't repeat her question, though he seemed to want to force her to do so; instead she stood stock still like a ballerina whose music had stopped. 'Oh! The bounty, my dear feminine Shylock? Double the usual rate if you get me the manu-script of an A-1 author. The traitors to our economy are out there pushing again for international copyright, led by that Brit lover James Lowell, and if they succeed *we* take the hit in what we are permitted by law to print.

'Take the late Charles Dickens, for instance,' he continued, 'I have reason to know that for one reader in England, he has ten here. I will go farther and say that for every copy of his works circulated in Great Britain, ten are printed and circulated here. We have made those copies affordable and widespread throughout the republic through what I call transmitting – what the ignorant call pirating – and have thus brought culture and learning into homes that would not otherwise be able to afford any. I may not live to see the day, but you will, when the best English classics will be sold in America for a dime. Never forget, we are the heirs to Benjamin Franklin, *we* are the true-blooded servants of this trade.'

This produced some nodding and general indifferent consensus from his audience as they stood to leave.

When the visitors passed as one body through the door in the railings to the stairwell on their way out, the clerks and accountants at their desks in the outer room stopped what they were doing and stared. Before Molasses crossed through the arched doorway, the Major took him by the arm.

'Aren't you through with us?' Molasses demanded.

'You're the best of your kind,' the Major said confidentially. 'The most persistent, so to speak.'

Molasses asked, 'How would you know?'

'Come, friend! You watch us. We watch you. It's said you had Thackeray's final novel before his own publisher in London.'

Molasses sneered with scampish pleasure at the memory.

'So. I have something special I want you to do.'

'I thought you wanted us to cooperate.'

The Major shrugged. 'Courtesy is courtesy, but business is business, my dear man.'

'You had something else to say or didn't you, Major Harper?'

'Keep an eye out for Osgood,' the Major said, tapping one of Molasses's buttons on his coat and dropping an extra double-eagle coin in the man's breast pocket.

'Osgood?'

'You want your big boodle from this? Come! Then pay attention. Keep an eye out for James Ripley Osgood. I told him I'd be watching him and you will be my eyes. He has something we need. I don't know what, precisely, I don't know where, but I can feel it in my bones.'

The very same Jack Rogers that the Harpers had sought in vain was at this moment only a few city blocks away from Franklin Square. He'd recently disembarked from a ship out of Liverpool and two days before had arrived in New York.

Around the dilapidated docks at the lower portion of the island of Manhattan, looking out on the crowd of sails, steaming ferries and busy tugs, he wore a sackcloth suit and was notable for not being involved in the habitual occupations of the tired workmen and the wretched wharf rats. The flabby brim of his wideawake was pulled low, shading his face; when he lifted his face into the light, an observer could see a plaster on his right eye and crisscrossed columns of false wrinkles and crow's-feet.

They were the same wrinkles he had applied around his mouth and forehead when disguised as George Washington. If spotted by any of Major Harper's agents – even other former members of Harper's Police – they would not make out much about him at first. But time was growing short for how long the old disguise would conceal him, and so far, it had all been for naught.

Though Osgood had made it clear he wanted nothing to do with Rogers, and Rogers for his part wanted nothing more to do with the Harpers or their money, he still could not give up pursuing the Dickens mystery under his own steam. The shame he felt confessing his motives and his role as Datchery to Osgood and Tom Branagan could not be the end of his part in the story.

Tom had made it clear enough that he would have had him arrested if he had remained around London to investigate. But Jack Rogers knew there were lucrative opium deals that permeated the New York harbour. Many were carried out by legitimate merchants engaged primarily in outfitting ships to Turkey to retrieve opium (as the English largely possessed a monopoly on the supply from India), then taking it to ports in China and the scattered Oriental islands. Yet a smaller portion brought their wares back into the American ports, and it was these traders, Rogers suspected, that had to be engaged in some connection with the opium fiends that had nearly finished him and Osgood off that night in the East End. Clues were thin, though, as Rogers wandered through the wharves and engaged in idle chatter about trading and ships, poking with his bamboo walking stick through piles of garbage (animal carcasses, old boots, large amounts of rotted vegetables tossed from passing ships). Sometimes he would sit and go fishing in the broken-down boats abandoned at the piers with the wharf mice, hoping to learn something other than the fact that the boys could swear like troopers.

Rogers removed a handkerchief and dried his nose and his eyes, both of which were leaking. His head throbbed. He wanted nothing more in the world than to relieve himself of the shooting pains. He wanted nothing more than to buy opium for himself. Not the watered-down, altered, and diluted stuff at the druggists but the pure raw crude poppy juice.

Though it had been a load off his heart to reveal his identity to Osgood and Tom Branagan, he had not told them the entire truth. He did not lie about who he was: Jack Rogers was Jack Rogers. This was precisely the problem. To Rogers, deception came quickly and naturally to protect himself.

It was not true, as Rogers had told Osgood, that he had not used narcotics for six months. In fact, the asylum in Pennsylvania where he had been sent by Harper had prescribed heavy doses of morphine – derived from opium – as a way to cure his habits. The morphine, while steering him away from crude opium, caused an entirely new state of dependence he indulged in every morning and night.

Rogers thought about something he had seen during the Civil War, when he had been recruited by a general for a series of secret missions. He had seen a surgeon on the Union side, riding on his horse and pouring liquid morphine into his hand. He would then hold out his hand and the soldiers would line up and lick his glove. This way the surgeon did not have to step down from his horse. It was a disgusting sight to recall. Rogers questioned whether he himself would ever sink so low as the glove-licking soldiers desperate for relief. He despised that proud expression of power he remembered on the face of the surgeon and felt himself its victim.

When people discovered Rogers was an opium habitué, they would sometimes say, *I have always wanted to try that. I should like to see what the visions of the opium eater are like.*

'You should not,' Rogers would tell them. 'You shall not have the dreams of Coleridge and the pleasures of De Quincey and then stop at your convenience. We are not opium eaters; opiates are man eaters. There is no stopping until the drug is willing to release you.'

Then they would talk of their stronger wills.

Rogers would shake his head ardently. 'Do not talk to me of will, man! For will is what I have lost, what has shrivelled and died inside of me! There are days when I cannot wind my watch, for my fingers feel as though they will fall off from their joints!'

In going to England, Rogers had sought to fulfil a lucrative mission for Major Harper. He also had known that *Edwin Drood* was set among the opium trade and had half hoped that seeing it through Dickens's eyes, he might gain some insight into his own dark history. Maybe, in Rogers's attempt to trick Dickens, Dickens had indeed transferred something to him in their sessions at Gadshill that could serve him now – some small sliver of his genius.

In any case, and for however impractical a reason, he could not now walk away from the mystery he'd been originally assigned to investigate. Since he could not remain in England safely, he'd determined that mixing among the opium traders on this side of the Atlantic might offer some clue to the connections he still hoped to make. This afternoon he finally recognised someone he saw out there. This person he recognised, strange to say, he had never seen before in his life.

Among all the scum working the opium trade at the New York harbour, it was an old Turkish sailor with a blue turban and short, shaggy white whiskers. It was the *Turk Seated Smoking Opium* – the statue Rogers had seen so many times at Gadshill in Dickens's summer study, now come alive! The same statue that had disappeared from

Christie's auction house in King Street. Only he was right here in the flesh. There was no denying the perfect verisimilitude of the statue, though the living man had grown older and more beautifully gaunt.

'If that wretched-looking creature is coming all the way from London to New York from that cesspool to this,' Rogers said to himself, 'it's likely that he's not ponying up money for the trip himself. And it's too much to just call coincidence. He's someone's messenger, someone who doesn't want to communicate by wire that could be stolen or read by an operator.'

Rogers followed him to a fish shed which the sailor entered. Rogers stopped at the window and pretended to adjust the plaster over his eye. The Turk passed an envelope into the hands of a slender man with heavy eyelids and a businesslike presence. The exchange was quick and silent and before long the two men had split up.

Rogers, waiting anxiously for a few seconds to pass, tucked his bamboo stick under his arm and followed the second man a few paces behind, even as he marked the direction of the Turk.

XXXI

LOWER PROVINCES, INDIA,
THE NEXT DAY, 1870

———◦———

HE RAINY SEASON HAD MADE itself known. Superintendent Frank Dickens decided to make a stop at an outpost with the small group he had personally selected from the Opium Detective Police. The English military officers welcomed them, and ordered their *khansáman* to arrange a light supper while they waited for the rain to quiet down.

'What brings you to these provinces, Superintendent?' asked their host, a young Englishman of strong build and amiable personality.

'An opium *dacoity*, to begin with,' said Frank. 'Worth many thousand rupees.'

The host shook his head. 'The blessings of civilisation do not come easily for our dark-skinned friends, I should say. Their rude morals allow their own people to steal the source of their future wealth. Ah, here we have a pleasant change of subject. Let us eat to your health!'

The Bengal policemen stared at the bowls of lumpy orange-red liquid that were placed in front of them.

'What is it?' asked one of them.

The host laughed. 'It is a type of liquid salad, my friend, a Spanish invention called *gaspácheo*. Among the Spaniards, it is employed as a way of reducing thirst and preparing for a hearty meal in the warm climate. It will keep away fever in the hot, rainy weather.'

After indulging in the strange lunch, Frank and his band continued by horseback until reaching a dry riverbank by a jungle. Consulting his hand-drawn map given to him by the inspector who had interrogated the captured *dacoit*, Frank stopped and dismounted.

'Remove the shovels.'

Procuring an elephant from a nearby police outpost, Frank inspected the area as his men dug at several different spots, while the rain would come down hard and then at regular intervals give way to the blazing sun. Though the activity was wearying, Frank could not help admiring the image of himself as the conquering European atop the awesome beast. He thought dismissively about his time being trained to work at *All the Year Round* and the disappointment of his father when he left. It was not that Frank could not manage the writing, he simply could not manage the boredom of it the way his older brother Charley could.

When he had been a schoolboy, his father had announced to Frank one day that he would teach him shorthand because it was a saleable skill, and that the great Boz himself had hung a shingle to do free-lance shorthand as a reporter in his younger days. The system, called Gurney's after its inventor, was difficult enough to train in, but Dickens had even 'improved' it with his own 'arbitrary characters' (various marks, dots, circles, spirals and lines) to represent words, making it more mysterious still. Frank would study carefully, certain he had made excellent progress, and then his father would test him by giving him dictation.

Charles Dickens would scream out a bombastic, ridiculous speech like he were sitting in the House of Commons, then interrupt himself in an entirely different voice arguing the opposite point of a more absurd and bombastic character. Frank would swear his father somehow talked over himself during these tests. Frank, trying his hardest to concentrate, would fall over laughing, and by the end of the parliamentary debate, both father and pupil were rolling on the rug in side-shaking hysteria. He resembled his father physically, more so than any of the other boys; but at those times he felt as though they were actual twins. Frank's page of shorthand, meanwhile, would end up like absurd, meaningless hieroglyphics.

Frank had heard that his diminutive younger brother Sydney, who was in the Royal Navy, had been nicknamed by his mess mates 'Little Expectations' after *Great Expectations* was published. Frank had never been meant to follow in his father's foot tracks, but he would not be seen to the world as a failure.

The first spot Frank had chosen in the sun-scorched ground yielded nothing, but after consulting the map again the squadron unearthed a mango-wood chest sealed in pitch. After another two hours had passed, five more chests, the total promised by the thief, were discovered.

Frank climbed down from the elephant. The heavy chests were soon lined up in a row. Meanwhile, a small crowd had gathered from the nearby village to watch.

'Get the natives away from here. They have seen that the thieves will not beat us, that is enough.'

But Frank's order was not heeded fast enough. Several of the native women had begun to dance and this was sufficient to distract the opium policemen. In the meantime, more natives were slowly emerging from the edge of the jungle.

'Rifles,' Frank said, then louder: 'Rifles up!'

At that moment, the band of natives charged with flaming torches and spears. Frank ordered his men to fire and, several volleys later, the raiders had fled back into the dense woods.

'They do not like white police in these districts,' offered a local policeman bemusedly.

Frank turned to his men, who were shamefaced at having been duped. 'Open the chests. I want each one examined thoroughly.'

'Rocks!' one of the policemen cried. He had discovered that about one-third of the lumps of opium in the chest had been replaced with stones of about equal weight. In the other chests it was the same.

Frank did not evince any surprise; he simply took one of the rocks and put it in his satchel.

XXXII

LIVERPOOL, THE DOCKS,
THE NEXT MORNING

———————◆———————

HE TRAVELLERS, NOW RESIGNED TO going home, felt fortunate to push off aboard the *Samaria* once again. Booking passage at such short notice would have been nearly impossible, as Osgood's passport had been held since the suspicious situation in which he'd been found after the incident at the opium rooms. Marcus Wakefield was himself embarking on one of his frequent business trips between England and America. In a matter of hours, and with great expense billed to the publishing firm, he had passage arranged for Osgood and Rebecca on the same ship. In conjunction with Tom Branagan's urgings through the police department, Wakefield employed his influence to release Osgood's passport for travel.

On the way to the harbour, Osgood and Rebecca sat with Wakefield in the merchant's coach. Tom and another police constable walked on opposite sides of the street so they could watch for Herman. Each of the two pedestrians held up his umbrella and kept his hat pulled down low on his face. There was no sign of Herman and the two Americans boarded with the tea merchant quickly and quietly.

Aboard the steamship, Wakefield was as solicitous a friend as ever, though both Osgood and Rebecca noticed a certain petulant charge to his demeanour.

'I am afraid since we last travelled my business has entered a period of great dullness,' Wakefield explained with a touch of embarrassment in the saloon to Osgood over tea. 'My partners are quite circumspect about general prospects. Enough of my gloominess, though. What about you, my friend? It seems you were rather burning the candle at both ends in England.'

'Indeed, I suppose I was,' said Osgood. 'What did you say this was, Mr. Wakefield?'

'Ah, it's called oswego. It's believed to have curative properties – good for the stomach and to prevent nausea. Do you like it?'

'It makes me feel plucked up already, thank you.'

'Well, I should say you are in quite better form than when I saw you in the company of the police in London, covered in rat bites!' Wakefield said, laughing. 'I pray this is at least a respite for dear Miss Sand. All she endured with her brother, Daniel. Awful, senseless tragedy, by the sound of it.'

'We shall always be grateful for your assistance, Mr. Wakefield. Even though it is now over.'

'Yes, yes, absolutely.' He raised his wineglass. 'To the health of us all now that this is over!' After taking a drink, he added, 'Now that *what* is over, Mr. Osgood?'

'A great disappointment,' Osgood answered.

Wakefield nodded regretfully, as if their business disappointments were the same.

Osgood smiled, appreciating the sympathy. 'Sit with me at supper, Mr. Wakefield, and I shall unburden it all to you then, if you shall hear it. I owe you that. One day I hope to be able to do you as decent a service as you have done for us,' said Osgood.

'Your trust is quite enough reward for me, dear Mr. Osgood. Quite enough!' Then Wakefield paused and seemed to have a tickle in his throat as he spoke again. 'Perhaps there is one thing you could do, if you're willing. But I hesitate to ask.' Wakefield fell silent, engaging in his habitual knee-tapping.

'I insist on it.'

'Pray, Mr. Osgood, a good word from you to Miss Sand about my character . . . Well, she respects you very much.'

'Why, Mr. Wakefield . . .' Osgood seemed lost deep in a troubled thought.

'I have grown to admire her a great deal, as I think you know. Will you do me this one favour?'

'I would not deny you any favour, my friend.' Osgood was about to say more when the bell rang from the dining saloon.

'Shall we continue this over our meal?' Wakefield suggested with a hearty smile.

Instead of going into dinner with the others, Osgood stood on deck at the railing, looking out at the brilliant gleam of the sea. He closed his eyes as the mist sprayed his unshaven face.

'Mr. Osgood? Are you feeling unwell?'

Osgood turned to look over his shoulder, but quickly turned back. It was Rebecca. He had not prepared what he would say to her.

'No, no,' Osgood said. 'I believe I am almost fully healed with London behind us, as a matter of fact.'

'Well, I suppose we should get to our tables for dinner.'

'Mr. Wakefield is a fine man. He has been a true friend to us, as you know.'

'What?'

Osgood said, 'I just wished to say that.'

'Very well,' Rebecca said, a little confused.

He wished he could explain to Rebecca. He wished he could find a way to express the feelings that had been so clear to him the night of his opium stupor when everything else had been a blur. Now, there were the rules again – his, as her employer, hers, given by the courts. Wakefield, for his part, had practically asked Osgood's permission when they had first met on this same ship. *Miss Sand is an excellent bookkeeper* was all Osgood had managed to say. An excellent book-keeper! Osgood sighed. 'I suppose, because he is English, the courtship of such a man as Mr. Wakefield would hold great appeal.'

'To have a decent man express his dedication to me flatters any woman. But I hope you would not believe of me that I would ever pretend to be in love with an English citizen in order to free myself from a decree, and trade one prison for another. Do you think if I loved a man, I would allow paper constraints, words in some law book, to stop me, no matter the consequences?' In the passion of her speech, a curl of her raven hair had fallen from her bonnet and clung to her lip.

'Perhaps I,' Osgood said, then paused as though he had lost track of his tongue. 'I *know* after you lost Daniel I thought too much of shielding you.'

Rebecca nodded her thanks for his honesty and held out her arm. 'I'm famished, Mr. Osgood. Will you walk me inside?'

She had not told him what their failure meant for her, that her life in Boston, and her time at the firm, would have to come to an end. Osgood, grateful for her reply, took her arm under his, and could feel his heart beating against the soft leather of her gloved hand, feeling they had all the time in the world.

XXXIII

NSURANCE INSPECTORS AND WORKMEN WERE moving in and out of what still remained of the main auditorium of the Surrey Theatre on Blackfriars Road. What had been London's grandest theatre had been reduced to a gloomy shadow of itself in a few short hours. The floor and walls were still smouldering. Tom Branagan entered and crossed through a labyrinthine series of charred and dirt-begrimed halls until he reached the carpenter's room.

'This is where it started?' Tom asked.

'Who's there?' answered a workman, before he saw Tom's blue coat and bright buttons of the police uniform. 'Oh, another bobbie? That's how it seems, yes, gov'n'r. We've already had the inspectors around investigating whether it's the work of an incendiary.'

'Did they tell you what they concluded?' Tom asked.

'There's always hazards around the theatre – sparks everywhere, fabrics that could ignite with a fiery look at them. The police didn't tell me nothing. Shouldn't you already know, gov'n'r?'

'They don't tell me,' admitted Tom. 'It's the constable's duty only to take out exposed property after a fire. To prevent robbery while the debris is cleared away.'

The workman, realising Tom's lack of authority, turned his back on him.

Digging through the black piles of rubble and old props, Tom found a placard. On it, there was listed the upcoming season of plays.

'*The Mystery of Edwin Drood*,' Tom said. 'That is being done at this theatre?'

'Aye, was about to open. Not any more, 'course. Not with the theatre burned and Grunwald dead.'

Tom shivered, remembering the name from Forster's complaints. 'Grunwald?'

'The actor. They found him trapped in the green room with his young assistant. The manager said he was practising the new lines in front of the mirror every night this week. Well, good thing the fire was in the middle of the night instead of the middle of a performance, gov'n'r, or we'd all have been roasted alive like them.'

'New lines? Right before it was to open?' Tom asked.

'They had just changed the ending to suit Grunwald. Now who knows when anyone will get to see it! Grunwald – he threatened to quit if they didn't allow him, I mean Edwin Drood, to survive in the end. Finally, the manager agreed, and forced Mr. Stephens, the writer, to give them a new conclusion over the grousing of Mr. Forster. Oh, that Grunwald had been going about telling everyone he knew. Why, that was just a few days ago, though now it seems another life altogether.'

Tom stared at the poster, then at the mass of ruins all around him.

The workman, now that he had become more talkative, seemed reluctant to stop. 'That Grunwald, he used to say nobody could understand his position who hasn't walked in the shoes of Edwin Drood, a man who only wanted to belong to a family. He said he was born for the role and would not permit Drood to die. He was a man obsessed, but then he was an actor. Rest his soul.'

'Good God,' Tom said to himself.

'What's that, gov'n'r?' the workman asked, cupping his ear.

Tom dashed out of the carpenter's room past a row of firemen.

XXXIV

T Queenstown in Ireland, where the Liverpool-to-Boston-line made port, Osgood was surprised to be a brought a lengthy cable by one of the *Samaria*'s stewards. It was addressed from a police station house in London.

'It is from Tom Branagan,' Osgood said, showing it to Rebecca in the ship's library. 'Arthur Grunwald was up to his neck in schemes. Look!'

Rebecca read the cable. Tom explained what the theatre workman had revealed about Grunwald changing the ending of the play. Moreover, after his visit to the scene of the fire, Tom proceeded to search Grunwald's lodgings, where he found a pile of drafts and revisions of the letter to 'my dearest friend' in Forster's possession about not finishing *Drood*.

'You had said the day you went to the Dickens auction that Mr. Grunwald was there,' Rebecca said.

Osgood nodded. 'It must have been Grunwald who left the letter in one of the boxes at the auction, so when it was found it would seem to have been overlooked in the crates and boxes of Dickens's belongings. He did not want any other "discoveries" to distract from his own ending of *Drood*.'

'If that letter you saw was forged . . . then what we believed before we left London could have been right,' Rebecca exclaimed. 'Dickens still may have written the second half first, after all!'

'Yes,' Osgood said excitedly.

'Then Mr. Branagan was right, too. We should have stayed in London to continue our hunt!' Rebecca exclaimed. 'We must wait here in Queenstown for the next ship passing through to Liverpool and return at once.'

'Hold, Miss Sand. There may be something else.'

Osgood put aside the cable and picked up the quill pen given to him by Forster. He turned it over in his hand, studying the soft feather and the sharp blue-stained nib. He poked his own fingertip with the sharp point.

'Have you ever been to the Parker House, Miss Sand?'

'I had delivered some papers to Mr. Dickens and Mr. Dolby during their stay,' Rebecca said.

'Do you remember what ink was provided on the writing desks there?' Osgood asked.

Rebecca thought about it. 'I took some notes written by Mr. Dickens back to the firm. They were written in iron gall, if I recall it.'

'Yes, iron gall, a black purple colour,' Osgood said, nodding. 'That is what they keep in all the Parker rooms for the guests. Dickens wrote his manuscripts in blue, as we saw of *The Mystery of Edwin Drood*. And the nib of this pen that he used for the book shows us, it is dried blue accordingly. Miss Hogarth told us that the Chief liked to use the same pen the entire way through the process of writing a novel.'

'Yes,' Rebecca replied, uncertain of Osgood's train of thought.

Knowing he was not yet being clear, Osgood put a hand up for her patience. He took up a magnifying lens from the shelf and lowered it on to the quill pen, squinting as he examined it. Then he stood, sat back down, and moved the moderator lamp to throw the light from a different angle.

'Do you have a knife?' Osgood asked.

'What?'

'A knife,' Osgood repeated.

'No.'

'No, I suppose you wouldn't. Can we find one?'

Rebecca exited the library. A few minutes later, she returned with a small pocket knife secured from the captain.

'Thank you.' Taking the requested tool, Osgood carefully put the blade to the end of the pen. 'Hold the lens over this spot, please,' Osgood said.

Peeling the surface of the nib, layers of blue ink fell away.

'There!'

The blue began to give way to layers of brown.

'Look,' Osgood said excitedly. 'Look what's underneath.'

'It's *brown*,' Rebecca replied with disappointment after examining the underlayers of the tip under the light.

'Just a moment, Miss Sand.' Osgood walked to a table at the other end of the library office and carried over a carafe of water and a stout glass. He poured a small amount of water into the glass, after which he swirled the tip of his finger until it was wet. He then removed that finger from the glass and rubbed the peeled nib of the pen. As it became wet, the dry brown slowly turned purple black.

'See!' Osgood said, displaying the evidence.

'It's black!'

'That's iron gall, the same ink supplied at Parker's! When iron gall dries and hardens, it turns to a brownish maroon colour. I think he used this pen in Boston,' Osgood declared. 'This may very well show Tom Branagan was right! *Drood* ended before it began! When Herman went to Gadshill and Forster's office, he was looking for the wrong type of clue – he shouldn't have been looking for a piece of paper that might tell him what Dickens had planned for the rest of the book, but the very pen itself with which he had written it. This ink points us not back to England but right where we're headed.'

'You think it possible he had written the second half first while still in Boston?' asked Rebecca.

'When I asked him if there was any place he hadn't seen in Boston, he said he wished to see the Harvard Medical College where the infamous murder of Parkman had occurred,' Osgood mused. 'He had also mentioned to us that he was preparing a new reading about Bill Sikes murdering Nancy from *Oliver Twist*. Perhaps the Chief had such murder stories on his mind, not only as a matter of local curiosity, but because he was already writing one himself! That is what brought Poe to his mind to begin with in his conversation on the train with Mr. Branagan and Mr. Scott!'

'Mr. Osgood, you've done it!' Rebecca exclaimed. 'Even if this is true, he didn't tell Mr. Forster, or anyone else that we know of, where those pages are. We wouldn't know where to begin to look.'

'Who else might he have told?' Osgood wondered out loud.

'What about Mrs. Barton!' Rebecca cried out.

Osgood looked over at her with surprise and shook his head. 'The deranged reader? I can't imagine a less likely candidate for him to entrust his secret with, truly.'

'I recall hearing at the office what Mrs. Barton had wanted that night. She was writing nonsense that she believed – in the disordered folds of her mind – *was* the next Dickens novel. She believed his next book had to be *her* next book: that they were one in the same, that the line between reader and writer had been erased. Mr. Branagan described Mr. Dickens having a gleam of sympathy in his eyes for the poor soul and he leaned in – after she had cut her own throat and it seemed every drop of her life was dancing out of her, she managed to ask about his next book – and he whispered to her.'

'But Mr. Branagan said he hadn't heard what it was Mr. Dickens whispered.'

'No, Mr. Osgood, but it might have been . . .' Rebecca said, bracing herself for the possibility and willing herself to propose it, 'if he was already writing *Drood*, it just might have been related to it, to put her at ease before she died. She may have received the answer we have been searching for – waiting for us back home in Boston!'

XXXV

BENGAL, INDIA

T HE RAIN HAD BEGUN AGAIN. At the jail in Bengal, this was a particular annoyance for the sentries on their rounds on the roof. On this day, the sentries were Officers Mason and Turner, of the mounted police patrol. As they passed each other, Mason paused to gripe.

'Three days in a row to have guard duty! It's not right, Turner, when you're a mounted man! That Superintendent Dickens is a damnable fool!' Mason cried, hanging on to his hat to keep it from blowing away with the wind. 'I thought he was a good man, I vow I did, until now.'

Turner stared up at the sky. Though it was the middle of the afternoon, it could have been midnight it was so dark; the flash of lightning, and then a fast peal of thunder shook the rooftop. The storm was as bad as they had seen all season. 'There aren't good men in the public service, Mason, I suppose,' he said with a bitter tongue.

'I'm going into the box until it stops. Won't you come?' Mason asked. 'Turner, what's that?' Mason was looking at Turner's carbine, with its bayonet fixed. 'You know you can't have the bayonet up here. It's in the rules. It can attract lightning.'

Turner screwed his eyes and looked away from Mason. 'That damned *dacoit* is in this jail. The one who stole the opium.'

'So?'

'They blame us for having let him flee in the first place, but he's more dangerous than they know. I'd like to speak with him.'

'We're on duty! Now come on into the box!' Mason shouted to be heard over the sound of the storm.

Before Turner could reach the door down into the prison, it

opened and a man stepped out. The crackling light from the sky showed it to be Frank Dickens.

'See here, Mr. Turner,' Frank said. 'You will be glad to know we recovered the stolen opium chests from where they had been buried in the ground.'

Turner's eyes showed signs of relief.

'The case is not closed though, I'm afraid,' Frank continued. 'You see, in the bungalow of Narain, the thief that leaped from the train window, I found several books – and annotations inside them. Records in the margins, actually, of transactions and bribes to officials, native and European. In another book was a record I have deciphered with great effort, of a recent bargain with you.'

Turner shook his head vigorously. 'I don't know what you mean!' Mason, coming back out into the rain from the shelter of the guard box, moved in closer and listened.

'You volunteered,' said Frank calmly, 'after the opium convoy had been robbed, so that you could see to it that the thieves escaped. However, with Mason at your side, you had no choice but to arrest one of them. You told Narain, when you were alone with him on the train, that if he said your name to anyone in the police, you would kill him. You told him if he wanted a chance at survival, he could jump from the train. He had a one in ten chance to live, I'd say.'

Frank removed a stone from his pocket and placed it in Turner's trembling hand.

Frank went on. 'Only the other thief, who goes by the name of Mogul, escaped. He had known nothing of Narain's arrangement with you until after the theft, and that was what their argument was about that detained them at the receiver's house. In fact, Mogul was so fearful of you that after I captured him, it was only when he saw you waiting outside the interrogation room that he confessed to the inspector. It was you that scared him far more than his trial on the *chabutra*. If you had caught him in the mountains, I have no doubt he would have met the same fate as his accomplice by your hand. I wish to know this. Was it Hurgoolal Maistree who was directing the scheme?'

Turner evaded Frank's glance.

'Ingenious,' said Frank admiringly. 'Maistree, the receiver, had instructed the thieves to take only a *few* of the opium balls from each chest, replacing the others with rocks like this one. This way, if the chests were found, we could consider the case finished and perhaps not even notice the rocks until later examination, when we were occupied with new excitements. Meanwhile, he had paid you to pass along information about when the convoy would be at its most vulnerable, and to ensure that his thieves were not captured. With the total number of opium balls he had received, for which he paid the thieves perhaps less than a third of their value, he would have enough to make a substantial sale to a smuggler, and a big profit for himself.'

'What is this about?' young Mason demanded hoarsely. 'Turner, tell Superintendent Dickens he's mistaken!'

By this point in the narrative, Turner's face had hardened and his hands stiffened on his bayonet, as if he would run his superior officer right through the chest.

Frank clapped his hands. Two police officers rushed on to the roof from the stairway below. They surrounded Turner.

'He was a darkie *dacoit!*' Turner shouted, his teeth grinding, his voice hollow.

Frank Dickens nodded. 'Yes, he was. This isn't about talking Narain into his jump – good riddance to him. You don't seem to recognise, Mr. Turner, that it is our responsibility to ensure that the opium trade moves freely and safely through Bengal and to China. In contributing to its disruption, you contribute to those who wish the European success around the world to fail. You leave room for smugglers and traders far less reputable than those our government chooses to make partners in these endeavours – harming not only the English, but the natives in India, in China, around the globe. It is Bengal's right to share in the prosperity of civilisation.'

Frank bowed with satisfaction, leaving his inferior officer prisoner of the other policemen.

'Damn you!' Turner screamed over a peal of thunder. 'Goddamn you and Goddamn Charles Dickens for bringing you on to this earth!'

Along the river Ganga, in the region bordering Bengal, was Chandernagore, a territory seized by the French years before. There in a palace sat a solemn Chinese man, called Maistree, in robes that sparkled as did the walls in delicate gold and silver leaf. Indian and Parsee servants brought him food and wine.

One of the members of a Chandernagore criminal family entered and reported that the stolen opium balls had been repacked into sardine boxes and were ready for transport. He salaamed and left Baboo Maistree in peace. Maistree had lost two men, Narain and Mogul, through the course of this theft – Narain leaping to his death, and Mogul sentenced to two years' penal transportation. Plus a mounted policeman had been exposed. It was a large treasure, though, and there were always more men in wait for the next one. It required far more effort by the Bengal police to find one of his agents than it took Maistree to hire ten more.

A tinge of worry might have been seen in a dull gleam in Maistree's eye as he swatted his spoon in his soup like an oar. He had not heard yet from the purchaser – whose name he did not know, for Maistree dealt only with the Parsee headman of the rugged sailors who came to take the disguised opium away. This man, Hormazd, Maistree knew, did not work on his own. He had always been reliable, though. Much of the palace where Maistree now sat had been built with money given by the unknown buyer. And as long as Maistree did not step one foot outside of Chandernagore, the English police in Bengal could not arrest him and the smuggling could continue.

So what could be wrong?

In fact, last time Hormazd had expressed a directive for Maistree to secure even more opium than the season before. Markets were opening, namely the United States. The purchaser wanted as much pure Bengal opium as could be smuggled out immediately, and the receiver should await their message with instructions for when they would pick it up.

Yet here the next shipment was ready. Where was the purchaser?

XXXVI

McLEAN ASYLUM, BOSTON,
LATE AT NIGHT

ALKING BRISKLY THROUGH THE CORRIDOR of the hospital, Rebecca Sand had braced herself for the bleak sights she knew to expect. It was hard, though, to keep that in mind, for the place seemed more like an English country home than a hospital for the insane.

Osgood had not even stopped at his home at Pinckney Street first or to see Mr. Fields at the office – he was too eager and asked to go directly to the McLean Asylum in Somerville.

'Are you certain you would not like to go home, Miss Sand?' Osgood had asked her.

'I am no more tired than you must be, I'm sure, Mr. Osgood. Besides, I don't think you'd be permitted inside the women's wing.'

'Of course,' Osgood said, and then paused wistfully. 'I am lucky to have you with me.'

The hospital was separated into its divisions for men and women, all of whom came from circumstances of great wealth and status except for the occasional pauper patient taken in charitably. No person of the opposite sex could enter a wing unless a medical professional. Rebecca could hear women screaming and crying, but others laughing and singing, and she did not know which set of noises most unnerved her soul. All the windows were barred, the walls inside the rooms muffled.

Reaching the privilege room, Rebecca was given a comfortable chair by a stout female attendant with a muslin cap and rosy face. Inside the dimly lit but lavishly furnished room, there sat a woman looping a finger through her thinned, greying hair. Much of it had been pulled out, the rest tied on top and dripping with sad, multi-coloured ribbons. A wide scarf was wrapped around her neck. She did not look up.

The attendant nodded to the visitor for her to begin.

'Mrs. Barton?' Rebecca asked.

Finally, the patient twisted her head in her direction. It was only momentary. She quickly returned attention to the wall.

'Succubus,' said the patient in an embittered register.

'Mrs. Barton, what I have come to ask is quite important. Urgent, in fact. It is about Charles Dickens.'

The patient's eyes slid upwards. 'They told me he is dead.' Her voice was creaky and whispery, not the vigorous shout it had been in Tom Branagan's encounters with her. Perhaps her injury had changed the range of her voice. As the inmate – or 'boarder', as patients were called here – leaned towards her visitor, she asked, 'Is it true?'

'Yes. I am afraid so,' said Rebecca.

Tears filled the patient's eyes. 'They won't let me keep any of his books in here, did you know that? These ill-mannered physicians here say it excites me too much. They wouldn't even tell me *how* he died, my Chief. *How* did the poor Chief's mortal parts die?'

'We don't want to excite her, miss,' the attendant cautioned before Rebecca could answer.

Rebecca heard in Louisa's voice a promise of something in return, if she could give her something satisfactory. Rebecca tried to recall all the details she could from Georgina Hogarth and Henry Scott and relayed them: Dickens coming in from the chalet after a long day's work, collapsing at dinner, being moved by the servants on to the sofa, the heated bricks at his feet, the doctors coming one by one and shaking their heads hopelessly as the family gathered and stood by him in his final hours.

'Now, as for Mr. Dickens's last book . . .' Rebecca said after this.

'*A New Book of Job by Charles John Huffam Dickens!*' Louisa howled out in her old yell. Clearly getting this close to the heart of the matter had put her in a different state of mind. Rebecca decided it was the wrong approach to try to tell her anything about her purpose.

'He whispered,' Rebecca said confidentially. 'Mr. Dickens did. The Chief whispered to you the night when you picked him up from the street in that coach, didn't he?'

After Rebecca had repeated the sentiment with slight variation several more times, Louisa nodded and said it was true.

'What was it he said to you?' Rebecca asked carefully.

She was nodding again and then she giggled. This was the satisfied giggle of a rich little girl of Beacon Hill at being given her first puppy. Rebecca, frustrated to her core, was about to shout. But it was not clear the other woman cared a fig about what anyone needed, even herself.

The patient pulled off the silk scarf from around her neck. There was visible a white, almost translucent scar across the neck, deepest on the right end, in the shape of an unfinished smile, which gave Rebecca the urge to run her hand across her own neck to check that it was in one piece. 'He was right. He looked like a poem,' Louisa said suddenly.

'Who did?'

'He looked like a poem, can't remember which poem though,' replied Louisa. Suddenly, she seemed to have an Irish accent, eerily like Tom Branagan's. 'Too many poets in America today!'

'Tom Branagan. What was Tom right about?' Rebecca asked gently.

'The Chief and that actress,' she muttered. '*Nelly*. He said the Chief loved her.'

'There have been many slanders about him in the press,' Rebecca said.

Louisa suddenly spoke as though the centre of attention at a Beacon Hill dinner. '"All well" means to come. "Safe and well" means not to come. While that nasty old widow was trying to steal the Chief away for herself, I took it so nobody else would steal it and print it in one of the profligate papers!'

Rebecca waited for more, shaking her head. 'I don't understand.'

'No, you *don't*! I'm sure you couldn't ever have understood, you're such a nice girl and dim witted.'

Rebecca, frustrated, looked for help at the attendant, who was sitting patiently. In response, the attendant removed a pair of keys and silently motioned for Rebecca to follow her to a closet door on the other side of the room, away from Mrs. Barton.

'This is where we place the materials that have proven too combustible to her mind, Miss Sand,' said the woman quietly, bending down and pulling out a red calf-leather book, only a few inches tall and wide, that could fit in a small coat pocket. 'She claims this was

Charles Dickens's diary. Said she had taken it from a trunk in the Westminster Hotel in New York.'

Rebecca held out her hand to the attendant. 'It did belong to Dickens, then?'

'We don't know,' the attendant answered. 'After all, it's written all in some kind of cipher! This bird would stay up at all hours staring at the page to understand it.'

'"All well" means to come! "Safe and well" means not to come!' Louisa exclaimed vigorously from the other side of the room.

'What do you mean, Mrs. Barton?' Rebecca asked. When she could not extract any answer, she turned to the attendant and asked if she understood.

'I should think we would, miss! This little bird crowed the same thing every night for two weeks. She claims she found directions to decipher secret language that Charles Dickens would cable to England whether this "Nelly" should come with him to America. If he cabled "all well", she would come. If "safe and well", she'd stay in Europe.'

'She didn't!' Louisa interrupted, her hands trembling and her chest heaving at the topic. 'She *didn't* come! You see? The Chief told her safe and well, do not come. He didn't truly love her after all! He had come to finally find his great true love! As his Mr. Redlaw would say to me, "Your voice and music are the same to me." That is why he found me. That is why he read to me all those nights at the Tremont Temple. Why he whispered to me after all those mean men had roped him into hating me!'

Rebecca knew she had to be careful if she wanted Louisa to say more and not exhaust herself to the point of being useless.

'Mr. Dickens – the Chief – wanted you to share with the world another message that he whispered to you the night that other man attacked you.'

Louisa seemed to consider this as she continued her steady nod. Suddenly, she stopped. 'Yes, wanted all of it shared. He spoke the truth – he saw the future at last,' she said.

'Yes! What did he say?' Rebecca urged her.

She let out an exhale that seemed to have been stored up for years. 'God help you, poor woman.'

Rebecca blinked. 'That is what he said to you? That is everything he whispered?' *That was all!*

'God help you, poor woman!' Louisa repeated more vigorously, and in a voice that had the heft of Dickens's.

'Nothing else? You are certain, Mrs. Barton?'

'And God *has*. The Chief always spoke the truth. God has helped me!'

God help you, poor woman. Dickens, there to bless the unfortunate! Rebecca, dejected, thinking of all the time they had lost by coming here on her suggestion, signalled the attendant. She could not help lamenting how disappointed Osgood would be in the intelligence she would have to report, yet she also knew she had to tell him right away.

Louisa, her wasting spirits appearing lifted by all the talk of Dickens, did not seem to want the interview to end yet. 'You were wrong, dear!' she said when the attendant began to escort Rebecca away. There were tears forming in Louisa's eyes. 'No street! No street!'

Rebecca told the attendant to wait.

'What do you mean, Mrs. Barton?' she asked, turning her attention with a fresh patience back to the boarder.

'You said I took him from the street. But that isn't true, not one whit. That carriage was stopped when I found it. That driver – trying to take the Chief away to who-knows-where!'

Rebecca considered this. They'd always thought Dickens had just hailed a cab to be taken for a late night drive before returning to the hotel. The fact that the cab was sitting empty suggested that Dickens had hailed it with some place – some errand – in mind. Did Dickens have a particular destination the night before he would leave Boston for ever? Rebecca was about to ask for more but Louisa was by this time determined to continue on her own.

'It was stopped on North Grove Street,' said Louisa. 'When he got back into the carriage, he didn't know *I* was driving it. Little did he know how our lives were destined to change for ever from that point! Can the candle help it, my dear? Can the candle help it?'

'North Grove Street?'

The waiting driver opened the carriage door for Rebecca. She climbed in and sat across from Osgood.

'It's the Medical College!' Rebecca cried.

'What – what do you mean? Was that what Mr. Dickens said to that woman?' Osgood asked.

'No, no.' Rebecca explained that Louisa Barton had tricked the driver as he was waiting for Dickens at North Grove Street. 'He wasn't merely going out for another of his breathers,' Rebecca said. 'He must have instructed the driver to go to the Medical College.'

Osgood thought back to the breakfast conversation between Dickens and Dr. Oliver Wendell Holmes.

Anything in Boston you haven't yet seen that you'd like, Mr. Dickens? Osgood had asked.

There is one place. I believe it is at your very school, Dr. Holmes. The place where Dr. Webster, whom I met twenty-five years ago, murdered Mr. Parkman in such extraordinary fashion. I would have staked my head upon it even then, that Webster was a cruel man.

'There may be something to find there,' Osgood said to Rebecca. 'He had seen it already. Knowing Dr. Holmes, he had probably given Dickens a very thorough examination of it. If he really went back to that dismal place before he left Boston, he must have had a reason.'

'Let us go at once then!' This excited utterance came from the lips of Marcus Wakefield. He sat in the seat next to Osgood.

Osgood turned to him. 'Mr. Wakefield, are you certain it is no trouble for us to use your carriage?'

Wakefield shrugged. 'Of course! I hired it for the afternoon, and I haven't any pressing business until late. It is a pleasure to be of small assistance to my two American friends. Let me send a runner with a note to my trading associate, and my chariot and my humble self will be at your disposal until you are entirely finished once and for all with your expedition.'

XXXVII

SGOOD, HOLDING A LANTERN, TOOK the stairs slowly down into the vault of the Medical College, following in the steps that Dickens had taken with Holmes that day in Boston. And steps he'd retraced that night before his assault by Mrs. Barton?

Osgood had left Rebecca in the idling carriage, though she had not wanted to stay.

'Mr. Osgood, please, surely I can help you search for any clues!' she had urged.

'We do not know where Herman is. I cannot in good conscience bring you into a place of potential danger,' said Osgood. 'I should not forgive myself if anything happened.'

'I will stay with her, Mr. Osgood,' Wakefield had said, nodding meaningfully and smiling gently. 'I will watch her, in case Herman is anywhere near.'

'Thank you, Mr. Wakefield. I shan't be long at all,' Osgood had replied. He had known that he had to fulfil this task, even though it would afford Wakefield the opportunity to confess his love to Rebecca. He had to find out what was inside for the sake of the firm's future, and he had to keep Rebecca safe, even if it all meant that in the process he would lose her affections to Wakefield before he could find a way to prove his own.

The publisher entered the building and reached the bottom of the wooden steps down into the vile-smelling dark vault filled with specimen jars and half-empty shelves. Why – if the lunatic in the asylum was right – had Dickens come back here alone, in the middle of the night, with only hours remaining in his stay in Boston? A line from the first instalment of *The Mystery of Edwin Drood* chanted itself in the publisher's mind: 'If I hide my watch when I am drunk,' it said, 'I must be drunk again before I can remember where.' Carrying the lantern in one hand, Osgood groped the shelves with his other. He searched the old demonstration table and the holes in the wall, felt behind spouts and sinks. He reached the furnace, from which the dreadful stink that filled the room emerged. It was where chunks of Parkman's body had once burned. Osgood hesitated and chased the thoughts inside his head. *This would be the perfect spot – the one place in Boston left behind, left untouched, while everything around it changed. Nobody wanted to remember such a hideous death. Boston left it a skeleton in our giant cabinet.*

Steadily, Osgood reached inside the furnace. His fingers traced the ashen, chemical-laden surface. It felt like pushing a hand through a storm cloud – leaden and empty at once. Then he brushed up against something solid, something that felt like the wrinkled skin of a dying man. Slowly, careful not to lose his grip, he pulled out a cracked calf-leather case.

He opened it. Inside was a stack of pages.

Osgood couldn't believe his eyes. He recognised Dickens's hand in iron gall ink at once. He was frozen in place holding his treasure. The feeling was so enormous that for a moment he couldn't bring himself to perform the most natural action known to him since childhood – to read. He could not do anything else but sit there on the cold stone floor from some irrational fear the pages would vanish before his eyes once he looked at them. It was not only the triumphant relief of bringing his quest to a successful conclusion. It was his whole future that he felt at the tips of his fingers. It was Fields, Osgood & Co. in his hands; it was all the men and women who relied on him. It was Rebecca.

And it was as though he had, for a few more seconds, kept Charles Dickens alive. The moment was invigorating. He thought of Frederick Leypoldt's question to him about being a publisher. 'Why are we not blacksmiths or politicians?' Here, here is why, Leypoldt. The truest act of the publisher was one of the discovery of what nobody else was looking for, one that would reawaken imaginations, ambitions, emotions. All of a sudden, he could not wait a second longer to know how Edwin Drood would turn out. Here, right here, all the answers in his hand! Dead or alive? Taken or in hiding? He turned up the light and shined it over the pages and began to examine them, struggling to see through the dust and thick darkness. But the brighter light of the lantern nearly blinded his darkness-adjusted eyes.

'Well, you've done it then!' Wakefield interrupted, appearing at the top of the stairs, carefully stepping down into the vault. He was covered by the darkness of the vault, and his usually friendly, airy mood seemed completely buried in the gloom. 'Have you found anything yet, Mr. Osgood?'

Osgood stood up.

'But why here? Why would he leave it here, Mr. Osgood?' Wakefield asked.

'He was scared to lose it,' Osgood answered.

'Scared?'

'Yes, he was scared, don't you see? Think of it. Dickens was about to leave Boston for ever the next morning. Every time he boarded a train, a ship, even a hackney, he grew cold with fear since the accident in Staplehurst where he almost perished. The passage back to England on the *Russia*, Dickens knew could be a dangerous voyage halfway across the world on the roughest waters in the ocean. Indeed, he would not forget that at the time of the dreadful train accident in Staplehurst, he had been composing *Our Mutual Friend*, the book before *The Mystery of Edwin Drood*, and had its latest pages with him. The newest instalment of it was still in the train compartment that he escaped, and he risked his life to climb back inside to retrieve it.'

'That was daring.'

Osgood nodded. 'That is not the only thing that would have been on his mind, though. There had been Mrs. Barton, who had broken into the hotel room – leaving behind a note demanding to speak to Dickens about his next book. There had been his pocket diary, stolen by her. There were the tax agents threatening to do whatever they had to in order to retrieve the money he was owed – to confiscate tickets or his personal belongings and documents. Dickens knew that if he boarded the ship with this in hand, he might never see it again. Moreover, back in England, he knew when he would begin publishing his mystery, there would be fierce demand to know how it was to turn out. A servant he had once trusted had broken into his locked safe at his office while he was away. There were dangers for Dickens, yes, for this manuscript, waiting everywhere. *This* spot, this dingy lonely place, may have been the only safe place on earth for these pages. They would reside here undisturbed until he was ready to call for them to be retrieved – which he would do when he finished the first half. But when he died suddenly, it was too late for him to communicate it.'

Wakefield applauded.

Osgood thought about Rebecca. He wished he had agreed to her coming along into the building so she could be beside him to share this moment. Then he realised.

'Where's Miss Sand, Mr. Wakefield?'

'Oh, don't worry, Mr. Osgood! I have my colleague watching Rebecca.'

Osgood nodded gratefully, though tilting his head at the informality of his patron's use of her Christian name. It meant one thing – she had accepted his declaration of love. Despite the heartache of thinking about this, Osgood still wished she were with him. This was an accomplishment by her every bit as much as by him – by her and for her. For all she endured with Daniel.

Osgood realised those words passing through his thoughts were not his own. *All she endured with her brother Daniel. Awful, senseless tragedy.* That had been Wakefield's phrase, in their conversation on board the ship saloon. A question entered Osgood's mind, for that moment pushing out the astonishing document he held in his hands and the gloomy cellar where he stood: How had Wakefield known about Daniel? Had Rebecca become that intimate with him to tell him? Osgood could not decide whether it was protectiveness, or jealousy, or suspicion of Wakefield that suddenly took hold of him.

'Remarkable, Mr. Osgood!' Wakefield was saying, laughing as though they had reached the climax in a riotous joke. 'And, lo, you've found these before anyone!'

A scene entered Osgood's mind from his first journey on the *Samaria*. Wakefield becoming his friend immediately. A rush of ideas, of facts. Wakefield had not just been on their steamer to London and back. Wakefield had *followed* them to London and back – just as Herman did. He and Herman had been in Boston at the same time, on the ship at the same time, and in London at the same time. Wakefield rushed to the police station after Herman's attack on him at the opium rooms.

'I think I should find Miss Sand now,' Osgood said quietly.

'Certainly, certainly,' Wakefield said.

'Will you be kind enough to stand guard over this for a moment?' Osgood asked, gesturing at the calf-leather case.

'I am your humble servant, sir,' Wakefield said. Just as Osgood had hurried halfway up the stairs, Wakefield added, 'Oh, but hold on. I have a gift for you I brought from London! In all the excitement, I nearly forgot! To repay you for all the books aboard our passages.'

'That is generous,' Osgood murmured, judging in a sidelong glance the number of stairs remaining to the door.

'Watch out!' Wakefield called.

He tossed the heavy object through the air. Osgood caught it to his chest with one hand. Unwrapping the paper, he bathed the lumpy object in the light of the flaring lantern. It was a yellow plaster statue that had once been listed for auction under the title *Turk Seated Smoking Opium*. The statue from the home of Charles Dickens.

'You said,' Osgood commented offhandedly, 'that the auction house had broken this.'

'Think of it as a farewell gift, of sorts, Mr. Osgood. Oh, and why should I guard a calf-leather case that I'd bet my best pair of kid gloves is empty? You did switch the pages into your own satchel already, didn't you?'

The loud echo of Wakefield snapping his fingers rang through the grim chamber. Two Chinese men appeared at the top of the stairs. One of the men scratched the back of his neck with his fingernail. Only it was no ordinary fingernail. The nail of the little finger on the left hand was between seven and eight inches long and perfectly clean and sharp, an appendage uniquely cultivated by the Chinese *scharf* for use in testing the counterfeit or genuine nature of specie used to pay for opium.

Rebecca, trembling, also appeared at the top of the stairs. Behind her, the silvery reflection of Osgood's lantern illuminated the jutting fangs of a Kylin's head.

Osgood backed down the stairs to the bottom, where Rebecca joined him for protection. Wakefield joined Herman on the landing above them. Herman bowed his head at Wakefield, putting both hands on his forehead.

'I told you, Mr. Osgood,' pointed out Wakefield, 'that Miss Sand was being carefully watched.'

'You arranged for Herman to assault me on the *Samaria* and for you to be the hero in the encounter, to ensure that I would trust and rely on you,' Osgood said. 'You have been partners with him the whole time. You attempted to win Miss Sand's affections so that she would reveal to you our plans.'

'You are awarded the premium! You know, you have an earnest habit of thinking the world around you is as well meaning as you are, my friend,' Wakefield replied. 'I admire that. Let us go somewhere more comfortable than this.'

'We shall go nowhere with you,' Osgood said. 'You're no tea merchant, Mr. Wakefield.' As he spoke, Osgood casually slipped the Turkish statue into his satchel, and felt the increased weight of the bag on his shoulder.

'Oh, I am,' came the reply from Wakefield with a muted laugh shared by Herman. 'Though not tea alone, of course. Tea, quite often, is how our friends in China pay for their opium shipments. Don't you see the larger picture yet, Mr. Osgood? No, you were always paying too close attention to sentences to understand the books – it has kept you insulated, worried over words that make no difference in the end, because the machinery of more powerful men overcomes you. When I was a boy, I was sent away from home. I found refuge with a relative, but I gained a restless spirit that has never abandoned me.'

As Wakefield spoke, Osgood swung his satchel hard, striking the businessman in the leg. He did not flinch. There was a metallic clang and the statue shattered to pieces in the bag.

Osgood and Rebecca exchanged a startled glance. Wakefield lifted his trousers and revealed a mechanism on his foot consisting of straps, joints, and cog wheels.

'My God!' Osgood blurted out. 'Edward Trood!'

Herman took two menacing steps closer to him.

Wakefield waved his Parsee protector away and, standing erect, glared at Osgood. He spoke in sharp bursts of Chinese to the two *scharfs*, who nodded and left the building. Then he turned back to Osgood.

'No, Mr. Osgood, I am not he. That *was* my name once, yes – I was cowering little Eddie Trood with the club foot when I was sent away from Rochester by the cruel despotism of my father. But that part of me is dead, and so is Eddie Trood. I began to erase him when

I escaped through opium ecstasies in the home of my uncle. But my body soon rebelled against it, placing me either in the agony of its power when I swallowed it, or in the depth of misery when I attempted to abstain from it. A physician advised me on the use of a syringe, a method that spread a greater sense of relaxation and deadening of the senses but did nothing to reduce my inner demand for it. It was a stimulation without satisfaction.

'Opium was an armour that kept me safe from the outside world but crushed my bones in the process. I was told that a sea voyage was the only way to force myself out of its control. After I sailed to China I was no longer enslaved. A new truth had come to me. An understanding of the unavoidable power of the drug – the need to oversee its arrangements not through the doctor or druggist but in the shadows and the cover of night. It was in Canton that a doctor fitted my foot with this. It corrected the position of deformity so that there is no noticeable deficiency in my step even under close scrutiny. That was when I knew I was ready to return to England a new man.'

Osgood's mind raced and his comprehension of their situation jumped three or four moves ahead. 'Then Herman never tried to kill Eddie Trood – you – for knowing the secrets of his drug enterprise?'

'My drug enterprise, Mr. Osgood,' Wakefield said, smiling. 'Herman has served as my agent ever since I helped him escape from the Chinese pirates. You see, in my travels, I determined that a smuggler, in order to survive long enough to prosper, would have to be an invisible man. On that basis, I started a new life when I came back, a life as Marcus Wakefield. Herman and Imam, our Turkish comrade, assisted in my scheme, but they were carpenters in its execution, and I, the lone architect. There was a young man who had at the time recently suffered the effects of an overdose of bad opium and died. We dressed the lad in some of my old clothes and Herman took a crowbar to the head so the body would not be recognised. One weekend, when my uncle was in the country, I went into hiding, while my collaborators tore down a wall in his home and hid the body of our false Edward Trood there.'

'Machiavellian to the last degree,' Osgood said, surmising his larger purpose. 'Then Marcus Wakefield would be feared.'

'Well, yes, precisely, only not Wakefield exactly. I used that alias in my ordinary course of business. As an opium merchant, I have used as many names in as many places as would suit my purposes: Copeland, Hewes, Simonds, Tauka. But nobody would ever meet the keeper of any of the names. They would hear stories – legends of his remarkable and terrible deeds, stories of the dead, starting with Eddie Trood who had tried to infiltrate his opium lines. Otherwise, there was invisibility, and men like Herman and Imam served as my hands and feet out in the world.

'So, too, did my means of transport have to achieve invisibility. Though there were not many countries like China willing to fight wars to prevent the import of opium to its people, there are many governments, like your own, gleeful to extract tariffs and hold inspections on incoming supplies of the narcotics. My organisation secured ownership of a line of steamships, the *Samaria* being the fastest, and specially fitted them not only so they could be converted to warships but with ample hidden storage space. Since ours is a passenger steamer, the customs officials would examine the luggage being brought on shore. But in the dark of the night, my crew would bring out the chests of opium, disguised in cheap vases or sardine boxes to deliver to the enterprising scoundrels in Boston, Philadelphia and New York. They would supply them to eager customers unable or unwilling to purchase their opium from doctors and pharmacists, who have in the last years been forced to record the names of every purchaser of "poisons".'

'Why Daniel?' Rebecca asked, shocked and overwhelmed by the betrayal. 'Why harm my little brother?'

Wakefield looked disapprovingly at Herman. 'I'm afraid, my dear girl, that his death was incidental to our purpose. After Dickens died, Herman had found an urgent telegram from Fields and Osgood at the office of Dickens's executor requesting all that remained of *The Mystery of Edwin Drood*. We set out for Boston immediately to intercept the shipment, and bribing a willing employee of yours named Mr. Midges, it was discovered that Daniel Sand had been assigned the task of receiving the latest instalments of any novels coming from England.'

They learned further from Midges – who was disgruntled at rumours of Daniel's having been a drunkard and even more disgruntled that women were taking too many positions at the firm – that Daniel was to be waiting at the harbour early in the morning for more pages of *The Mystery of Edwin Drood*. The ship from England was already docked. But by the time Herman detained the young man in the too-heavy suit, Daniel had suspected he was being followed and had nothing in the canvas sack hung from his shoulder. And to their astonishment, he would take no money in exchange for telling them where he had hidden the pages.

'No, sir,' Daniel had said. 'I am very sorry, I cannot.' They had led him into the second storey of a warehouse on Long Wharf where they stored smuggled opium.

Wakefield had put a hand on the young clerk's shoulder. 'Young man, we know you've had some troubles in the past with certain intoxicating agents. We surely wouldn't want your employer, who trusts you with such important errands, to know about *that*. We're not some cheap reprinters looking to steal copy. We just need to see what's in those Dickens pages, and then we'll give them back.'

Daniel hesitated, studying his interrogators, then shook his head vigorously. 'No, sir! I must not!' He was repeating, 'It's Osgood's! It's Osgood's!'

Herman lunged forward, but Wakefield signalled him to stop.

'Now, think carefully, my dear lad,' Wakefield had urged, the friendly expression on his face flagging, and a fog of violence replacing it. 'How disappointed Fields, Osgood & Co. would be after putting their faith in you to find out who you really are beneath that youthful and charming face. An inveterate drunkard.'

'Mr. Osgood would be *disappointed* if I didn't do my job I'm paid for,' the boy had said bullheadedly. 'I would rather account for my history to Mr. Osgood myself than to fail his instructions.'

Wakefield's full smile returned, almost breaking into a warm laugh, before he gave the slightest flick of his hand.

Herman tore open the clerk's shirt and cut shallow, straight slits into his chest with the Kylin cane's shimmering fangs. Daniel winced but did not cry. As the blood dripped, Herman let it fall into a cup and then drank it down in front of Daniel with a rising grin until his lips were bright. Daniel, recovering from the pain, shook hard but tried staring straight ahead.

'For God's sake,' Wakefield had said. He cracked Daniel over the head with a bludgeon. Daniel crumpled to the floor.

'Can't you see,' Wakefield had explained to Herman, 'you could beat this boy until his head rolls off and scare him until his hair stands up on its ends and he wouldn't say a word this Osgood hadn't authorised? He is a lesson in loyalty, Herman.'

At this, Herman grunted irritably.

Wakefield instructed Herman to inject the lad with opium and release him on to the wharf. If Wakefield's instinct was right, in his confused state the boy would go to retrieve the pages wherever they were hidden. But his senses would be impaired enough to allow Herman to easily overtake him; and, to make the affair even cleaner, if the boy reported the theft to the police they wouldn't listen because he'd be stuck in the aura of the drug.

But Daniel, upon retrieving the bundle from a stray barrel, lost Herman in the crowded piers of the wharf and the commotion of the waterfront. When Herman grabbed him at Dock Square, Daniel pulled away and was struck by the omnibus. There were too many people around for Herman to get the papers. But Wakefield joined the circle of observers around Daniel's body and heard the name of Sylvanus Bendall, the lawyer who would greedily confiscate the pages.

'You were there,' said Osgood to Wakefield with an unexpected tinge of envy. 'You were there when poor Daniel died.'

'No,' Rebecca whispered, horrified by the thought and the new vividness of her brother's final moments.

Wakefield nodded. 'Yes, I was among the many curious spectators as he expired. The poor boy still called your name, Osgood. By the time Herman retrieved the pages from Bendall – the two-penny lawyer carried them around with him on his person, leaving us little choice how to serve him – we learned even those later instalments of the serial, the fourth, fifth and sixth, had no reliable clues to the ending of the book. We were about to return to England. Then our stool pigeon in your firm told us that you were going to sail to Gadshill to find the end of *The Mystery of Edwin Drood*. Why do you think it was so easy for Mr. Fields to get you passage at the last minute, my dear Osgood, when he decided to send you? The *Samaria* was the only liner with any room left – because I made certain of it. Because the *Samaria* and all its crew belong to me.'

'When Herman disappeared in the middle of the ocean, where had you hidden him? The captain, the stewards, the ship detective all looked for him,' Osgood said.

'They work for me. Me, me, Osgood. Herman no more disappeared in the middle of the ocean than you did. It didn't occur to us that you'd pay a visit without escort days after the charade of locking him up. He was safely stored away in our secret rooms below the captain's quarters as he was on the passage back to Boston we've just completed. But by that point you trusted me, dare I say, with your life. As well you should have. Herman protected you in London from the opium fiends when those fools attacked you for your purse and he left you where you were sure to be given help. He saved you.'

'So I could live long enough to find what you were after.'

Wakefield nodded. 'In the meantime, my entire business began to suffer – payments gone unmade, opium managers avoiding my suppliers. Why do you think those opium fiends salivated at the sight of you? They'd kill any stranger for a shilling. The whole field of opium dealers had become dry as they all read *The Mystery of Edwin Drood* in its serial parts along with the rest of the world.'

'But why?' Osgood asked.

'Because my trade had very quickly recognised in Dickens's words what you've unearthed, the story of Edward Trood, and saw in those hints of Drood's survival a looming danger to our enterprise. Nor could we afford any further attention on the "murderers" of Trood – that is why Herman stole the statue from the auction house. That Turk, in the statue, you see, was done by some interfering artist of the real man, Imam, one of the opium pushers who helped conceal "my" body. We didn't need Imam's face on display at the biggest auction to be held at Christie's in the last hundred years! This attention to everything related to Dickens's final days and book was all nothing less than disaster!'

'If people believed Trood was alive,' said Rebecca, 'your organisation could collapse, be overtaken by doubts, because of your lie that started it. People began to believe that the supposedly murdered Trood was alive and knew your secrets.'

Wakefield waved his hand in the air. 'You see Mr. Osgood, your bookkeeper is a natural woman of business. Yes, it's true. If it was believed that Eddie Trood had not died, it meant he could be out there somewhere waiting to use his knowledge to bring us down. Yet that is not all that has haunted me since Dickens picked up his pen to retell my story. After the case of Webster and Parkman of your city became famous, the methods it also made famous spread. The skeleton of Parkman was identified by his teeth. Since then, death does not bring an end to all things. And if the police were to hear the tales that Trood might be alive and decide to dig up the grave of

Edward Trood? Would they determine it was not Trood, and then what? If that was not Trood lying beneath the earth, where was he? You can imagine the entertainment Scotland Yard would have with that question. You can imagine how free I would be to move about London – my old self suddenly resurrected! Arthur Grunwald convinced the Surrey to perform just such an ending in their production of Mr. Dickens's book, so Herman burned it down early on the morning of our departure. A shame, though, that Grunwald had to be in the green room, I did enjoy him as Hamlet at the Princess. You see, even Herman and myself are not always perfect.

'Of course, I read Tom Branagan's wire when we made port at Queenstown. The captain directed it towards me upon my instructions before you saw it. What a dear soul your Constable Tom is, to find proof that the letter to Forster was Grunwald's forgery. That letter would have been a great interference to us.'

'These six instalments,' Osgood said, gripping the satchel with the remainder of Dickens's novel tightly. 'That's all you want, then, to destroy these?' Osgood folded his satchel into his chest.

Wakefield laughed. 'If only there were happy music,' he mused suddenly. 'Yes, that would put all our minds at ease. What do you say, Ironhead Herman?' Wakefield extended his hand and Herman took it, being swept across the room, dancing a brisk waltz around Osgood and Rebecca. 'Are we graceful enough for you, Osgood?' Wakefield asked, laughing and bowing.

It was a chilling scene to watch the two killers waltz around the warehouse. Strangest in the tableau was this: Ironhead Herman was ready to look like a fool on command of Wakefield. If Herman were a killer who respected only brutality and force, what were the depths of Wakefield's own brutality to have that kind of hold over him? The meaning of it sunk into Osgood. The dance, step by step, made one thing clear as noontime. They would die there.

'Please, for mercy's sake, let Miss Sand go free,' Osgood said prayerfully.

Wakefield examined his captives, saying, 'I am not the terrible man you must now imagine. My curse in life is to have the vision others do not. I can understand what your government and mine still cannot. People are beginning to make a devil out of opium and opium use; in their minds the opium eater is as unreal and unwanted as a human vampire. They have protested the morality of the trade with

China. Before long the Americans and the English will hold opium accountable for all their own faults and pass more rules and regulations. China has finally surrendered their will against the drug and will grow the poppy themselves to feed their people's appetite. Besides, with the opening of the Suez Canal, every damned little *parleyvoo* with a tugboat can get to China without any skills or knowledge of trading: the coasts will be positively overrun. It is your own people who clamour for supply, with scores of soldiers – Yankee and Rebel alike – returned to their homes under the spell of injury and the need for relief and ignored by a society that has moved on with commerce and progress while those brave souls wither. Now with the hypodermic, any man or woman who wishes will provide themselves with the medication and enjoyment they can no longer find in the devouring cities without artificial assistance. America is the land of experimentation – a new religion, a new medicine, a new invention – if there is something to transform, Americans will throw away all constraints with the freedom of self-indulgence. Alcohol makes man into beast, but opium makes him divine. The syringe will replace the flask and be an unfailing remedy in the pocket of the businessman, the bookkeeper, the mother, the teacher and the lawyer who suffer the curse of modern cares. What do you think of it, Osgood? Oh, I know your trade is books, but it all comes down to this: to know your customers, to know how they wish to make their escapes from this bleak world, and to make sure they can't live without you. The modern brain will wither without finding a way to join excitement and numbness. We have sought the same thing through Dickens, you and I, to protect ourselves and the people we depend on. No, I seek nobody's death.'

'Daniel Sand depended on me,' Osgood said, 'and I could not protect him.'

'But I could have,' Wakefield said, 'if he had not been so set on your approval.' He turned solicitously to Rebecca, 'My dear girl, I'm afraid you've gained too much intelligence today to live freely without causing me some degree of future consternation. You have fascinated me from the moment I saw you. We have both been made invisible by unjust forces. Damn the rules of your divorce, damn the little position Osgood has thrown at you for half pay, the peasant labourer he made your brother into: come with me back to England, you will have all you ever ask for, all you deserve. That is why I have unfolded everything for you now. I'd want you to understand all the reasons for what has happened, so that you could consider my offer honestly once and for all within your heart.'

Rebecca looked up from where she sat, first at Osgood, then at Wakefield. 'You killed Daniel! You are nothing but a scoundrel and a liar! A woman could have loved Eddie Trood, with all his faults in the face of a hard world, but never a fraud like you!'

Wakefield's face turned red before his hand went flying out across her face. To his apparent surprise, she did not cry when he struck her. 'I shall not give you the satisfaction, Mr. Trood,' she said bitterly, seeing in his raging eyes his anticipation. 'I'll weep for my brother, not for anything you could do to me.'

'Ungrateful female,' Wakefield said, turning away from her and replacing his hat on his head. 'You have done fine in training her in your species of high-handed failure, Mr. Osgood. Very well. You have made your bed, Rebecca; now you may both lie in it.'

Wakefield turned his back to them.

'Your father!' Osgood said.

Wakefield slowed his steps.

'Your father misses you, Edward,' Osgood continued.

Wakefield sighed longingly. Then, as he turned around again he laughed, harshly this time.

'Thank you. I shall have to see to it that my old man never tells another soul my story who may pick up on the clues as you have done. We'll be paying him a visit back in England, be sure, and Jack Chinaman, and your friend Branagan, too.'

Wakefield disappeared up the stairway.

Herman stood grinning toothlessly and raised his walking stick. He swung it at Osgood's satchel, scattering the floor with the pages of the final six instalments of *Edwin Drood*.

XXXVIII

'PLEASE HORMAZD, WE CAN WORK out a bargain,' said Osgood pleadingly to Herman.

'This isn't a Jews' marketplace,' replied Herman, momentarily pausing at his given name. 'No bargains.' He seemed to contemplate the beastly animal head on his walking stick for a moment. Then he glowered at his prisoners. 'The only thing I'd regret, Osgood, is that Mr. Wakefield insisted on trying to persuade her to come with us. Waiting makes me angry. I may even finish you off with my bare hands.'

'Why have you despised me?' Osgood demanded.

'Because, Os*good*, you think you can be friends with everybody by flashing your smile. You think everybody can be like you.' Herman's answer flew out of his mouth like a confession, showing his real mind more than he intended.

'It's Mr. Wakefield who has made you who you are, Herman!' Rebecca said persuasively. 'He made you into a pirate.'

'I was born one, lassie.'

A torrent of footsteps on the stairs. When Herman turned to look over his shoulder for Wakefield, his smug smile dropped away. Osgood recognised a look of confusion in the face of his captor. In a flash, Osgood lunged at him, throwing himself on to Herman's back and putting his arm around his eyes to blind him. Herman growled out and prised Osgood's fingers with his iron grip. Osgood landed on his feet and put up his fists in a boxing pose. Just then, a club slammed against the back of Herman's turbanned head.

326

Behind Herman, gripping the hook and bill club, stood the man Osgood once knew as Dick Datchery: Jack Rogers.

There was a sickening sound as the club resounded against Herman's skull. But Herman didn't budge, blinking meditatively.

'Ironhead Herman,' Osgood whispered.

'Ironhead?' Rogers repeated in a worried tone.

Herman revolved around slowly to face Rogers, readying his walking stick. Realising the man was still unhurt, Rogers thrust the spike at the tip of the club into Herman's sternum. This stunned Herman. He dropped his cane and fell to the floor on his knees. With a shout, Rogers swung the club again as hard as he could against Herman's head. It smashed into splinters and sent the hook and spike flying across the room in bits. Herman dropped on to all fours and, drained of strength, blinded by his own blood, he collapsed flat on top of his walking stick.

'Rogers!' Osgood cried, looking from Herman to the former Harper's policeman. 'How did you know . . . ?'

'I told you I would repay my debt to you, good Ripley,' said Rogers, breathing heavily. 'I'm a man of my word.'

Osgood threw himself on the floor and began to gather the scattered pages of *Drood*.

'No time, Ripley! There's no time for any of that!' Rogers called out. 'Where's Wakefield?'

'He's already gone – probably back to his ship,' Osgood said.

'Come along!'

Securing his treasure in his satchel, Osgood hesitated to take the hand Rogers held out to him.

Rogers seemed prepared for this. 'Because it was my duty, I deceived you in England when my conscience told me otherwise. Now my duty is to follow my conscience above all else. You must trust me – your lives depend on it.'

Osgood nodded and stepped over the motionless Herman on the way to the door. Rebecca paused for a moment, tears in her eyes. She looked down at the man on the floor and she brought her heel down on to his back again and again.

'Rebecca!' Osgood took her in his arms. 'Come along!'

Osgood's embrace returned her to the present situation and its dangers. She felt more grounded at once with his touch.

Rogers spoke rapidly as they made their way up the stairs. 'Ripley, there is great danger about Wakefield – he makes frequent trips between Boston, New York and England, but I believe the only tea he trades is in his own cup.'

'What did you find?' Osgood asked.

'By following his men, I have located a mountain of evidence which we must take to the police, of a string of attacks and murders perpetrated by his agents to protect his enterprise.'

'Dickens's words were the only thing that he thought could bring him down,' Osgood said.

'He *was* right,' Rogers corrected him. 'Now we shall do it. Thank heavens I found you in time, Ripley. Stand here with Miss Rebecca.'

As they reached the top of the stairs, Rogers motioned for Osgood and Rebecca to wait. He looked outside for any sign of Wakefield. Determining the way was clear, he waved them to advance. His hired carriage idled across the street in case any one from Wakefield's gangs of hirelings had watch on the building. The way appearing clear, Rogers signalled for the rescued pair to get into the carriage. As Rogers and Osgood helped lift Rebecca inside, there was a grunting sound from behind them and a shiny object gliding through the air. It was a furiously reappearing Herman, standing at the door to the building, his arm completing the arc of a throwing motion.

Rogers looked up just as the bowie knife pierced his neck. His body plummeted from the steps of the carriage on to the pavement. Rebecca tripped on the bottom of her dress and nearly tumbled down to the street.

'Rogers!' Osgood cried. He kneeled by his rescuer's side, but the man had bled to death in an instant. 'No! Rogers!'

The driver cursed and took up his reins and threw back his whip.

Rebecca's ankle had twisted but she still hung on to the handle of the coach. Osgood pushed her back on to the steps and she pulled herself into the carriage just as the horses started into a trot, spinning Osgood away.

'No – Mr. Osgood!' Rebecca cried out, reaching out her hand.

Osgood shouted to the driver to go as fast as he could as the dust and gravel swirled around him in its wake. Herman would only be able to pursue one of them, and it was Osgood who had the satchel with the manuscript. At least Rebecca would be safe.

Osgood ran up Washington Street, grabbing his bandaged ribs as he went, while trying to ease his painful breathing. The Parsee was going to kill him and nothing would stop him; he would demolish anything in his path to do it. Osgood broke into a run with Herman on his heels.

Ahead was the Sears Building, which Osgood knew well as it was the location of his bank. Outside the front door, there was a janitor with a ring of keys locking the front door of the building. Osgood hoped he could make Herman lose his trail inside and escape. He pushed past the janitor and into the building.

Osgood had reached the other side of the main corridor where he could see another door to the street. Pray the janitor hadn't yet locked it! As Osgood moved closer, the door shook and slowly opened – to reveal the silhouette of a roguish figure with an uncombed beard and a cocked hat. Another opium pusher from the *Samaria* sent for by Wakefield? Osgood halted in midstep.

Echoes of Herman's running footsteps seemed everywhere, above, below, on every side. Osgood turned one way, then the other, not knowing which corridor to choose. Instead, he rushed to the centre of the hall and pulled open the door to the elevator. Then Osgood realised: no elevator operator, not at this hour! The boys didn't sleep in these little rooms, however cushioned and decorated they were. He had been inside many times in the course of everyday business to be carried up to his bank on the seventh floor. Would he remember how he had seen the lads do it?

His head tilted to the side at the sound. The mounting whir of steam pumping; the loud clank clank of chains and metal. Herman slid to a stop in the hall. He surveyed his surroundings: stairs on either side of the building. He ran towards the far end, following the whistling sound of the steam rising up above him.

Osgood quickly formed his plan. He would stop the elevator on a floor midway up the building, hurry out of the elevator and down the stairs, exiting the building while Herman was still searching inside.

The Sears elevator was what they called a moving parlour. The car had a domed ceiling with skylights and a chandelier elegantly suspended from it. The gas apparatus connected to the chandelier was concealed by a lightweight tube. The rest of the car could have been the corner of a Beacon Hill parlour. Underfoot was thick carpeting, and sofas lined each of the three sides of the car. Atop the French walnut panelling, gilded on its perimeter, were large polished mirrors.

The levers didn't look easy to operate and in actuality they were even more difficult than they appeared – Osgood manipulated them into a jerking, halting movement that immediately made him regret his plan. Stopping it was even harder, but Osgood managed to make the machine halt close enough to the fourth floor.

Osgood climbed out of the elevator and dashed to the stairway, where he began to descend before hearing footsteps rising up towards him. It was him! Osgood turned and tried to exit back to the fourth floor but he had lost ground, and Herman was close to grabbing his ankle. The publisher created enough distance to exit on the sixth floor instead. Heaving for breath, Osgood scrambled to the elevator door and pulled the platform lever to call for it from four. Blast that slow steam pump! *Please, faster* . . . The elevator arrived and Osgood threw himself bodily inside, smashing his torso hard against the floor.

As the door swung closed, Herman was bearing down on him. Extending his walking stick – the door slammed on it. Osgood, for a long second, found himself eye to eye with the golden face of the Kylin, the lusty horn bursting from its head and its empty onyx eyes. It had been so demonic and chilling. Closer up it lost its power. It seemed a silly gold trinket. Osgood yanked the cane with all his strength by the Kylin's prickly neck. He fell back in the car with it in his hands and the door shut. Osgood kicked at the lever with the toe of his shoe and started the car down.

Osgood hoped he would be far enough ahead (thirty seconds?) of the mercenary that he could get out of the building. But as he listened to the whirring steam below, he thought of the brave Jack Rogers, of foolish Sylvanus Bendall; he thought of poor Daniel on the coroner's cold table; he thought of Yahee's haunting terror; he thought of Wakefield's coldness as he had danced the waltz, of the threats to silence William Trood and Tom; and he thought, too, of Rebecca. Then he knew, without the slightest doubt, that he could not simply run from the building and leave Herman free to find them again. For a moment, Osgood was astonished by his own determination. Herman had to be stopped. He had to be stopped once and for all *here*.

Osgood passed the first floor. His skills with the lever having improved every moment, he softly brought the car to a stop in the basement. He stepped away from the car to the adjoining engine room where it was controlled and kicked hard without result at the steam pipe that powered the elevator. Then he took the walking stick and pounded it again and again until the valve dented and then broke – the walking stick cracked, decapitating the monstrous golden visage. Osgood returned to the elevator and crouched, waiting, his eyes on the stairwell, his breathing laboured and shooting around his fractured ribs, where the dressings underneath his shirt had loosened and ripped and made him feel as though his body would crack in half at any moment. As Herman appeared at the basement door and hurled himself forward, Osgood pulled the door shut and adroitly shot the elevator up at the most reckless speed.

As the car launched into the air, a geyser of steam shot out of the broken engine and sprayed into the charging figure of Herman. Blinded, dazed, the mercenary shrieked and fumbled around in a circle, stumbling into the shaft.

Up above, Osgood panicked. The elevator car was swaying and groaning, its steam power compromised. He abruptly stopped it at the fifth floor, not quite even with the platform, but he tumbled out anyway, grunting in pain as he made contact with the wood floor. Just then, the chains unravelled and the empty car rushed down as though in a dead faint. Herman, curled up in a stupor in the shaft and trying to crawl away from the burning steam, looked above him just long enough to see the car before it smashed on to him. The force was so great that the hulking form of the mercenary's body broke through the floor of the elevator car, as the chandelier and the skylights shook free and rained a thousand shards into him.

Both dizzy and profoundly awake, Osgood rose to his feet, looking down the elevator's shaft. An explosion left a layer of flames at the bottom. He was tucking away his satchel, when he was grabbed by the shoulders.

'No!' Osgood screamed.

'Halloa! Are you well, man?'

It was the scraggly, messy-bearded man Osgood had seen at the bottom of the building, the beard now apparent as a rusted red colour.

'You looked to be under some distress at the door,' the man

continued, his hands groping at Osgood's shoulders, arms, and around the satchel as though to check for wounds.

'I must send for the police,' Osgood said. 'There's a man injured down there—'

'Already done!' the man with the overgrown beard cried. 'Already sent for, my dear man. Though not much of that fellow down there is left, by the looks of it. Elevators! Why, I won't get in one myself, not with those demonstrations at the fairs killing one or two passengers at a time, and on a good day. They should be abolished, says I. Now, how can I help you? I have a wagon out front. Where can I take you?'

Was the rust-coloured bearded man another janitor? Then the publisher realised: this stranger matched the description of Molasses, he of the rainbow-coloured beard who operated among the notorious Bookaneers and claimed the fame of having secured Thackeray's *The Adventures of Philip* before the world.

'Hand it over,' said Molasses, a change passing over his face as he caught the glint of Osgood's recognition. 'Don't know what you have there exactly, but the Major would probably pay triple for whatever it is. And you're in no shape for a tussle, not tonight.'

Little does he know what Harper would pay! thought Osgood. He knew there were no police coming, at least not by this man's doing.

There was a moan from far below them. Another explosion came from the engine room, and the flames shot another floor higher. Osgood realised from the dampness of his flesh that the heat was closer. Soon the gas line that had lighted the elevator car would burst open and the whole place and everything inside it would be roasted.

As Osgood backed away towards the elevator shaft, he noticed Molasses's face suddenly turn fearful. The literary pirate's hands raised slowly. Osgood whirled around and saw Wakefield coming from the stairwell. He was pulling Rebecca by her arm and had a pistol to her neck. Her arms and face were bruised, her dress torn in multiple places.

'Rebecca!' Osgood exclaimed in shock.

'I am afraid your dead hero's hired hackman went a little wild from all the commotion, Osgood,' Wakefield said. 'The carriage tipped over, but don't fear – I was there to come to your damsel's aid, just as I have yours so many times now.'

'Let her be, Wakefield!' Osgood cried, then quickly added, as calmly as possible: 'You can still get down there. *There is still time to save him.*'

Wakefield peered down at the flames lapping the darkness from six floors below, where the broken body of Herman struggled. 'Doubtful he'd survive that, I'd say, Osgood. There are plenty of other fire worshippers that would serve me for a profit.'

'He is your friend,' Osgood said.

'He is a cog in my enterprise, as your search has been. Now, I shall tell you what *I'd* like. You drop that satchel down into those flames, and I'll allow your silly girl to live.'

'Don't, James!' Rebecca cried. 'Not after all that has happened!'

Osgood mouthed to her that it was all right and smiled reassuringly. He held the satchel out over the shaft.

'Very good move, my boy. You can take orders after all.' Wakefield smiled. 'Don't worry, Mr. Osgood, the world will not be deprived of Dickens's ending.'

Osgood looked at him with confusion. 'What do you mean?'

'After we have destroyed this, I plan to find Dickens's ending myself, of course! At least, how I would like it – with Edwin Drood's body discovered to be quite dead and gone in a crypt in Rochester. Would it surprise you to learn I am acquainted with the greatest forgers and counterfeiters, Mr. Osgood? From samples of Dickens's handwriting I will have my men create six instalments of the finest literary forgery ever attempted, a class beyond the amateur production of Mr. Grunwald. I am certain John Forster will be only too happy to have this, as it agrees with his own professions about the book's finale. There is only one problem. We must be rid of Dickens's real ending before I can forge my own. That is how you are about to help me.'

'Lower your pistol from her first, Wakefield,' said Osgood. 'Then I will do as you ask.'

'You are not in command here!' Wakefield roared, shaking Rebecca's arm violently.

But Osgood waited until the pistol strayed slightly away from her neck. Osgood nodded to his adversary for the gesture, then let the bag drop, but kept hold of the top of the strap so that it dangled precariously over the flaming pit of the elevator shaft.

'For me, this would have been my finest publication, Wakefield,' Osgood said meditatively, in the voice of a eulogy. 'Only conceive of what a treasure it would have made! Not only to have rescued my firm from our rivals but to have done proper justice to Mr. Dickens's very last work and restore it to the reading public. But for you, the ending of *Drood* is even more. It's your life. Isn't it? These last six instalments could destroy you, since all eyes around would have been on their every word.'

'And that's why you'll drop it!' Wakefield yelled, losing the remnants of his composure. 'Let it go!'

Two more big explosions burst the air from below . . . the final moans from a roasting Herman . . . the flames exhaling up and licking at the ironworks of the shaft, turning it into a gigantic open chimney and reminding Osgood all his choices were gone.

'Drood?' Molasses, said, gasping at the realisation. 'That's *Drood* in there?'

'Quiet!' Wakefield yelled. 'Come, Osgood.'

Osgood nodded obediently to Wakefield. 'I will let go, Wakefield. I promised, and I do as I promise.'

'I know it, Osgood.'

'But you must hope,' Osgood continued, 'that whole way between the Medical College and here I didn't stop for a moment to switch it for some worthless papers, or stuff this with leaves or blank stationery. Are you confident enough that I would destroy what I've searched for all this time, even for the sake of a woman? Are you absolutely certain?'

'I am, Osgood. You love her.'

'Yes,' Osgood said, unhesitating. Rebecca for a moment lost all her terror. 'But tell me, Mr. Wakefield,' Osgood continued, 'would you find it anywhere inside of you to ever do that, to destroy everything you've wanted to protect someone you love?'

Wakefield's eyes widened, his brow poured sweat. Slowly, he stepped towards Osgood. Now he trained his gun on the publisher as he inched towards the satchel.

'Don't think of moving a muscle, Osgood,' said Wakefield, steadying the gun at Osgood's forehead. The publisher nodded his head in surrender. Osgood's gaze shifted to Rebecca, and in that moment he looked in her eyes she knew what to do.

Here Wakefield slipped his hand into the satchel and out came the thick bundle of papers covered in iron gall ink, with yellow shards of the plaster statue clinging to it. He held the gun steady, in one hand, while with the other he brought the pages to his face. After a moment of quiet suspense, a dark shadow passed over his expression. Awkwardly using two fingers of his gun-holding hand, he flipped the page back to see the next one, then the next one, then finally skipped ahead to the last one.

His face concentrated, then contorted with a baffled entrancement. As everything but the manuscript seemed to drift from Wakefield's sight, Rebecca raced forward. She pushed Wakefield from behind with all her strength. Man and manuscript entangled. His instincts empowering him, Wakefield's hand gripped the ironworks and he raised his pistol at Osgood's head with his other hand – but the fire below had sent the heat through the iron, and now steam rose from under Wakefield's ungloved hand. His hand yielding, Wakefield went plunging down the elevator shaft, all the way down in a screaming drop into the inferno. As he fell, the pages fluttered through the air around him. They fed the flame like fresh wood in a winter hearth. Wakefield crashed and shrieked inhumanly.

In his last moments, his eye seemed to fall on one of Dickens's final pages just as it curled into ashes. And all was devoured as one.

Osgood, ashen pale, hugging his rib cage with his arms, dropped limply to his knees in exhaustion, terror and relief. He watched the pages below them in various states of demise and ashes. To breathe was utter agony.

'Mr. Osgood!' Rebecca called out. She pulled him out of the way just as Molasses lunged forward on to the edge of the elevator shaft. The Bookaneer was reaching for any stray pages.

'*The Mystery of Edwin Drood*!' the Bookaneer called out. 'Even one page would be priceless!' His hat tumbled off and caught fire as another explosion from the engine room shot up towards them.

Osgood pushed himself to his feet and leaned into the red hot shaft, grabbing the back of the Bookaneer's collar and coat, the bottom of which was already singeing.

'One page!' the man was repeating. 'Just one!'

'Molasses! It's gone! It's already gone!'

Osgood pulled Molasses backwards as the engine room exploded once more and this time filled the buckling elevator shaft with a solid column of fire. Osgood had taken Rebecca into his arms as they watched from the precipice of the fifth floor.

'Quickly!' urged a newly sensible Molasses as the fire and steam spread.

As the three survivors ran down the stairs, Molasses periodically cried out in lament for the lost pages. 'You couldn't, could you? How could you allow him to destroy the end of *The Mystery of Edwin Drood*! The last Dickens, in a column of smoke!'

The poor Bookaneer, unwilling to accept the defeat, followed behind the firemen as they trooped into the building pulling their hoses from their nearby engines. In the meantime, Rebecca helped Osgood to a kerb across from the building. He sat and coughed violently.

'I shall go for a doctor,' said Rebecca.

Osgood held up a hand to plead for her to wait. 'I hope the lady shall not be offended,' he said at the first moment he could find his voice. He scraped the ash and grime off his hand, then inserted his hand under his torn shirt, into the bandages around his chest.

He took out a thin collection of papers flattened against his skin.

Rebecca gasped. 'Is it . . . ?'

'The final chapter – while I was in the elevator alone, I hid it. Just in case . . .'

'Mr. Osgood! Remarkable! Why, even without the rest of it, just to have the ending will change everything. What is Edwin Drood's fate?' She reached out her hand, then hesitated. 'May I?'

'You have earned it as much as I, Miss Sand,' he said, passing the pages to her.

As she looked down, she passed her hand over the first page of the chapter as if its words could be touched. Her bright eyes glistened with curiosity and amazement.

'Well?' asked Osgood knowingly. 'What do you think of it, my darling? Can you read it?'

'Not a word!' she said, then laughed. 'Oh, it's beautiful!'

XXXIX

———— ✦ ————

HARLES DICKENS HAD KNOWN HE had to be better than all the others. He was not yet twenty years old and was trying to compete with the more experienced corps of London reporters. It had been their mission to provide verbatim reports of the speeches of the most important members of Parliament and the chief cases at Chancery.

There were two primary questions surrounding them: who could write the most accurately, and who could write fastest. The Gurney system of brachygraphy, or shorthand, brought him under its magical, mysterious spell. *Brachygraphy, or an easy and compendious System of Shorthand* rested on and under his pillow. It permitted an ordinary human, after some close training and prayer, to condense the usual long-winded language of their fellow beings into mere scratches and dots on a page. The reporter would copy down an orator's speech in this cobweb of markings, then rush out the door. If outside the city, in Edinburgh or some country village, he would bend over his paper while being driven in a carriage, scribbling furiously under a small wax lamp as he transformed on to blank slips of paper the strange symbols into full words – occasionally sticking his head out the window to prevent sickness along the rocky passage.

The green reporter, Dickens, mastered the Gurney, just as his father had once done in brief employment as a shorthand writer, but that was not enough. Young Dickens altered and adjusted Gurney – he created his own shorthand – better and quicker than anyone else's. Soon, the most important English speeches were always certified at the bottom of the page by *C. Dickens, Shorthand Writer, 5, Bell Yard, Doctors' Commons.*

That was how he could write so much, even half a book, in the small cracks of a full schedule while in America. That was the only way his pen could keep pace with his mind and reveal the fate of Edwin Drood.

The Gurney system had years ago been replaced by that of Taylor's and then by Pitman's. Rebecca had been trained in Pitman's at the Bryant and Stratton Commercial School for women on Washington Street before applying to be a bookkeeper. Fields and Osgood, after depositing the pages from the satchel representing the last chapter of *The Mystery of Edwin Drood* in their fireproof safe at 124 Tremont Street, did consult some of the first-rate shorthand writers in Boston (several of whom, themselves the brainier Bookaneers, had been the ones attempting to copy down Dickens's improvisations at the Tremont Temple before Tom Branagan and Daniel Sand stopped them). They would show them only a page or two, for purposes of secrecy, and did not tell them the provenance of the document. No luck – it was useless. The system, even for those very familiar with Gurney, was too eccentric to decipher more than a few scattered words.

They sent confidential cables to Chapman & Hall seeking advice on the matter. Meanwhile, quietly, Fields and Osgood made preparations with their printer and illustrator for a special edition of *The Mystery of Edwin Drood,* complete with the exclusive final chapter.

The first week after the retrieval of the manuscript there were endless consultations and interviews with the chief of police, customs agents, the state attorney and the British consulate. Montague Midges, denying all accusations, was immediately dismissed from his post and interrogated by the police about his conversations with Wakefield and Herman. The *Samaria* was boarded by customs and an eager tax collector named Simon Pennock, using the information gathered by Osgood and the late Jack Rogers, and every member of the crew was taken into custody. The Royal Navy had been alerted and over a matter of months the majority of Marcus Wakefield's operation was dismantled.

One morning, Osgood was called into Fields's office where he was shocked to be staring straight into the mouth of a long rifle.

'Halloa, old boy!'

The double-barrelled rifle was hanging loosely behind the shoulder of a burly, ruddy man in a tight-fitting sporting outfit with high leather gaiters, knee breeches and a cartridge belt around his wide waist. Frederic Chapman.

'Mr. Chapman, forgive me if I wear a look of astonishment,' Osgood began. 'We sent our cables to you in London not two days ago.'

Chapman gave his mighty laugh. 'You see, Osgood, I was in New York on some dull business for the firm, and on my way in full force to a shooting party in the Adirondacks when my the hotel messenger stopped me at the train station with a cable from my office in London passing along your intelligence. Naturally I boarded the next train into Boston. I always liked Boston – the streets are crooked and the New Englandism is down to a science. I say, these' – he delicately picked up the small sheaf of pages with care and awe – 'are simply remarkable! Imagine!'

'Can you make sense of it, then?' Fields asked.

'Me? Not a single speck, not a single word, Mr. Fields!' Chapman declared without any diminished excitement. 'Osgood, where did you go? There you are. Say, how is it you came upon this?'

Osgood exchanged a questioning look with Fields.

'Mr. Osgood is our most diligent man!' Fields exclaimed proudly.

'Well, I should think this proves it,' said Chapman, resting his hands on his cartridge belt. 'I could use men like you, Osgood. My clerks, they're worthless and hopeless creatures. Now we must set in motion a plan to *read* these at once.'

Fields told him how the shorthand writers they'd consulted could not make it out, and they did not want to give them too much of it to see.

'No, we mustn't let anyone else get wind of this. Clerk!' Chapman leaned out the door and waited for anyone to appear. Though it was one of the financial men who presented himself, Chapman snapped his fingers and said, 'Some champagne in here, won't you?' Chapman then closed the door on the confused man and insisted on shaking both men's hands again with his hunter's iron grip. 'Gentlemen, I have it! This shall be historical! Long after we are all – pardon the morbidity – out of print permanently, our names will be honoured for this. The end of the last Dickens, for all the world to see! *That* is a triumph.

'I happen to know several court reporters who worked alongside Dickens in the capacity of shorthand writers thirty years ago; in some cases, they competed with the younger rival, attempting to replicate his altered version of the shorthand technique. Some of them, though their heads have grown white with the creeping of age, still live retired lives in London and are known to me personally. I have no doubt that for the right price their success in "translating" this text will be assured.'

'Upon my word, we shall contribute liberally to such a fund,' Fields said.

'Good. I'll book my passage back early to deal with this without delay,' Chapman said. 'Say, you have made a copy of the chapter, haven't you?'

Fields shook his head. 'The truth is, this shorthand is of such a strange design, I fear any copies could be worthless. Dashes and lines and curly symbols not replicated exactly would render a word or paragraph potentially indecipherable. It would be like an illiterate copying out a page from a Chinese scroll. Perhaps with two or three of the best copyists checking each other. The best copyists in Boston are also the greediest, and it would be a risk to entrust them.'

'You did not even make a copy for yourself?' Chapman asked, surprised.

'Mr. Fields cannot, with his hand,' Osgood said. 'We didn't know you were coming, Mr. Chapman. I would have tried, but I am afraid even the attempt could take weeks.'

'And tracing it is out of the question,' Chapman noted, 'for these papers have not exactly been well kept, wherever it is you found them, and the chemicals of tracing paper could tamper with the ink. No matter, the original shall be safe' – here he stopped to caress the end of his rifle – 'even from your so-called Bookaneers. Let them try me!'

Chapman put the chapter in his case. As soon as the transcription was complete, Chapman would send a private messenger in whom he had complete trust to deliver the fully transcribed pages back to Boston, so the Fields, Osgood & Co. edition could appear well before any pirated editions.

'Tell me – for a lark – before we finally know the truth, what do you think, Osgood?' asked Chapman as he prepared to depart from the office, his assistant handing him his overcoat and brown felt hat with its jaunty blue ribbon. 'Tell us, do you think Drood lives or dies in the end?'

'I don't know whether he lives or dies,' answered Osgood. 'But I know he is not dead.'

Chapman, shouldering his rifle, nodded but moved his mouth in a rehearsal of confusion at the enigmatic response.

Some minutes later, after their guest's departure, some impulse or feeling gripped Osgood. It made him get up from his desk. He stood looking down at the palms of his own hands and the various scars from their adventures.

He could not have said why, but he was soon walking down the hall; hurrying down the stairs, dancing around the slower climbers; bursting through the reception hall, past the shining glass cases of Ticknor & Fields and Fields & Osgood books, out the front doors; pushing past the line at the peanut vendor and the Italian organ grinder, looking out, looking at the tourists to Boston in bright bonnets and light hats loitering under the shady elms of the Great Mall along the Common, looking over at squirrels scrambling for lost crumbs and pleading pitifully for donations of other scraps, looking for Fred Chapman in the dappled light of the summer scene. Osgood got as far as the tents pitched by the travelling circus, which were sheltering exhibitions of overheated animals and myriad humanity.

It is impossible to claim to know what James Osgood thought to have said had he caught up with him. It wouldn't have mattered, though, because the strapping visitor from London and the pages in his case were already gone.

SIXTH INSTALMENT

All that was left of 'Edwin Drood' is here published. Beyond the clues therein afforded to its conduct or catastrophe, nothing whatever remains; and it is believed that what the writer would himself have most desired is done, in placing before the reader, without further note or suggestion, the fragment of 'The Mystery of Edwin Drood'. The tale is left half told; the mystery remains a mystery for ever. – 1870 edition, *The Mystery of Edwin Drood*, the first six instalments only, published by Fields, Osgood & Co.

XL

BOSTON, DECEMBER 1870,

FIVE MONTHS LATER

———◆———

ROSSING THE ORNATE LOBBY, THE man with the flowing white beard made a graceful stop at the front desk.

'Is Mr. Clark in?'

He addressed this question to a definitively New England shop boy, whose dream was one day to turn thirteen years old and another day to write a book of his own like the ones in the shining glass cases. For now he was content to be sitting and reading one. 'Guess he ain't,' was his reply, too absorbed to break his concentration.

'Can you say when he'll return?'

'Guess I can't.'

'Mr. Osgood or Mr. Fields, then?'

'Mr. Osgood's out on business, and Mr. Fields, he's not to be disturbed today, guess I don't know why.'

'Well,' the caller chuckled to himself. 'I entrust these important papers with you, then, sir.'

The lad looked up at the documents and took the card that sat on top with a surprised and astonished expression.

'Mr. Longfellow,' he said, jumping to his feet from his stool. He stared at the visitor with the same intensity he had reserved for his book. 'Say, old man! Do you mean to say you are really Longfellow?'

'I am, young man.'

'Wall! I wouldn't have thought it! Now, how old was you when you wrote *Hiawatha*? That's what I want to know.'

After satisfying this and the shop boy's other burning questions, the poet turned towards the front doors as he secured his heavy coat, lowered his hat, and braced himself for the wintry air.

'My dear Mr. Longfellow!'

Longfellow looked up and saw it was James Osgood coming in. He greeted the young publisher.

'Come upstairs and warm a while by the fire in the Authors' Room, Mr. Longfellow?' suggested Osgood.

'The Authors' Room,' Longfellow repeated, smiling dreamily. 'How long since I idled there with our friends! The world was a holiday planet then, and things were precisely what they seemed. I've just left some papers for Mr. Clark that needed my signature. But I ought to return to Cambridge to my girls.'

'I shall walk with you part of the way, if you'd allow it. I have my gloves on already.'

Osgood put his arm through the author's as they walked up Tremont Street through the blustery afternoon. Their talk, interrupted at intervals by the freezing gusts, soon turned to *The Mystery of Edwin Drood*. The Fields, Osgood & Co. edition had just been published a few months earlier.

'I believe I interrupted your shop boy's enjoyment of Drood's tale,' Longfellow said.

'Oh, yes. That's little Rich – he hadn't seen a schoolroom before two years ago, and now reads a book a week. *Drood* is his favourite so far.'

'It is certainly one of Mr. Dickens's most beautiful works, if not the most beautiful of all. It is too sad to think the pen had fallen out of his hand to leave it incomplete,' Longfellow said.

'Some months ago I had in my possession the final pages,' said Osgood, without exactly intending to. What would Osgood tell him about it? That Fred Chapman had taken the manuscript back to England? That an accident had occurred on board the ship and destroyed several pieces of baggage including the trunk carrying *Drood*? 'Cruel misfortune intervened,' Osgood commented vaguely.

Longfellow paused before replying, pulling Osgood's arm closer as if to tell him a secret. 'It is for the best.'

'What do you mean?'

'I sometimes think, dear Mr. Osgood, that all proper books are unfinished. They simply have to feign completion for the convenience of the public. If not for publishers, no authors would ever reach the end. We would have all writers and no readers. So you mustn't shed a tear for *Drood*. No, there is much to envy about it – I mean that each reader will imagine his or her ideal ending for it, and every reader will be happy with their own private finale in their mind. It is in a truer state, perhaps, than any other work of its kind, however large we print those words, THE END. And you have made the best of it!'

Indeed, their edition of *Drood* had been a resounding success by any measure and beyond every expectation, sending the publishing firm scrambling to print enough editions to keep up with demand. It had seemed that stories had trickled out into the trade – apparently beginning with a Bookaneer who called himself Molasses – of Osgood's remarkable search for the book's ending. Pieces of the narrative of this quest, some entirely true and some wild rumour, were put together in a lengthy series of articles by Mr. Leypoldt in his newly titled magazine, The *Publishers' Weekly*, as the first of his stories of the soul of publishing, which brought thousands of new eyes on Leypoldt's magazine and led to the narrative being retold by the major newspapers and journals in all the cities. This attracted enormous attention and interest in their edition of *Drood*, turning the name Osgood on the title page into a selling point – while the pirated editions by Harper eagerly hawked by the pedlars and bagmen gathered dust. The Fields & Osgood editions filled the front windows of bookstores, banishing the Indian prints and cigar boxes to the back shelves.

The added attention by the trade journals not only helped sell copies of *Drood*. It brought in fresh new authors who wanted to be published by a man like Osgood – Louisa May Alcott, Bret Harte, Anna Leonowens, among others. Osgood was currently discussing arrangements for a novel with Mr. Samuel Clemens.

It was all a revelation in the trade. The firm was poised not only to survive but to flourish.

Returning to 124 Tremont after parting from Longfellow, as he hung his hat on a peg, Osgood was greeted by the reliable clerk who had replaced Mr. Midges. 'Mr. Fields wants to see you at once,' he said.

Osgood thanked him and started to take his leave before the clerk called after him. 'Oh, Mr. Osgood, the operator has stepped out. Do you require assistance with the car?'

Osgood glanced at the firm's newly installed elevator on the east wing of the building. 'Thank you,' he said. 'I'd just as soon take the stairs.'

On his way through the corridors, he looked for Rebecca, who had some weeks earlier been promoted by Fields from a bookkeeper to the position of reader. The usual reader had fallen ill for two weeks. Rebecca had impressed Fields examining the manuscripts submitted to the *Atlantic*.

Since their return from England, Osgood and Rebecca's contact had been the model of professional distance and propriety, all doors of communication between them open for anyone to see. But they had both marked their desk registers. May 15, 1871, approximately six months from the present: that would be the date the clock would wind down for her divorce to be as official as the gold dome of the State House. The wait proved to be a source of immense excitement. The secret was thrilling and increased their love for each other. Each day that passed brought them twenty-four hours closer to the reward of an open courtship.

When he entered the senior partner's office, Osgood sighed in spite of himself and their renewed successes.

'More extraordinary sales numbers for the last Dickens today,' Fields said. 'Yet your thoughts seem lost far away.'

'Perhaps they are.'

'Well, where, then?'

'Lost at sea. Mr. Fields, I must speak my mind. I think it possible Frederic Chapman's baggage had no accident at all.'

'Oh?'

'I do not believe those pages were involved in an accident. I possess no evidence, only suspicion. Instinct, perhaps.'

Fields nodded contemplatively. The senior partner had the general mark of exhaustion on him. 'I see.'

'You think me unjust to the gentleman,' Osgood said cautiously.

'Fred Chapman? I know him no better than you to judge him a gentleman or swindler.'

'Yet you don't seem the least bit surprised by my radical notion!' Osgood exclaimed.

Fields looked over Osgood calmly. 'There *were* reports of a flood aboard that steamship in the wires.'

'I know. Yet you've suspected it, too,' Osgood said. 'You've suspected something else from the beginning. Haven't you?'

'My dear Osgood. Have a chair. Have you read Forster's book on Dickens's life?'

'I have avoided it.'

'Yes, he hardly wastes any breath on our American tour. But he does print the text of Dickens's contract with Chapman.'

> *If the said Charles Dickens shall die during the composition of the said work of* The Mystery of Edwin Drood, *or shall otherwise become incapable of completing the said work for publication in twelve monthly numbers as agreed, or in the case of his death, incapacity, or refusal to act, it shall be referred to such person as shall be named by Her Majesty's Attorney-General to determine the amount which shall be repaid by the said Charles Dickens, his executors or administrators, to the said Frederic Chapman as a fair compensation for so much of the said work as shall not have been completed for publication.*

Osgood put the book down. 'It is as the Major said, that books would be mere lumber. Chapman gets paid twice!' he exclaimed.

'Correct,' Fields said. 'He earns the money from the sale of the book and he gets paid from the Dickens estate in compensation for the book being unfinished. On the other hand, if he waved the final chapter around for the world to see, the executors – Forster, who likes Chapman not a bit, considering him another unworthy competitor for Dickens's attentions – would argue that even without the entire final six instalments, the last chapter proves Dickens *did* finish and that the estate did not owe a farthing to Chapman. And that's not all. Think of it, won't you? A new Dickens novel is a new Dickens novel – as remarkable as that is. Yet an unfinished Dickens novel is a mystery in itself. You see the speculation, the sensation! The attention that gets for Mr. Chapman's publication is invaluable.'

'Nor does he contend with pirates, as we do without copyright for Mr. Dickens over here,' Osgood said.

'No, he doesn't,' Fields agreed.

'Do you think the pages we gave him, that last chapter, still exist, then?'

'Perhaps an accident did destroy them. We shall never know. Unless – well, you say he gets paid twice, very true. But he *could* get paid three times in the end. If a day should come, perhaps months, perhaps ten years from today, perhaps a century, when a firm of Mr. Chapman's or his heirs needs money, they could publish the "newly unriddled!" ending to *The Mystery of Edwin Drood* and cause a roar among the reading public! The novel's villain would finally be convicted for good.'

Osgood thought about this. 'There must be more we can do.'

'We have. We have made our own success out of this, thanks to you and Miss Sand.'

Osgood realised only now that Fields had been clutching a pen in his pinched hand. 'My dear Fields, why, you must not strain yourself writing. You know Mrs. Fields ordered me to watch that you take care of your hand. I can call your bookkeeper in again, or I'll do it.'

'No, no. This one last thing I must write myself, thank you, if I write nothing else ever again! I am tired and will go home early today and sleep like your old tabby cat. Mind, I have a present for you first, that's why I called you in.'

Fields held up a pair of boxing gloves. Osgood, laughing under his breath, wondered what to say.

'You'd better take them, Osgood.'

Fields pushed a piece of paper across his desk. On it, painfully scrawled in his own hand, was a preliminary design for stationery. It read:

James R. Osgood & Company. 124 Tremont Street.

'This talented and charming young lady helped me with the design,' said Fields.

Rebecca came to the doorway smiling in a white cashmere dress and a flower in her hair, which was in black ringlets coiled high on her head. Osgood, forgetting to restrain himself, took one of her hands in each of his.

'How do you feel, my dear Ripley?' she asked breathlessly.

'Yes, don't be shy,' Fields said, 'what do you think of it? Honest now. Are you surprised, my dear Osgood?'

The shop boy knocked at the door struggling to hold up an awkwardly wrapped package almost as big as him.

'Ah, Rich,' said Fields. 'Ask Simmons to send a note to Leypoldt telling him we have news for him to report. What is that?' he asked of the parcel. 'We're very much occupied at present with some celebratory tidings.'

'Guess it's a parcel. See, it's addressed to . . .' the shop boy began, pausing uncertainly. 'Wall, to "James R. Osgood and Company", sir.'

'What?' Fields exclaimed. 'Impossible! What kind of modern-day

Tiresias could know about that already? What kind of man with more eyes than Argus?'

Osgood slowly unwrapped the layers of paper, which were cold enough from the package's winter journey to be thin sheets of ice. Emerging from underneath it all, an iron bust of a distinguished Benjamin Franklin with his sidelong, wary, bespectacled gaze and pursed lips. 'It's the statue from Harper's office,' Osgood said.

'That's the Major's prize possession!' Fields said with surprise and bewilderment.

'There's a note,' Osgood said, and then he read it aloud.

Congratulations on your ascendancy, Mr. Osgood. Take good care of this relic, for the time. I shall claim it back when I come to swallow your firm. Always watching, your friend, Fletcher Harper, the Major. At the top of the note was the emblem of the eternal Harper torch.

'Harper! How did he find out already? Get a hammer!' Fields declared. 'Damn that Harper!'

Osgood shook his head calmly and gave an even smile. 'No, my dear Fields. Let it stand here. I have a good feeling that it shall remain ours from this time onward. I have not felt this lighthearted since I was a boy.'

HISTORICAL NOTE

———————◆◆————————

O N JUNE 9, 1870, CHARLES DICKENS died of a stroke at fifty-eight years old at his family estate. He was arguably the most widely read novelist of his day. After his death, some observers blamed his deteriorated health on the arduous nature of his farewell tour of the United States, while others pointed the finger at the strain he was under from his last book. Before collapsing, he had written the first six of twelve instalments planned for *The Mystery of Edwin Drood*, literary history's most famous unfinished novel.

The Last Dickens aims to portray Charles Dickens and the atmosphere surrounding his life and death as accurately as possible. Dickens's language, behaviour and personality as they appear in this novel incorporate many actual conversations and actions. The re-creation of his landmark farewell tour of the United States (1867–68) is based on visits to sites like the Parker House where Dickens lodged in Boston (now the Omni Parker House) and was enlarged by research into letters, playbills, newspaper accounts and recollections by participants like George Dolby and James and Annie Fields. Thus, most of the tour's incidents depicted here are historical, including Dickens's rescue of the stranded animals and his visit with Oliver Wendell Holmes to the Harvard Medical College.

The stalking incident portrayed in the same chapters is based on an actual series of encounters involving a well-to-do Boston admirer named Jane Bigelow, from whom Louisa Barton is drawn and fictionalised. A tax collector blackmailed the Dickens staff while plotting their arrests for evasion of the federal entertainment tax. Dickens's pocket diary for 1867 indeed disappeared in New York around the same time, turning up without explanation more than fifty years later at an auction (today it forms part of the New York Public Library's Berg Collection).

Historical characters in this novel include James R. Osgood, the Fieldses, the Harpers, Frederic Chapman, John Forster, Georgina Hogarth, Frederick Leypoldt, Dickens's tour staff – Dolby, Henry Scott, Richard Kelly, George Allison – and Dickens's children – Frank, Katie, Mamie – all of whom are re-created here from investigation into their personal and professional lives. Fictional characters, including Tom Branagan, Rebecca and Daniel Sand, Arthur Grunwald, Jack Rogers, Ironhead Herman and Marcus Wakefield, are developed from research into the era. Rebecca reflects the real achievements and challenges in a new class of single working women in mid- to late-nineteenth-century Boston as well as that of divorced women. The international opium trade and its manifestations in England and British India as portrayed here, as well as the book trade, reflect historical turning points.

The firm of Fields, Osgood & Co. became the authorised American publisher of Charles Dickens in 1867, a move that ignited controversy with rival publisher Harper & Brothers. Dickens did offer Queen Victoria to tell her the story of *The Mystery of Edwin Drood* ahead of the public, but she apparently declined the preview. With *Drood* incomplete, theatrical dramatisations and 'spiritual' sequels appeared and multiplied. Rumours began that Dickens had completed more of the novel than what had been made public. While Osgood's attempt in *The Last Dickens* to trace clues to the rest of Dickens's novel is a product of imagination, many of its key elements grow out of history and scholarship. Dickens closely modelled his novel's opium den and characters on an actual London establishment he visited that was managed by a woman named Sally or 'Opium Sal'; also, possible sources for his story of Edwin Drood's disappearance include a Rochester legend about human remains of a man's nephew found in the walls of his house. The landlord of the Falstaff Inn, located across from Gadshill estate, was William Stocker Trood, who had a son named Edward. Dickens's statue, *Turk Seated Smoking Opium* was sold at auction along with his other belongings at Christie, Manson & Woods in London on July 8, 1870. The statue, along with the quill pen Dickens used to write *Drood*, can be viewed today at the Charles Dickens Museum in London; his walking stick with the screw in its handle is at Houghton Library, Harvard University.

The Mystery of Edwin Drood was published in book form in late 1870 in London by Chapman & Hall and in Boston by Fields, Osgood & Co.; the Boston publication was followed by an unauthorised edition from Harper & Brothers in New York. As shown here, the end of 1870 saw Fields retire and Osgood becoming proprietor of James R. Osgood & Co. In 1926, Chapman & Hall indicated that it still kept their original agreement with Dickens for *The Mystery of Edwin Drood* locked in a safe, but would not share it. Less than a year later, Chapman & Hall claimed they no longer could locate the agreement. In the many years since Dickens's death, various pieces of new evidence have shed little light on Dickens's intentions for *The Mystery of Edwin Drood*. The questions about the novel and its ending are as strong today as ever.

ACKNOWLEDGEMENTS

In writing a novel set in a cutthroat era of the publishing industry, I am blessed that behind this project there are such generous publishing professionals, my literary agent Suzanne Gluck – endlessly dedicated and dexterous – my editor Jennifer Hershey – insightful, creative and challenging – and a zealous champion in Gina Centrello. I'm fortunate to have benefited from the further input and guidance of Stuart Williams at Harvill Secker. Support and imagination came from so many individuals: at Random House, Lea Beresford, Sanyu Dillon, Benjamin Dreyer, Laura Ford, Jennifer Huwer, Vincent La Scala, Libby McGuire, Courtney Moran, Gene Mydlowski, Jack Perry, Tom Perry, Carol Schneider, Judy Sternlight, Jane von Mehren, Annette Melvin, Beck Stvan as well as Amy Metsch at Random House Audio; at Harvill Secker, Matt Broughton, Liz Foley, Lily Richards, Ellie Steel; at William Morris Agency, Sarah Ceglarski, Georgia Cool, Raffaella De Angelis, Michelle Feehan, Tracy Fisher, Eugenie Furniss, Evan Goldfried, Alicia Gordon, Erin Malone, Elizabeth Reed, Frances Roe, Cathryn Summerhayes, Liz Tingue.

I've relied on my superb reader's circle for judgment and ideas, once again composed of Benjamin Cavell, Joseph Gangemi, Cynthia Posillico, and Ian Pearl – who have proven they are impervious to being bothered by borrowers to their genius – and joined this time around by additional brilliant talents Louis Bayard and Eric Dean Bennett. Gabriella Gage provided invaluable assistance in a cross-section of complex research, fortifying the project with her persistence, resourcefulness and patience. Susan and Warren Pearl, Marsha Wiggins, Scott Weinger and Gustavo Turner were present throughout to encourage both work and rest. And my gratitude to

Tobey Pearl, who from the first to last word helped me through all hills and valleys of the process.

I bow to more than a century of scholarship on Charles Dickens and *The Mystery of Edwin Drood*, especially all that has appeared in the *Dickensian* and *Dickens Studies Annual* journals, and the writings of Arthur Adrian, Sydney Moss, Fred Kaplan, Don Richard Cox, Robert Patten and Duane Devries, with the latter three scholars kindly fielding additional questions through private correspondence. I've had the privilege to benefit from the resources of Harvard University Library, the Boston Public Library, the Bostonian Society, the Philadelphia Free Library, and the Dickens Museum in London.

This novel is dedicated to all of my English teachers.

The Castle of this Ogress ~~and it was so windy that it~~ was
in a steep bye street at Brighton, and it was so windy that it sounded like
a great shell, which the inhabitants were obliged to hold to their
ears night and day. There were two other small Boarders in it; one
Master Bitherstone from India; and one Miss Pankey. Master Bitherstone objected
so much to the Pipchinian system, that before Miss Pankey had been established
in the house five minutes he privately ~~asked him~~ if he could give him any
idea of the way back to Bengal. Miss Pankey was then in

durance in the Castle Dungeon for having sniffed three
times in the presence of visitors, at one o'clock when
there was a dinner — chiefly of the farinaceous and
vegetable kind — ~~this~~ this young Prisoner (she was a
mild little blue eyed morsel of a child, who was
shampoo'd every morning and seemed in